Cat's Café

Book One of the
Eagle Rock Trilogy

Ralls C. Melotte

 FriesenPress

One Printers Way
Altona, MB R0G 0B0
Canada

www.friesenpress.com

ISBN
978-1-03-913351-8 (Hardcover)
978-1-03-913350-1 (Paperback)
978-1-03-913352-5 (eBook)

1. *FICTION, HISTORICAL*

Distributed to the trade by The Ingram Book Company

For Richard Morse, whose integrity and friendship through our business partnership made my retirement dreams possible; Jon Hockenyos who was as fine a mentor as I've ever known, and whose invitation to help create a magnificent working HO model of the Feather River Canyon Division of the Western Pacific Railroad in his basement over the last 40 years imparted in me an enthusiasm and curiosity of the ways early railroad construction changed the West; and for my mother E.V. Melotte, who instilled in me a love for the written word.

Preface

Inspiration for Cat's Café and the Eagle Rock Trilogy came in a few lines of an Idaho Museum of Natural History book on the geology of Eastern Idaho. A brief mention of William Murphy and his wife Catherine, a toll bridge, and a bar room shooting became the saga of Catherine Callaway and the many real-life trailblazers she would meet finding her way in the American West.

Over approximately 40 years, according to researchers Paul Link and E. Chilton Phoenix, Catherine Murphy, who became Catherine Harkness after her first husband was shot in a bar by the local sheriff, and husband Henry O. Harkness "built a farming and ranching empire, a power generation facility, a flour mill, and a hotel to serve the new railroad." These remarkable accomplishments inspired me to write about the challenges faced by men and women attempting to become self-sufficient in the wild, often lawless, West in the late-19th century.

Through the trilogy, Catherine will strive to become a successful business owner and join real-life leaders of the day in advancing women's rights and expanding areas of tillable land through the use of canal systems. Their heroic pioneering spirit, courage, and grit live in the DNA of all who followed.

One of the joys of writing historical fiction is researching the social, cultural, political, economic, and physical landscape of a region. I found as much satisfaction discovering first-person records, maps, and blogs by writers with a shared passion for the Old West as I did creating a realistic story to weave into actual events. You can read my background research on real-life characters and my justification for the characters I created in the back of this book and online at www.rallsmelotte.com, Home of the Eagle Rock Trilogy. It really was an amazing time in our country. I invite you to take a look, leave a comment, and subscribe for updates. — Ralls Melotte

Acknowledgements

I owe the fun of discovering Idaho's rich history to my wife Stacey and her sister Melissa Neiers who know Idaho very well, and to the Museum of Idaho for guidance and resources. Stacey's son Levi Hastings created the cover and logo art.

And my special thanks to DiAnne Crown for sculpting this work with her editing genius and wordsmithing, for creating a website from the ground up, and for launching my social media.

It's been amazing to see this all come together.

Cat's Café

Eagle Rock, Idaho Territory, 1879

Prologue

Thursday, June 26th, 1879

"What kind of man are ya? Where's your sense of honor? You promised me you were gonna kick those damn Callaways out before the railroad got to Eagle Rock. In two weeks they're gonna celebrate the new bridge opening on July Fourth and you ain't done a damned thing! I've been hazin that greenhorn Irishman jus like I said I would, but I'm gonna lose a fortune if you don't pony up[1] and put a spoke in their wheels[2] so's I can move into that saloon!"

The short, scrawny man with long, greasy, blond hair and several missing front teeth had worked himself into a lather as he yelled at the gentleman across from him sitting behind his stately mahogany desk. But by the end of his tirade, Edgar Potts' bluster was gone. His face had turned from bright red to ghostly white as the tall, stern, dark-complexioned man behind the desk rose slowly from his chair. From the expression on Potts' face, you might think he was watching the devil rise up from the underworld.

There was nothing other worldly about Luther Arnold Armstrong, though. Standing erect behind his desk, Luther was an imposing six-foot-three inches and quite striking in his black, three-piece suit, freshly starched white shirt, and gleaming gold cuff links. His pocket-watch chain reflected the morning sun and occasionally glinted into Potts' eyes. All in all, Luther was quite real enough for Potts.

---

1 **Pony up** – *hurry up*
2 **Spoke in the wheel** – *to make it difficult for someone to do what they planned to do*

Luther's coal-black eyes bored into Edgar Potts with a look of hatred and disgust while his jaw and neck muscles worked back and forth as if trying to swallow something foul. He slowly raised one arm and pointed a finger at Edgar, his arm noticeably shaking as he tried to control his anger. "You!" he roared. "You have the audacity to question my honor, you sniveling little piece of rotting bat shit. You come into my home! *My home!* And claim I have not met my end of our bargain? Who do you think you are?"

The owner of the Potts Establishment for Fine Spirits, known simply as Potts' Saloon, had already jumped up in alarm and was starting to back up to the closed door of the office.

"Sit down!" Luther roared.

Edgar quickly returned to his seat, avoiding looking directly at Luther, his eyes fixed on the front of Luther's desk.

Luther leaned forward with both hands on his desktop and then abruptly slammed one fist down on the desk hard enough to make Potts wince. In a slightly more controlled growl, he continued, "Let me remind you of our agreement."

"I'm sorry, ah, I'm really sorry," Edgar stuttered, hoping to avoid the oncoming indictment. "I was in such a shindy[3] I might've got a little out of line."

But Luther was already coming around from behind the desk. "Stay in that chair, you little shit, and shut up while I re-educate you! You are not going anywhere until I know we understand each other."

By this time, Potts was studying the floor, wringing his tightly clasped hands between his legs.

Luther just stared at Edgar for another long moment and then leaned down until his face was level with Edgar's. He raised Potts' chin with one finger so they were looking eye to eye.

"What I recall of our agreement is this." Luther raised one finger up to a point directly in front of Edgar's eyes. "One: I gave you the building you are presently in for the modest cut of twenty percent of your profits, so you could compete with the Callaways and run them out of their dwindling resources."

He raised another finger in front of Edgar. "Two: I paid for the inventory to get you started with the understanding that you would pay me back over the next several months."

---

3   **Shindy** – *uproar, confusion*

He raised a third finger. "And three: I demanded that my ranch hands and the railroad crews stop going to Patrick's Saloon and use your new Establishment for Fine Spirits."

Edgar leaned forward and started to speak, but Luther pushed him back in his chair and continued. "That was six months ago! Now let's go over what you have done. One: You have given me a couple of small bags of coins expecting me to believe that's my cut of the profits without a single bit of evidence from what you are calling your books."

Luther was using his fingers in front of Edgar's face again to make sure he was getting the point. "Two: You haven't given me one red cent for the inventory! And three: The men say your drinks are watered down and the beer tastes like skunk piss! At this rate, Patrick's won't have any competition at all."

Luther paused, staring directly into Potts' eyes. "So just exactly what is it that you have contributed to our so-called agreement that you claim I have not honored?"

Edgar started mumbling a response, but Luther cut him off again. "Oh shut up, you moron! I don't really want to hear your excuses."

Luther stood up and walked back and forth in front of Potts for several moments, grimacing each time he looked down at him. "Now I have to fix this mess. Shit!"

He sighed, sat down back at his desk, and motioned to another man who had been standing quietly at the back of the room, observing the whole discussion.

"Here is what we are going to do. Cloyd here and his brother Billy are going to escort you back to your saloon and you are going to hand over all of your recordkeeping. Tonight, my ranch manager is going to go over it with me to determine just what your profits have been." Luther leaned forward with both elbows on his desk and said in a quiet, reasonable tone, "Tomorrow morning, you and I are going to have another little chat. I suspect you have been scamming me for the last six months and I expect to get all my money back. I am sure that Billy and Cloyd would be pleased to find some effective ways to encourage you meet your responsibilities."

Then he banged his fist on his desk again and yelled, "Now get the hell out of here before I kick your sorry ass all the way back to that wretched saloon."

Edgar jumped up from his chair. "Ya know Mr. Armstrong, I knows yor a fair man and yor right. Ah, I just haven't done the best job keepin up my books. Ah, ya see," he stammered, "I have gotten, ah, jus a little behind. Ya jus gimmee a few days to get'em in shape and you'll jus see how hard it's been for me ta getcha yor money. But I'm sure I'll be able ta pay ya back by the Fourth."

Just before Luther swiveled his chair around to stare out the window behind him as if considering Edgar's offer, Potts saw a small smirk form on his face.

Without turning from the window, Luther said, "You know Mr. Potts, I am certain if I give you a few days, your books would certainly be more understandable and probably support the difficulties you are having." Then he turned around abruptly to face Potts. As a look of outrage crossed his face, it was clear his seething mood was about to erupt again. "And I also know that I would be looking at a shitload of lies, you little weasel!"

He looked up at Cloyd. "Is Billy still outside?"

"Yep, Cap'm," Cloyd drawled. Cloyd was short man, slim and wiry, with a dark, lined complexion weathered by the sun. He looked really mean as he moved toward the door to head Edgar off. You could see the well-defined tendons in his arms moving beneath his skin as he opened the office door while simultaneously restraining Potts from bolting out. He was well-known for violence when provoked as well as whenever Luther allowed him to dem- onstrate what would happen if someone disobeyed orders. Blocking the door with a nasty smirk on his face, he seemed to be enjoying the moment.

"Have Billy escort Mr. Potts to his saloon but tell him not to let Potts touch his books until you are there. You and I need to talk for a moment."

Edgar made one more attempt with Luther. "Shorly we can work somethin out? I'll getcha your money," he exclaimed in a voice filled with panic.

"You'll do exactly as I as I have just said! Do you understand?"

Edgar nodded meekly.

Luther stared coldly at the cowering man. "Now get out."

Billy was just outside the door, almost a foot taller and 150 pounds heavier than his brother, with a demeanor that was the exact opposite of Cloyd's. He had an almost angelic, round face and the mind of a six-year-old. He had been born simple-minded. But the extra 150 pounds he carried was all muscle, and he did anything and everything his brother asked. Nobody messed with the two brothers. Billy lifted Edgar by one arm and carried him out to the front porch with Edgar's legs frantically pin-wheeling trying to reach the floor. Cloyd shut the door and sat down across from Luther.

There was a long moment while Luther gazed out the window again con- sidering his options. Finally, nodding to himself, he turned and spoke quietly to Cloyd. "That little rat-bastard has been a pain in the ass ever since I picked him to manage that saloon. I knew he was stupid, but I didn't expect him to be this stupid."

He sighed and shook his head. "I guess I should have expected this. He has done nothing to force the Callaways out of their saloon. He is a worthless piece of shit and we don't need him anymore. It's time to fix this saloon problem ourselves. I recommend you start thinking of an accident that will befall him. I suggest that it occur on the Fourth when there will be a lot of chaos and confusion around here."

Cloyd chuckled. "You think he can come up with the money?"

"What books he might have won't tell us anything, but I suspect he has salted away a pretty pile and I aim to get it back before we cut him loose. Bring back whatever he's got. I want you and Billy to ride him hard and scare the shit out of him. Tear his place apart. There has to be a large stash of money hidden somewhere. Maybe we can get some of what he owes us, although I suspect he has drunk most of the profits. Just don't let him run off."

Cloyd chuckled again. "I'm sure Billy and I can make that little runt pretty nervous. I think you will get back more than you expect."

Luther laughed. "Yes, I am sure you can. Lord knows you have had enough practice. But I still have to deal with the Callaways. I don't believe my plan to starve them out is going to work fast enough. I think it's time for that damned Irishman to go as well. It would be convenient if he were involved in the same accident as Potts. I am sure Callaway's arrogant, aloof wife won't stay in Eagle Rock a minute longer if her husband is found to have fallen into the Snake River in a drunken stupor and drowned. Wouldn't it be something if the two saloon owners in town got into a fight on the new railroad bridge and knocked each other off? Once Patrick Callaway is out of the way, Lady Callaway herself certainly won't want to run a saloon alone. I'll offer her a modest amount, just enough to pay her way back to her kin in Louisville, and we can finally claim the last bit of property downtown that my idiot surveyors didn't lock down for me when we set up this town."

Luther got up, came around his desk, and gave Cloyd a pat on the shoulder. "You think about what I have said. I know you and Billy can handle this. Now get that little ass-wipe back to his saloon and make sure you tear the place up to find any paperwork or hidden cash that will help us put the last nails in his coffin."

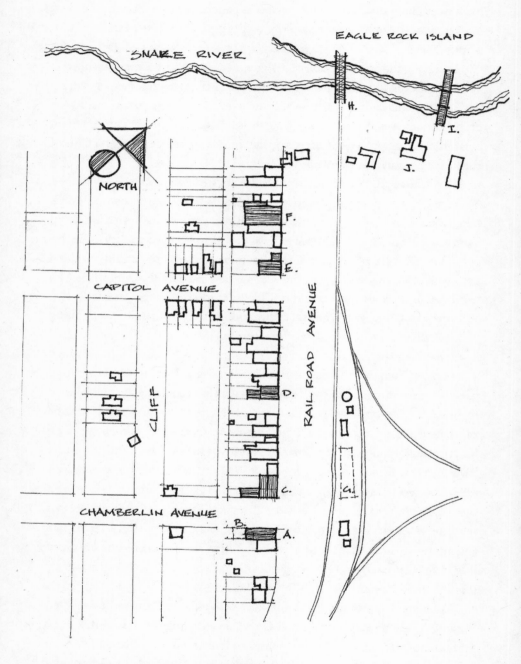

Hand drawn street plan showing locations of buildings, track right-of-way and river taken from an 1882 survey. (Drawn by Ralls Melotte)

LEGEND

*(*Indicates actual locations of buildings and structures with known Owners. Owners of other buildings are entirely fiction but all these structures were present on the 1882 survey)*

A. Patrick's Saloon *(Potts' Saloon and Luther Armstrong's ranch are on the other side of the river and not shown.)*

B. Proposed location of Cat's Cafe

C. Anderson Brothers' Warehouse

D. Eagle Rock Register – Ellington Harper, Jr, Proprietor

E. Eagle Rock Hotel – Dexter Highsmith, Manager

F. Eagle Rock Livery – Shorty Smith, Owner

G. Proposed location of permanent Railroad Depot*

H. East Bridge of the Utah & Northern Railroad*

I. Taylor's Bridge*

J. Robert Anderson's first structures *(serving people crossing Taylor's Bridge)**

Chapter One
One week later, Thursday, 9:30 PM, July 3rd, 1879

The abrupt sounds of gunshots and stampeding horse hooves outside the saloon brought a death-like silence to the room full of drunken railmen and miners. Even Sheriff Zane Gunther seemed taken by surprise, probably from the effects of steady drinking for the last ten hours. He stumbled off his stool and yelled in his slow drawl, "What'n the hell is goin' on out there?" Pulling out both his pearl-handled .44-caliber six-shooters, he started for the saloon doors.

With that, the rest of the crowd started talking and got up to see the commotion. The first ones to the windows exclaimed, "Shit! It's the Clancy clan!" Warning shots from Zane's six-shooters quieted the crowd. Drunk as he was, pulling those guns out of his swivel holsters, he might easily pick off one of the riders by accident, but no one in the saloon was too worried about that. A dead Clancy was good riddance and one less thing to worry about at night.

The sheriff nearly emptied both guns, firing randomly in the air, then proceeded to yell at the riders. "We don't have no use foh y'all pot-lickers.[4] Go back up there in them hills with the rest of the heathens where y'all belong!" His blustering drew fits of laughter from the riders.

Towering over Zane astride a horse at least eighteen hands high, the eldest son of Ben Clancy rode up to the sheriff and laughed directly in his face. "All right, Mister Big and Mighty Sheriff. This time we're a-clearin out. But

---

4   **Potlicker** – *a thoroughly disreputable person*

rememba, our pappy will be outta the Fort Henry hoosegow[5] tomorrow, so ya'll be seein a lot more of us in the future. That oughtta make ya shiver in your boots tonight," he sneered. "Ya might wanna consider a new profession cause'n the Clancy clan's back an we're ready ta dish out a heap-a payback."

With that, the riders started whooping and firing their guns in the air again. They turned and rode noisily out of town, leaving Eagle Rock's main street, saloon, and sheriff in a cloud of dust. Zane stood slack-jawed and watched them go. He had forgotten that Ben Clancy had finished his jail time for the clan's last escapade. Even in his present drunken stupor, he recognized things could get a little dicey for a lawman in this hick town, particularly since he had been the one to put Ben in jail. It might be a good time to lay low.

Turning to look back at the men peering at him from the saloon, he decided to mosey down to his office and alert the deputies. If the Clancys did return tonight, it would be wise to have his deputies on duty while he slept off a long hard day of drinking.

The pre-celebration for the Fourth of July town party tomorrow had been in full swing until the confrontation outside. In just a few minutes, the mood inside the saloon abruptly changed. The appearance of the Clancys was bad news and the party ground to a halt for the night. Everyone hoped the sheriff would be sober by tomorrow and things could be a little more joyful.

But, if the rest of the crowd was disappointed to call it a day, one person in the saloon was more than a little relieved. Catherine Callaway had been trying to keep up with the rowdy crowd's demands for the last two and a half hours. Fortunately, Henry Willett had stepped in to help or things could have gotten out of hand. When the last customer left, Catherine collapsed onto a chair and moaned, "Where is Patrick? Why didn't he come back? I can't do this by myself."

Henry walked over to her, pulled up an overturned chair, and sat down across the table from her. "You know how he gets carried away with his storytelling," he said. "You told me yourself he's been drinking heavily lately. I suspect he lost track of time and is at Potts' Saloon spinning yarns."

"But I need him here!" Catherine wailed. "What if you hadn't dropped in? Those two fights could have become barroom brawls without you to break them up." As tears began to streak her face, she banged her fist on the table and

---

5   ***Hoosegow*** – *jail*

got up. "I never planned on this! Patrick wanted the saloon. Not me! I can't deal with this chaos."

She sat down again, sighed, and looked directly at Henry. "I really was so glad to see you tonight. You were wonderful, taking over the way you did. You didn't have to do that. You could have been celebrating with the rest of them, but I really need someone to handle this place. Patrick doesn't seem to get that or..." She started sobbing. "Or, he just doesn't care!" she said angrily.

Henry stood up and gently took a hold of her wrists. "I am sure there is a good explanation for his disappearance and this will all look different to you in the morning. Do you want me to help you close up?"

Catherine slipped her wrists from Henry, looking a little uncomfortable. "No," she said. "Patrick can clean up this mess himself when he feels like coming back. I have already done my share."

Henry smiled at her. "Well then, I'll be going. Bar the doors behind me and then you go directly to bed. You look exhausted."

Catherine smiled at her friend. "Thank you again for helping. It means a lot to me."

After Henry left, Catherine assessed the damage. She just couldn't go to bed with the saloon looking this bad, so she sighed and started picking up the overturned chairs. Half an hour later, she had washed and put away the glasses and mugs and swept the floor.

"There, that is finally done," she said to herself and took a moment to look around the saloon. It had been a long hard day for her while her husband had been taking his so-called walkabout to scout out business at the other saloon. That had been at seven o'clock this evening and he had never come back. She hated the saloon, and right now she was pretty sure she hated Patrick.

Still, tonight had been the first time since they had arrived in Eagle Rock more than a year ago that they would actually break even, and tomorrow would bring in a nice profit if this was an example of the attention the saloon would get for the Fourth of July weekend. She had been praying for this, had actually counted on Patrick being right for once, and had prepared for the event. But she hadn't expected him to wander off just as the crowd descended. Where was that man? They should have opened a café, like he promised.

Patrick Callaway had already decided to move west when he met Catherine Callaway in her father's Louisville, Kentucky home at a large, festive

Thanksgiving party. One month later they eloped on a night train to Salt Lake City to start a new life together. Patrick soon became disenchanted with Utah and they moved on to the new railroad town of Eagle Rock. He had promised they would open a café and she could cook meals using her mother's recipes. But as soon as they arrived in Eagle Rock, Patrick announced he had changed his mind and intended to open a saloon. Admittedly, his personality and storytelling were truly more suited to a saloon than a café. He could tell a good story and was always surrounded by people goading him to tell more. So, although Catherine had no interest whatsoever in tending a bar and managing a saloon, her duties began as soon as they opened Patrick's Saloon.

Soon after, when turnout was surprisingly low at his new tavern, Patrick made a point of visiting the other saloon in Eagle Rock to see what kinds of crowds they were getting. Of course, Catherine thought, they did need to size up the competition, and it was easy enough for her to take over the bar-tending duties for the few customers who frequented their saloon back then. But this was going to be a very big weekend for the town, and Patrick had gone visiting again just as the crowd was picking up. One of them was needed in front to tend the bar and manage the room while the other stocked and restocked supplies for the holiday crowd. It was Patrick who had decided to spend the last of their money to stock up on all of the whiskey, beer, and food they could buy for the three-day weekend, but the celebrating had started early and he was nowhere to be seen. Early in the evening, he'd left for what he promised would be a quick twenty-minute walk.

Exhausted and upset, Catherine checked the back-door lock, glad she had insisted that real doors be installed inside of the front, bat-wing saloon doors. She climbed the ladder to the small room above the saloon that served as their only private space—the space that was to become a proper apartment as soon as they could turn a profit. A lot was riding on this weekend.

On one hand, Catherine was relieved there was a good chance they were finally going to make back some of the money her father had loaned them. Patrick had demanded that she request money from her father to build a café. She had agonized the last few weeks over having to go back to Louisville and admit to her father that they had not only lost all the money, but they'd lost it on a saloon rather than a café. Now it appeared they were going to have enough money from the celebration of the Fourth to stay in Eagle Rock.

But life out west was hardly anything like she had imagined, and life with Patrick had not been anything like she thought it would be either. He had been so romantic, so attentive, so caring when they met at her father's Thanksgiving party. His stories of travels and adventures up and down the east coast were marvelous. And his idea of heading west to leave behind the stuffy, pompous Louisville atmosphere had thrilled her at the time. Drawn in by the attention, romance, and promise of adventures to come, she hadn't imagined how hot, dirty, dusty, and wild the West really was. It had frightened her some but, as a new, good Christian wife, she felt bound to abide by her husband's decisions and hoped everything would work out.

What bothered Catherine most were the rumors about the yarns Patrick told when he wasn't with her—stories that weren't quite as humorous to her as the ones she had been drawn to in Louisville before they got married. Recently, they seemed to focus more on gambling and loose women, which the local menfolk found very entertaining but suggested that Patrick had not been completely truthful with her. Of course, they were just rumors, weren't they?

What was obvious to Catherine was that her husband was bewitched by Fannie Smiles, the dark haired, dreamy eyed, full-figured bartender at Potts' Saloon where Patrick had headed this evening and, she was convinced, many other evenings. But he had never been gone this long before, and he had certainly never left her stranded with so many customers. She got into bed and tried to stay awake until Patrick came home. She would make it clear to him in no uncertain terms that this could not happen again.

Her mind returned to her rescuer Henry Willett and their growing friendship. Thank goodness for him. She and Patrick had met Henry on the wagon train they had joined to travel from Ogden, Utah up to Eagle Rock. Patrick had insisted they buy all the supplies they needed while in Ogden, since he was convinced the cost would be less than trying to buy them in Eagle Rock, a town still unconnected to the railroad at the time. Hauling supplies from Ogden made sense. Altogether, eighteen prairie schooners[6] and six Conestoga

---

6   ***Prairie schooner*** – *smaller, lighter version of the Conestoga wagons used by 19th-century pioneers.* ***Conestoga wagon*** – *heavy, horse-drawn freight wagon found in many wagon trains, pulled by four to six horses, mules, or oxen. They could haul as much as six tons of freight.*

wagonloads of families, bullwhackers,[7] and adventurers had joined the wagon train to make the trip north. Everyone was convinced that the newly formed Utah and Northern Railroad, backed by the Union Pacific, and the ongoing extension of that line northward would open up an opportunity for new wealth and freedom.

Patrick and Catherine had needed two wagons to haul all they had purchased with her father's money, so she was required to drive one of them herself. She was accustomed to riding horses but had never driven a stiff, rigid framed, steel-wheeled wagon pulled by oxen. The days were dry and hot, and the unrelenting wind kicked up dust from the wagons ahead of her. It covered her clothes, hands, hair and face, and permeated everything in the wagon. Even the oxen were matted with sweat and dirt. She had thought the trip through the mountains would be beautiful, but she rarely saw them through the suffocating clouds of dust. And when she did, looking through the dusty haze made them seem dark, gloomy, and foreboding. The buzzards circling overhead in search of dead and dying animals made her even more uncomfortable.

Instead of the adventure Patrick had promised, she found the trip frightening, and got no relief when they stopped for the night. The more seasoned travelers filled the evening with campfire tales of hostile Indians in the area.

By the third evening, her nights were filled with nightmares. She tried to dream about her peaceful rides on her pony as a child in the pastures around Lexington and Springfield, but the dreams always ended up with vultures and buzzards feeding on dead animals in a hot, burnt landscape. Each day on the trail was more wearisome than the last, and she began to regret ever listening to Patrick's promises. She hoped when they finally got settled in Eagle Rock, she could ride quietly on some local trails and experience the wildlife and scenery without the noise, dust, and weariness she was feeling.

Patrick assigned Catherine to building a fire and making a large meal that could be shared with the others. He fraternized with the other travelers, brought as many as a half dozen of them each evening to Catherine's fire for dinner and drinking, and regaled them with his colorful tales of life in the east. Those early relationships became just about the only customers they'd had until this evening.

---

7   **Bullwhacker** – *a driver of an ox wagon or other heavy freight wagon used in the early settlement of the West.*

Along the way, Patrick had convinced two surveyors responsible for laying out the land rights for the new town of Eagle Rock to help him secure one of the best lots for their café. Only later did Catherine find out he had been planning a saloon, never a café, all along. She had asked him how he managed to get such a good location but he never really gave her a very believable answer. It was only later that he had let it slip that he had outwitted the surveyors in cards and proposed the trade of a good site in exchange for what they owed him.

What finally made the trip bearable was Patrick's request for Henry to take over driving Catherine's wagon when one of the wheels came loose. Catherine found Henry to be one of the only gentlemen on the trip and welcomed his company and conversation. The friendship had continued once they got to Eagle Rock and he was one of the few who regularly frequented their saloon.

In the time that they had been in Eagle Rock, besides Patrick and Henry, the only other educated and reasonably polite gentleman she had encountered was the town's mayor, Luther Armstrong. Another man, a new arrival, Ellington Harper, Jr., seemed all right but she really hadn't formally met him. The rest of the town was filled with dark and dirty, oil-covered rail men; Chinese laborers who looked strange and frightening to Catherine; burly, bearded, rough-speaking trappers with very few social skills who spent most of their time alone in the mountains; grizzled men searching the streams for gold; a desperate collection of promiscuous single women; and the only really attractive woman in Eagle Rock—the vivacious and flirtatious Fannie Smiles.

Catherine eventually fell into a troubled sleep filled with dreams of women wooing Patrick at Potts' Saloon.

Chapter Two

Thursday, 11:30 PM, July 3rd, 1879

"As soon as you finish those dishes Sandy, let's pack up and get out of here." Fannie had just finished straightening up Potts' Saloon and she was ready to get back to her room across the river in Eagle Rock.

"Actually, I just finished," Sandy answered, "but I still need to set up the back bar."

"Forget it! We have worked long enough. I don't know where in the hell our ignorant Edgar has got to, probably still arguing with Patrick Callaway, but he can finish up in the morning when he finally shows up. Hang up your apron and let's get going."

"I don't know why Edgar insists on arguing with Patrick," Fannie continued. "So what if he owns a saloon on the other side of the river? If Edgar didn't water down his whiskey and try to sell that piss-poor beer, he wouldn't have so many customers rushing to cross the river now that the bridge has been completed. I thought he was going to lose it when Patrick said he would buy everybody a round of good red-eye whiskey[8] so they could find out what they're missing here. If Sheriff Zane hadn't been in the crowd, I think they would have gotten into a real bruiser of a fight, but it looked like Zane had been actually trying to get those two riled up into some kind of argument.

---

8   ***Red-eye whiskey*** – *a rather wicked combination of alcohol, burnt sugar, a little chewing tobacco, and possibly red pepper, gunpowder, arsenic and muddy river water. More processed and properly aged whiskey had a red tint from being aged in oak barrels. Some saloons might have served their own homemade whiskey as described but with coloring added to pass it off as red-eye.*

Did you notice how he kept egging Patrick on? The stories just got wilder and more fantastic, and it didn't help that Zane was buying everyone rounds. When Edgar grabbed Patrick by the throat, I think he would have choked him to death if Patrick hadn't pulled out that huge Bowie knife of his so fast. I've heard he always carries that monster knife strapped to his calf. It was just a good thing Zane got Patrick to clear out of here when he did."

The two women headed toward the rear door. Fannie paused just before she was about to open it. "You know, come to think of it, Edgar and Zane left about the same time as Patrick, and neither of them ever did come back."

Sandy just laughed. "You know that lazy bastard keeps a stock of the good whiskey in his room. He probably doubled back and used the back door to his apartment. He doesn't like overworking himself and I think he spends a lot of time back there." She flashed her eyes at Fannie. "You know what he says. He has 'book work' to do."

Fannie laughed at this. "Book work, my ass! I don't think he evens knows which end of a pen to write with. Oh shit! I've left one of the oil lamps on. You go ahead. I'll find my way home."

In the minute it took her for her eyes to adjust to the dark again as she stepped outside, Fannie sensed movement behind her. Before she could turn around, two large hands grabbed her from behind and squeezed her breasts.

"You bastard! You scared me half to death."

A deep base voice whispered in her ear. "Ya ready for a long, rough ride tonight? I got plans foh you."

"Oh Carl. Not tonight. I had a hell of a day and tomorrow will be worse. Let a poor working girl have a rest. And why do you always have to grab my tits? Couldn't you just greet me with a simple kiss?"

Carl Clancy spun her around, grabbed both cheeks of her ass, pulled her tight against his hips, and gave her a deep kiss. Fannie could tell from his hardness below her waist that he must have been imagining the evening while waiting for her. When they separated, he said with a catch in his voice, "Now, come on Fannie. Be reasonable. I've been a-waitin for ya out here in the dark foh at least half'n hour. We can just do it up against the wall of the saloon if you wanna make this quick."

Fannie held his broad shoulders at arm's length, leaned back, and looked up at him. "Oh for God's sake, I guess we can do better than that." His wet, lingering kiss had awakened a deep, lustful desire in her. She was getting less tired by the minute. "If we're going to have a go at each other, I would rather do it on a nice, soft bed. But not my bed. You know how noisy we get. And," she added, "if you're going to kiss me like that, I wish you'd not drink so much of that rot-gut whiskey beforehand. It tastes terrible."

Carl looked across the river to what there was of the business section of Eagle Rock. "Thundernation! This burg is really jumpin. It looks like ya have a real swingin celebration goin'. This place was dead the last time I came down. I rode here tonight with Ben, Jr. and the rest of the gang, and Ben was really pleased to see all the new opportunities in this town. We counted two saloons, the new bank, a depot, the hotel, and word's out there'll be a whorehouse soon. Pa'll be mighty pleased ta be seein this town has built up so fast right in our own back yard."

"Now don't you be gettin involved any more than you have to with your thieving brothers, Carl. You don't want to get thrown into the calaboose for a year like your pa. Whatever would I do for entertainment?" Fannie asked, smiling. "I might have to go out lookin for a new young stud. There are more comin to town every day on the train."

Carl smiled down at her and pulled her roughly to him again. "Ya know I can take care of mahself and stay outta trouble most of the time. And don't you be gettin any wanderin ideas, Ma'am. I'm keepin an eye on you." He gave her bottom a firm squeeze, followed by a quick swat.

Fannie swatted him right back. "Don't you be callin me Ma'am, mister. I'm not that much older than you. Now, how are we getting to your cabin? If you are really up for a romp, we gotta get a wiggle on."

Carl laughed, picked her up, threw her over his shoulder like a sack of horse feed, and carried her behind a shed at the back of the saloon. "Pappy told all us boys to eithah pick a young cowgal with a big rump ta make babies or an older, experienced widow that would really appreciate a romp in the hay with a young buck."

All the time he was talking, Fannie was putting up a fake fight, demanding to be put down, pounding his back with her fists, and quietly cursing him. A large horse with an oversized saddle was behind the shed. Carl lifted Fannie up and dropped her down onto the horse like she weighed nothing at all. She was always amazed at how strong he was. And handsome. Powerful chest, slim waist, tight ass, deep-blue eyes, and that sultry smile that could melt an iceberg.

"You'll be noticin I brought Ol Swayback and our special saddle. Only thinkin of you."

Fannie looked down at him. "Right, only thinking of me. You just like the tight fit when we both have to squeeze into this saddle."

He smiled. "Well, ya could always jus walk ta the cabin, but I might be sleepin befoh ya git there."

Carl didn't wait for her response but stepped up easily onto the front of the saddle. Fannie knew he enjoyed riding with her behind him in this saddle because she was forced to press herself tight up against his back with her crotch pressed against his ass. The bouncing ride always got her horny, if she wasn't already. He wriggled his butt against her to get all the way into the saddle and started riding east into the low hills with Fannie's head resting on his back.

Fannie had been entranced with Carl ever since the first time he had entered Potts' Saloon. But when she found out he was a Clancy, she had tried not let her interest show. The Clancy clan lived in the mountains east of Eagle Rock. They were all outlaws and constantly involved with horse and cattle rustling along with other illegal activities. They were a really mean bunch of mountain men and women, a grizzled, tough, scary family of sons and daughters, cousins, uncles, and an assortment of other relatives. But the worst of the bunch were the old man, Ben Clancy, and his brother. They were rotten to the core and ruled the family with iron fists. Ben was the brains of the bunch and had a keen mind for theft and crime.

Carl was the youngest of Ben's four boys and two girls by eight years. He had grown up less wild and crazy, was never mean, and was sometimes even thoughtful. One night, when Fannie had sampled a little too much alcohol, she had been sufficiently beguiled by Carl to let him follow her to her apartment. What followed was the most outrageous, exhausting, and satisfying sex she had ever known. Considering her background, that was quite remarkable.

Carl wasn't all that imaginative, but he had incredible staying power and proved to be a quick learner. Really rough and wild sex was always followed by unusually sensitive conversation for a man and a lot of touching, giving an almost a boyish side to his personality, and this usually led to another round of lovemaking. Carl provided the most carefree and deeply sensual sensations Fannie had ever felt with a man. But it was too noisy for the neighbors. After their first time, she had faced a number of complaints and was almost evicted. After that night, she made it clear to Carl that they could not continue to meet in her one-room apartment. But there was no way she would go to the Clancy homestead either. She admitted she was quite frightened by his family and wanted nothing to do with them. So, Carl had agreed to build a small cabin in the hills closer to Eagle Rock, away from the clan, where they could have their clandestine meetings and make as much noise as they wanted. He liked to call it their Ace in the Hole[9] and was quite proud of his somewhat primitive love-nest.

Carl spent a lot of time alone out in the open valleys east of Eagle Rock, rounding up the cattle and horses the clan had acquired. He was only involved with a few of the clan's criminal activities and never in a very significant way. Consequently, his time with Fannie was sporadic and unpredictable. Whenever he arrived, it was always a surprise, and it usually started with a two-handed greeting from behind. Fannie was proud of her full figure and generous bust, and Carl had always been in awe of her beauty and remarkable hour-glass figure. His familiar greeting tonight had started on their second night together when he whisked her off to his almost complete cabin. It was still missing a roof, but the sky was clear and the stars were amazing. For her, it was a welcome respite from the monotony in this two-bit town. The combination of outrageous sexual abandon coupled with caring, conversation was always a welcome relief for her in this new frontier.

Fannie decided she would sleep in tomorrow. That deadbeat Edgar Potts could set up the back bar himself. She was going to have an even longer night than she had planned, and she would be sore tomorrow but it would be worth it. She sighed and gave Carl a little squeeze below his belt.

Carl chuckled. "Whoa lady! We ain't there yet."

They both laughed and rode on into the night.

---

9   *Ace in the hole* – *hideout or hidden gun*

Chapter Three

Friday, 9:00 AM, July 4th, 1879

Wheeeeeeewoo!! Wheewoo!! Wheewoo!! The shrill whistle of Engine 101 silenced the noisy drinkers already packed wall-to-wall in Patrick's Saloon for the holiday. The blast was ear piercing as the train fired up to roll into town. For a moment, the only sound in the room was Catherine's whispered "Drat!" when the glass she was washing slipped from her hands and fell back into the dish bucket, splashing soapy water all over her new dress. Catherine had meant to put on an apron, but the crowd of celebrating drinkers had kept her behind the bar ever since she had opened up. The silence was broken by one slurred voice yelling, "Dar she is, boys! Bout ta cross our bridge. Let's go greet'er good and proper."

With that, a cacophony of shouts and curses filled the room again. Chair legs scraped the rough wood floor, some tipping over as men clambered up and drained last precious drops into gaping mouths, slammed down empty glasses, and pushed away from their tables. The saloon was filled again with the boisterous sounds of drunken men ready for a celebration.

The Fourth of July weekend was starting off with a bang. Right on time, the shiny, wood-burning, narrow-gauge 4-6-0 was crossing the very bridge these men had been working overtime to complete for the last several months. This spindly-looking steel structure provided a way for the railroad to cross the Snake River in the eastern Idaho Territory and open up a path to the Montana mines and all the wealth these men were convinced was buried in those hills.

Truth be told, half the excitement was watching to see whether the bridge would even hold up. Not having seen many steel bridges, many of these men had placed bets as to whether a fully loaded train could cross the bridge without collapsing into the river. They were more familiar with wooden railroad bridges, which looked far more substantial. But this didn't keep them from celebrating their first three days off this year. Most of them had been celebrating since yesterday afternoon when they had gotten off early, and the official arrival of the train was the grand kickoff for the food, drink, and gaiety everyone had been anticipating for weeks.

The 101 had been oiled, greased, and carefully washed yesterday afternoon. For maximum visual effect, chief engineer, Joel Gustvenson, had quietly taken the 101 and half a dozen flat-bed cars across the bridge late yesterday evening so the engine could enter the town center over the bridge from the west in full view of the depot. What could be more impressive than seeing this mighty train billowing black clouds of smoke and bursts of steam rolling across the new bridge to the center of town? A formal ceremony dedicating the new bridge would be held at the temporary train depot kitty-corner to Patrick's Saloon.

The saloon's prime location was no accident. Unscrupulous and unrepentant, Patrick had tricked and bribed the early surveyors during their long wagon train ride north to get it. Now, his plans had finally come to fruition. Today, there would be a street festival unlike anything before in this sleepy little town of Eagle Rock, including speeches by Mayor Luther Armstrong and Brigham Young, Jr. himself, who had arrived from Salt Lake City with much fanfare on the regularly scheduled, late-afternoon train pulling three brand new passenger cars filled with people ready to party. Young had spent the night at the mayor's ranch on the west side of the Snake River and would speak this morning to kick off the festivities. Patrick had explained to Catherine that he expected to recoup much of their investment before the weekend was out.

As the crowd of miners, train men, laborers, ranch hands, fur trappers, and other locals that hung out looking for free drinks climbed over each other to get through the swinging saloon doors, Catherine breathed a sigh of relief. She'd had to open much earlier than planned, but a crowd had gathered outside her doors and started loudly chanting in unison for her to open up. The whistling of the 101 amounted to her first break this morning. And Patrick was still gone.

She looked over the room and let out a small moan. The saloon was filled again with upturned chairs, glasses on the floor, tabletops littered with cigar butts, with spilt whiskey and beer everywhere. If Patrick did not show up soon, it would be another difficult day like last night, especially with the cooking she had planned. In anticipation of the Fourth of July weekend, Patrick had acquiesced to her wish to serve food and allowed her to gather all the ingredients for an elk stew. She had planned to prepare it last night, but with Patrick wandering out and not returning, she would have to do it this morning. The last thing she wanted was to spend the remainder of the day behind the bar, but until Patrick came back, the stew would have to wait.

Up to this point, Patrick and Catherine had operated the saloon without any outside help, but never before had they experienced so many customers. Most of the locals liked to spend time at the other saloon. It was located across the river, closer to the tent shanty town that provided temporary housing for the railroad men. Having a saloon on the same side of the river as the temporary housing meant the rail men didn't have to pay the toll to get across Taylor's Bridge which, up until now, was the only bridge across the Snake River in all of eastern Idaho. Patrick had predicted that as soon as the railroad bridge was completed, more customers would come to their saloon in the middle of the small business district of Eagle Rock. It would also be a draw to the dreadful hotel, the only stop for overnight accommodations in the area and home to the worst food anywhere. But one step at a time, he liked to say of the promising new town. When Catherine questioned if it was safe to cross a railroad bridge since there wasn't a walkway yet, Patrick scoffed.

"These men have been walking rails for years and are certainly sure-footed enough to get across that bridge without falling off," he laughed. "And with the prospects of beer, whiskey, and an evening with some of those new working girls who arrived in the last few weeks, they will be coming over in droves."

Catherine had observed first-hand just how "sure-footed" these men were once they had spent a night drinking continuously. She was concerned that the trips back to the railroad shanty town could be pretty hazardous for the men.

But, from the look of the crowds last night and early this morning, it appeared that Patrick's prediction had been correct. Of course the announcement Catherine had put in the local, one-page newspaper advertising a Fourth of July reduction in the cost of whiskey shots probably helped as well. But, if Patrick did not get back soon, she was going to have to find some help. This was too good an opportunity to close the doors, but she would lose the money she'd spent on the side of elk if she didn't start cooking soon. Where on earth was she going to find help on the Fourth?

And where was that damned man?

Chapter Four

Friday, 9:00 AM, July 4th, 1879

The day was already heating up and it felt to Jeremiah that the mid-morning winds would soon swirl street dirt and debris into miniature dust devils traveling eastward down the town's main street. Yes, it would be another hot and gritty day, he thought, as he stood nursing what was left of his beer, leaning against the front wall of Patrick's Saloon where he'd been since just before dawn this morning.

Jeremiah found that the early morning was the only comfortable and relaxing time of the day. The sun took its time to rise over the Rocky Mountains to the east and most of the town was usually sleeping off a hard drunk from the night before. After cold nights under the shadow of the Snake River Mountains, mere foothills when compared to the Rockies farther east, he would walk to the town early in the morning, seek out a bench in front of Patrick's Saloon, and settle in to warm up and watch the sunrise. The sun wouldn't warm the small hut he shared with his mother near a wash east of town on Sand Creek for another half hour. Jeremiah liked this routine but, then again, this saloon had never been as busy as it was this morning. That might be a problem for him. Crowds often were.

The depot across the street from the saloon was a temporary, wood-frame building up on wood blocks, soon to be replaced by a much grander structure according to the town leaders. Surrounding the building were the two tracks of the new Utah & Northern Railroad; a main line in front and a passing siding behind, along with a short spur heading north toward the location where maintenance buildings would soon be built to serve the future railroad yard.

A row of dilapidated huts in a long line north of the tracks served as the temporary housing for the railroad maintenance men. The railroad construction crews were housed in tents on the other side of the river. On the south side of the street along the next block west was a line of roughly built, one-story wood structures with false fronts hastily erected to impress would-be investors. These comprised the bulk of downtown Eagle Rock. Towering above them in the middle of the block was the two-story Eagle Rock Hotel, although it looked just as temporary as the depot. Only Patrick's Saloon looked relatively well built and boasted both a long canvas overhang and boardwalk across the length of its front. It even had a second story that, unlike the hotel, did not look like it would fall over in the first big wind.

This was the first Fourth of July in Eagle Rock, a town that had been hurriedly thrown up last fall as the railroad had established this location as its division point and maintenance headquarters on the planned route under construction from Franklin, Utah to the Butte, Montana mines. Railroad men, freelance miners, fur trappers, and all sorts of rough-looking men had been arriving every week with dreams of fame and fortune, along with wranglers, unsavory looking waddies[10] and saddle bums[11] drawn to the new ranches. The miners and trappers had driven out the few Indians in the area who had not left for the Blackhawk reservation south near Fort Henry.

For young men like Jeremiah, the center of town was an exciting place to be. It was also much safer in town than across the river in the railroad construction crews' shanty town. The roughneck railroad construction crews, unlike the railroad mechanics and engineers found behind the depot, were an unruly group who had a tendency to start fights in the only saloon on that side of the river and gang up on outsiders. Unfortunately for Jeremiah and his mother, this included the few remaining local Natives.

Tall, lanky Jeremiah had features that more closely resembled his Shoshone mother than his French trapper father, or so he had been told. His father had long since left one night in search of a quieter patch of wilderness to the west and never returned. Even with the Christian name his mother had given him,

---

10   **Waddies** – *hired men who tend cattle and perform many duties on horseback, cattle rustlers, cowboys who drift from ranch to ranch*
11   **Saddle bums** – *drifters*

hoping to avoid the attention of bullies in the new town, Jeremiah had grown up as the target of drunken insults and, more than occasionally, violence.

There was little left in Jeremiah's glass; what there was had gone flat, and he couldn't afford another one. He was just deciding it might be time to find a less obvious location if he wanted to enjoy the festivities away from the locals' jeering and insults. He had earned the nickname Slink for his ability to keep from drawing attention.

Jeremiah had awakened early this morning in anticipation of the train's arrival. He had seen this powerful engine before as it brought passengers and goods up from Ogden and Salt Lake City, but he had never seen an engine this large and heavy cross what looked like a very rickety bridge. The steam engines and workings of the railroad had fascinated him from the very first day they'd started bringing men and equipment to lay the roadbed for the Union Pacific's Utah and Northern Railroad.

Abruptly, the shrill whistle of the 101 and the slowly accelerating chug… chug…chug of the massive steam pistons signaled the arrival of the engine at the bridge. The train pulled a number of flat cars festooned with red, white, and blue bunting across its benches and railings. For the moment, Jeremiah could only see billowing clouds of black smoke and soot shooting skyward like the hammerhead storm clouds he had seen in the mountains. But he knew what it would look like; he had snuck across the railroad bridge last night and had watched it being decorated. It would come into view soon to cross over the river.

Just as abruptly, the double doors of the saloon swung open as a crowd of loud, rowdy men scrambled out to see the train. "Get outta our way, Slink!" yelled a burly lumberjack Jeremiah had had run-ins with before. The man gave Jeremiah a shove, causing him to trip over one of the benches set along the front wall of the saloon and into the dirt and horse-dung-covered street. "This ain't no celebration for half-breeds. This here celebration is for real, hard-workin Americans."

The crowd of men laughed as they walked around Jeremiah. Another kicked dirt in his face and said with scorn, "I don't know why he hangs around here all the time. He should stay where he belongs up in those hills with the rest of the crazy Injuns."

Jeremiah got up and dusted himself off as the men joined the growing crowd in front of the depot to watch the train come over the bridge, effectively blocking Jeremiah's view of the train's arrival. *Just another day in Eagle Rock*, he thought.

Since the saloon was now empty, he decided to go inside and stay out of the way. As everybody continued to drink, things would probably get worse. He might have to head back to his mother's shack and hole up for the rest of the day, but he really wanted to get up close to Engine 101. Maybe later he could get a better look.

As he entered the saloon, he was surprised to see that two men had stayed inside: Henry Willett and old Smiley Jack. As usual, Smiley Jack was curled up in the back corner sleeping off a hangover. Henry was up at the bar telling the pretty Mrs. Callaway about his departure as bookkeeper of the Johnson ranch. Jeremiah had overheard the men in the bar talking about this earlier.

"I just couldn't work with him any longer, Catherine." Henry was saying.

Jeremiah decided to take a chair next to Smiley, in case he tried to get up before he was fully capable of negotiating the length of the saloon from the back to the front door. Smiley was known to fall flat on his face after several shaky steps, trying to get to the bench in front of the saloon. Doc Jones would have to be summoned, and since Doc was probably hung over himself, he would come in using foul language that always upset Mrs. Callaway. Jeremiah would have liked another beer, but he had spent all he had on the first one, and it really wasn't all that good. Someday, he would find enough money to buy shots of whiskey. They had to be better than this beer.

After he sat down, Jeremiah couldn't help hearing the conversation between Henry and Mrs. Callaway.

"Do you really think it's wise to leave your job before you find another one, Henry?" Mrs. Callaway asked.

"Well, it may not be a good idea, and working for him as a cowhand when I got started was just fine, but I'm afraid that, well, let's just say, I don't want to be involved in that mess of books he's got me working on. Some of the entries I have found just don't add up. I'm sure I can find something else to do."

"Well, I am sure you know what you are doing but I sure don't know what *I'm* going to do." Although Mrs. Callaway was holding a glass she had started drying, it looked more like she was wringing her hands. "Honestly Henry, I've gone from furious to worried. Where could he be?" Catherine leaned in close to Henry and confided quietly, "I have never felt comfortable in this town and now, with Patrick missing, I am even more alarmed. All these rough, rude men and the drinking and the gunfire and there are even Indians…I'm frightened. See that young Indian at the back of the saloon? He is always hanging around out front. It's creepy. We heard so many horrible stories about Indians on the wagon train coming here. You heard them. And now one is actually in our saloon. If Patrick were here, he would escort him out right quick, but I just can't do that. He hasn't done anything bad, but I am afraid."

"Catherine, that's Slink. He's just a teenage boy who happens to be part Indian and part White. He hangs out in this town because there isn't anything to do or anywhere else to go. I've run into him many times. He is really good-natured and wouldn't harm a fly. You've got no worries with him around."

Catherine didn't look convinced. "Well, if you say so, but he always seems to be creeping around."

"He's learned that from experience, Catherine. Most of those rough men you mentioned don't like Indians. He's wise enough to know he has to be careful. Half-breeds are even lower than the Chinese in the pecking order around here. I'm afraid he gets bullied a lot. Just about everyone gives him a hard time, but he never acts up about it. He seems pretty mature if you ask me. He got the nickname Slink because he tries to stay to himself and keeps out of everybody's way. He's really a good kid. You're far safer around him than a good many of the men you have been serving at the bar."

Catherine looked over at Slink and nodded but still seemed dubious. Then she noticed she still had a glass in her hand. She set it down, picked up a tray, and started around the bar. "I have to pick up all this mess, clean the tables, wash the glasses, and restock the bar. I don't know how it will get it all done by myself."

In his usual calm, quiet voice, Henry responded, "I'm sure Patrick is all right, holed up somewhere with some of the men, and lost track of time. As I've said all along, he does like to spin a yarn."

"Lost track of time! You've got to be kidding. He never even came back last night! I was supposed to be making elk stew for the lunch crowd this morning, not acting as a bartender."

Henry looked surprised but decided not to comment on Patrick not returning home last night. To change the subject he asked, "Really? You were going to start cooking meals for the saloon? Have you done that before?"

Catherine collapsed in one of the saloon chairs, put her elbows on the table and cradled her head. When she lifted her head to look at Henry, she said sternly, "Patrick promised me before we left from Ogden that I could cook and run a café. But then once he got here, he decided it had to be a saloon. Now I think that's what he had planned all along and he knew I wouldn't come here if he told me what he was really going to do. We will be in big trouble if we don't make a profit during this celebration." She banged her fist on the table, and then grimaced and started massaging her hand.

"I bought most of the side of elk and the fixings to make a stew for this afternoon's lunch and dinner. It will spoil if I don't start cooking soon." It looked like she was going to start crying, but she fought back her tears, stood up and started picking up more glasses.

Henry got up from the bar stool and went over to touch her on the shoulder. "I will go out and find Patrick. Don't worry. I'll get him back here." He looked at Jeremiah and Smiley Jack in the back of the saloon. "In the meantime, maybe Slink here could help you clean up the place."

"Slink," Henry turned and asked the young man, "you think you could do something useful rather than hiding over there in the corner with Smiley? Maybe you could help Mrs. Callaway pick up these glasses and sweep the floor."

Slink was surprised he had been noticed and turned to Catherine. "Why, why sure Ma'am. I'd be fine to helpin out. You just tell me what needs a-doin'. I'm shur-nuff not doin' nothin else." He got up and walked over to Catherine, who looked a little alarmed and backed up a step.

Jeremiah smiled at her and carefully took the tray from her hands. "I'd be right glad to be helpin out, Mrs. Callaway," he repeated.

Catherine gave him a small smile. Jeremiah thought it was the most beautiful smile he had ever seen. He turned to start picking up the rest of the glasses, but Catherine touched his arm to stop him.

"I do need help Slink, and I will pay you. But if Patrick does not get here soon, I may need help all day. It's just not fair for me to ask you to work on the Fourth of July."

"Ah, don't worry, Ma'am. I've already been told the Fourth ain't a holiday for us lowly half-breeds."

Catherine put her hand to her mouth in surprise. "Well, that's just outrageous. Who told you that?"

Jeremiah shrugged. "It don't matter, Ma'am. I wanna help."

Catherine looked closely at him and then sighed. "Well, I still hope Patrick gets back here, so you can go out and enjoy the festivities. At least you'll have some coins in your pocket as well."

She looked around the room. "I'm going to restock and clean up the bar if you will clean up out here."

Slink looked puzzled. "I thought you were going to cook elk stew."

Catherine shook her head solemnly. "I have never cooked elk stew before and I really don't think I have time to learn now. I should have started last night."

Slink looked at her, then looked down at the floor, pursing his lips together, obviously thinking about how to say something. "Well Ma'am, I know someone who can make a really fine elk stew if you're interested."

"Really? But today? I can't just ask someone to drop everything and come cook for me on the Fourth of July." She thought for a moment. "But who were you thinking of?"

Slink smiled. "My ma. She's a really fine cook and she makes all kinds of stews, but elk stew is my favorite. She ain't doin' nothin today because a lot of the men wanted their best bib and tucker[12] cleaned for the Fourth. She's been working mighty hard the last two days to keep up."

"Well, she has already worked hard enough this week. I can't ask her to work today."

Jeremiah smiled and shook his head. "What I'm meanin is, Mrs. Callaway, she loves to cook. She would be glad to cook all day for you. She would much rather cook than clean clothes. Let me talk to her and I'll betcha she'd be here all smiles in the blink of an eye."

Catherine breathed in deeply and gave Jeremiah another one of those wonderful smiles. "Slink, you go ahead and ask her and tell her I will pay her well."

Henry had been watching the discussion and winked at Catherine. "I'm going to go look for Patrick. You look like you are in good hands. I'll drop back by as soon as I find him."

"Thanks Henry. That would help me a lot. You tell him he needs to get back here right now!

But as Henry and Slink turned to leave the saloon, Catherine stopped them. "Henry? Slink? Could you possibly take Smiley Jack to wherever it is he lives?

---

12 **Best bib and tucker** – *best clothes*

He came in late last night as I was closing up. He was really drunk but also seemed terribly frightened and kept babbling about something and wouldn't leave. I was exhausted and wanted to go to bed so I gave him a beer and told him he could sleep in the saloon. He kept repeating something over and over, but he was mumbling so much, I really couldn't understand him. Something like, "Thase poosht." It was all so slurred, I guess it could have been anything. I would like him to be out of here if we really are going to serve food today."

Slink smiled. "I know where his shack's at and it's on my way to my ma's. I'll take him."

Catherine smiled at Slink. "That would be wonderful of you. Your pay starts right now, whether your mother wants to cook or not. And thank you Henry, for looking for Patrick. He is probably just passed out somewhere sleeping it off like Smiley here. That man will be the death of me."

Henry waved back at Catherine as he held the double doors open for Slink. Slink had already lifted Smiley into a somewhat vertical position and was guiding him out the door.

"We'll find him. Don't worry, although I suspect he might be in for some blistered ears once he shows up," Henry laughed.

He winked at Catherine before he let the doors shut. She smiled and thought to herself, *What a nice man. This day may work out after all.* Putting her hands on her hips, she gave an exasperated sigh. "Even without my wayward husband."

Chapter Five

Friday, 9:30 AM, July 4th, 1879

After the two men left, Catherine went into the back room to restock the bar only to find the barrels and crates far too heavy for her to move. "Mercy! How am I going to get anything done?" she cried out. She sat down on one of the kegs in frustration, and then realized she could ask Slink to do the heavy lifting while she straightened up the saloon. He would be back soon.

Ten minutes later, Slink entered the saloon with a huge grin on his face. A short, heavyset, older woman followed close behind with her eyes downcast.

"Mrs. Callaway, this is my ma, Crow Feather." Slink looked down at his mother and said quietly, "Now tell Mrs. Callaway what ya told me, Ma."

The woman looked up at Catherine with large dark eyes that darted all around the saloon, taking in the room for the first time. Then, in a slow monotone and with carefully spaced words, she said, "I wud be mos please to cook foh you."

"Ma'am, are you sure this is all right, asking you to help just because my husband didn't show up?" Catherine asked Crow Feather.

The older woman turned to Slink with a look of panic and then turned back to Catherine and repeated just as slowly, "I wud be mos please to cook foh you, Ma'am."

Slink chuckled and put his arm around his mother. "She's not real good with English, Ma'am, but you should've heard her on the way over here tellin me in our language all the things she could cook for you. It would be hard to tell by lookin at her right now, but she's really excited about this. She practiced that speech most the way here. You just show her your kitchen and point to what you want cooked and I know you'll be happy."

He turned to his mother and said quietly again, "It's gonna be all right, Ma. Mrs. Callaway won't bite."

Crow Feather's big eyes turned toward Catherine again and a tentative smile formed on her lips.

Catherine laughed. "Of course, yes, everything will be all right. And I will pay you for your help. Let's go back to the kitchen and get started."

Slink looked around the saloon with a frown. "I thought you wanted me to straighten up the saloon? You're not a'needin me now?"

With one hand on Crow Feather's shoulder, leading her to the kitchen, she turned back to gesture for Slink to follow. "Oh I do! But what I really need is a strong, young man to haul all those heavy barrels and crates up to the bar so I can restock. Come with us so I can show you what I need."

With that, Slink flashed Catherine a big smile as she led both of them through the small vestibule to the kitchen in the back of the saloon. Crow Feather was the first to go through the kitchen door but stopped abruptly and stared in awe at the room. She turned and started speaking animatedly to her son while gesturing around the room. After a moment of rapid exchange between the two, Slink looked at Catherine and explained, "My ma says this is the biggest room she's ever cooked in and it has so many pots and pans. She's not sure which ones she can use."

Crow Feather moved the rest of the way into the room and stared at everything with big eyes full of wonder. Catherine laughed again. "She can use anything she wants. You see, I thought we were planning to open a café when we came to Eagle Rock, so I brought everything I might need to open up a small restaurant." She sighed. "So far, the only thing I have cooked are meals for Patrick and me. It will be good to put this kitchen into operation. If your mother has any questions about anything, I'll be glad to help."

Slink translated Catherine's instructions for his mother and went with Catherine to start moving the barrels from the storage room at the back of the kitchen. By the time Catherine returned to the kitchen, Crow Feather had found the side of elk and vegetables and was exclaiming rapidly in the language of her tribe all the different ways she could prepare the stew. Of course Catherine didn't understand anything. As Slink came through the room with a case of whiskey, Catherine asked him to please tell his mother she could prepare the stew any way she wanted. She was sure it would be just fine. After another quick exchange between Slink and his mother, Crow Feather turned to Catherine and with a large smile this time, made a small bow, turned back to the crates of vegetables, selected a knife from the rack on the wall, and started vigorously chopping vegetables. Catherine noticed Crow Feather had started humming to herself and seemed completely at home.

Back in the saloon, the noise of the festivities across the street had grown to a low roar of cheers, catcalls, and even a few gunshots. Catherine shook her head. Why did Westerners shoot off their guns whenever they became excited? She had never experienced this in Louisville. It was probably instigated by the sheriff. He seemed to be completely at ease shooting his guns for just about any occasion. Catherine was beginning to wonder about his life before coming to Eagle Rock.

Just then, Henry came back into the saloon. He didn't look happy.

"Did you find him?" Catherine asked.

"No," Henry responded, "but it appears he spent a considerable amount of time down at Potts' place last night. Nobody will tell me much, but just about everyone agrees he was there for at least a portion of the evening."

"Well, he told me about scouting about the town to see why so many of our early customers haven't been back lately, but surely it wouldn't have taken all night." Catherine started wringing her hands again. "I'm getting worried."

"I wish I could tell you more." The last of Henry's words were drowned out by an extraordinarily loud cheer from the crowd outside."

Catherine looked flustered. "What on earth is going on out there?"

"I think the mayor has just introduced the Honorable John W. Young. He is about to make a speech. You probably won't hear him again this close to home. You might want to take a break and hear what he has to say."

Catherine looked oddly at Henry. "You used the word 'Honorable,' which sounds like a sign of respect, but you don't look like you mean it. Isn't he the leader of the Mormon Church, a well-known preacher? What's wrong?"

"Brigham Young, Sr. was the leader of the Mormon Church, but the leadership has been a little unstable since he passed. John Young is as extreme in his politics as he is in his religious viewpoints. I haven't met him, though I have had a few encounters with some of Brigham Young Sr.'s followers that I find disturbing and distasteful, but I still want to hear what he has to say. Come with me and decide for yourself. It's not often you will see him up here in this part of Idaho so far from civilization. He really prefers the ease and sophistica-tion of the old states[13] on the east coast."

"I'd like to but I had better get ready for my hoped-for onslaught once the speeches are over. Thanks for looking for Patrick, Henry."

"Try not to worry. I'm still looking. He will probably show up for the speeches. I will report back as soon as I have something to share."

"Thanks Henry. I know you're trying."

As Henry left the saloon, Catherine turned to see how Slink was faring. "What an awful name." She hadn't meant to say that out loud and abruptly put her hand over her mouth. "Oh, I am so sorry," she stammered, and set down her broom. "What a terrible thing to say. But, unless you really like the name, I would like us both to find better names to address each other."

Slink looked a little embarrassed. "Well, Ma'am, I can manage with that name since that's what everyone calls me."

"Is that the name your mother gave you?"

Slink laughed. "No, no. She calls me by my Indian name, but we agreed that name may only cause more trouble around here. Unfortunately, the American name we picked don't seem to fit in much better."

"Well, what name did she pick?"

"Jeremiah, but I think folks 'round here think that that name is too uppity for me."

Catherine stopped leaning on the bar and looked surprised. "I think that's a beautiful name."

"Well, Mrs. Callaway, that might be the problem. I don't pretend to be beautiful."

Catherine thought about this and then her face brightened up. "Do you mind if I call you Jay? That would be short for Jeremiah."

The young man looked startled, and then a big smile spread across his face. "I think I'd like that mighty fine, Ma'am."

"And," Catherine went on, "my first name is Catherine, but even Catherine seems too formal if we are going to be working together. Why don't you just call me Cat."

"All right, Mrs. Callaway. I'll try."

Catherine frowned. "Jay?"

---

13   **The old states** – *the original thirteen states*

"Ah, Cat," Jeremiah stammered. "That's what I meant to say, but it just don't quite feel right, like it's just not respectful enough for someone like you. But I'll try."

They both smiled at each other and then started to laugh. Catherine was aware of just how much she and this quiet, sullen young man had loosened up around each other in the last hour. She had accepted his help when Henry had volunteered him and he seemed like a genuinely nice young man after all, especially when he relaxed enough to smile a little. And he came with a mother who apparently knew how to cook.

Only time could tell how this new arrangement would turn out.

Chapter Six

Friday, 10:15 AM, July 4ᵗʰ, 1879

With two people working together, the saloon was back in order more quickly than Catherine had thought possible. She began to realize that even when Patrick was there, he didn't actually do much. He spent most of his time sharing his entertaining stories with the customers. Admittedly, his personality drew in customers but, with Jay carrying some of the workload, things were a lot less overwhelming for Catherine. She checked in with Crow Feather and found her ingredients were already fragrantly simmering in a large stew pot. Had they started earlier, they could have had homemade bread to go with the stew, but Catherine felt that that was really too much to ask this late in the morning.

Catherine's thoughts turned to the speaker outside. Henry's comments about John Young were bothering her. This would be a good opportunity to meet the man, and as Henry said, decide for herself what she thought. She and Jay had completed the straightening up of the saloon and were ready for customers. Maybe they could catch the tail end of Young's speech. They could stand near the back of the crowd and leave when the speech was almost over.

"Jay, we don't have much else that needs to be done. Why don't we go listen to what Mr. Young has to say?"

Jay didn't say anything at first. "Ya know, Mrs. Callaway..."

"Cat," she corrected him.

Jay seemed a little flustered. "I'm sorry, uh, Miss Cat. I'm just not used to callin a white woman by a nickname."

Catherine noticed he'd called her "Miss Cat" and decided that would be close enough for now.

Jay hesitated before continuing. "My ma suggested I might want to stay away from the people who follow Mr. Young."

"Jay, this is a free country and Mr. Young is a Christian. I have heard his beliefs are a little different from most Christians, but he believes in God and Christ. You shouldn't be concerned. I want you to come with me and you can see for yourself if he is as great a speaker as people claim. The crowd out there is certainly making a tremendous fuss over him."

When she stepped outside, Jay reluctantly followed. Cat was surprised to see how crowded the street was. The entire northeastern part of the territory must have turned out to see Eagle Rock's famous guest. She and Jay certainly weren't going to have to worry about getting back to the saloon when the speeches were over. The only space for them was no more than ten feet outside of the saloon. They could stand on their own boardwalk and see just fine.

Fortunately, the town had built a tall platform in front of the temporary depot so Young could be seen above the crowd. He was very distinguished looking. When they walked out of the saloon door to find a place, he had just paused in his speech so he could be heard above the noise and cheers of the crowd. Catherine was glad she'd made the decision to see him in person; after forty-five minutes he was still going strong. As the din died down, he continued in a loud, high-pitched voice.[14]

> Cain became jealous of Abel, and he laid a plan to obtain all his flocks; for through his perfect obedience to his father he obtained more blessings than Cain; consequently Cain took it into his heart to put Abel out of this mortal existence. After the deed was done, the Lord enquired of Abel, and made Caine own what he had done with him. Now says the grandfather, I will not destroy the seed of Michal and his wife; and Cain I will not kill you, nor suffer any one to kill you, but I will put a mark upon you.

---

14   *The indented text is actual excerpts from a speech on Slavery, Blacks and the Priesthood given by Brigham Young, Sr., February 5, 1852.* **The original spelling and punctuation have been corrected to reflect contemporary usage.** *The entire speech can be found in the LDS Church Historical Department, Salt Lake City, Utah and on the internet.*

If Catherine was surprised to find that Young was using the Eagle Rock Fourth of July celebration to preach a sermon, she was utterly shocked by what came next.

> What is that mark? You will see it on the countenance of every African you ever did see upon the face of the earth, or ever will see. . . . But let me tell you further. Let my seed mingle with the seed of Cain? That brings the curse upon me, and upon my genera-tions—we will reap the same rewards with Cain. In the priesthood I will tell you what it will do. Where the children of God mingle their seed with the seed of Cain it would not only bring the curse of being deprived of the power of the priesthood upon themselves but they entail it upon their children after them, and they cannot get rid of it. . . Therefore I will not consent for one moment to have an African dictate me or any of my Bren with regard to Church or State Government. I may vary in my views from others, and they may think I am foolish in the things I have spoken, and think that they know more than I do, but I know I know more than they do. If the Africans cannot bear rule in the Church of God, what business have they to bear rule in the State and Government affairs of this Territory or any others?

Catherine began shaking her head over the direction this speech was going. Why on earth had she brought Jay out here to hear this? What must he be thinking? It was only a short step from the Mark of Cain on Africans to Indians and any other non-white people.

> But say some, is there anything of this kind in the Constitution the U.S. has given us? If you will allow me the privilege of telling right out, it is none of their damned business what we do or say here. What we do is for them to sanction, and then for us to say what we like about it.

> I have given you the true principles and doctrine. No man can vote for me or my Bren in this Territory who has not the privilege of acting in Church affairs. Every man, and woman, and child in this Territory are Citizens; to say the contrary is all nonsense to me. The Indians are Citizens, the Africans are Citizens, and the Jews that

come from Europe, that are almost entirely of the blood of Cain. It is our duty to take care of them, and administer to them in all the acts of humanity, and kindness. They shall have the right of Citizenship, but shall not have the right to dictate in Church and State matters.

You could feel the excitement in the crowd rising to the fervor in Young's voice. People were shouting "Amens" and "Hallelujahs" all around Catherine. She had had enough. She and Jay must leave. But as she started to turn back to the saloon, Catherine was startled by the presence of a leering Sheriff Zane standing right behind her.

"Ain't he plumb[15] boss?[16] Ah jus love ta hear him talk. Yeee-haaa, what a ride! This is just Simon pure.[17]" And with that he pulled out both of his well-used six-shooters and starting firing into the air again. Many of the men in the crowd joined in.

Outraged, Catherine's mind raced to decide whether she should stay and avoid drawing attention to Jay or turn around and reprimand the offensive sheriff. She suddenly squealed and turned to glare at Zane, but he had sauntered off right after giving her a firm pat on her bottom. Jay looked alarmed.

"It's all right, but we should leave shortly," Catherine said as her face started to turn red. She straightened her dress and turned back to face Young.

As for our bills passing here, we may lay the foundation for what? For men to come here from Africa or elsewhere; by hundreds of thousands. When these men come here from the Islands, are they going to hold offices in Government? No!

Many members of the crowd yelled back, "No!"

It is for men who understand the knowledge of Government affairs to hold such offices, and on the other make provisions for them to plow, and to reap, and enjoy all that human beings can enjoy, and we protect them in it. Do we know how to ameliorate the condition of these people? We do!

---

15 **Plumb** – *completely, totally*
16 **Boss** – *the best, top*
17 **Simon pure** – *the real thing, a genuine fact*

This time most of the crowd responded with a much louder, "We Do!" and more shots were fired.

> Suppose that five thousand of them come from the Pacific Islands, and ten or fifteen thousand from Japan, or from China. Not one soul of them would know how to vote for a Government officer. They therefore ought not in the first thing have anything to do in Government affairs.
>
> What the Gentiles are doing we are consenting to do. What we are trying to do today is to make the Negro equal with us in all our privilege. My voice shall be *against* this all the day long. I shall not consent for one moment. I will call them a counsel. I say I will not for one moment *allow* for you to lay a plan to bring a curse upon this people. I shall not while I am here!

The entire crowd had been cheering through most of Young's last sentences and a chant of "John W. Young! John W. Young!" had started. Guns were being fired into the air, the train whistle started blowing in time with the cheers, and the depot bell chimed in. The noise was deafening.

"That's it!" Catherine took Jay by the arm. "We're leaving." Catherine stormed into the saloon, pushing the bat-wing double barroom doors so hard they slammed against the walls. "What an arrogant, pompous bigot! I have never heard anything so disgusting. He has no right to call himself a leader of a religious faith!"

Jay had a small smile on his face as he thought about Catherine's outburst. "Now Mrs. Calla...Miss Cat, I mean, I guess ya just ain't been round these parts long enough to know about them Mormons. And ya know, not all Mormons are quite so, uh..." He struggled for the right word.

"Repugnant?" But just then, she began to notice a tantalizing aroma wafting into the saloon from the kitchen. With a look of wide-eyed wonder she whispered, "Do I smell homemade bread?"

Jay was looking a little sheepish. "I hope you're not upset, Miss Cat. My ma's homemade bread is the best anywhere. She told me she was going to make it if she had time. I didn't know if I should mention it but, ya know, it tastes mighty fine with stew."

"Oh, this is wonderful!" Catherine took in a slow, deep breath of the savory fragrances coming from the kitchen. "We have to open the front doors so people will smell this. Oh! And I have to get my sign out! I made it yesterday but forgot about it in all the rush this morning. I'll add the bread to it!"

Catherine quickly left and came back with her new window sign:

Homemade Elk Stew
FREE Fresh Made Bread with a two-bit shot of whiskey.

She set the sign board in the front window and turned to Jay. "Maybe that will keep them sober longer," she said with a wink. Then her smile turned to concern. "Jay, I don't want you to be upset, but I think you had better stay in the kitchen once that terrible speech is over. That despicable man has got this whole town worked up and I'm not sure what might happen once those men start drinking. Some of them get way too excited once they have a few licks of whiskey in them. How about if you stay in the vestibule between the saloon and kitchen? I'll call in the number of servings I need and you and your mother can put them on a platter on the shelf in the vestibule. Thank goodness I decided to serve family-style. I'll pick up and serve the platters and bring back the dirty dishes when I come back for the next order. Do you mind washing dishes?"

"That's just fine, Miss Cat." He had become uneasy during the speech, too. "I was wonderin while we was list'nin to Mr. Young if it was such a good idea for me to stay in town. I would be glad to help ya out in the kitchen, though. And Ma would never be able to get your orders straight anyway."

Catherine took another deep breath of the delightful aroma of fresh bread, smiled, and said, "Great, then let's get moving."

A roar of cheers and blasts of gunshots signaled the end of the speech. Before she could get behind the bar, and just as Jay had moved into the darkened vestibule to the kitchen, her first customers burst through the doors. They responded just as Catherine had. Each inhaled a deep breath and exclaimed, "Is that the Elk stew? And, I want the bread and whiskey, too."

As the first men inside found seats, more poured in and reacted similarly to the wonderful aromas of their dinner to come. The men shared laughter and wisecracks as Catherine and her helpers tried to keep up with the demand. The day looked like it would be a great success—everything Catherine needed it to be. Only one thing would have made it better.

What had happened to Patrick?

Chapter Seven

Friday, 2:00 PM, July 4ᵗʰ, 1879

"Ya sure have a fine-ass selection of ceegahs, Luthah," Zane Gunther drawled as he leaned back in a wicker chair on Luther Armstrong's back porch. He rested his boots on the top of the mayor's porch railing. Gunther, the unlikely sheriff Luther had brought to Eagle Rock, and Jake Edwards, the depot manager, had just finished a large T-bone steak and baked potato lunch at the mayor's home west of the Snake River and were enjoying some of Luther's scotch and Cuban cigars. As a good Mormon keeping up appearances, Luther was not drinking with his guests, but he did keep an excellent collection of alcohol for entertaining as well as a hidden decanter at his desk for his own enjoyment from time to time. Zane drew a deep draw from the cigar and blew a perfect smoke ring over the porch rail. As the ring widened behind Luther's home, he pursed his lips and blew a fine stream of smoke through the ring with a final puff that drew the ring into the tail of the stream of smoke as it drifted out toward the corral behind Luther's home. He loved showing off his "smoke rope through the hole" trick.

"Ha! Mah daddy taught me ta blow smoke rings with the awfullest tastin ceegahs in the world. They surely did smell like pig shit compared to yoahs, Luthah," Zane chuckled. "Mah daddy was right famous for his smoke rings, but he could nevvah match ma 'smoke rope through the hole,' and that really pissed him off. Ah just loved gettin undah his skin. He sure was one real asshole."

The three men were watching five of Luther's ranch hands trying to calm down a wild new horse. Dust flew high above the small corral about 200 feet from their vantage point on the porch.

Zane drawled, "That new horse is a real bangtail.[18] Looks like they're not havin much luck with him, Luthah. Ah don't know why ya keep on a-usin that crippled Injun to break yoh horses."

"Even with one stiff leg, Bear Claw has more success breaking horses than all four of those other so-called cowboys out there," Luther answered

"Well, Ah jus don't be thinkin it looks right, ya hirin an Injun to do cowboy work. Y'all an Ace High[19] gentleman, ya ah, Luthah. Ya surely gotta be flush enough ta hire a team of real wranglers, not some low-life mudsill[20]. Ah wager he's jus not cut out to uncorkin a bronc[21]."

Luther just smiled and said, "We'll see."

Zane took his boots off the rail and leaned forward to ensure Luther's attention. "Why weren't ya at the hullabaloo for Mistuh Young? Ya missed a mighty fine, razzle-dazzle speech there. Ah sure like ta hear him talk. It's like magic a'comin outta his mouth. Why, the entire crowd was jus hangin on every word. Ah bet they ain't heard nothin like that befoh. He had them hook, line, and sinker. Now, Ah have to admit, it took some work on mah part ta get them stirred up like ya wanted. Ya wudda been right proud ta see me loosen up the crowd. Ah wish ya had been there, Luthah. Ya tol me ta get'em excited an Ah did just what ya said. It was just great. They wudda listened to that man all the afternoon. Ah'll bet there aren't many that can hold a candle to that man." Zane paused and then laughed. "Ah don't a-know why he left so quick, though. It was like he thought he might miss the afternoon train outta here."

He turned to Jake. "Surely y'all weren't gonna let the noon train leave before he got on, was ya, Jake?"

"Nah, we had already told the engineer he wouldn't be leaving until the crowd broke up. Hell, a good share of the crowd was standing on the tracks. But why didn't ya stay for the speech, Mr. Armstrong? Weren't ya the one who invited him in the first place? Ya high tailed it out after ya introduced him."

Luther smiled. "Well, I hope my departure wasn't that obvious to everyone else. You're right. I talked him into coming, but I can't say he was very cooperative. You would think, being a Mormon community this close to the mines in Montana, he would have jumped at the chance. But John Young is nothing

---

18   **Bangtail** – *wild horse; mustang*

19   **Ace High** – *first class, respected*

20   **Lowlife mudsill** – *thoroughly disreputable person*

21   **Uncorking a bronc** – *breaking a horse*

like his father. Brigham Young, Sr. was a real public speaker. He wouldn't have needed your help to get the crowds excited, Zane. Our crowd would have been eating out of his hand, so I am glad you were there to fire them up."

Zane took another drag on his cigar. "Ah guess Ah should-a spent some time in Salt Lake City befoh his daddy passed. Ah canna imagine anyone talkin bettern what Ah jus heard. Mistuh Young sure doesn't sound like he'd a'take any shit from them Injuns, Darkies, Chinks, or anyone else that snuck into this great nation. No-sirree-bob, he mah kinda man."

Luther chuckled. "Well I am glad you found the event so inspiring. I hope everyone else feels the same. If so, it was worth the effort to get him here." Then he looked out to the corral. "Zane, it looks like Bear Claw has successfully mounted our new horse."

"Mounted, sure, but look at'im. That Injun ain't no wrangler. He a'bouncin up and down on that horse like he gots hot coals in his britches. Ah still say he's a'gonna be flat on the ground chewin gravel any moment now. Ah'd put mah money on it."

Zane pointed his cigar at Luther. "Ya know, just about everyone round these parts came out for that speech. Ah even saw the pretty Mrs. Callaway takin in the doin's. Boy, she's a right fine sight. Ah'd sure like ta get undah her skirts ta see that fine ass of hern." He winked at Jake. "Ah already know first-hand it's pretty firm. And she'll be missin havin her man about the house now. She's maybe needin a little attention, if ya knows what Ah mean. I gotta notion…"

Jake had a puzzled look on his face as Luther cut Zane short. "You know Zane, I can hear a lot of gunfire across the river in Eagle Rock. Don't you think you should head back to establish some law and order?"

Zane jumped out of his chair. "Yessirree Mayuh. That's just what Ah'm a-gonna do. Ah'll crack some heads and get everybody straightened right out." He got a calculating smile on his face. "Ah'm ya man when it comes ta law and order. Most likely be some cowpokes and rail men in the pokey[22] tonight."

Zane slapped both his guns in their holsters, winked at Luther and strode off the porch. Once out of earshot, Jake drew a deep breath and muttered, "I'm sure glad that man had somewhere to go. He is so full of bullshit. And half the time I'm not really sure what he's saying. He's damned hard to understand."

---

22 **Pokey** – jail

"Even when he's sober," Luther agreed, chuckling. "From the south, no education, a hardscrabble life[23]—he comes by it naturally. He was actually born in the south, a rebel no less. Losing the war was hard on him. He lost everything, farm, wife, kids, slaves, you name it. It was gone or burned to the ground. He just packed up and wandered west."

"What was he talking about—Mrs. Callaway missing Patrick? I know Pat's been missing, but people are saying he just ran off with Fannie. Surely he will show up soon?"

Luther shrugged. "Zane can get just about anything wrong. He gets worked up easily."

"That's a fact. You know," Jake said, "we're lucky that slew of bullets he fired into the air today didn't drop down right on top of Young's head. He's pretty wild with those guns of his. I've heard some crazy stories that he was the ringleader of some bandit gang on the west coast before he got here. You think there's anything to that?"

"Actually, it's true, Jake. He was the leader of the gang of stagecoach robbers called The Innocents that wreaked havoc up and down the California coast," Luther answered.

Jake looked shocked. "No kidding? Zane made it out of there? I thought they finally tracked them down and hanged'em all."

Luther sighed, "All but Zane. He escaped to Salt Lake City, joined the Mormon Church, and made a big donation on the condition that the Church bishops would spread it around he'd been hanged in some small, remote town in Utah. Young, Sr. asked me if I needed a man with expertise in gunmanship. What could I say?"

In truth, Luther had recruited Zane himself to assist his own thugs in doing his dirty work, but he didn't admit that to Jake. "Don't worry, I have a lot hanging over his head. I can keep him under control. And while you're here, Jake," Luther continued, bringing the conversation around to the real point of the afternoon meeting, "if you have time, I would like to go over a few things that could benefit both of us. Do you have time to talk in my study where we will have a little privacy?"

"Sure thing," replied Jake. "You're the boss."

---

23 **Hardscrabble** – *involving hard work and struggle*

As they got up, Jake looked out at the corral. Bear Claw was easily guiding the new horse around in tight figure eights. It was already looking like a made horse.[24] Luther would have won that bet with Zane, but they both knew Zane would have tried to wiggle out of it. That man was just a lot of blow and no depth. Still, if he really was the leader of the notorious gang said to have murdered several dozen innocent men, Jake was going to make it a point to stay out of Zane's way and humor him whenever he had to.

No point in calling out Zane's outrageous boasts and bluster.

---

24   ***Made horse*** – *a horse that is an expert at his job, a highly desirable horse*

Chapter Eight

Friday, 3:00 PM, July 4th, 1879

Luther led Jake into his study. He was pleased that Jake was obviously impressed. Luther had gone to great expense to recreate the feel of his father's formal study back in New York City. For Luther, his father represented the quintessential professional businessman—a shrewd, authoritative, financial genius in full control of all affairs, both business and personal. The time young Luther spent in his father's study listening in awe to this great man were some of his most cherished childhood memories, and he sought to instill his own sense of power and authority with every feature of this study. The effect was not lost on Jake.

Dark walnut bookcases lined the interior walls. Each held rows of dark, mostly unread, leather-bound volumes displayed for their appearance of knowledge and age. A large humidor on a beautifully carved, dark mahogany desk held Luther's favorite Cuban cigars along with a handsome cast iron R.J. Reynolds Tobacco Co. Browns Mule Plug tobacco cutter. The only other thing on the polished desktop was a line of expensive fountain pens and an impressive leather-bound Book of Mormon. The immaculate desktop display was prepared to look exactly like his father's, with the exception of the Book of Mormon. The desk and Luther's opulent, hand-carved throne chair evoked the same feelings of power and authority Luther had felt toward his father. In the corner, a high-backed, upholstered swivel chair faced two large windows where one could look west out over the vast high desert behind Luther's ranch. Luther sat down behind his desk and motioned for Jake to sit in the ornate chair at the window. He noticed Jake appreciating the stark but peaceful vista through the windows.

"I know," Luther said. "It's vast, endless, and beautiful but dry, desolate, and useless. It seems a shame that all this land is only good for cattle, and then, only for land near the few grade-level access points along the river. I wish the Snake could be diverted and spread out rather than rushing by in one, deep torrent below those steep, rocky banks. There's money to be made if we could sell that land with water access. We could have ranches from here all the way to the Oregon Mountains." After a moment of reflection, he came to his point. "Jake, I have a proposition for you."

Jake stopped gazing out the windows and turned back to face Luther. "I'm all ears. I recall you mentioned some possible future opportunities when you suggested I come north with you to become the depot manager. What do you have in mind?"

"Brigham Young, Sr.'s sons drove a hard bargain with Gould's Union Pacific when the UP bought the Mormon Church stock of the Utah Northern Railroad. The sons insisted the Mormons get the best of the opportunities that would become available as the railroad progressed north, as well as a fifteen-percent discount from every transaction with the new Union & Northern Railroad. It was to include land sales, the best sites, transportation costs, and, above all, preferential treatment for any employment opportunities."

Jake chuckled. "That figures. Brigham Young, Sr. had a reputation for expecting special treatment, so I guess his sons would be no different. I'm glad it was you that negotiated with them. I would have been inclined to show them the door. So what did you do?"

"We argued, of course. I knew they were asking for more than they expected, but we had to go through the motions. And, acting on behalf of Gould as the middleman, I had the advantage of claiming that 'those arrogant UP managers' would never go along with their proposal. But since the UP bigwigs knew I had worked with Brigham Young, Sr. on the construction of the Transcontinental Railroad and continued to have a good relationship with both Jay Gould of the UP and speculator Joseph Richardson, a financier Gould liked, it turned out to be easier to get the UP to a more reasonable discount for members of the Mormon Church than I had anticipated. Negotiation Lesson Number One, Jake—keep parties separate throughout negotiations," Luther said, smiling and confident in his role as chess master of this game. "Then you get the best terms for yourself."

Jake looked puzzled. "But we haven't given out any discounts to Mormons. Did they back off?"

"No, that was the beauty of my counter-proposal. I told them that the UP management wouldn't give them any more than an eight percent discount because the UP needed revenue to get the railroad up and running again. The southern leg from Ogden to Franklin in the Cache Valley was losing too much revenue to keep afloat. I made it clear the most the UP would accept was an eight percent discount."

"I'm surprised they accepted that."

Luther smiled. "They didn't."

"So what happened?"

Luther leaned back in his chair. "Here is where I need your oath that nothing leaves this room. And I can make it well worth your while." He got up and started pacing back and forth. "When I went to Gould and Richardson, I had already prepared them that this haggling was how the Mormons dealt with all negotiations. I explained how they were asking for a fifteen percent discount and I wasn't sure they would accept anything less than ten percent."

Jake looked puzzled. "Ten percent?"

Luther stopped pacing and sat down on the front edge of his desk. "As I said, Jake, this is the art of negotiating. It is best done with only one side at a time. That way neither party knows what the other party is really thinking. Gould wanted to come to Salt Lake City and ram the Mormon offer down their throats. I pointed out that once Young's sons felt they were being manipulated, they would dig in their heels and we would get nowhere. It worked."

"Well, it's a damned good thing. What would you have done if he had come?"

"Negotiation Lesson Number Two. Know both parties' real interests before you start. On the UP side, I knew Gould had no interest in getting on a train to travel clear across the western plains just to get caught up in an argument with a group of men he knew were bullheaded and had no business sense. He is in love with the east and all its luxuries. He just wanted a railroad line that would get him the profits from the Montana mines. On the Mormon side, I knew Young's sons wanted to crow to their people about what they obtained from the UP. They would brag about their outstanding negotiating skills with the stuffed shirt UP managers for excellent discounts and job opportunities for their brethren. I also knew they were still heavily involved with all the legal issues over the Mormon policy of multiple marriages and really didn't care what the discount was as long as they could tell their brethren they got something. What they really wanted was more land settled by Mormons, and John Young needed money to continue the latest railroad line he was building to southwestern Utah."

"So, we *are* going to discount all Mormons fifteen percent?"

"Absolutely not! I suggested the UP go no higher than ten percent and demand that the discount not be part of the deal until the bridge across the Snake was built. Of course, what we will do is simply make small, incremental increases to our fares, starting soon, so the UP can recoup what is lost by the discount. To make the deal more acceptable to the Mormons, I suggested that the UP interview and hire qualified Mormons for the depot managers up and down the line. Gould thought it over and asked me to try harder but, if that was the only offer they would accept, I could go with it. I then came back and told Young's sons that Gould was insulted by their offer and would consider no more than a ten percent discount and that the railroad couldn't afford to provide the discount until the Snake River Bridge was in place. Of course, they fumed until I told them the UP would agree to hire Mormons to be depot managers and they finally, begrudgingly, accepted."

Jake looked even more puzzled. "Let me see if I've got this. The Mormons get a ten-percent discount, which is better than eight percent, can hand out jobs to their brethren, will wait for the discounts until we finish the bridge... and we can quietly adjust the prices soon. That's pretty clever. Sly, really."

Luther smiled and went back to the chair behind his desk. He looked solemn. "More sly than you might realize. This is why I expect your confidence in these matters. You see, I also arranged for us to handle all of the accounting for these transactions. We will control who keeps track of all income for the Utah & Northern Railroad. I explained to Gould that, although I was convinced that the Mormons would accept the proposal, I didn't trust the new hires they were going to provide. I wanted all the depot managers to send the cash and receipts to the Eagle Rock Depot and we would send the cash and summary with backup documents as needed to the UP on a daily basis for fares along with a monthly summary for cargo. I said I trusted you and I wanted you to be the lead depot manager and my assistant accountant, and that both of us would need a raise to do the additional paperwork for all Utah & Northern Railroad fares and cargo. This way we could offer lower salaries for all the other depot managers only doing minor paperwork, and that extra would be more than be enough to cover the cost of the two of us doing the additional paperwork. I, of course, will be reviewing all of the paperwork before it's sent east to the UP."

A smile started to form on Jake's lips. "So, both of us get a raise, but also some additional work."

"I explained that a fair amount for this additional work would be a ten percent increase to our present salaries and they would have the comfort of knowing nothing funny was going on with the books. And, the Mormon Church won't have direct access to the U&NR finances."

Luther opened up the humidor and brought out two fat Cuban cigars, snipped off one end of each with his cigar cutter, and handed one to Jake. "That's not all. A little extra work for a nice ten-percent raise is certainly worth it, but I have also planned for a little extra profit for both of us."

They lit their cigars and each took a deep draw. The room started to fill with smoke and, as the western sun began to filter through the haze, Jake asked, "How do you get cigars from Cuba?"

Luther smiled. "It's no wonder Zane likes these cigars. I didn't bother to tell him these are the same cigars my father smoked in his study when I was a young man. You are smoking an *El Principe de Gales*. In 1856, Martinez-Ybor started his cigar company in Havana, Cuba. Back when I was growing up, my father was able to purchase Cuban cigars directly from Cuba. When the United States government put a tariff on Cuban cigars, Martinez-Ybor moved his plant to Key West, Florida, brought his Cuban workers, used Cuban tobacco, renamed them *Prince of Wales* cigars and avoided the tariffs. It's no wonder they taste better. They are."

Jake chuckled at this. "Yep. Zane would have gone off on another tangent. I was glad you found a reason for him to go back to Eagle Rock. And, back to your proposal, everything you have suggested sounds good to me."

"Well, there's more," replied Luther. "If all of the receipts for fares and cargo come to your office, we are talking about a large sum of money to be accounted for. It will be more work, but I suspect that, with both of us doing an excellent job of accounting for all the receipts on a regular basis, no one in the UP will notice if they get shorted a small amount here and there. I suspect we could clear another five percent of the income and still show a sizable profit for UP now that the bridge is open and the income from fares and cargo is going to increase rapidly from all of the additional traffic. I would like to gain a little more for all the efforts I have put in to get to this point and I suspect you would, too."

Luther knew by looking at him that Jake was mulling this over with a bit of wonder as well as a little skepticism. "You probably have questions."

Jake was rubbing his jaw to hide a nervous twitch that had started as it always did when he was presented with new ideas that could be a little dicey. He remained silent a moment before answering. "With all due respect, Mr. Armstrong..."

"It's Luther, Jake. If we are going to be partners, we should both be on a first-name basis."

Jake sighed. "With all due respect, Luther, just how exactly do we keep this quiet?"

"Ah. You've asked a very good question. It is really quite simple. You see, by being the lead depot manager, although all fares will be paid to each of the originating depot managers up and down the line, all money received will be itemized — including which fares were discounted — and sent up here by train. Your new responsibility will be to collect all receipts and cash here in Eagle Rock and prepare a daily summary ledger to send to UP headquarters in New York, but you will lose a small percentage of the receipts before preparing the summary. I recommend they be burned, discreetly of course."

Then Luther closed the deal. "I was thinking that with this extra money, you could build a house on that acreage you bought some time ago just north of my property. You could use a couple of my ranch hands to help if you'd like. Then you could bring your wife and kids to Eagle Rock. What do you think?"

Jake was shaking his head in amazement. "My God. It sounds crazy but it could work."

"And if you're interested," Luther worked the conversation back around to the new house, "I heard Henry Willett just left the Johnson ranch and may be looking for work. I could extend you a small loan to hire him and you could have your family up here within a few weeks. You may want to think about this some more, but I think we're in agreement here, Jake," Luther said, standing up to signal this conversation had come to a conclusion.

Jake got up out of his chair and shook Luther's hand. "Consider me on board, Mr. Armstrong. Ah, I mean, Luther. Thank you for trusting me. I might have some questions once this has rattled around in my brain for a day or two, but I really think this is a great plan. Thank you."

Luther smiled as he walked Jake to the door. "Don't let me keep you from the festivities. Now, I believe you have a little more to celebrate. Just remember, tight lips."

"Don't worry Luther. I don't want to mess this up. I have too much to lose!" As Jake stepped out the door, he suddenly turned. "By the way, I forgot to ask. Why didn't you stay up on the podium with John Young during his speech and why did he take off so soon? You would think he would have wanted to spend more time here."

Luther shook his head dismissively and walked with Jake onto the front porch. "You know, Jake. John is not an easy man to understand. Unlike his father and the other brothers, he doesn't spend much time in the West. He did mention over breakfast this morning, though, that he is not used to the heavy food we eat here."

"You probably served him some of your fine beef with lots of potatoes."

"Of course I did. We had thick steaks, baked potatoes with lots of good, extra greasy gravy, but I also shared one of my Western cigars with him. I think that may have been the real problem. He isn't used to Western food or cheap Western cigars and I wasn't about to share a *Prince of Wales* with him. I save them for my real friends. And partners."

Jake smiled. "Well, I am right proud to be one of your friends and it looks like we are going to be partners, too. I gotta admit, you can be pretty tricky, but I like your ideas. They suit me just fine."

Luther shook Jake's hand again. "Now you go celebrate and think about bringing your wife and kids up here."

"You bet. This has been a great day, and the weekend has just started."

As Jake headed off through the dusty yard toward town, Luther dropped his collegial demeanor. His face assumed its usual hard, calculating lines. Jake was a pawn in his game, and everything was proceeding in due course. As he walked back to his office, Jake's comments about being sly and tricky repeated in his head. He took another pull on his cigar as he turned to watch Bear Claw lead the new horse back into the stable.

"Jake," Luther said to the empty room, "you have no idea how sly and tricky I can be."

Chapter Nine

Friday, 4:00 PM, July 4th, 1879

Luther went back to his desk, proud of what he had accomplished already this day. He pulled out a whiskey tumbler and a decanter of Old Forester bourbon from the lower drawer, poured two fingers of Kentucky's finest, took a small sip, and sighed with satisfaction. Luther didn't drink in public, but this didn't keep him from enjoying a modest amount of some of the world's finest bourbon in the privacy of his own home. It had truly been a good day so far. Great progress on many fronts.

The discussion with Jake had been on his mind for many days. He knew he could not start giving out discounts to Mormon passengers without providing an explanation. In the formative stages of the new Utah & Northern Railroad, he had pushed the management and the Mormon Church hard to have Jake hired as the Eagle Rock depot manager.

He told the UP officials that Jake was a dependable Mormon Luther had known for some time, fair and honest, and that this choice would encourage the Mormons to negotiate. He told Young's sons that, under his tutelage, Jake could be molded into a good Mormon leader. In reality, he knew that Jake was pretty simple minded, easily led, and quite disenchanted with the whole Mormon culture, petty cliques, and ultra-conservative atmosphere of Salt Lake City. He wanted out but wasn't really ready or financially able to cut the strings that tied him to the Mormon Church. Luther knew he could gain Jake's loyalty with a better paying job and the opportunity to move far away from Salt Lake City. Jake would see Luther's ambitious plans as one of the benefits to what was already going on within the Mormon community in Salt Lake City. In fact, if

Jake had thought about it, he might have considered skimming a little extra for himself without splitting the money with Luther once revenues from the railroad expansion increased. So Luther had been pretty sure Jake would go along with the plan, but you never really know how someone is going to react until you present it in person. Well, this was just one more step in a long-range plan that was finally coming to fruition.

Luther took another sip of bourbon and smirked as he thought about how his grand plans had all started.

When he was a teenager, his father had frequently shared his business plans and family challenges with Luther in his study, usually with a little bourbon and, later, a fine cigar. Luther's great-grandfather had arrived in New York more than seventy years earlier to escape religious persecution in Europe. He had changed his name from Soren Pederson to Samuel Armstrong and started a small lending company but hid his beliefs from everyone except his own family. His wealth grew slowly but steadily and the financing trade was handed down through the family to Luther's father. Through the years, his family's Jewish customs were no longer followed as faithfully and only in the privacy of their home. His father had ultimately decided to join the Lutheran church to improve his status in the business community.

Luther had grown up in the ease that came with wealth in New York. His father, Arnold Roger Armstrong, an aristocratic banker and financier, had dealt with many of the capitalists of the east coast, including Joseph Richardson, a notorious financial speculator with connections to the steel and rail barons.

Luther's father wanted the public acceptance that came with his Lutheran affiliation, but Luther was more interested in the growing number of new, fundamental religions. He was particularly drawn to the teachings of Joseph Smith found in the Book of Mormon. In the early1860s, when it was clear that the Union Pacific was going to build the eastern portion of the Transcontinental Railroad terminating somewhere near Salt Lake City, Richardson suggested to Jason Gould that young Luther Armstrong would be an excellent candidate to be hired to assist in the purchase of railway rights around the western terminus of the proposed Transcontinental. His interest in Mormonism could be useful in enlisting Brigham Young, Sr.'s support of the UP.

Luther accompanied several of the surveyors to the Salt Lake City region and found that Young was indeed very willing to provide the UP with Mormon labor if the railroad line was extended through Salt Lake City and the UP would assist the Mormons in extending new rail lines both north and south of Salt Lake City once the Transcontinental was completed. Through numerous railroad planning meetings with many of the bishops and Young himself, Luther learned enough about Mormonism to want to convert. He was drawn to the strong leadership, the sense of brotherhood and the emphasis on supporting all members of the church, particularly the more business-minded. The opportunity of having multiple wives in a strongly patriarchal society was equally appealing. And the Mormon connection solidified a fit of both Luther's skills and long-term financial goals in the west. During these meetings, Brigham Young shared his dream for a railroad connection to the north to the Cache Valley in upper Utah and southeastern Idaho where there were several growing Mormon communities that needed better connections to Salt Lake City and room for additional communities away from the distractions of Gentiles.[25]

While still working for the UP, Luther had set up a household in Ogden, Utah, the probable western terminal for the UP and a strong Mormon community north of Salt Lake City. To improve his chances of a leadership role in the Mormon faith, he married a wife chosen for him by the local bishop. When Luther found out that the Union Pacific Railroad would pass north of Salt Lake and the western terminus of the UP would more than likely be near Corinne, Utah, he asked his father for funds to privately invest in land in that vicinity under a false name so the UP wouldn't be aware of his purchases. In 1869, when the Golden Spike ceremony[26] transpired near Promontory Point, Utah, the UP made Corinne a major hub for any future trade to the Montana mines. Luther's land jumped tenfold in value. As the UP invested in Corinne, Luther sold his property. He was able to pay his father back and was left with a very comfortable addition to the portion of his inheritance he had already obtained from his father.

Not long after the Transcontinental was completed, Young approached Luther and suggested that he explain to Gould it was time to start construction

---

25 **Gentiles** – *conventionally defined as a person who is not Jewish; but the Mormons regard their members as the true Hebrews, so the word "gentile" for them refers to any person, including Jews, who is not a Mormon, according to the Book of Mormon.*

26 **Golden Spike ceremony** – *At completion of the Transcontinental Railroad, a **golden spike** was forged. All four sides were engraved with commemorative information and the top simply read: "The Last Spike."*

of the railroad connection to the Cache Valley as had been agreed upon. Luther had expected to be part of this construction but was quite upset when Gould explained that the Union Pacific could see no profit in joining the Mormons in this undertaking.

"But that was all part of the arrangement that you had agreed to in order to obtain the Mormon labor for the Transcontinental," Luther reminded Gould during a trip he made back to Gould's office in Omaha.

Gould's response shocked Luther. "Times have changed and I am not sure there is any longer an advantage in honoring that agreement. The board has decided to invest in more profitable ventures. You have to be able to move with the times, my boy. But you did a fine job in arranging that agreement. That's why we gave you that sizable bonus."

Thus, Luther's plans to become a part of the railroad business were brought to a screeching halt.

The Mormons were furious with Luther for not being able to talk Gould into honoring their agreement and eventually, using volunteer Mormon farm labor, decided to build their own railroad, the Utah Northern connection to Salt Lake City and the southern portion of the Idaho Territory. But once the railroad was extended as far as Franklin, the Cache Valley farmers had gotten what they wanted, and there was little interest in extending the railroad farther. The Mormons had gotten funding for the railroad extension from Joseph Richardson in exchange for stock, a contact Luther had made for them earlier. This resulted in Richardson having controlling interest in the railroad, but he was lacking capital to continue building due to a lack of profits from the railroad line completed to date. Luther had predicted this and felt Richardson and Young's sons had been naïve to expect anything else.

With the railroad stalled at the very southern edge of the Idaho Territory, Luther began to develop his next scheme to get a piece of the railroad. He was not ready to be bypassed again in profiting from this western expansion, nor was he interested in helping Joseph Richardson get a part of any expansion of the Utah Northern Railroad.

Chapter Ten

<u>Two years earlier</u>

10:00 AM, Thursday, July 12, 1877,
Jay Gould's Omaha office

In the early spring of 1877, Luther left Ogden, Utah and traveled east on the Transcontinental Railroad to Omaha, Nebraska, to meet with railroad magnate Jason Gould (later known as Jay Gould). In securing Mormon labor for Gould to advance his western rail line, the Union Pacific, Luther had demonstrated he was a man who could get things done. The two men shared the same hard-nosed business sense, which sometimes included questionable ethics, so Luther easily received an audience with Gould.

Once he was ushered into Gould's office, he was pleased to find that several high-ranking administrators and financiers of the Union Pacific Railroad were there to hear his proposal. Among others such as Sidney Dillon, these included Benjamin Richardson, a speculative investor Gould favored, not to be confused with Joseph Richardson of New York. Luther considered the number and rank of those present a good sign. Of course, it helped that he had suggested that the Union Pacific (UP) had an excellent opportunity to capitalize on a number of mistakes the Mormons had made in the construction of their line, the Utah Northern Railroad (UNR.) Luther knew that Gould and his partners viewed Brigham Young, Sr. as more of a pawn than a partner, and they were eager to expand their holdings in the Utah Territory at just about any cost. Luther also knew that Brigham Young, Sr.'s sons might be overextended by their railroad expansion southwest of Salt Lake City and could be looking for financial assistance. He was convinced that there was an opportunity to acquire the Utah Northern and expanding the Union Pacific line beyond Utah into Idaho and Montana would be seen as a high priority.

After an exchange of pleasantries between fellow railroad men, Gould got down to business. "Now exactly what have you been scheming about out there in the Wild West? You have been gone from the civilized part of America so long, I'm curious to see just how shrewd you've become and what these opportunities might really be." Gould gave Luther a sly wink and turned to the other men in the room. "If you didn't know, this is Arnold's son, who came to us asking to be a surveyor when we were starting to lay out the route to Utah for the Transcontinental. He not only was of great assistance on the surveying team, he cozied up to the Mormons and got the attention of Brigham Young, Sr. himself. Thanks to Luther's natural charisma and innate negotiating skills, we enjoyed nearly free labor from the Mormons. We would have had great difficulty getting to the finish line in time without his assistance. Let's hear him out." He turned back to Luther. "So what have you got for us, son?"

Luther smiled. This was starting out well. "When I came to you last time with my proposition to assist you with the Mormon situation, I wasn't really sure it would be an overly profitable venture in the short run, but I thought it would be the beginning of a good inroad to the financial expansion opportunities in the west. This time, I know there is a profitable venture available for anyone willing to take a modest risk. I will be candid. It is so good, I am hoping you will let me be part of it. I was squeezed out of even a minor role in the construction of the Utah Northern Railroad after I set the Mormons up with Joseph Richardson's backing, so I have a good incentive to make this work.

"I am sure you are aware that the railroad has gone nowhere since reaching the Cache Valley," Luther continued. "I know it's floundering and will not get any farther. Joseph Richardson has money invested in the Utah Northern, but the management of the railroad is in the hands of farmers who don't see the future the way you gentlemen do. They're not businessmen. There is a distinct possibility Richardson will not get his money back, at least not for a very long time. The Mormons are more concerned with supporting their own efforts and don't see the future beyond their own immediate settlement needs. As it is, this doesn't bode well for Richardson's investment, but I have an idea on how to turn this around so the UP could profit from this opportunity."

Benjamin Richardson had started frowning and cut Luther off. "To be honest, Luther, I am personally not in favor of any investment in Mormon projects. As they have clearly demonstrated to Joseph Richardson, they just don't seem to understand that we need to get our investment back and make a reasonable profit. They certainly haven't shown us that they value this goal as highly as we do."

Mr. Gould responded, "I'm pretty sure Luther understands our opinion of investing in Mormon projects and has brought us something we might still find interesting. Let's give him a little leeway to see what he has come up with. Go on Luther."

"I can assure you I would never suggest investing anything further in the Utah Northern Railroad." Luther paused and smiled at each of the men in the room before continuing. "Unless I thought you were going to get your investment back tenfold. Here is my idea."

Now he had their attention.

"With Thomas Edison and George Westinghouse[27] competing against each other to cash in on the untold wealth electricity is going to bring them, copper is going to be worth almost as much as gold. Everyone looking at the future is aware of this. And where is the largest known source of copper? In the Montana hills. Getting that raw copper ore to the industries that need it could be a golden opportunity for any railroad that controls a direct line to the mines. But, at present, the Mormons control the closest railhead[28] in Idaho leading to Montana, their own Utah Northern Railroad. They just don't realize what they've got."

Luther could see the men growing more interested. "Now, John Young has control, on behalf of the Mormon Church, of the Utah Northern Railroad, the UNR, but he is in the middle of another railroad expansion to the southwest of Salt Lake City and he is running out of funds. Their construction on the UNR has already started toward Soda Springs, the destination Brigham Young, Sr. wanted as the terminus for that railroad where several Mormon leaders, including Brigham Young, Sr., already owned property. They had planned to

---

27 *See Chapter Notes*
28 **Railhead** – *a point on a railroad from which roads and other transportation routes begin.*

make it their own private cash-cow resort and spa retreat. But, that extension will never be completed."

Gould looked puzzled. "It sounds like they have considerable incentives to get the job done. Why don't you think they will complete it?"

"The Mormons only build railroads with volunteer labor from Mormon farmers. They can only raise funds from Mormon farmers, and the farmers have no interest in spa retreats. They know the land north of the Cache Valley is high desert, completely unsuitable for farming or nearly any other profitable use. William Preston, who has superintended the construction to date, knows how to raise money for materials from farmers who want rail connections to their communities, but has no idea how to build a railroad without free labor. There are no farmers north of the Cache Valley. It is a desert! The railroad construction that was started 1872 has come to a standstill and I predict it will go no farther. But someone eventually, is going to extend a railroad line to Montana."

Richardson still had questions. "So, you are suggesting that we give them additional funds to complete the line to Soda Springs with the understanding that a line will also be built up to the Montana mines? That seems pretty risky even though the eventual payback might be good."

"Absolutely not. I recommend you buy the Utah Northern Railroad from the Mormons and extend that line directly to the Montana mines yourselves. With that expansion, you will control the entire length of the rail line from the Montana mines all the way back to the east coast, and you will enjoy all of the profits from transporting the raw materials coming out of the mines in Montana—gold, silver, copper, and whatever else they find in those hills. The UP will have a monopoly on the distribution of these minerals for years to come."

The room was silent. Luther could tell they were thinking so hard he could almost hear them. And he wasn't even to the good part, yet.

Richardson grabbed a sheet of paper off of Gould's desk and started adding up numbers. After a moment, he shook his head. "At current interest rates, the initial investment could easily wipe out any future profits."

Luther was unphased. "What if I told you I can help you buy the entire length of the present Utah Northern Railroad for two bits on the dollar? Try running the numbers with that."

The room went silent again.

Gould started chuckling. He got up, went to his desk, opened up his humidor, and asked, "Would anyone else like a cigar? I have known Luther long enough to know he would not suggest something so outrageous without a rabbit up both sleeves. I, for one, want to hear him out. And Luther, you will be glad to know that I prefer the same cigars as your father always had on hand. Please try one of my Cuban Prince of Wales cigars."

Luther smiled. "Yes, thank you. I will share how this can be done once we have come to an agreement, but let it be understood that for my efforts I expect to become an employee of the new railroad and have ten-percent ownership of this division of the Union Pacific Railroad."

Richardson had been frantically scribbling numbers on his sheet of paper. He looked up and said, "If Luther has any real evidence that we can buy the Utah Northern for two bits on the dollar, I will wholeheartedly support the purchase. But the devil is in the details. I want to hear how this can be done."

The next half hour was spent with the men in the room listening in rapt attention to Luther's explanation. In the end, Gould asked that champagne be added to the elegant lunch about to be served, so they could properly celebrate the UP's youngest stockholder.

Luther rode back to Ogden in one of Jay Gould's plush, private cars, staffed by a butler and personal chef, and stocked with a dozen Cuban cigars from Gould's humidor. It was the luxury Luther had been dreaming about since he'd pinned his future on becoming a bishop in the Mormon Church.

When this outrageous plan had first caught his imagination, there were already long-standing bishops in the local communities around Salt Lake City, so he knew he was going to have to establish himself in a new community. He started taking trips into Idaho, looking for logical routes to extend the railroad to Montana rather than Soda Springs. He determined that the only reasonable river crossing was at the location of Taylor's Bridge near a small outpost named Eagle Rock. From there, the railroad could travel north along the west side of the Snake River through rolling desert all the way to the mines of Montana. Eagle Rock was a logical division point for the proposed railroad, being located about midway between Ogden and Butte. Luther spoke with the Anderson brothers, who had an outpost in the area, and verified that they too, were unaware of any better crossing. Although this area was unsuitable for farming, it seemed an excellent location for ranches along the west side of the river and the perfect location for Luther to obtain a bishop-level position.

By early 1877, Luther had become sufficiently confident that the Mormons were not going to extend the Utah Northern any farther than Franklin and Brigham Young, Sr. was now so caught up in legal battles over his possible role in the Mountain Massacre[29] and lawsuits over his position on polygamy that he was paying very little attention to the lack of progress the Utah Northern was making. When Young, Sr. died, his son, John W. Young, was in the middle of construction of the Utah Central and the Utah Southern, rail lines running west and south of Salt Lake City, and he had little time for the Utah Northern. That was when Luther decided to approach Gould with his plan for the UP. It was to be based on chicanery and deception, but his presentation had won their approval and they agreed he could begin immediately upon his return to Ogden.

As agreed in the meeting with the UP executives, Luther started anonymously spreading half-truths in Utah and Idaho, suggesting that the Utah Northern Railroad was becoming insolvent and might go bankrupt. Working quietly in small communities up and down the Utah Northern line, Luther encouraged local farmers who were stockholders in the UNR to consider selling their stock while they still could recoup some of their investment. In the meantime, Luther had recommended that Jay Gould and Sidney Dillon of the UP quietly purchase Joseph Richardson's bonds and as much of his UNR stock as they could as soon as the stock prices started dropping. Not aware of the UP's plan of purchasing the UNR and hearing the rumors of possible bankruptcy, Joseph sold his bonds and some of his stock at a serious loss in order to protect himself if the railroad really went under. Since the locals could see that progress on the railroad had come to a halt, within several months, Gould and Dillon were able to buy the majority of the stock and bonds of the UNR for $480,000, or about ten cents on the dollar, but they still had to purchase the remaining stock owned by the Mormon Church. Due to the precipitous drop in the stock value, the UP was able to get the remainder of the stock when Brigham Young, Sr. died. John Young controlled this stock and he needed the cash to complete the Utah Southern.

In December of 1877, the Utah Northern Railroad was ordered to be sold as the result of a suit from the Union Trust Company of New York, which, not coincidentally, represented Dillon and Benjamin Richardson. It was sold for

---

29 *See Chapter Notes*

$100,000 at an auction on April 3, 1878, to UP employee S.H. Clark. The court ordered that Clark distribute the purchase price to the creditors of the Utah Northern Railroad, none other than Dillon and Benjamin Richardson. Clark admitted he was a representative of both Dillon and Richardson, so the cash from the sale of the railroad was simply turned back over to the parties that purchased it, resulting in the purchase of the UNR costing the UP nothing. Dillon, Richardson, and an unnamed silent partner immediately formed the Utah & Northern Railroad, the U&NR. The former Utah Northern Railroad, an asset worth well over three million dollars, was taken as part of a hostile takeover for about $800,000, considerably less than two bits on the dollar, just as Luther had suggested. In this way, Luther, the silent partner who had orchestrated the idea for the takeover, could obtain two parts of his scheme: a partial ownership and the title of administrator for the new extension of the railroad from Ogden, Utah to Butte, Montana.

Although the residents in the area knew Luther was the administrator of the new Utah & Northern Railroad, no one was aware he was also the source of the UNR's downfall. The legal maneuvering involved to create the new Utah & Northern was without debt, and the fully laid track extending from Ogden to Franklin could be used as collateral to issue bonds to extend the track farther north. As more track was laid, this too could be used as additional collateral, guaranteeing that the full length of planned track work would be completed with a small cash outlay from the UP and without having to depend on volunteer Mormon labor, something Luther thought was ill fated from the beginning.

All that remained was the bishop position. As Luther was negotiating with the UP in 1877, he had privately agreed to John Young's request that he obtain property for the Mormon Church on the west side of the river near Taylor's Bridge, in exchange for a bishop position. He requested, and was granted, permission to be appointed mayor of the new town of Eagle Rock, located on the east side of the river and, at the same time, became the most likely candidate to be the leading Mormon in Northeastern Idaho, which at that time was a large area with only a modest Mormon population.

When construction started for the new U&NR, Luther sent surveyors ahead to lay out the location of the new town with a depot, warehouse, maintenance shops, roundhouse, and city center. Although the UP and Mormons would obtain land rights to land on either side of the new railroad right of way, he told the surveyors that he wanted to acquire control of as much of the property around the future depot site as possible as well as additional land on both sides of the river for his own private development. Luther had planned from the beginning to make his next fortune as the mayor of Eagle Rock with absolute control of the development of the new railroad town for the UP and the opportunity for the expansion of the Mormon Church in Idaho to hasten his advancement in the Church as rapidly as possible.

Young's sons be damned.

Chapter Eleven

Friday, 8:00 PM, July 4th, 1879

Luther was startled out of his reverie by a loud banging on his office door. Zane burst in and exclaimed, "We found Potts' body! It got snagged on a rock in the Snake 'bout five miles downstream."

"Who found it?"

"Ah sent a coupla mah deputies back down the river ta look this afternoon."

Luther growled, "Have they told anyone?"

"Nah! Ya told me ta keep a lid on it til we talked."

"Good. And what about Callaway? Haven't they found him yet? Your deputies don't seem to be doing a very thorough job. Didn't they go out this morning?"

Zane dropped into one of the chairs facing Luther, apparently oblivious to Luther's sudden foul mood. "Well, Ah didn't wanna leave too early til we found Smiley and squared away what he saw. After some discussion, he agreed he only saw'em fall inta the rivvuh. Then Ah only sent mah two best men, since Ah diddin wanna word spreadin round. Ah thought ya would like mah plan—not lettin the cat outta the bag, if ya know what Ah mean." Zane was feeling quite satisfied.

Luther leaned across his desk and stared directly into Zane's eyes. In an even lower growl he said, "The *plan* was that you weren't going to let yourself be seen pushing the two of them off the bridge! Our story was going to be that you were close enough to the bridge to hear them fighting with each other but couldn't stop the fight in time. Then, you would be able to go down and retrieve their bodies, both bodies, immediately so you could confirm that they were both dead. Now we still don't know for sure that Callaway isn't just injured but still alive somewhere. What's your 'plan' for that?"

"Well boss, don't ya fret so. Ah sent mah men back out and told'em ta keep a-lookin. We'll find'im soon enough."

"Nightfall will be on us soon. If he comes straggling back here, I'm blaming this whole fuck-up on you. I recommend you station your deputies on either side of the river, so if that damned Irishman has survived we can catch him and finish the job before he gets to town. There is just enough commotion around here tonight that if your men can stay alert and far enough south of town, you might actually get this job done right this time."

"Well, ah, ya know, Boss, Ah've had those guys a-workin all the day long and they surely would like ta enjoy the festivities."

Luther rose abruptly from this desk and slammed his fist down on the desktop hard enough to knock the top off of his humidor. "What's the matter with you? Do you not realize what a mess you've created? Damn it, Zane, we might have a really pissed off Patrick Callaway straggling back into this town ready to claim you attempted to kill both of Eagle Rock's bartenders. It's going to be hard to cover that up. *You*, you lazy bastard, are personally going out tonight and not coming back until we have proof that Callaway is dead. I don't give a damn if any of your staff see the festivities tonight."

All confidence gone that he could talk his way into Luther's good graces now, Zane looked increasingly uncomfortable. He leaned forward in his chair, rubbing his hands together and staring at the floor. "Ah'm sorry, boss, but there is no moon shinin tonight. Clouds have rolled in. It will be pretty hard ta see anything or find anyone after sunset. And Ah really don't think he cuddah survived that fall. An even so, the water is up and runnin fast. He wuddah hit a rock or tree and drowned bah now."

"Is that right? You know that for a fact? And what if he is still alive?" Luther was pacing back and forth in front of his desk. He had looked out the window and noticed that it would get dark soon. The fireworks would be a pretty good distraction since most of the crowd was already drunk. He mulled this over and then sat down at his desk again.

"OK. Here is what you and your deputies are going to do. If he is alive and comes back to town, you still have to have someone on both sides of the river tonight to hold him. Assuming he really is dead, first thing in the morning you are going to take your deputies and organize a search party. That means there will be no drinking until we have found Callaway. You and your men have to at least look concerned over this tragedy. Am I clear?"

Very disappointed with these orders, Zane got up slowly and grumbled, "Ah'll be doin what's gotta be done."

And with that, he left Luther to consider what he would say to Mrs. Callaway.

Chapter Twelve

Friday, 9:30 PM, July 4th, 1879

The noise of the fireworks had started ten minutes ago, nearly drowning out the yelling and shooting going on just outside the saloon doors. They were supposed to have started at nine o'clock but they had been late. Catherine was ready to go to bed and had counted on the fireworks to draw the last of the drunks out of the saloon. Patrick had always kept the saloon open longer, but she was worn out and ready to close the doors long before nine. It was the usual chaos in the saloon, chairs overturned, tables in disarray, the floor sticky and slick. Her strength to get through a rough day finally gave way to emotions. Before she could break down in tears, she hurried into the kitchen.

In the kitchen, she leaned against a counter, drew a deep breath, and tried to regain her composure. Actually, from a financial point of view, Patrick had been right. The day had been an amazing success. With Crow Feather and Jay helping, they had sold out of the food and she had kept up with both the dining service and the bar. But she hated working the bar. Many of the men were difficult at best, rude usually, and occasionally downright scary. Patrick had tended to the difficult drinkers in the past, and, thankfully, Henry had stopped by at a few fortuitous moments and escorted drunken men out of the saloon before they caused any trouble. But many of the prominent town folk had visited the bar for the first time and some of those encounters were not pleasant, including a confrontation with Mr. Anderson. Robert Anderson was one of the founding citizens of Eagle Rock and now owned the bank and warehouse. He demanded to know where Patrick was, but what could she tell him? Catherine had no idea what had happened to Patrick, and this only made her more upset. Mr. Anderson would just have to wait to have any business conversation with Patrick. Dick Chamberlain, another early settler of Eagle Rock and a known womanizer, arrived a little later. He leered at Catherine, made off-color comments, and stared at her breasts most of the time he was in the saloon.

Catherine had never seen many of the other men before. There were mountain men, trappers, and gold miners who stayed up in the hills east of Eagle Rock; ranchers and cowboys, covered with dust and smelling like horses and sweat; and rail men and rail construction workers with sweat-matted hair and foul breath. Almost all had shaggy beards, filthy clothes, pungent body odor, and extremely bad manners. They all needed a good bath. They too spent much of their time leering at Catherine and making comments to each other that brought outbursts of laughter. She was convinced that they were all making jokes or sharing dirty thoughts about her.

Sheriff Zane was the worst. Catherine was convinced he was the source of much of the laughter at her expense. He made a point of grabbing her hand when she waited on his table and moving just enough to bump into her as she tried to get past him to other tables. All of this made her even more upset about Patrick walking out on her. Yet she was also concerned that he might be in real danger or actually hurt. When the fireworks finally started, she was relieved to be able to shoo out most of the drinkers. She set down the broom she had carried with her into the kitchen, straightened her apron, took another deep breath, and went back into the saloon.

Two tables of drinkers had stayed on after she announced she was closing. They had been loud and crude and had been complaining loudly for more whiskey for the last half hour after Catherine had announced she had run out.

"Gentlemen, I explained earlier I would be closing once the fireworks started and I have run out of both whiskey and beer. You will have to leave."

One of the more inebriated railmen sneered at Catherine then raised his glass and slurred, "Hey Pretty Lady, when ya gonna get me anotha whiskey? Or am Ah gonna have ta put ya ovvuh my knee to get ya to behave right proper?"

With that, the men at both tables started laughing again. One of the other railmen tried to stand up with his empty glass held high to propose a toast, but he didn't have enough balance to stay upright and fell back into his chair. "Ah'll toaz to that! Ah think we all awtta havva shot at her. She looks like she's a-needin a liddle masculine encouragement."

More laughter. Just then, Henry walked into the saloon. The rail men hadn't noticed and kept at it. They all started pounding their glasses on the tables. One yelled, "Mo' whiskey or show us some tits!"

Another responded, "Hell no. Mo' whiskey or show us some ass!"

And everybody howled.

"*Enough!*" shouted a stern voice from the front of the saloon. Henry's grim face stared down the last of the hecklers. "That is no way to talk to a lady. Every one of you get your deadbeat asses out of here now or I will call the sheriff back in here."

The first man to speak chuckled just loud enough for everyone to hear. "Lotta good that'll do." He turned to one of the other drinkers and whispered, "Ah heard the sheriff braggin jus this afternoon he couldn wait ta get unduh the sheets with pretty Missus Callaway."

Henry withdrew his gun and fired one shot into the ceiling. The loud report and falling ceiling fragments shut everybody up. "*Out!* Right now! This saloon is closed for the night."

With a considerable amount of mumbled complaining, the men shuffled out the door. It took half of them to carry out the one drinker who couldn't stay upright on his own.

Catherine slammed the bat-wing[30] doors shut, swung the security doors shut, and dropped the wooden board down to secure them. Then she sat down in the nearest chair and burst into tears. Henry moved another chair to her table and sat down. Hesitating a moment, he put one of his hands over hers.

Jay and his mother had come out of the kitchen. "Is everything all right, Miss Cat?"

She quickly withdrew her hand from under Henry's.

Henry replied for her. "Everything is all right now."

"Oh Henry," Catherine wailed. "Everybody's got a worse story about what's happened to Patrick! He's disappeared with Fannie Smiles. He was in a fight with Harry Potts. He has run off with Potts' whore. He fell off the bridge. He's

---

30 ***Bat-wing doors*** *– partial, double doors that swing in both directions. They were practical in western saloons since they provided easy access, cut down the dust from the outside, allowed people to see who was coming in, and provided some ventilation. They also shielded the goings-on in the saloon from the "proper ladies" who might be passing by. But there is no way to secure them.*

never coming back." She looked pleadingly at her friend. "Have you heard anything, Henry? I just don't know what to do or think!"

Henry's voice was soft and soothing. "You know how gossip spreads. I doubt any of that is true. These people are just jealous. And look at what you did today! My God, did you really sell out of whiskey?"

"We sold out of everything! My stock is completely gone." Catherine's mood improved slightly as she wiped away her tears. "Thanks to Jay's mother, we used up all of the elk, the vegetables, and almost all of the flour! She made four enormous pots of stew and I don't know how many loaves of bread and we still ran out." She turned toward the kitchen. "Crow Feather, it was wonderful stew! How can I thank you enough? And Jay, I could have never kept up with the dishes and cleaning if you hadn't been here, even if Pat had been behind the bar. You were a huge help."

Recovering from her outburst, she got up and went over to her cash box. "I told you I would pay you, and you both put in railroad hours so I am paying you railroad wages, with a bonus." She put a number of large denomination coins in a bag and handed them to Jay. "You earned this. Please split it between the two of you. And, regardless if Patrick ever comes back, I would be pleased to hire you again, if you will say 'yes.'"

Ignoring their cultural boundaries, she gave both Jay and Crow Feather a genuinely appreciative hug. "Now go home and get some rest. You deserve it."

Jay's face had turned bright red and he looked even more embarrassed by the hug. He had not opened the bag but could tell by its weight that it was a generous amount. "You don't be need-in ta give us this much, Miss Cat. I think Ma and I both enjoyed being useful."

"I said you deserve it and I have plenty left to restock the saloon, if that is what I decide to do."

She smiled at them and led them to the door Henry had unbolted, but when Henry opened the door, Mayor Luther Armstrong was standing there. Luther smiled and said, "Well, thank you Henry. I was just coming to bring Mrs. Callaway an update on the search for her husband."

"Oh my God!" Catherine blurted out. "You found him. Is he all right? Is he hurt? Why didn't he come with you?"

Luther looked uncomfortable. "Well, we didn't exactly find him, but Sheriff Gunther has been talking all day with our revelers. What he has found out so far is a little confusing but, of course, most of the people he talked to were pretty hungover. You might want to sit down. This isn't exactly good news."

A look of alarm spread over Catherine's face and Henry led her back to the chair she had been in. Neither Jay nor his mother left but went to the back of the saloon and sat quietly to listen.

Luther began. "We don't know for sure what happened. There certainly has been a lot of talk. You know your husband was a pretty colorful storyteller, who could spin some pretty tall yarns, possibly imagined and exaggerated. The consensus seems to be that Edgar Potts got into a loud argument with your husband early last evening and somehow or another, the two of them ended up on the bridge in a scuffle.

"Now I know for sure that your husband was bragging about your cooking and encouraging the drinkers at Potts' to leave his saloon and come over here last night. Edgar has a pretty bad temper if he gets embarrassed, and it seemed like your husband was going out of his way to embarrass him in front of his customers. In the past, I have seen Edgar become violent in similar situations.

"Although everyone seems to have varying accounts of what happened next, most agree that both your husband and Edgar were headed to the bridge after many of Potts' customers left to come here. There could well have been a scuffle of some sort between the two of them on the bridge. Mrs. Callaway, do you know if Patrick can swim?"

Catherine groaned. "No, he is deathly afraid of water. Oh my God. Is he really dead?"

Luther leaned over and touched her shoulder. "Now Mrs. Callaway, we don't know that, but it is certainly a possibility and I felt you would want to know. The sheriff has already gone up and down both sides of the riverbank a ways, but it's too dark to see anything. We haven't found Patrick or Edgar.

"There still may be some hope," he continued. "Most of the men the sheriff talked to were just about as drunk as Smiley Jack usually is. These are not dependable witnesses so we'll keep looking. I have instructed the sheriff to form a posse with some of my men and search both sides of the Snake downstream as soon as it is light tomorrow morning. We should know then what really happened. In the meantime, I want you to know I will do everything I can to help. If you need anything, please get a hold of me. If you want, at my expense, I will tell Mr. Harper to send a telegram to your family in Kentucky so they can help you decide what to do next. But let's wait until the search party comes back tomorrow morning. Who knows, they may have good news for us."

Catherine had regained some of her composure. She looked up at Luther and asked very quietly, "I heard that Fannie Smiles is missing, too. Can you tell me if that is true?"

Luther looked a little embarrassed. "Well, it is true. We haven't found her either, but that isn't necessarily related to your missing husband. She has gone missing a number of times in the last six months."

"Yes, I see," replied Catherine. "But, as bad as it seems, it would be better if Pat had run off with her than to have fallen off the bridge and drowned."

Henry stepped in and took hold of her hand again. "Catherine, there are too many questions and not nearly enough answers for us to know what happened. What you need right now is to get some sleep. You have been working non-stop for two days. You will be able to cope with this much better tomorrow when you have gotten some rest. Don't you agree Mr. Armstrong?"

"I do. Please try not to fret about this any longer tonight. Maybe I shouldn't have come over, but I thought I had a responsibility to tell you all of the efforts we have been making. You get some sleep and we will talk again tomorrow."

Catherine stood up and, after a confused moment, reached out and shook Luther's hand. "Please don't misunderstand me, Mr. Armstrong. I do appreciate all you have done and your counsel seems very wise. I am just really tired and am not myself."

"Don't worry about how you have been acting. You are under considerable strain and, no matter how this comes out, I will continue to provide for your best interests in any way I can. I will be going now. You get some rest."

As Luther left, Jay came forward with his mother and waved at the upturned chairs and tables with dirty glasses. "Miss Cat, don't you worry about this mess. My ma and I will be back tomorrow morning and we will clean this up for you. You gave us too much money and we need to help you out. He's right. You go get some sleep."

Catherine looked over the room and her shoulders slumped. "I am too tired to argue with you now. Let's talk tomorrow morning, but not too early."

As they were leaving, Henry went behind the bar and found a single bottle with a little whiskey left. He rinsed out two small glasses and filled them with the remainder of the whiskey. "Looks like you didn't completely sell out of everything. I think we both need a nightcap."

Catherine walked over to the bar, lifted one of the glasses, and downed it and started coughing violently. "Yuck! This stuff is awful! How can anyone drink it?"

Henry sipped his and smiled. "Actually, Catherine, this is really good red-eye whiskey. Haven't you had any before?"

"Never," she said, shaking her head. "I saw how Patrick and all the rest of the men acted after drinking any kind of liquor and swore I wouldn't touch the stuff, but these last two days have definitely caused me to reconsider. I deserve this drink, although I might not think so tomorrow morning."

Henry chuckled. "Really Catherine, you won't get a hangover from one shot. I gave you the drink to help you sleep and, since you have never had liquor before, that one generous shot should do the trick. Bar the door behind me and go to bed."

At the door, Catherine reached out to touch Henry's shoulder. "Thank you for all you did today. I really needed a lot of help. And wasn't Luther just wonderful? What a nice man."

Henry said yes, but as he walked away from Patrick's Saloon, he shook his head at Cat's naivete. She had a lot to learn about living in the West. This wasn't a very good place for a young, pretty, aristocratic single woman from Kentucky. She was going to need a man in her life to survive out here. He smiled to himself. He'd have to think more about that.

This could turn out to be an excellent opportunity for him.

Chapter Thirteen

Saturday, 8:30 AM, July 5th, 1879

Catherine bolted upright in her bed, shielding her eyes from the bright sunlight flooding the room. *What was that noise?* She had been awakened by a noise coming from downstairs. There shouldn't be anyone downstairs. Hadn't she barred the front doors? What time was it? She rubbed her eyes and tried to wake up completely. She had slept so hard. Then she stopped breathing to listen more closely. There was the noise again. It was definitely someone talking softly in the saloon downstairs. She had to wake Patrick.

As she started to roll out of bed, her legs became entangled in the sheets. After some fumbling, she found that her legs were actually tangled up in her dress. Had she not undressed to go to bed last night? She even still had on her apron. What had happened last night? She must have just fallen into bed. After carefully untangling her apron, dress, and sheets, she stepped onto the floor of their bedroom loft above the kitchen. That's when she remembered. Patrick was not there. He might never be there. A deep sob rose in her throat just as another sound of voices came from below.

She took a deep breath, swallowed the sob, and quietly tiptoed over the ladder that led down to the kitchen storage room in the back. Peeking down, she saw the back door was partially open. In her haste last night, maybe she hadn't barred the back door after all. The cash box! Had she brought it upstairs? Is that what they were after? She could now hear two people whispering to each other. She carefully went back to her bed and lifted the spread to look under the bed where Patrick had told her to always put the cash box and the loaded rifle every night. Thank God, it was there, filled with more cash than they'd ever had.

Knowing that the money was still safe, she grabbed the rifle and crept back to the ladder. Holding the rifle and her dress with one hand so she didn't trip on the ladder steps made her somewhat clumsy and much too noisy. She had insisted that Patrick put in a real stairway to their loft but he claimed there wasn't enough room. It was at times like this she realized real stairs were needed for more than just convenience. The last thing she needed right now was to Warn intruders of her presence, or, worse, to fall flat on her face on the floor below.

Finally down, she looked tentatively around the corner of the storeroom into the kitchen. No one was there but, to her surprise, dozens of dirty dishes and glasses had been stacked on every horizontal surface. She didn't recall doing that last night. Henry's shot of whiskey must have affected her memory more than she realized. Walking quietly, she managed to get through the kitchen without disturbing the stacks of dishes and enter the small vestibule between the kitchen and the saloon. She could hear the voices much better now. There were definitely two people moving about in the saloon, probably looking for the cash box. There certainly wasn't any remaining beer or liquor to steal. Since there were two of them, she would have to scare them off. Preparing to fire a warning shot, Catherine raised her rifle and used the barrel to part the curtain between the vestibule and saloon. She got her first look into the saloon as she started putting pressure on the trigger and braced herself for the loud discharge of the rifle.

"Miss Cat? Are you up?"

Catherine froze.

"Jay? Is that you?"

Why on earth had Jay broken into her saloon? What was he looking for? And who had he brought with him? She should have known better to trust an Indian.

Catherine lowered the rifle, set it on the counter in the vestibule out of sight but still close enough to reach if she had to escort Jay and his friend out of the saloon. Then she got a good look into the saloon.

There were Jay and his mother with armloads of dishes and glasses heading directly toward her. Catherine was stunned until she remembered that Jay had said last night the two of them would come back to help clean up. Her face turned bright red from embarrassment. She had almost fired a warning shot at them. Her knowledge of guns was not great. She could have hurt them. But with the embarrassment also came relief. No one had broken in to rob her. It was clearer than ever that trying to operate a saloon without Patrick was just out of the question.

Jay was looking at Catherine with a look of concern on his face and Crow Feather was just looking terribly frightened. "Are you all right, Miss Cat?"

Catherine held up both her hands and gave a startled cough and a small shake of her head. "I'm fine, just a little sleepy. I must have overslept. Let me freshen up and I can help you. You certainly didn't have to come back this early."

"Oh, Ma and I get up with the sun. We have been up for hours. I'm sorry if we woke you, but the back door was unlocked, so I figured you wouldn't mind if we got started."

Catherine saw that Crow Feather was still frozen in fright. "Crow Feather, everything is all right. I really appreciate both of you coming to help, and we have plenty of time. I won't be opening up today, or the next few days, until I decide if I want to restock my inventory. In fact, I may not open at all unless we find Patrick."

Crow Feather finally gave a small smile. Catherine smiled and reached out to pat Crow Feather's hand. "Just give me a moment in the kitchen to freshen up, and we can tackle this mess together."

As Catherine closed the curtain and turned to wash up, she saw the rifle on the counter. She grabbed it, took it into the storeroom and hid it behind some empty barrels. Then she drew in a deep breath to help her calm down. She would have to act more sensibly, and she would start by accepting Luther's offer to telegraph her father for help.

It only took a little more than an hour for the three of them to finish cleaning up the saloon and the kitchen. As soon as Catherine unbarred the front entry to air out the saloon, numerous miners, trappers, and railroad men trailed in for a drink. Many inquired about lunch but Catherine told them she was closed. Jay suggested she might want to order more supplies first thing since she clearly had customers, but Catherine was undecided. She hadn't given up on the sheriff's search party finding Patrick but, if they didn't find him, she would need money to get back to Kentucky.

Mr. Ellington Harper, Jr., the owner of *The Idaho Register* dropped by as well. "Mrs. Callaway, I'm so sorry to hear about Patrick. I wonder if I could speak with you."

Catherine quickly stopped what she was doing. "Have you heard something about Patrick?"

"Only that the search party has not returned." He gave Catherine a warm smile. "But I might be able to help a little bit. Could we sit down and talk?"

Catherine looked puzzled but offered him a chair at one of the tables. She wiped her hands on her apron and sat down across from him. "But what can you do?"

"Well, I can arrange to have a special edition of the paper ready late this afternoon with a small article about Patrick being missing, including that we are looking for him. There might be someone out there who could help us search or provide some new information. My paper will be seen as far south as Franklin. Who knows? It can't hurt."

"Oh my, I hadn't thought of that. Of course it could help. What would you like to know?"

"To make the article interesting to my readership, I will need a little background on Patrick, and on you. It is more likely that readers will want to read the article if it has some personal information about the two of you. You are not the first to find your husband missing from a possible accident. They would be interested to find out how a young couple like yourselves ended up in Eagle Rock. I understand you are from a grand family in Louisville, Kentucky, but I know little about Patrick."

Catherine hesitated. "Actually, I guess I know Patrick less than I thought I did. He has certainly changed since we arrived here. I only met him a little more than a year ago. We were married on our train trip to Salt Lake City." She blushed. "Of course we had already decided to get married, but I left Louisville rather abruptly and Patrick found a minister on the train who agreed to marry us. It all seemed so romantic at the time but I guess, looking back, it might appear to be a little foolish. Patrick was so dashing and full of life. He had such grand dreams and the idea of starting over in Salt Lake City sounded very exciting to me at the time. He kept saying that we could do anything in the new American West and I believed him."

Catherine paused, looking down at her clasped hands. "I guess it was more of a dream than actual reality." She looked up at Ellington. "Patrick wanted to open a café in Salt Lake City. Well, actually, I wanted to open a café and Patrick said it would more likely be profitable if it was a café for the lunch crowd and a bar for the evening crowd. We quickly learned that the Mormons around Salt Lake City frowned on liquor and Patrick was convinced we could do better up here in Eagle Rock. He said, with the establishment of the Utah & Northern Railroad division headquarters and maintenance facilities here in Eagle Rock, we could be the first to set up our café and be ahead of any competitors. We did turn out to be first, but it took a long time before we really had enough customers and Patrick never thought it was the right time to start the café."

Ellington was taking notes as Catherine spoke. He frowned. "If you were planning on opening a café, why is this called Patrick's Saloon and why did you serve food for the first time yesterday?"

Catherine leaned back in her chair and took a deep breath before responding somewhat bitterly. "Well, I don't really think Patrick ever had any intention of opening a café." She made a face, slowly shook her head and then firmly said with a small grimace, "Patrick clearly wanted a saloon. In fact he likes to gamble and I think he really wanted a saloon with gambling, not a café at all, but he wouldn't admit it to me or I wouldn't have asked my father for the money we needed to start this business." A tear appeared on one of Catherine's cheeks. She put her hands over her face. "I've said too much."

Ellington reached across the table and laid one of his hands on Catherine's. "Now there, I didn't mean to get you so upset. Let's not talk about this any further. I was just trying to help."

"But what about the article?" Catherine wailed. "I need to know if he's alive, or hurt, or needs help!"

Ellington responded soothingly. "I will write an article with the information I have. Your saloon and your noonday lunch is the talk of the town. I hope you keep cooking for our townspeople. I will write a very complimentary article and it will go out this afternoon. Luther Armstrong told me Patrick was last seen wearing his patriotic red, white, and blue striped shirt, which should be easy to identify. Is that correct?"

"Yes, yes, he was very excited to be celebrating the Fourth of July and had bought that just for such an event while we were still in Salt Lake City," Catherine answered. "I'm sorry I broke down," she added after a moment and took a handkerchief out of her apron to wipe her eyes. Sitting up straight in her chair, she looked directly at Ellington. "I should control myself better. I really appreciate you doing this. It could help." She sniffed, "And I certainly need the help right now."

Henry had come into the saloon as Ellington and Catherine were talking but had sat down quietly near the front door. He got up, came over to them, and pulled up a chair near Catherine. "And there are many of us who will help you, Catherine. Of course you are upset, but we will all work together to help you decide what to do next. There just isn't much we can do until we know where Patrick is." He turned to Ellington. "Your idea of an article about Patrick going missing is a fine one. I'm sure it will help."

Ellington got up to leave. "I am going to start on this right now. It will go out this afternoon. You have my word on this, Mrs. Callaway. And Luther told me about his offer to help you get word to your family. Anytime you want, you come over to the newspaper and we will send out a telegram."

Catherine and Henry rose. "Thank you so much for coming. I really don't want to contact my family until I know what has happened to Patrick, but you have been very kind."

Chapter Fourteen

One hour earlier - 7:30 AM, July 5th, 1879

An hour earlier, Ellington Harper, owner of the local newspaper, was carefully walking across the new railroad bridge on the way to Luther Armstrong's ranch on the other side of the Snake River. He didn't understand why there weren't more accidents when drunken men made their way back to the construction camp on the west side of the river. Walking the ties was difficult and required one's close attention. They were too close together to step naturally from one tie to another and too far apart to step on every other tie.

Once on the other side of the bridge, he reflected on yesterday's events. The chaos of the celebration had been evident throughout Eagle Rock's main street. Streamers, trash, boots, and hats, as well as a number of sleeping drunks, were scattered all over the area. Ellington chuckled as he thought about the town-wide celebration. It had been a rather successful event and only three residents got injured. Harvey Smut had gotten into an argument and shot himself in the foot while trying to un-holster his gun; a visiting elixir salesman broke his arm when he fell out of his window in the hotel while trying to pull down a banner that blocked his view of the brothel ladies marching to the café down Railroad Avenue; and Jimmy Brown got his wrist slashed after claiming one of the Richard brothers on the railroad crew lived up to his unfortunate nickname, "Little Dick." Everyone was aware that the mother of the two Richard brothers had been drunk during each delivery and had inadvertently named both boys Richard after their father. Since the first one born was a considerably larger man than the younger one, the locals distinguished the two with the nicknames "Big Dick" and "Little Dick" respectively. The older brother didn't seem to mind, but the younger was pretty touchy about the nickname.

Doc Jones, drunk as always, was still able to patch up all three, including a cast for the salesman, while continuously consuming most of the "medicine" in his bag. Sheriff Zane was more sober than usual and locked up the three injured men and Little Dick for the remainder of the night for disturbing the peace. This was highly unusual since it was normally Zane and his deputies who were disturbing the peace. Ellington was surprised by Zane's behavior and decided to look into this further. For a small Western town of railroad men, cowboys, trappers, and miners where there was at least one shooting injury a day, this could be considered a pretty tame event. Fortunately, the Clancy clan had not shown up. There hadn't even been any fatalities. He would congratulate Luther on that at breakfast.

He wondered again about that invitation for breakfast he had received late last night from Luther, though. Normally, this meant Luther wanted something. If nothing else, Ellington could quiz Luther on the various rumors that were spreading around town about the status of Patrick Callaway and Fanny Smiles. As the mayor, Mormon leader, and representative of the Utah & Northern RR with close ties to the top brass of the Union Pacific, Luther seemed to have control of just about everything in this town. And a visit for breakfast at the Luther ranch was always the opportunity for a good, but heavy, meal. The slop available at the Eagle Rock Hotel was a joke. Fortunately, Luther's ranch was easy to get to, just on the other side of the river with a commanding view of the town from the low bluffs above the Snake River. By walking across the new railroad bridge, Ellington wouldn't have to pay a toll at Taylor's Bridge. Maybe he should contact Bob Anderson about a story of the building of the bridge. He had heard that the original name for the small settlement Matt Taylor and Bob Anderson started was Taylor's Crossing.

A few minutes later, Luther's live-in maid met Ellington at the front door. Ellington was pretty sure the maid would soon be Luther's next wife. She had come up with him from Ogden and he only had one wife at present. As the probable future bishop of the territory, he was certainly entitled to more than one.

The dark-haired young woman, probably fifteen years younger than Luther, smiled at Ellington and said, "C'mon in, Mr. Harper. Mr. Armstrong is in the dining room."

When Ellington entered the dining room, Luther was already seated, writing in a journal and drinking his morning coffee.

Without looking up from his writing, he said, "Glad you could come, Ellington. Please sit down. Rachael has prepared steak and eggs for us. But excuse me for just a moment as I collect my thoughts. I have some ideas for your paper."

"I am always looking for good ideas, Luther," Ellington said, smiling. *Just as I thought. He is going to tell me what I should write today.*

Rachael brought the men large plates of steak and eggs, fried potatoes, and a platter of freshly buttered bread with marmalade probably shipped all the way from San Francisco. It was obvious from the pat Luther gave her on her bottom that she was more than just his maid.

After an exchange of congratulations over the success of yesterday's celebration, Luther got down to business. "It's important that we get the word out so everyone in the territory knows just how successful yesterday's event was. In addition, I want the bishops in Salt Lake City to understand how far we have come in putting this town on the map. I will continue to need their financial backing in order to deliver job opportunities for more Mormons and encourage them to move to our town if we are to grow to the extent I have planned. Your valuable contribution to our success will be to put this in print so all of your readers will know just how advanced this community has become. To that end, I have jotted down a few ideas you may want to include in your paper."

After looking over the list, Ellington folded it and slipped into his vest pocket. It was two pages of generally self-congratulatory references to Luther's achievements on behalf of Eagle Rock.

"This, as always, is very helpful," Ellington said, dutifully playing his part in the familiar scene. How soon do you want me to get this out?"

Luther leaned back in his chair, paused, and nodded to give a sense of gravity to his answer. "Although I would like this to get out as soon as possible, I believe the whole situation surrounding the disappearance of Patrick Callaway is even more urgent. You know Patrick has been a thorn in my side ever since the Callaways arrived. I am still angry my surveyors allowed him to purchase a prime location on the main street without telling me. But hard feelings aside, we have to look out for our citizens. I think you should put out a small special edition making people aware of his mysterious disappearance, and the sooner the better. Today if possible. Do you think you can get that done?"

Ellington frowned. So that was it. As usual, Luther always asked for complete and total support of all his decisions, regardless of the efforts and inconvenience caused to others.

"I suppose it could be done but I really need a little more information. I know that a search party was formed. Have they had any luck? Shouldn't I mention Edgar Potts as well?"

Luther sighed. "Of course you can put in a note about Edgar, but I am more concerned about Patrick. You know his wife is the daughter of an aristocrat in Louisville and I am sure they will be concerned. I don't think Edgar has any relatives or kin that I know of." He got up. "I need a cigar. Would you like one?"

Ellington hated cigars but knew better than to decline and nodded politely. It was just understood—if you were invited to Luther's ranch you had better appreciate his tastes in alcohol and tobacco.

"I'll be right back. You will really like these."

Ellington quickly finished the rest of his steak and eggs before he was required to smoke a cigar that would leave a foul taste in his mouth for the remainder of the day.

When Luther came back, they went through the traditional ritual of lighting up and, after a deep draw on his cigar and a satisfied smile, Luther explained what he felt probably happened to the two men.

"As close as we can tell—and this is all off the record, I don't want you printing this—Patrick and Edgar Potts got into some kind of quarrel that turned into a brawl on the new bridge late the night of the third. Those two have been at each other's throats for quite a while. You would think with only two saloons in the town, they could figure out a way to get along. Potts' Saloon has been losing money under Potts' management for some time and I suspect he has been blaming Callaway for his own poor business skills. At any rate, it appears they both may have fallen off the bridge into the Snake during the scuffle. It's running high and fast from late runoff so, even if they were to survive the fall, it's unlikely the either of them could fight that current and avoid the boulders. We haven't found either of them yet, but surely they have drowned. I suspect it is just a matter of time before we will find their bodies down river. I would like you to write a short article on Patrick with a description of what he was last wearing, just in case anyone comes across him. You should probably include a description of Edgar as well. Someone may remember what he was wearing, but don't spend too much time on that. I really want this out today."

As Luther was talking, Ellington took notes. "Is there anything else you think should be in this article?"

"You know, I think you should talk to Mrs. Callaway. I think if you make the story personal with a little background material on the couple and how they ended up out here, it would make her feel a little better. I have already offered to pay for her to telegraph her family back in Louisville. I understand her family is part of the aristocracy of that state and it would probably be best if she goes back to them as soon possible. A young, attractive woman like that doesn't belong in Eagle Rock just now without a man to protect her. The sooner she goes home, the safer she will be. She certainly can't run that saloon alone, so how would she support herself?"

Ellington reviewed his notes and then asked, "I think they may have put everything they had into that saloon. How is she going to leave that behind?"

"Well that's a good question, but I believe, if nothing else, I can find a buyer for the saloon. That would give Mrs. Callaway all the money she needs to get back to her family. I can help her out with the negotiations, but I don't want to bring it up until we have definitive information on Patrick's death. No need to worry the pretty woman with the difficult details of a land transaction."

"Don't you think making the article without the background information on their choice to come to Eagle Rock would be better? I could just focus on the descriptions of the two men, which I am sure would get everyone's attention. Interviewing her right now could be pretty upsetting for her. I'm sure she is probably having second thoughts about coming out west."

"No. I really want you to talk to her today and I need that special edition out today as well." Luther chuckled to himself. "It's important that she understand that we are all willing to help her. She also has to come to grips with the idea that it would not be very good for her to stay in Eagle Rock. The sooner we get that point across to her, the better off everyone will be."

And with that, it was clear to Ellington that the breakfast was over. But just before Ellington left, Luther added, "Oh, you better mention that Fanny Smiles is also missing."

Ellington nodded. "But won't that look a little odd, naming her missing along with Patrick and Edgar?"

"Edgar is a good-for-nothing low life and meant nothing to anybody. No one is going to miss him but, people are asking about Fannie."

Ellington left a few minutes later, trying to come up with a logical reason to interview Mrs. Callaway without upsetting her more. Certainly, she wouldn't appreciate having Fanny Smiles' mysterious disappearance showing up in the same article with Patrick's. He shook his head in frustration. One thing was clear in his mind. The sooner Mrs. Callaway accepted her fate and left Eagle Rock, the sooner someone would have access to the best saloon location in Eagle Rock. He was pretty sure that would also be the best result for Luther Arnold Armstrong. Luther always seemed to come out ahead every time he was involved with some business transaction in Eagle Rock.

Both Potts and Patrick going missing on the same day was an interesting coincidence.

Chapter Fifteen

Saturday, 11:30 AM, July 5th, 1879

Henry was talking quietly with Catherine, trying to calm her after Ellington's interview, but Jay decided he would disturb them anyway.

"Miss Cat, Mr. Willett? My ma made some soup. Could I bring it out now?"

Catherine turned, looking confused. "How could she make soup? We are out of everything. I guess I really do have to at least buy some supplies so we can eat."

Jay chuckled. "My ma can make something out of just about nothing at all. You have more leftovers in that kitchen than she has after shopping for fresh vittles. She made a broth from the elk bones and dumplings to go with it. She was worried you hadn't eaten today. I hope it's all right." He smiled and shook his head. "She loves to cook and your huge kitchen is bigger than our entire home. When she's in there, she thinks she's died and gone to white man's heaven. I think she would sleep in there if you let her."

Catherine got out of her chair and squeezed both of Jay's arms. "You two have been just wonderful. I don't know what I would have done without your help. Tell your mother to bring out four bowls and we will all have lunch together."

Jay paused before responding. "Well, ah, I think Ma would rather eat in the kitchen. She'd be too nervous to eat out here with as fine a lady as you. We will be happy to eat in the kitchen."

"Well, you just do what you think is best for your mother. But, if Patrick comes back and we stay here, I will insist that both of you eat with us on occasion."

Jay served the elk and dumpling soup, and Catherine and Henry were amazed at how good Crow Feather's meal of "just about nothing at all" could be.

"I do believe, Catherine, your new cook is the best in this territory," Henry said between bites. "This is better than anything that's ever come out of what passes for a kitchen down at the hotel. What a dump. You would think that with the new railroad station and all the railroad traffic, someone would put together a better eating establishment."

Catherine pursed her lips. "When my damned husband manages to get himself back here, I will demand he build the café he promised me. And I will hire Crow Feather and her son to help me. I am certainly not going to work this awful saloon anymore. I just don't like working behind a bar. You, Jay, and Crow Feather are the only good things about it."

She looked crestfallen. "But what if he never comes back? What can I do? This is all so terrible. Patrick can't swim. He could have already drowned. I can't run this saloon alone. You saw what happened last night with those terrible men. I have never been so scared."

"Now look here. You need to settle down and take each day one step at a time. We will deal with what happens next once we know something certain about Patrick. I took a job to build Jake Edwards' new home late last night—he got a promotion and is going to bring his family up here as soon as it is finished—so I have a steady income for the next month and can spend evenings here to help you out with the bar and knock a few heads together if anyone gets out of line. What would you think about taking Crow Feather and Slink on and running this saloon as a café for breakfast and lunch? At least until we know more about Patrick."

Catherine composed herself and nodded. "Well, at least we would all be eating well if I gave Crow Feather free rein in the kitchen." She smiled. "I knew my way around an eastern kitchen pretty well, but she knows this area and this crowd much better than I do. That elk broth and dumplings today, and everything she made yesterday were all delicious!"

The saloon doors opened. Robert Anderson, owner of the Anderson Brothers Trading Post and Bank walked in and began speaking before Catherine could tell him they were closed. "Ma'am, the supplies and lumber your husband ordered have arrived. Where do you want them?"

Catherine looked startled. "What supplies? What are you talking about?"

Henry stood up. "What's this about, Bob? Patrick isn't here and Mrs. Callaway wasn't expecting any deliveries."

"I heard about Patrick, but I have a signed contract and a wagonload of lumber and supplies that needs to be delivered and paid for. Patrick was very clear about what he wanted. He said I should get it delivered as soon after the Fourth as I could since he would have the money to pay me then. You know, I normally ask for the money up front, but he promised he would have everything after the Fourth. And he must have been right. Ma'am, you sure looked busy yesterday. Anyway, can I just put it on your back lot?"

Catherine stood, to try to take control of the situation. "I don't know what this is about, Mr. Anderson. You will just have to wait until Patrick shows up and discuss it with him."

Now Henry looked concerned. He turned his back to Anderson and spoke in a low tone to Catherine. "I'm thinking this is for the gambling hall he was going to build out back. I thought you knew. I'm sorry to be the one to tell you. He has been talking about this all over town. I was at Potts' Saloon when he was bragging to anyone and everyone about how his saloon would soon be the first gambling hall in Eagle Rock. I think that is what got Potts so angry that night."

Catherine's face had gone white. She put both her hands over her face to cover her embarrassment. No, he had talked about what they might do if the Fourth was profitable, but he certainly hadn't mentioned adding a gambling hall.

Mr. Anderson was clearly not interested in Catherine's problems. He was ready to get paid and get going. "Ma'am, I can drop off this stuff in your back lot and give you a day or two to settle this account, but I need to know when I will be paid."

Henry spoke up. "Bob, could you just store it in your warehouse across the street for now until we can get to the bottom of all of this. Mrs. Callaway really has her hands full dealing with this place. Certainly you can understand that."

Mr. Anderson ignored Henry and looked directly at Catherine. "My warehouse is already full and I need the wagon for another delivery. The way I see this, I met the conditions of a contract your husband signed with me and I expect to get paid, whether your husband ever shows up or not. I can't afford to sit on that much merchandise and just about everyone else in town is aware that your husband is probably already at the bottom of the Snake River. I still need to get paid."

Henry jumped up and stormed over to Mr. Anderson, snarling, "You will get paid. Take that wagon load and get out now, you bastard, before you cause any more damage."

"I'll put it in your back lot, but I will need to know when I will get paid," Anderson repeated, and he marched out of the saloon. Henry returned to Catherine, who was staring in a daze at the table where they had been sitting. She was shaking and her eyes were unfocused.

She looked up at Henry, fear in her eyes. "Does everyone in town think Patrick is already dead?"

Henry sat down and took both her hands in his. "No one has any real idea what has happened to Patrick. It's all talk. Anderson just doesn't want to lose money on those supplies. We can work something out."

Catherine had tears in her eyes. "What if he really is dead?"

Henry tried to reassure her. "I think you would be surprised about how many friends you have in this town who would be willing to help out. And we don't know yet where Patrick is. He could walk into this saloon any minute."

And just then the saloon doors opened.

Catherine jumped up expectantly, and then gasped and exclaimed with a grimace, "Oh! *You!*"

Chapter Sixteen

Saturday, 12:30 PM, July 5th, 1879

There stood the seductive Fannie Smiles wearing a snugly fitted blouse unbuttoned halfway down her chest and a long, bright red satin skirt clinging tightly to her full hips and thighs.

In a low, angry voice Catherine asked, "What are you doing here?"

Undeterred, Fannie confidently walked in and approached Catherine and Henry where they were sitting. "I just heard about Patrick and what people are saying about the two of us. I've heard the scuttlebutt[31] and it just goes to show how the locals like shooting their mouths off. I came to tell you myself, it's not true. I think Patrick is a fine gentleman, and he keeps us entertained at the bar with those stories of his, but I would not run off with your man. Someone should be out looking for him."

Catherine was a little taken aback and was going to ask just exactly what Fannie's interest was with her husband, but it seemed her concern for Patrick was real, and that in itself was comforting. "I'm sorry I was rude," she said. "I have been under a lot of stress. And, yes, the sheriff has ordered a posse to go looking for him."

"Then I think we should all be concerned," Fannie responded. "I wouldn't trust that pig to do anything useful unless it was in his best interests. I'm sure he's not seriously looking for Patrick. Can I sit down?"

Catherine gave Henry a small nod. He pulled a third chair to the table. Fannie sat down, leaned forward, and continued in a low voice. "I wouldn't

---

31 **Scuttlebutt** - rumors

count on much assistance from that man at all. I have had many ugly encounters with our dimwitted sheriff. I'm sure the only way he finds his boots in the morning is to trip over them. He hangs out in Potts' Saloon when he should be attempting to establish a little law and order in this town. Unfortunately, he wouldn't recognize law and order if it came riding into town with a herd of mustangs. And a gentleman he ain't. I'd be surprised if he hasn't groped you already. It's his favorite pastime."

Catherine looked shocked. "Well he has!" Her face turned red as she looked at Henry. "I mean," she stuttered, "well, he did act awfully familiar with me."

Fannie chuckled. "You probably mean he gave your ass a squeeze? That's nothing. But you better slap him good or he'll start squeezing your tits next. And after that, he'll be thinking you're his property, and I can tell you, once he starts, he's not likely to stop until he gets what he wants. You got to be real careful around that man. He is always looking for a way to get under a woman's skirt."

Catherine looked shocked. "You don't mean that do you?"

"Of course I do! That and shooting off his guns is all he thinks about. He is a mean man with nothing more between his ears than the constant thoughts of how to bed every good-looking woman he meets, as well as some of the not so good looking ones."

She turned to Henry. "And if you're as attracted to Catherine as you appear, you should stick around here to protect this young lady."

There followed a rather embarrassing moment of not a sound in the saloon except the soft banter between Jay and his mother in the kitchen.

Henry recovered first. "Well," he started, "Catherine and I were just talking about that. I suggested I come over in the evenings to, ah…look over things and make sure no one gets out of line."

Fannie looked at Henry. "And what do you propose to do about the rest of the day? The sheriff wanders all about town bothering people all day long, and now he's talking about buying Potts' Saloon."

She turned back to Catherine. "I have an idea that might help us both. It's the other reason I wanted to see you today. It may not be the best time to bring this up, or it just might be. Here's what I propose. I've quit working at Potts' Saloon, or whatever it is going to be after Zane gets a hold of it. I certainly won't work for him, so I need something to do while I decide what is next for me. I have a little savings put away so I can get by for a while and I would like to help you here. If you would have me, I will work for free for a while. I know saloons, I know how to handle myself in this crowd, and I like tending bar. You could focus on the food side of your business and handle the money. Put me to work serving liquor and keeping the ruffians in line. At least until Patrick gets back. If he doesn't, and it works out with us, maybe we can make some long-term arrangement. You are going to have to make money in the meantime and I can help. It's a lot to think about, and it's sudden, I know. But, what do you think?"

Catherine didn't know what to think. When Fannie had entered the saloon, Catherine had been ready to throw her out. But the offer did give her a way to get by for now.

She was a little flustered. "This has all happened so fast. I need a little time to think, but I appreciate your offer. I did think Patrick was with you." She looked down at her tightly clasped hands. "You are right," she admitted. "I'm sure you would be better at managing the saloon. I'm just not cut out to be behind a bar."

"Right now, you're not. But you look like a pretty smart lady. It won't take you long to learn our ways out here in the West. You should do well. We could do well. You think about it. And, if you've really sold out of all your supplies, you'd better start ordering more. You made quite an impression on the towns-folk yesterday. They'll want more of that good food."

Henry gave Catherine an encouraging smile.

Fannie got up and looked around the saloon. "This place is a little too small for a café and a saloon, but I am sure we could figure something out. Think hard on this. It just may be time for the people of this dusty spot in the road to start enjoying a few of the finer things, like a meal they don't choke on!" and she turned and walked out of the saloon.

After taking in Fannie's retreating figure showing through the filmy skirt as she passed out the door with the sunlit street in front of her, Henry shook his head and turned to Catherine. "Well, that might be your answer."

"I would have never guessed she would want to come to my rescue. Can I trust her?"

"I don't know Fannie that well, but I have watched her handle unruly men in a saloon. She can be pretty tough. And she certainly is right about the demand for your food. Here is a chance for you to get your café going and keep the saloon going as long as you choose to. If I were you, I certainly would consider it. My offer still stands, but I will be busy during the daytime. Having her here would give you the help you need when I can't be here. And, if Slink and Crow Feather will stay on, you would have help in the kitchen. This place really could be a gold mine, if that's what you want."

Catherine was silent for a moment. "I do need to order supplies, even if it's just for my own meals for now. I might as well get liquor too and see if I can run the saloon until Patrick returns.

Henry put his hand over hers and smiled. "You are already looking better. I am leaving on the late afternoon train for Ogden to buy supplies for Jake Edwards' house. If you put together a list, I can buy your supplies while I am at it and you can open back up by early next week. What do you say?"

Catherine managed a small smile. "Why not? I am not getting anything done just sitting here. I need to go see if Jay and Crow Feather will help." Then she suddenly looked shocked. "But what about the building materials Patrick ordered? I definitely do not want a gambling hall."

Henry smiled. "Well, it is inevitable that there will be a gambling hall in this town. I'm sure it would be profitable."

Catherine grimaced. "It wouldn't be if the primary person losing money was Patrick! I doubt I could keep him from gambling away any profits we made."

"Well, let's just deal with one issue at a time. And you probably should get in touch with Fannie," Henry added. "Her offer is too good to pass up."

Catherine had gotten up and began seeing the saloon as Fannie had. "She's right. This place is a might small, but it could work. My father always said when you're down, pick a project, put your heart into it, and walk any uncertainty out of your life. I think he would be proud of me right now."

She smiled at Henry. "Give me an hour. I'll talk with Crow Feather about that supply list.

She marched into the kitchen with a new resolve.

Chapter Seventeen

<u>Two days later</u>

Monday, 9:30 AM, July 7th, 1879

"What in the hell are you talking about? What do you mean Patrick's Saloon is going to reopen tomorrow? Who in the hell is running it?" Luther's face was bright red with rage.

The sheriff had just barged into Luther's office and was leaning against the door frame. "That gawdamn Fannie Smiles up and left Potts and talked Mrs. Callaway inta openin Patrick's Saloon themselves. Of course," Zane said in a mocking voice, "the sign in the windah says, 'Until Patrick comes back.' So, when are we gonna tell the pretty Mrs. Callaway that her darlin husband ain't a'comin back? That he's dead fish food at the bottom of the Snake?"

"Hold your tongue you idiot!" Luther looked Zane in the eyes. "We still don't really know that he's dead. And why? Because you screwed up. And we won't know he is dead for sure until *you find his body!* And when's that going to happen? You created this mess. What are you doing to fix it?"

"Ah, c'mon Mistuh Ahmstrong. You an Ah both know that man's dead as a dohnail. Nobody could suhvive that fall. An iff'in he did, he surely wuddah drowned. We's a-wastin time tryin ta find his body. Let's just teller and run that bitch outtah town. I want mah saloon!"

Luther had been sitting very still at his desk, staring into his cup of coffee. His taut, composed expression allowed Zane the short show of bravado. But when Luther looked up, the glare now on Luther's face made it clear he was about to have another one of his infrequent but explosive outbursts.

Zane quickly decided it was a good time to be somewhere else. He started to back out the office door. "Ya know," he stammered, "This might-int be the best time ta discuss this. Ya probably have other things on your mind right now. Maybe Ah should come back later."

"You get your fucking ass back in here and sit down." Luther was pointing at the chair directly in front of his desk.

Zane knew he had overstepped and had better placate Luther quickly if he wanted to avoid a severe reprimand. Luther knew too much about his background to allow him to get really pissed off. "Uh, yes Suh," he said meekly as he took the indicated chair.

Teeth clenched into a stern grimace and openly glaring now, Luther slowly rose, walked around his desk to stand menacingly behind Zane, and placed both hands on Zane's shoulders. He squeezed firmly to make it clear Zane wasn't going anywhere until they were through.

Zane flinched. He had been in this position before and it hadn't gone well. He started to speak and Luther barked, "Shut up! I will be doing the talking."

Luther leaned down and talked quietly, directly into Zane's right ear. "I want you to listen to me. No interruptions. No long-winded explanations. No half-assed excuses," he said, volume slowly rising. "This is your last chance to keep from finding yourself strung up by steel hooks pierced through your chest muscles," he continued, threatening the extreme, well-known Indian torture. "Don't talk. Just nod if you understand."

Zane's head was bowed and his face white. He quickly nodded. He had seen this punishment first-hand last year when a rail foreman had double-crossed Luther. Luther told Zane to kill the man with the help of some of the meaner Indians still in the area. He had Cloyd escort Zane to make sure he followed his instructions. Luther meant it to be a vivid example of what happened when somebody disappointed him, although Zane accepted it as a lesson for himself as well. He had thrown up when the man finally died.

Luther leaned back up and continued in a slow, dead calm voice. "You killed two civilians from our community, or at least you have repeatedly told me you killed them. That's punishable by hanging. I'm sure I can convince Smiley Jack to change his story back to what he initially claimed and testify that you pushed them off the bridge. And you have already bragged all over town how you are going to become a new saloon owner. So, in summary, I can find witnesses to testify against you, your boasts prove you had a motive, and your abrasive, reckless reputation will precede you into the courtroom. What chance do you think you would have of not being strung up like a carcass of beef if I were to decide to bring charges against you?"

Zane vainly raised his hand, apparently asking for permission to speak.

Luther firmly grabbed one of his fingers, clenched it hard, and started bending it backward as he leaned down to speak softly into his ear again. "Don't talk. Just listen."

After a long pause as Zane paled, Luther let go of Zane's finger and continued. "Now you might think you could avoid this predicament by claiming that I had something to do with this murder. But no one will believe you. I am a member in good standing with the Mormon Church, dedicated to the enrichment and moral guidance of our followers. I am the well-respected mayor of this town and a leader with the backing of the very influential, top management of the Union Pacific Railroad, as well as the most important members of the Mormon Church. Who are you going to call in your defense? And if you were brought to trial, I would make sure that this got the attention of the members of the Mormon Church who think you are already dead. And for good reason. What about all those people your gang killed in California, just to name one territory you terrorized? If people found out that the terrible leader of the Innocents gang was alive and kicking, what chances of surviving a trial do you think you would really have? Or maybe I should just introduce you to our new U.S. Marshal. I am sure he would like to meet you."

By this time, Zane had sunk down in his chair and was breathing hard.

Luther continued in his low, even tone. "But I have good news for you, Zane. I would never cause you to go to trial. You know why?"

Luther's voice changed suddenly and this time he yelled in Zane's ear as he squeezed Zane's shoulders hard. "Because I don't have time to waste on you! If you cannot follow a simple set of instructions, you are of no use to me. I certainly don't want our fine community, or myself, to be dragged through the mud by the ugliness that would come out of a drawn-out court battle about you. I would rather have Billy and Cloyd take you out in the desert and have some fun with you before they fed you to the coyotes. Do you understand what I am saying? A simple yes or no is all I expect from you."

Zane was clearly shaken, but he whispered a quiet, "Yah."

Luther let go of Zane's shoulders, patted him on the back and murmured, "Good boy." He walked back to his chair behind the desk, sat down, and continued in a deceptively bright tone. "You, you alone, not the ignorant buddies you have picked for deputies, are going out within the hour and you are going to find the body of Patrick Callaway. You are not returning to Eagle Rock until you have proven that we are done with that loudmouth Irishman. I want his dead body here in Eagle Rock so I know Mrs. Callaway understands that her husband is dead and can no longer protect her from the harsh realities of a wild western town. She needs to understand that there is no reason for her to stay in Eagle Rock any longer. When you can bring me clear evidence that Patrick Callaway is dead, you will be in a somewhat better standing with me again, but not until then. Are we clear?"

Zane nodded. And with that, Sheriff Zane was given permission to leave Luther's office.

He was observed a little later heading out of town with two rifles, a bed roll, and a grim look on his face.

Chapter Eighteen

Monday, 11:00 AM, July 7th, 1879

Catherine, Crow Feather, Jay, and Fannie had been talking excitedly since ten that morning. Plans were coming together. Catherine had gotten up early and drawn up signs announcing:

"The Re-opening of Patrick's Saloon <u>and Café</u>, featuring the best beer and whiskey in Eagle Rock and more REALLY GOOD HOMEMADE COOKING, Breakfast and Lunch."

She was proud of the way using all capital letters had made the phrase *"REALLY GOOD HOMEMADE COOKING"* stand out. Her first sign wasn't as impressive and she had run out of room on the signboard so she turned it over and tried again with smaller, bolder capital for special emphasis on the cooking. Jay and his mother had come over about nine and, while Crow Feather prepared a breakfast with whatever she could find in the kitchen, Jay and Catherine posted the signs all over Eagle Rock. Now Catherine was discussing her supply order for the new menu with Fannie and Jay.

Catherine frowned as she looked over the list she had made out last Saturday. "I hope I ordered enough flour and corn meal. Every batch of Crow Feather's bread seems to disappear in minutes no matter how much she makes and I'll bet the breakfast corn muffins will as well."

Jay smiled to himself, proud of his mother, as Fannie said, "This all looks good to me. I'm glad you ordered the better brand of beer. That swill at Potts was awful even before he watered it down. But, if you do re-bottle good beer with a little water, you can call it the house beer for the cheapskates who want more quantity than quality."

Catherine wasn't sure. "Won't I lose money that way?"

Fannie smirked. "Honey, you got a lot to learn about saloon keeping. You water it down as you re-bottle it and charge less, but you sell more to the numbskulls. It's a slower drunk, so they drink more. You sell more, make more profit, and will stretch your inventory. You just let me take care of that."

"Oh! When you put it that way, it does make sense."

Catherine and Jay were both getting an education about bar keeping.

"When is all this stuff supposed to get here?" Jay asked, concerned about getting the large order of barrels and crates safely into the back storeroom behind the kitchen.

Catherine referred to her notes again to check what Henry had written down as the arrival schedule for the new inventory. "Henry says it will be on the four o'clock train today. That should give us enough time to check it and get it stored away before we start cooking early tomorrow morning."

"That's all well and good but remember, Young Lady," Fannie answered in a tone that let Catherine know she wasn't asking a question, "I'll be handling the bar and don't plan to open it until ten. That's already too early for me but this town's drunks like to start as early as possible. You are just going to have to deal with them until I get here. And don't expect any cooking and serving food from me. It will be better for all of us if I stay out of the kitchen," she said, smiling now.

"Don't worry," Catherine said to her new partner. "I don't plan on opening the bar until you get here, even if it means I lose some early morning customers. I don't mind serving liquor during the noon hour, but I don't think we should be serving while people are eating breakfast. And you could be putting in a long day if the night crowd drinks too long. I'm not planning on keeping the bar open as long as Patrick did. Staying open late into the evening just seems to promote more fights and disagreements as the night goes on. I wanted Patrick to close early, but he wouldn't hear of it. And I get to make those decisions until Patrick gets back. You can take breaks when things settle down after lunch and I should be able to keep things going. If we were to have a turnout like we did on the Fourth of July, it could get really hectic, but opening on a Tuesday, a workday to boot, I suspect things will go a lot slower."

The chatter went on like this for another hour through the early lunch Crow Feather served them, and by noon all four of them were worn out from laughter, planning, and excitement.

While the four finished their lunch and planning for the day, a different sort of meeting was in progress out at Luther's ranch as Luther and Cloyd made their own plans to send Mrs. Callaway packing.

Chapter Nineteen

One hour earlier

Monday, 10:00 AM, July 7th, 1879

An hour earlier, Ellington had just sat down in the Eagle Rock Hotel for either a late breakfast or early lunch. He wasn't sure which, but since early this morning, he had only eaten a couple slices of stale bread at his printing shop while preparing the article for Luther about the Eagle Rock celebration. At breakfast Saturday, Luther had made it clear his highest priority was the distribution of a notice for local residents to be on the lookout for the missing Patrick Callaway. But, as soon as that had been distributed, Luther started complaining that Ellington was not working on the Eagle Rock celebration news release fast enough. Typical.

Ever since his arrival in Eagle Rock, Ellington had known that working with Luther was going to be a challenging and often unrewarding experience. When Gould had suggested that an enterprising young newspaperman might find Eagle Rock an excellent example of a rapidly growing Western town, he also steered him to Luther Armstrong. It didn't take Ellington long to see Luther's influence and willingness to wax eloquent about the great things that were happening in northern Idaho, particularly Eagle Rock. But he wasn't a pleasant person to be around and could be very tight lipped, even mysterious, about the less favorable aspects of life in the territory. Ellington found it difficult to get objective, complete information.

He suddenly gasped as he almost choked over a nasty object he had nearly swallowed in the gruel the hotel was serving today. Muttering a foul word, he spit the offending glob from his mouth onto the table and wiped his mouth with a napkin he had brought, since to his knowledge, the hotel didn't own a single napkin, or cleaning cloth, for that matter. Ellington's palate wasn't what anyone would consider sophisticated but, even to his tastes, this food was disgusting on its very best day. He had almost gotten used to it until Mrs. Callaway offered the town a taste of real cooking. And now her saloon was reopening with breakfast and lunch service. This was the best news he'd heard in months.

He was just about to get up and see if he could interview Mrs. Callaway again about her decision to reopen the saloon when Cloyd and Billy walked by with their bowls of this god-awful gruel. They were in the middle of a dis-agreement—interesting since Billy rarely argued with Cloyd about anything—when they sat down in an alcove just around the corner from Ellington's table. Although the alcove had the appearance of being a private space, Ellington always picked the table just around the corner from it on the chance that he might be able to over hear the latest gossip in Eagle Rock. Much to his satis-faction, both Billy and Cloyd continued arguing after they sat down. Always on the lookout for an article for his newspaper, Ellington pretended to keep eating while he made mental notes of the conversation.

Cloyd was getting frustrated. He was speaking quietly, but Ellington could hear him clearly.

"Billy, how many times have I got to go over this with you? We've got to get moving. I agreed to wait until you had breakfast before we took off, but Luther wants us to ride down to Franklin with the wagon this morning to talk to the depot manager and pick up Luther's supplies."

Billy's response wasn't quiet or guarded. In his high, childlike voice he asked, "But why?"

"Dammit! Keep your voice down or we will leave right now and you will go all day without breakfast. Do you want that?"

"No, I want to eat now," Billy whined, more quietly this time. "But can't it wait? That wagon will be heavy. Bunny's already tired from all the riding we did yesterday. She's too tired to pull a wagon."

"Jesus, Billy, she's just a horse. That's what horses do. They pull wagons and carry things."

"No, she's a pony, not a work horse," responded Billy. "You don't make Fury pull the wagon," he added accusingly.

Ellington had to cover his mouth to keep from chuckling. Cloyd rode a large black stallion he'd named Fury. The name was appropriate since it had the temperament of an untamed racehorse. He looked like a child sitting on top of a horse seventeen-hands high.[32] Billy had picked out a small, thirteen-hands pony he'd named Bunny. His legs almost touched the ground when he rode her. His 300-plus pounds did seem a little much for the pony but he certainly loved her. When Ellington had asked him shortly after arriving how he came up with the pony's name, Billy confidently said the pony looked like a cute, furry bunny. Then he had looked oddly at Ellington as if to suggest he didn't understand why Ellington would have even asked such a question.

But it was Cloyd's next comment that caught Ellington's attention.

"Look Billy, Luther told me that we would be picking up a ton of food and liquor supplies: flour, meat, potatoes and carrots, apples, probably some sugar, milk, good whiskey, and beer. Of course it will be heavy. But we will go slow and take a little for ourselves on the way back. We could try out the whiskey and get one of the barmaids to make up some real stew tonight. It certainly would be better than this slop. What do you say?"

Billy was slow to respond, but it was obvious he was considering the offer. "Could Bunny have an apple, too?"

"Sure thing, Billy. She can even have a couple of carrots. She likes carrots, don't she?"

You could actually hear the smile in Billy's voice. "Bunny loves apples and carrots."

"There. It's all settled. Now eat up so we can get going. The sooner you finish, the sooner Bunny gets some treats."

Ellington had heard enough. None of this made sense, but it did point to some more, possibly underhanded work by Luther. If Luther was ordering a large inventory of food and alcohol, why wasn't it simply shipped to Eagle Rock?

The newspaperman got up, left his meal uneaten on the table, and headed out for a walk along the tracks heading south out of town where there was a

---

32 **Hands high** – *a horse's height is measured in "hands," a measuring unit of four inches. A horse is measured from the ground to the highest point of the withers, the ridge between the shoulder blades of the horse. Horses and ponies are the same species but are differentiated by height. A horse is at least 14.2 hands high whereas a pony is less than 14.2 hands.*

little shade and he could think. This took him directly past Patrick's Saloon. The reopening sign on the door stopped him in his tracks. That was surely it!

Ellington began piecing the threads together. To reopen, Mrs. Callaway would have to restock the bar and buy all of the needed foodstuffs. With few good sources in the area, she would look to a supplier from somewhere south. Henry Willett had left in a hurry for Ogden Saturday to get supplies for Jake Edwards' new home and would be able to pick up a delivery for Mrs. Callaway. Everyone knew that Henry was sweet on Patrick's wife and he had been making a number of inquiries about the whereabouts of Patrick ever since he disappeared. There could be three stories in the making: the reopening of the saloon by Mrs. Callaway, the misplaced supplies at the Franklin depot, and a possible romance between Henry and, likely, the new widow. Admittedly, they hadn't actually found Patrick's body yet, but everyone except Mrs. Callaway was confident he had drowned after the fight on the bridge several days ago. It would be just a matter of time before she accepted that. And she was sitting on some of the best prime real estate in the territory. This was going to make a good number of people interested in Patrick's fate. Especially Luther Armstrong.

Ellington decided he would have to be careful with the handling of the food and supplies story. Was it possible that Cloyd and Billy were actually picking up supplies Mrs. Callaway had ordered? That would certainly put a damper on her opening the cafe again. He did recall how adamant Luther had been about getting Catherine back to Louisville. He didn't like getting crosswise with Luther, but this certainly needed to be looked into.

Rather than his usual long walk to think after a meal, if you could call that a meal, he decided he would step into the saloon and discreetly determine if Mrs. Callaway had ordered supplies and was expecting them soon. He liked Mrs. Callaway and was confident he could charm her into some information and maybe a little more. He had always been successful when it meant charming attractive young ladies, and who knows where this could lead?

This day had all sorts of possibilities.

Chapter Twenty

Tuesday, 4:30 PM, July 8th, 1879

"Jake, what could have happened? Henry told me our supplies would be on this train. What do you mean there was nothing?"

Catherine was shaking she was so upset and Jake appeared just as concerned and was nervously rubbing his jaw. Catherine, Fannie and Jay had gone to the train depot early and waited for their shipment to be off loaded but, after checking twice, Jake had explained there was nothing on the train for them.

"You are sure it was the four o'clock train, not a later one?" Jake had rarely had this happen before and was getting a little anxious. He too was looking forward to the café opening again. While the conversation continued, Ellington just happened to show up. After listening briefly to the issue, which turned out to be a little confusing with everyone talking at once, he suggested that Jake authorize a telegraph message to be sent out to see if they were dropped off at the wrong station.

Jake was even more disturbed by this. "Oh no. I couldn't do that without Luther's approval. I wouldn't know which station to contact. There are a dozen depots between here and Ogden."

"Well, we all know Henry Willett is a trustworthy guy. If he says he put them on the four o'clock train, I think we have to believe him. This is pretty important, Jake. Why don't you check with Luther?"

Jake looked perplexed but finally said he would, once he had logged in everything that did arrive. Ellington turned to Catherine and said he would check with the owner of the telegraph office to see if he could also make some contacts.

Catherine looked confused. "But I thought you owned the telegraph service."

Ellington smiled. "No, I own the newspaper. The owners of the telegraph equipment allow me to use my office as a telegraph service center for Eagle Rock. That helps me get the news from surrounding areas and they pay me a small stipend for having the service located at my office. I'll go there right now and contact them."

Catherine and her friends saw no point in waiting at the depot any longer and went back to the saloon to determine what to do next.

Actually, Ellington had already contacted the Ogden depot manager. The Union Pacific had made the telegraph arrangements for him as a favor to start a newspaper in Eagle Rock so he had the authority to use the telegraph as he needed. He just didn't want Luther to know this. The Ogden depot manager had already sent a reply to Ellington confirming that Catherine's shipment had been put on the train that was supposed to arrive at 4:00 PM. He was as upset about the lost freight as everyone else. Ellington had not wanted to mention this in front of everyone because he was now even more convinced that Luther was behind all of this. As soon as he got to his office, he sent a telegram to the Franklin depot where he knew Cloyd and Billy were headed. The message read:

SHIPMENT OF A LARGE ORDER OF FOOD PRODUCTS,
LIQUOR AND BEER ORDERED TO BE DELIVERED TO MRS.
CATHERINE CALLAWAY ON 4:00 PM TRAIN TO EAGLE
ROCK MISSING /STOP/
POSSIBLE INADVERTENT DROP AT YOUR DEPOT /STOP/
PLEASE CHECK AND RETURN STATUS IMMEDIATELY /STOP

Ellington figured he could claim he was confident the Utah & Northern RR would not want to get the bad name of having supplies dropped off at the wrong depot. Luther wouldn't be able to come up with a legitimate reason to complain about this without tipping his hand. He really didn't want to get on the wrong side of Luther, but this had the smell of a dirty deal.

Thirty minutes later Ellington got a return telegraph message.

ORDER DROPPED HERE /STOP/
LOADED ON THE 8:00 PM TRAIN TO EAGLE ROCK /STOP/
SORRY FOR THE MIXUP /STOP

Ellington smiled. Success. He would go tell Catherine.

Later that day, about the time the missing freight arrived at Eagle Rock, Cloyd and Billy finally arrived at the Franklin depot. Cloyd had deliberately delayed their arrival long enough to justify staying overnight. He had plans for the night at a local brothel. The evening foreman was on duty and, since the day shift didn't want to advertise that they had inadvertently taken off the wrong freight, the night supervisor knew nothing about any missing freight. He said he would have to talk to the day supervisor in the morning. Cloyd was furious for deliberately delaying his arrival to Franklin but blamed it on Billy's leisurely breakfast. Billy was so upset that Bunny was not going to get an apple or a carrot that Cloyd finally admitted to Billy they could spend the night at the brothel he and Billy frequented just to quiet Billy down. He would talk to the day supervisor in the morning before he had to face Luther.

In the meantime, Ellington made a point of arriving at the depot before the arrival of the eight o'clock train. As the passengers departed, Ellington noted just how many there were. Eagle Rock was rapidly becoming a destination for more than just rail men and miners. Yet another good story.

Catherine, her friends, and Henry Willett were already there. Ellington insisted on accompanying Jake, who had stayed late to make sure the problem was resolved, and they inspected the freight before it was unloaded. As Ellington suspected, a torn piece of a bill of lading was stuck on top of the original bill of lading. Ellington asked Jake about this and Jake agreed that it looked like someone may have misdirected the freight because the original bill of lading had listed the destination correctly. Henry went out to advise Catherine that everything had arrived intact, just late.

When Jake brought the multiple barrels of freight out to Catherine, they all cheered.

"It must have been an accident," Jake told Mrs. Callaway. "Most of the depot managers are pretty new at this and they must have been confused." Jake even provided a cart to help them transport the freight over to the saloon. He was quite upset this had happened on his watch.

The signs went up again announcing that the café and saloon would be open for breakfast at seven and lunch at noon the next day, and the saloon would open at ten. Catherine was too excited to sleep that night so, when Jay and Crow Feather arrived at five the next morning, Catherine was already up and busy. She arranged the saloon with the additional tables and chairs she had scrounged up the afternoon before and helped prepare breakfast for the first customers of the morning.

In Franklin, Cloyd was just waking up. When he found out what had happened to the freight shipment, he demanded that the depot manager telegraph Luther and provide an explanation. Luther didn't want to draw any more attention to this latest fiasco, so he told Cloyd and the depot manager everything was all right and it was good that everything got straightened out. To keep Cloyd quiet about the event, he suggested that he and Billy spend an extra day in Franklin since they weren't needed in Eagle Rock just yet. Cloyd had known what Luther was planning and knew he would be upset, but Billy was delighted to spend another day in Franklin when Cloyd agreed to find some apples and carrots for Bunny.

Back in Eagle Rock, after Luther had sent a response to Cloyd, he sat in his office for an hour, seething. He still had to get rid of Catherine Callaway. That piece of property was too valuable to be outside of his control and was going to eat into his profits. He would meet with Cloyd again and come up with a foolproof plan to run that woman out of town once and for all. The longer this went on, the greater the possibility she might decide she could run the saloon herself.

He would just have to scare the wits out of her.

Chapter Twenty-one

Wednesday, 7:15 AM, July 9th, 1879

Ellington headed over for breakfast at the newly opened café first thing the following morning. A line of locals and new arrivals from last night's train chattered on the covered boardwalk in front of the saloon, eager for what everyone was claiming to be the first decent breakfast ever served in Eagle Rock. Last night, the eight o'clock train had many more passengers than usual. Ellington's office was directly across from the depot, which made it easy for him to monitor the new arrivals and watch for any possible news items. He had planned on dropping in on Catherine to warn her that she might have more customers than she had planned for, but the length of the line outside of Patrick's saloon made it clear that the dining room was already filled to capacity even with the extra tables Catherine had squeezed in.

To see inside through the front window of the saloon, he had slid between several of the people waiting to enter. Those in the back shouted, "Hey Ellington! Back-a the line!"

Shorty Smith, the livery owner at the very back, yelled, "You will have to get behind me if you want any grub!"

Ellington smiled at them. "Don't mind me, men. I will just come back a little later, but don't you all eat everything up. You're in for a treat."

Old Gerald Wyesinki guffawed, showing a toothless mouth. "Ah'll be leavin mah mohnin bacon foh ya, Mistuh Ellington. Ah canna chew it anyhow." He laughed again. "Ah jus want some nice smooth oatmeal without any strange lumps in it foh a change."

Everyone in line laughed at that and then there were some cheers when Mrs. Callaway came out to let four more diners inside. Ellington tipped his hat to Catherine, winked, and told her he would come back later if there was any food left.

Catherine was all smiles and a little breathless. She leaned over and whispered in his ear. "Crow Feather is cooking up a storm but at this rate, we will only have enough supplies for a couple of days! Where did all these people come from?"

"I tried to tell you last night, but you seemed a little distracted. Anyway, having too many customers shouldn't be something to complain about."

"My goodness, no, but I'm going to need more help." The noise from the hungry line of men was growing again. "Men, just be patient. We are not going to run out of breakfast today, but I am asking everyone not to dally too long at the tables, so everyone gets a chance. I'll be out here as soon as I can clear another table. I do have two more spots at the bar if you don't mind standing."

Five men immediately exclaimed in unison, "I'll take it!"

Catherine gave Ellington a wide-eyed look and shook her head before motioning the first two of them through the saloon doors.

Ellington turned to consider where to go next. He could head back to his office and wait for the crowd to clear out a bit. Perhaps he would go out to Luther's instead—give Luther a chance to thank him for the glowing write-up of the July 4th celebration. That special edition had been distributed all the way down the Utah & Northern line to Salt Lake City and there had been a noticeable increase in passengers arriving in Eagle Rock ever since. Mormon farmers were arriving every day bringing their large families, looking for land. Along with them were more railroad men looking for work, gold mining prospectors, and numerous salesmen and entrepreneurs.

Ellington hoped Luther would be inclined to underwrite another similar article, this one focusing on the advances the railroad was making toward Montana with the help of the additional rail workers. According to Jake, an unscheduled train from the south had arrived late last night carrying a large crew of Chinese rail workers Luther had hired away from the Western Pacific. The group had been quietly hustled off to a new encampment across the river, probably to avoid any issues between the locals and the Chinese workers, Ellington thought. He might be able to put a positive spin on this new development by pointing out that the track construction would accelerate with these additional workers, and this would bring even more business to Eagle Rock.

He finally decided to go over to the hotel, but most certainly not for breakfast. Never again if he could help it. No, he would do some scouting for news. He had reflected last night about the increased number of travelers that had gotten off the train. Obviously, Luther had anticipated this because two more engines were due to arrive in the next week to add more routes to the train schedule. The railroad now had sixteen engines and several new passenger cars to support the increase in traffic. This all meant more possible stories for Ellington and a significant increase in possible circulation. He had been advised to keep the newspaper free, but to charge for advertising. With the increase in circulation, there would be more advertising and he could slowly increase the price of advertising. He wasn't greedy, but he had been rapidly using up his nest egg to keep the paper going.

One of the groups coming off the train last night that had caught his attention were five women and one man who dressed and behaved distinctly differently from the others dressed in the plain, dull garb of the Mormons and rough work clothes found on railroad men and miners. Four flashy, well-dressed women had been escorted off the train by a dapper gentleman with a manicured handle-bar mustache, wearing a three-piece suit and bowler hat. This was certainly not another farm family. Judging by the low cut of the dresses, coiffed hair, and highly made-up faces, the women looked more like working women to Ellington. De-boarding behind this group was another older woman and what might have been her daughter, also well dressed, but quite the opposite of the first group. Wearing a tailored, dark-gray skirt and matching vest over a high-necked white blouse, she appeared somewhat stern compared to the flamboyant foursome. She stared resolutely forward, only barely concealing a look of disgust as she ushered the younger woman accompanying her to the hotel. As the four resplendent ladies headed for the hotel, waving and flirting with the local men, she held back to avoid appearing to be part of the same crowd, as if there would be a question. Probably a church lady, Ellington decided, like others who had come to save the rough bunch of miners and rail men.

With this many new passengers, the hotel would be overflowing. Ellington expected there could be at least two good stories here and it was time to get to work. He checked to make sure he had put his notepad and pen in his vest pocket and headed toward the hotel, musing that it was about time for Eagle Rock to build a second lodging facility. There seemed to be numerous opportunities to make a fortune in this small town. Managing a better hotel would be an excellent way to gather even more information from all the travelers. Then he laughed to himself. He already had enough to keep him busy. He certainly didn't have time to operate a hotel, but somebody should.

Putting that thought out of his mind, he set about deciding how he would approach Dexter Highsmith, the hotel owner, to wheedle out of him juicy information about his new guests. He would pay for it if he had to. But Highsmith was such a sleazy man, it never took much for him to reveal what he knew. With the fresh flow of cash from so many new arrivals, he might be even more forthcoming than usual.

The hotel dining room was full, and Highsmith was struggling to keep up with all of the demands. Undoubtedly, the crowd was complaining about the rooms, or beds, or insufficient wash water, and certainly the miserable fare. Rather than wait for a moment with Highsmith, Ellington got a cup of coffee and looked for diners who might be willing to talk. He recognized the dapper gentleman he had seen escorting the overdressed women. The man was sitting alone at one of the tables, so Ellington introduced himself and asked if he could take the other seat.

"Why of course," the man replied, clearly in good humor despite the breakfast. "I see you limited your morning breakfast to possibly the only item on the menu worth having. This food is despicable!"

Ellington laughed as he sat down. "The coffee is not much better, but I have never found anything strange floating in it. I have been in Eagle Rock long enough to know better than to look forward to a breakfast in this hotel. You really should try the saloon down the street. They just opened for breakfast and lunch and I can already guarantee the food is much better. By the way, my name is Ellington Harper, Jr. It's good to see new faces in Eagle Rock."

The man reached out to shake Ellington's hand. "Jasper Lightworth's my name." He pushed a bowl of sloppy looking, grayish oatmeal to the side of the table and wiped his mouth with a white silk handkerchief. "Once I have gotten my appetite back, I think I will go try the new place. So what brought you to Eagle Rock?"

Ellington laughed again. "I was just going to ask you the same, but I can go first. I am from Omaha. I wanted to start a newspaper but there was too much competition back there. I have always wanted to see the West and I heard that the Union Pacific was starting a new town as the division headquarters of the new Utah & Northern Railroad. I have always believed that the railroads are the new economic force in America so I decided that this might be just the right place for me to start a business."

"Ah. So it was the opportunity to become an entrepreneur. And that is good news to my ears because that is the same reason I decided to come here, although you need not worry. I will be no competition for you, and you may be interested in what I am planning. I'm sure you would agree, wherever there's a concentration of working men, there is a strong need for female companion-ship without, shall we say, long-term expectations."

He leaned closer to Ellington and whispered in a low voice so others would not hear. "I have a potential partner here, a gentleman in an influential posi-tion, who has advised me there are no establishments presently to fill this need. You may have noticed the four lovely ladies over there on the other side of the dining room. They are ready to work. I am supposed to have a meeting later this morning to finalize our arrangements and to set up an establishment that should be able to entertain the local male residents in all capacities. I suspect the railroad will be pleased with this addition to the town's prosperity. I have always believed that happy men make better workers. And more workers make for better profits, for everyone." He gave Ellington a conspiratorial wink.

Jasper leaned back in his chair, looking at the serving line where another diner, the soberly dressed woman from the train last night, was complaining loudly at the food choices. "And if she is an example of the females available in this town, our addition will be a welcome one."

He had nodded his head in the direction of the women in a gray cape loudly accusing Dexter of serving food riddled with bugs. "I want to speak to the owner of this establishment. I cannot bear to eat this food."

"Is she always so abrasive?" Jasper asked.

"I really don't know," Ellington replied. "I think she just arrived on the train last night."

"Well, now that I think of it, I noticed her on the train, too. I thought she was returning home. She seemed to have a high opinion of herself and gave my girls a hard time." He leaned forward again and whispered in a low voice,

"She might be one of those new female evangelists. If so, she could be a real pain in the ass."

By this time the four "lovely ladies" had come to Jasper's table. One of them gave Ellington a warm smile and a wink, but then turned to Jasper and announced loudly, "We will not eat here. The food is horrible and, if that miserable woman from the train ever finishes berating the owner, she could turn on us again. We want a real meal."

Jasper smiled as he stood and said with a flourish. "Ladies, meet our savior with a knowledge of local eating establishments. May I introduce you to the owner of the local gazette, Mr. Ellington Harper, Esquire. Leave it to a newsman to know where to get a good meal." He motioned to Ellington, who had quickly risen to his feet.

He gave a short bow to the ladies and explained, "Actually, it is Ellington Harper, Jr. I'm not a lawyer but just the second member of my family with that name."

Jasper continued, undeterred, "But, you will see, Ellington Harper is a refined gentleman of undeniable reliability and has suggested we would find far better fare at the saloon down the street. I suggest we go there promptly."

The lady who spoke first smiled again at Ellington and put forth her hand with even a bigger smile. "You are our knight in shining armor to save us from this place." She turned to the three other ladies. "I am sure we all agree we will be forever indebted to you for this assistance, and who knows what that might lead to." She winked at Ellington again as the other three women giggled.

Jasper gathered the ladies together and turned to Ellington. "You have just met Bella, the most precocious member of my entourage, but I do hope you will come to our establishment to meet and get to know all of the ladies." Turning to the women, he continued, "Ladies, let us take our leave before we have another encounter with the witch at the buffet."

Bella gave a little curtsy to Ellington, bowed low enough to reveal a substantial cleavage, smiled, and flounced off with Jasper and the group. Ellington, somewhat red-faced and just a little flustered, stood frozen for a moment but was brought back to his senses when the stern, gray cloaked lady passed him and gave him a hard glare.

"You should be ashamed of yourself, gawking like that. A grown man! Certainly not a gentleman. I can see this town is full of sin. But you just wait.

Things will change soon!" She shook her finger at him and then stalked out of the dining room.

Ellington raised his hand to his mouth to cover a grin. He had been right, he thought to himself. There were at least two really good stories here. Eagle Rock was not yet aware of what the railroad had just brought them.

With that, it was time for breakfast. It would be worth it to stand in line, but, if he went directly, he might end up in line directly behind Bella. "I better wait a few moments," he mumbled to himself. "I'll go visit Luther first. There will be time to talk to him and still get back for a late breakfast."

He wasn't convinced he could maintain his "gentlemanly" conduct if he had to stand in line behind Bella very long.

Chapter Twenty-two

Wednesday, 9:30 AM, July 9th, 1879

Catherine staggered into the kitchen, dropped the tray loaded with dirty dishes onto the bench and leaned with both hands on the edge of the bench to catch her breath. She wiped perspiration from her forehead and flushed cheeks.

"Are you all right, Miss Cat?" Jay asked. "Can I help you?"

"I'll be fine in a moment, Jay. The line is no longer out the door now and things are finally slowing down. This makes me think I shouldn't have prayed so hard last night for such a good turnout. Do we have any food left?"

Jay looked over at his mother and after a brief nod from her replied, "Well, we've already gone through three days' worth of breakfast supplies that we thought would last us through the weekend, but maybe there will be fewer people the remainder of this week. Don't worry, Miss Cat. My ma can find something to make for Friday and Saturday if you keep getting this many customers."

Catherine shook her head. "If this keeps up, I'll need more help in the dining room. Are we prepared for lunch? That's only a few hours away."

After another brief discussion in a language Catherine did not understand, Jay smiled.

"Ma has already started. We will be ready to start serving at noon, Miss Cat. She is cooking twice as much as we planned to make sure we have enough. I hope that is all right. She says we can save anything we have left for tomorrow's lunch."

Catherine straightened up and smiled. "That's wonderful! Thank you. We might just make it because of you two." She gave each of them a grateful pat on the shoulder and turned to go back into the dining room just as Fannie walked into the kitchen.

"My God! You still have a full house out there. Has this been going on all morning?"

"I didn't expect you so soon, but I could sure use your help. This rush hasn't let up since we opened the doors and we had to open early."

"Well, give me an apron and I will do whatever I can. I came early to make sure the bar was stocked. We are still opening up the bar at ten, aren't we?"

Catherine took Fannie by the shoulders. "Thank you for coming. Yes, you're right. But it would be better if you got the bar organized as soon as you can. I think the sooner you can open it, the sooner we can focus on getting lunch together."

"Well that is all well and good, but you better get out there. A loud woman wearing a cape, in July of all things, is causing a real ruckus. Real high and mighty. Probably one of those temp'rance crusaders. It would be good to get her out of here before we start serving liquor."

Catherine straightened her apron. "Oh dear. All right. I'll go."

When she stepped into the dining area, actually the same room where they would be serving alcohol in thirty minutes, there was the gray-cloaked lady commanding everyone's attention. She had apparently come for breakfast but now stood shouting in the middle of the room.

"What kind of place is this that serves the likes of you?" she demanded with her left hand on one hip and outstretched right arm pointing hard at four decadently dressed women sitting together with a well-dressed gentleman, all talking and laughing merrily. "You're undoubtedly here, primped and painted at this hour of the morning to lure the men in this town to your evil ways. Oh yes. I see you. You flaunt your despicable morals and bring down the morality of all of those around you. I thought this was a dining room, but now I see it's a den of iniquity, complete with a bar and all the woes that intoxicants bring to those who imbibe."

The rant did nothing to dampen the table's mood, but the rest of the customers had gone silent and stopped eating. Catherine noticed an alarmed Ellington standing near the loud lady and motioning to her to get the woman out.

The lady continued, "Who is the owner here?"

Catherine walked over. "Good morning. Might we talk outside while everyone else finishes breakfast?"

The lady wheeled around, made a face and exclaimed, "I want to talk to the owner, not a waitress!"

Catherine straightened. "My husband and I are the owners, but he is out. So, if you want to talk to an owner, you will have to put up with me. Now let's go outside." With that, Catherine took her by the elbow and led her out to the boardwalk.

The lady had an indignant look as she turned back toward the door to face Catherine and finally noticed the sign: Patrick's Saloon. "So it is a tavern. I see the sign now. I walked right past it in that line. That explains the bar. And the ladies. But Patrick's? You're an owner of this outrageous establishment?" She was just beginning to quiet down.

Catherine tilted her head. "I am. You think I shouldn't run a café?" Her quiet composure put the woman on the defensive.

The woman sputtered, "Well no, I mean, yes! This establishment serves alcohol!" She was trying in vain to regain the high ground, but Catherine was now fully in charge of the conversation.

"Patrick is my husband. He owns this saloon. Well, we own this saloon. He has been missing for six days and may have been injured. In his absence, I have been running the saloon, and just today, began serving breakfast. It is my hope that with better food in everyone's stomachs, they might not be as inclined to drink so much. As for the clientele, we'll serve anyone who comes in for breakfast and minds their manners. Of course, you could always eat at the hotel if you prefer."

This short speech sobered the lady considerably. "I'm sorry. I'm sorry to hear about your husband, but I don't approve of alcohol and the places that serve it." She smoothed her cloak, no less determined, but calm at last. "My name is Rebecca Mitchell. I just arrived from Chicago on last night's train. I'm a missionary here to save Mormon and other heathen souls. I can already see there's an urgent need to rid this territory of the demon drink and the houses of ill repute that go with it." And then she became even more alarmed and exclaimed, "I won't eat in that hotel. I wouldn't serve that food to swine. And I couldn't even get a room there."

"My name is Catherine Callaway," Catherine answered, thinking this woman needed a new approach if she had any hope of ridding the territory of anything. She was rude and insulting, and she couldn't even eat breakfast in the same room with the sinners she planned to reform. "I'm sorry that you couldn't get a room, but as I understand it, that is not a very nice place. Have you found someplace to stay?"

Rebecca nervously looked down and smoothed out her dress again. "I found an abandoned room at the back of one of the buildings on your main street and my daughter and I are staying there until we find something better."

Cat smiled. "Sometimes that's the best you can do. Would you prefer me to bring breakfast to your room? You could eat in privacy there with your daughter."

Rebecca turned and grabbed Catherine's hand. "I don't know what I thought I would find here. I suppose I shouldn't be shocked by sinners, but I truly was surprised to see the dining room was really a saloon, and those women...out in public ..." She paused. "Yes, I would appreciate that very much, at least until I learn my way around here. I want to do God's work, but I don't have much experience, well, any experience out here. I think I'll take a day to unpack and rest from the trip. Do you serve lunch and dinner? I will pay you in advance for your kindness."

"You will have to pay for the meals but delivery will be free if you are willing to wait until around two o'clock for your lunch. I suspect the noon hour will be very busy and I may not be able to get away sooner. It will be one large meal since we do not serve an evening meal."

Rebecca sighed. "I guess that will have to do." She was back to her former self. And with that she turned and marched down the street, lifting her dress and high-stepping over piles of fresh horse manure.

Catherine sighed with relief. Another crisis averted. She turned to go back into the café where the sounds of raised voices told her Fannie was already serving beer and whiskey.

As she entered, Ellington approached her with a wide smile and clasped both of her hands. "Congratulations! You handled that like a pro! It's hard for me to believe you haven't run a café before. What aren't you telling us, Catherine?" he asked with a wink of appreciation and more than a little irony.

Catherine laughed. "Never! And I don't know what got into me. I just knew I had to get her out of there before the liquor started flowing."

"Well, offering to deliver her meals was brilliant. You obviously can think on your feet. Very important when serving the public, especially this crowd of characters and roughnecks."

"Oh, I may have just been feeling greedy. I don't want to lose a paying customer and she certainly looks like she can afford the meals. She even offered to pay in advance!" Catherine grinned. "But I'm sure I won't be making any money on alcohol sales from her."

They both laughed at that.

As they moved through the café, Fannie gave her a nod from the bar, which was now crowded with customers. Catherine noticed that Ellington was still holding one of her hands. She wasn't so sure this was proper, but it was comforting. She listened to him as they walked.

"Well, one thing is certain. We won't ever have to wonder what our new missionary lady thinks about anything, especially Jasper Lightworth and his 'professional' ladies."

Catherine turned to look at him. "They really are? Professionals? I thought that was just the crazy idea of a high-strung easterner not used to the West." She glanced back at the group. "Well, they are overdressed." Then she looked at Fannie with a small frown. "Fannie's a little overdressed, too, really. Anyway, I hope that group doesn't intend to open a brothel. They would probably serve liquor and that could really undermine my business."

My business, Ellington noticed. He could see she was already developing a keen business mind. Good for her.

Catherine looked back at Ellington and smiled at him but pulled her hand away.

Ellington looked embarrassed. "I'm sorry. I was just so proud of you."

She continued smiling and looking directly at him. "That's all right, Ellington Harper, Jr. She gave him a little nod, smiled and continued, "A lady should be able to take a little comfort wherever she can get it. I have certainly needed it since the Fourth. Now I have to get back to work. This owner has tables to clear."

As she turned and walked to the only empty table, Ellington noted that she had as splendid a figure as any of the four women at Jasper's table. He sighed and wondered why he was noticing her in this way. She was a married woman.

But with Patrick missing, was she really?

Chapter Twenty-three

Wednesday, 4:30 AM, July 16th, 1879

Fannie awoke to find Carl nibbling on one of her breasts. He would soon want more, and so would she.

She had arranged to meet Carl late last night and had told Catherine she would be late coming in. Catherine had reopened the saloon a week ago and the crowds had not diminished one bit. To keep up, they had hired Sandy, the server who had worked with Fannie at Potts' Saloon. She was looking for work now that it was only open part time. Sandy would open the bar this morning so Fannie could spend some time with Carl. Fannie had also encouraged Catherine to start looking for more help for the cafe or soon they would all be run ragged. Of course, Catherine was holding out for Patrick to show up, but they were all losing hope.

Fannie opened her eyes and ruffled Carl's mop of hair resting on her breast. "Didn't you get enough already? You kept me up half the night. It isn't even light yet."

He let go of her nipple and looked up at her. "Ah, come on, Fannie. Until last night, it'd been days since we had a go'round. You know how much I miss you," he said as he rolled on top of her. He never wore anything to bed and it was quite obvious he was more than ready.

She sighed. "I need to find an older man, one without so much energy." But she knew what they needed. Their lovemaking had been wild last night, but this time she would make him go slow and easy. Sometimes a woman needed to have time to leisurely enjoy the moment. She would give him what he wanted, but make sure he reciprocated to her satisfaction.

When Fannie awoke in Carl's bed later that morning, alone this time, it was overcast and raining and she could hear sounds of cooking and smell bacon and eggs sizzling in the fireplace. She stretched. *Mmmm, Carl.* Still willing to please her.

One of the benefits of working at the saloon was not having to cook. Catherine insisted on feeding all her crew, and no one could turn down Crow Feather's cooking. Fannie had never been much of a cook and this was a benefit she hadn't planned on when she went, tail between her legs, to ask Catherine for a job. That had been a terribly embarrassing moment, but she knew she couldn't stay at Potts' Saloon with Zane, and now it looked like she wouldn't have any awkwardness with the missing Patrick. He had been entertaining, but not a very good lay, and she really didn't want Catherine to know she'd been right all along about the two of them. Her real love, if you could call it that, was Carl, who, judging from the delicious smells coming through the door, was fixing her breakfast. She was sore, but also happy and quite satisfied.

She pulled on a short cotton chemise and joined Carl at the fireplace. "That bacon smells good. I love it when you cook for me." Putting her arms around him, she kissed his bare back. The muscles around his shoulders flexed as she rubbed her cheek against him. He made it a habit to wear as little as possible and she enjoyed looking him over when she had the chance.

"Keep that up and I might have to toss you back in bed," he murmured.

She slapped him on his firm butt. "Not until I've had this wonderful breakfast, you won't."

Once breakfast was ready, they took their plates of slabs of fried bacon and mounds of scrambled eggs outside to sit by the stream that ran in front of Carl's cabin. Fannie noticed Carl had been unusually quiet during the meal preparation and his mood hadn't changed once they started eating.

She waited until they had finished most of their meal before breaking the silence. "You're quiet. Something the matter?"

Carl didn't look at her at first but finally put down his plate, more somber than she'd ever seen. "There's a bad rumor a-goin' around. I want ya ta hear straight from me it ain't true. Mah fam'ly ain't involved."

Concerned, Fannie put down her plate. "In what?"

"Rumor is the Clancys are gonna burn down Patrick's Saloon." Carl looked up at Fannie. "We would never. Even if Pappy wanted to, I wouldn't stand for it. But we never even been talkin 'bout burnin down anything in Eagle Rock, 'ceptin maybe Sheriff Zane's jailhouse."

"Well, who's saying that?"

Carl looked perplexed. "Pappy's been lookin inta it, and we ain't sure, but we're thinkin it's Zane tryin ta frame us and lock us all in the pokey so he don't have to fret about us makin his life miserable. That man is a pain in the ass."

Fannie was disgusted. "That sounds like Zane. And even talk of it around here is enough to round all of you up.

Carl nodded. "If anyone was ta burn the saloon or even jus start a fire, ya know everyone is gonna blame us. And I tell you what. This whole thing has Pappy in a real mean way. It's pretty jumpy up there. A whole lotta yellin goin' on."

Fannie thought about this for a while. She hadn't heard any mention of this rumor, but she had noticed a lot of secretive conversations going on around the town and wondered if Catherine had heard anything. She put her hand on Carl's knee. "Who did you hear this from?"

"Hell, we heard it down in Blackhawk. Seems people of Eagle Rock may be the only ones that haven't heard it."

Fannie began thinking aloud. "Then it would have to be someone who travels a lot. You know Zane has been gone for some time now. He could be anywhere. But I don't think Zane could come up with this on his own. He's really not smart enough." She thought about it a little longer.

"If the people of Eagle Rock don't know about this rumor, nobody will be trying to get to the source. But, if people from surrounding towns do hear it, they will be the first to speak out if there actually is a fire. And…" She stopped in horror, the full realization unfolding now. "Catherine wouldn't be forewarned, so a fire started late some night could trap her upstairs in her bedroom!"

This was just too devious for Zane to dream up himself. The beauty of the scheme was, even though the Clancys had no real interest in Eagle Rock, that little show of the clan riding into town, kicking up dust, making threats was all anyone would need to pin this on them. Zane could start the fire and have the entire clan locked up before the smoke cleared.

Now Fannie was really alarmed. "We have to stop this. And I need to warn Catherine."

Carl shook his head in frustration. "What are you suggesting? I ride into town and say we're not going to start a fire no one's even heard of? I'd be a laughingstock for miles, and so would my pa. No! I won't do it."

Fannie was still thinking. "No, you're right. And we can't go to the sheriff. Who else is there? Somehow, we have to handle it ourselves. Besides the fact that I don't want you to get in trouble, I like my job at the saloon. Catherine would be crushed if it caught on fire, if she even survived. Once she came to accept that Patrick is gone, she would head straight back to Kentucky."

They didn't jump back into bed after breakfast after all. Fannie wanted to talk to Catherine as soon as possible. She couldn't think of any way to fix the problem but hoped the two of them could find some way to protect the saloon.

Could Zane really have come up with this scheme on his own?

Chapter Twenty-four

Wednesday, 11:15 AM, July 16th, 1879

Carl dropped Fannie off at the eastern edge of town a little before noon and she went directly to the saloon to see if she could meet with Catherine before lunch. She found Catherine discussing last-minute arrangements at the bar with the Sandy, the new server.

"Catherine, we need to talk."

Catherine turned and smiled. "Oh there you are. I didn't expect you until later. I hope..." She stopped when she saw Fannie's grim expression. "Is something wrong?"

"I found out something awful and we need to discuss it right now. Can we go up to your room?"

"Well yes, of course, if it's that important." Catherine turned to Sandy. "Do you think you can manage?"

"Of course, Mrs. Callaway. I have done this before."

"Just call me Cat. I'm glad you are here. We need you." She turned back to Fannie. "OK, let's go upstairs, but just for a few minutes. The noon rush is about to start."

When they got to the kitchen, Fannie asked, "Cat?"

"Catherine turned and smiled at Fannie. "Yes. I think it's time for my friends to call me Cat. It's a nickname my father gave me as a little girl. I've always like it and if we are going to work together on a regular basis, Catherine just seems too formal. I call you Fannie. Do you mind calling me Cat?"

Now Fannie smiled. "No, not at all."

Once up the ladder, Fannie and Catherine sat down on the bed and Fannie told her what she had learned.

"Burn down the saloon?! Who would do that? And why?" The questions poured out of the now agitated and alarmed Catherine. She jumped up off the bed and started pacing around the small room. "I don't believe this," she said, shaking her head. Then, "Who told you this? And why would anyone want to do this?" She stopped pacing and faced Fannie. "We have to tell the sheriff."

"Catherine. . .I mean, Cat. We have to stay calm so we can think clearly. I heard it from a friend who has his own concerns in the matter. I think I know who is spreading this rumor and, if I'm right, the last person we want to tell is Zane."

By this time, Catherine had her head in her hands, sobbing softly.

"I'm as concerned as you are, but crying isn't going to help. We need to come up with a plan."

"I never should have stayed. I have to leave. If Patrick ever comes back, he can find me in Louisville." But she did stop crying, dried her eyes, and straightened up. "You really think Sheriff Zane is behind this? Why would he do that?"

So Fannie explained what she and Carl had discussed.

Catherine looked puzzled. "Who is Carl?"

Shit, Fannie thought. "Carl Clancy. We have been spending time together and, according to what he's heard, it will be pinned on his family. But they aren't behind it. Carl would know if they were, and he would tell me. I believe Zane is trying to frame them and he is spreading this rumor while he is supposedly out looking for your husband. You saw how he reacted when the Clancy boys came into town the night before the Fourth. He's scared to death of them. We don't know where he has gone, but he has had a lot of time to cook up this scheme and cover a large area of the Snake River south of Eagle Rock with this rumor."

"Wait, you don't believe Zane is actually looking for Patrick?"

"I'm sure he is covering his ass by spending some time looking for Patrick, but I'll bet money he is using this time away from Eagle Rock for his own benefit and to spread this rumor as well. If the rumor was started around here, don't you think we would have heard it by now?"

Catherine still looked confused. "But why?"

"Potts' Saloon hasn't done well since your husband's saloon opened up. Zane is too lazy to manage a saloon, so I think he wants yours. He probably doesn't want to burn your saloon down as much as he wants to scare you into leaving Eagle Rock so he can take over here. Not that he would run this place any better than Edgar Potts. I won't work for him and neither will Jay and Crow Feather. He would lose money here, too. But right now, you have to stop sniffling and help me think. We need a plan in a hurry."

Now Catherine was angry. "He wants my saloon? What a mean man. How could he?" Then the enormity of the problem settled on her. "I haven't even paid Mr. Anderson for the building supplies Patrick ordered and now they could get burned up. I'll never be able to leave."

Fannie frowned. "I thought you were going to pay him with the money you earned from the Fourth of July."

"Well, that is what I had planned. But when we decided to reopen the saloon, I used most of that money for more food and alcohol. Since then, I have saved up most of the money, but not all of it."

Fannie started pacing. "I forgot about that huge pile of firewood out back. Even an amateur could light up the town in minutes with that pile of lumber. With a good wind, it could catch the buildings across the street and the next block too. It wouldn't take long for the whole town to go up in flames."

Fannie stopped pacing and turned to Catherine. "Do you know who owns the building across the street from you?"

"The depot?"

"No, no, no. The building directly across the street from that temporary lumber yard of yours." She pointed out the small, south-facing window to the large pile of lumber Mr. Anderson had left.

"Well, yes. That is one of Mr. Anderson's warehouses. It's pretty big, but he told me he didn't have enough room to store Patrick's order because it was already full."

A slow smile formed on Fannie's lips. She nodded, then exclaimed. "Great! That's it. We need to talk with Mr. Anderson."

"What for? I can't talk to him. He treated me like dirt and I still owe him money."

"Listen to me. It's just what you said. It is chock full of Mr. Anderson's inventory. He will have a personal stake in this."

Catherine's eyes lit up. "Oh Fannie, that's brilliant! He may not care much about my supplies; I have to finish paying for them whether they burn up or not. But he won't want his warehouse burned down."

Fannie sat down on the bed next to Catherine. "You have to talk to him today, but you can't tell him about Carl and me. Let's come up with a different story." She frowned briefly, and then smiled again. "Maybe...maybe tell him I overheard one of our loose-tongued customers from down south talking about it after a few too many. That takes care of how you came to hear about the rumor. Now, I know John is still Mr. Anderson's night watchman ..." Fannie registered the look of surprise on Catherine's face.

"John? And who is he?" Catherine asked.

Fannie shook her head. "Let's just say we were friends for a while before I met Carl. Anyway, it shouldn't be a problem for John to keep an eye on your saloon, too."

Catherine nodded her head. "I could try to find him right after our noon rush. But what do I tell him? He's already upset with me and doesn't seem like a very reasonable man. It would be better for Patrick to go see him."

Fannie shook her head at that. Her immediate thought was that the saloon would likely be a pile of ashes before Patrick showed up.

"Treat him like the big man in town." She stretched out the words "big man" for emphasis while raising her eyebrows. "A leader of the community. Share how concerned you are that a fire in the middle of town would not only delay your supply payment but could be devastating to everything and everyone in Eagle Rock—a town he has helped build. And be sure to ask him if there has been any preparation to form a fire brigade for the town. We both know there's no brigade, but you plant the idea and he can take the credit. He'll love that. Men do. And it might just save this place."

Catherine was nodding her head, thinking Fannie not only knew an awful lot about men, she also seemed to know them well. "I'll try Fannie." Then with more conviction, "I guess I just have to."

As Catherine headed down the ladder to start serving customers, Fannie shook her head. *That poor girl,* she thought. *She'll have to do this and everything else if she wants this place to survive. And when is she going to accept that she is the sole owner of this saloon?*

Chapter Twenty-five

Two days later, Friday, 10:15 PM, July 18th, 1879

Luther was sitting alone in his robe in his office with only the desk lantern on. He loved spending time in this room, so connected to memories of his father, surrounded by books and dark wood. But tonight, as sporadic lightning flashed and rain beat on the windows from a very unusual desert rainstorm, Luther felt dismal sitting here. Zane had come back the day after he'd left and explained that he couldn't go down both sides of the river without help so Luther had agreed he could take a few men he trusted with him. Since then, Luther hadn't heard anything from Zane, and Patrick's Saloon was clearly doing better every day. He would have to come up with yet another plan to get rid of Mrs. Callaway, soon.

This freak storm had been threatening all day and had finally roared in earlier this evening. Luther had gone to bed depressed but was too restless to sleep, so he got up and served himself two fingers of bourbon. That had led to two more fingers of bourbon and then two more after that, so he was a little light-headed when his brooding was interrupted by loud pounding on the front door. As he got up, he misstepped and managed to spill what was left in his glass onto some paperwork on the desk. This put him in an even more foul mood, and he was really pissed that anyone would disturb him at this hour.

"Just a goddamn minute!" he roared. "And this had better be good!"

He finally got the door unbolted, still cursing, but he stopped mid-sentence when he saw who it was.

"Ah found'im." Zane croaked. He was leaning against the door frame looking exhausted. His shirt was soaked and stuck to his chest, a steady stream of water was draining off his battered Stetson, and his boots were covered with mud. "Ah foun Patrick's body. Can Ah come in?"

Instantly sober and alert, Luther wanted to hear the whole story, but Zane was going to make a mess of his front entry.

"Yes, but take your boots off first. Better yet, go around to the back and I'll open the back door. There is a mudroom just inside where you can take off those wet clothes and clean up. I'll get you a robe."

While Luther waited in his office, he thought through what he needed to know from Zane and how best to get this information to Catherine Callaway so she would leave town as soon as possible. A few minutes later, Zane entered the room in a robe. His hair was still wet and standing up on end and he was carrying his dripping saddlebag.

As Zane dropped into a chair, setting the saddlebag behind the chair, Luther asked his first question.

"If I understood you correctly, you found Patrick's body. That had better be why you're here."

Zane slowly lifted his head to gaze at Luther. He had dark circles under his bloodshot eyes. Finding Patrick must have been harder than Luther had expected.

"Yup" Zane grunted. "Just as Ah tried ta tell ya last week, Patrick mustah drowned as soon as he hit the water. His damn body floated down the Snake for almost thirty mile befoh it caught up on some sunken tree branches. Ah had mah men fanned out on both sides of the river ta make sure we didn't pass'im by if he had survived, even though Ah knew better, so it took us much longer than if we had just followed the river south. Bah the time we found'im, there weren't much left ta his body so we decided not ta try haulin'im back."

This story had just taken a bad turn to Luther's way of thinking. "What?! You didn't bring the body back? How am I supposed to prove to Mrs. Callaway that he's really dead?" Furious, Luther jumped up from his desk. "I made it clear. We need the body! Where did you leave it? Damn it, Zane. Go back out and bring back that body!"

Zane slowly raised his head to look at Luther with obvious irritation. "All was left of Patrick's body was mos'ly bones and bloated meat. No real way ta even prove it was 'im. No good to y'all anyways. What was that gonna prove?"

"Damn!" Luther exclaimed, privately worried now that maybe it wasn't even Patrick after all. Pushing forward, he said "You should have found him sooner."

Zane smirked. "Ya told me ta bring back proof. And Ah told ya Ah would. Ah didn't let ya down Mistuh Ahmstrong. Instead of yellin at me, ya should be thankin me for how Ah handled this here situation. Very clever iffn Ah do say so mahself."

Taking this approach with Luther had never gone well before, but Zane didn't let last time's finger bending slow him down tonight. He leaned back and reached for the saddlebag behind his chair. He opened it and pulled out a muddy rag. "Here's your proof."

Luther stared in disbelief. "A muddy rag? That's your proof? What in the hell am I going to do with that? You should have ..." He stopped mid-sentence. As Zane unfolded the rag, it became obvious it was the torn remains of Patrick's red, white and blue Fourth of July celebration shirt. It was in shreds, missing one sleeve, covered with faded blood stains and barely recognizable as a shirt. But the red, white, and blue clearly identified it as the shirt Patrick was wearing the evening he went missing. Anybody who had been wearing that shirt would have to be dead.

"Well I'll be damned!" Luther exclaimed, "That should work." He smiled for the first time this evening. "Nice job, Zane." A rare compliment. But then his frown returned, "But where is the rest of the body now?"

Ever conscious of his house and furnishings, Luther winced slightly as Zane lay what was left of the muddy shirt on the floor next to his chair. "Mah boys are buryin the remains. His face t'wernt much ta look at. Mostly fish food. Vultures had already picked out his eyes and tongue when we found'im. We stuffed'im in a sack loaded with rocks and dumped'im int'a a deep pool in the Snake, but Ah recommend we say the river was so strong the body got swept away from us befoh we could get it onta the shore."

So, Zane is recommending strategy now, Luther thought. But he let him carry on.

"Here's how Ah suggest we tell liddle Miss Callaway. It was early evenin when we found'im. This here shirt pulled off his body as we were pullin'im outta a tangle of branches. That's when we knew it was him. We tried to move the body, but ya know how strong the Snake River current is. Bah this time it was dark as a cave without any sign of a moon. He was swept away and we nevvuh saw'im again. How do ya want me to tell the grievin Mrs. Callaway?"

Luther moved back to his desk chair and spun around, apparently in deep thought as he stared out at the lighting streaking across the landscape. It was raining even harder and there was a constant drumming sound from the rain on his roof. This was even more disconcerting since they seldom had rainstorms like this in the high desert. After a few moments, he turned back to Zane.

"That's a good start, but I think we can do better. This rainstorm is going to help us. Does anyone else know you found him?"

"We talked with a lotta farmers, did anyone see'im. With that shirt of his, he was easy ta describe. But we diddin actually find'im until late evenin, and we have kept ta ourselves since then."

Luther nodded his head with one hand cradling his chin. "What about your men?"

"Ah toll'em Ah'd split the reward with'em but I would be listnin and string'em up if they ever said anythin to anybody."

"Fine, fine. You have done well. Hold off reporting your sighting of the body until tomorrow. With this downpour, it would be understandable that you would have difficulty getting the body to shore and that the Snake could easily send it downstream to never be seen again. You could come off as heroic in all of this—a storm, dangerous lightning, a rising river. This is good. I will wait to take this news to Mrs. Callaway until mid-morning. I will also have Ellington write up an obituary for Patrick to make it all official. I will make sure he understands what a magnificent effort you and the boys made to recover what you could."

"Magnificent"—Luther repeated, already playing to the crowd. "And I think it's time for me to send my own telegram to Mrs. Callaway's family suggesting that they encourage her to come home. This could work out really well for all of us."

Zane was smiling. "Ah jus knew youdda be pleased about how Ah handled this so well. Ah done told the boys you might have a little somethin more for all of us. It's been a hard time foh us."

Luther frowned, "For doing your job? Well, I suppose if you and your boys can get your stories to line up, I can find it in my power to thank you all for your efforts with a bonus."

Zane got up from his chair with a groan. "They're gonna be right pleased ta hear that. Now Ah need some sleep, if you're done with me."

Luther held up one finger to signal Zane to stay put. "You know, why don't you stay here tonight? I would rather you not be seen by anybody else until tomorrow morning. It will make our story better. I have a spare room you can stay in. And if you need anything to eat, you can find it in the kitchen. I will have Rachael launder your clothes first thing tomorrow."

"Well, that's a right fine idea. Ah'm sure dead on mah feet 'bout now."

"Where's your horse?"

"Ah put 'im in your barn so nobody be seein' im."

"Good. I'll tell my stable hand to dry down the horse and feed him," Luther escorted Zane to the door of his office. "Just head down that hall to the first room on the right. I will see you for breakfast in the morning. And again, good work. I was too abrupt when you first arrived."

As Zane walked down the dimly lit hall, Luther retreated back into his office. He needed to think this through carefully to make sure all the details were consistent. Luther's face slowly formed into a wide grin. Finally, they could confirm that Patrick was dead. And Luther had what he needed to get rid of that damned pain-in-the-ass woman. The best saloon location in town was about to be his. He just needed to be convincing enough in his account to Mrs. Callaway that she wouldn't just leave—she would flee.

A moment later, he chuckled. The image of Patrick's face eaten by vultures should do the trick.

Chapter Twenty-six

Saturday, 6:30 AM, July 19th, 1879

Catherine was in the kitchen with Crow Feather and Jay when she heard loud pounding on the saloon doors. "Oh dear!" she exclaimed. "Is it seven o'clock already?"

Jay looked confused as well. "I don't think so, Miss Cat."

Catherine took out the pocket watch her father had given her when she was a young girl. "No, it's just barely six thirty." She looked a little irritated. "Someone can't tell time. I'll go tell whoever it is to come back later."

She opened the door to find Shorty Smith, the livery owner. "Good morning Mrs. Callaway Ma'am," he said, clearly shy around her. "May I speak with you?"

Even when she calmly explained that breakfast would not be served for another half hour, Shorty wouldn't be put off. "I really need to speak with you now," he insisted. He had always been polite and seemed so nervous this morning that she didn't want to offend him.

"Well then, let's not stand out here. Please come in. I don't want the saloon doors open or people will think we are already serving breakfast and we just aren't ready yet." Catherine moved to the bar but didn't sit down, hoping Shorty would understand that this conversation would have to be brief.

Shorty seemed hesitant but finally mustered the nerve to speak. "I'm really sorry to bother you, but I am hoping you can help me out. The bullwhackers that drive the wagon trains up to Butte have decided to make Eagle Rock their home base for a time. The railroad has taken away most of their customers from Salt Lake City but, at least until the railroad completes the line to Butte, they still need to haul goods from here north. They want to use my livery stable to feed and house their horses and oxen in between trips, but I don't really have a good place for them to eat."

Catherine already understood where Shorty was going with this, but she let him continue.

"With my livery full up, I will be making enough money to offer them breakfast when they're in town. I wanted to ask if you could provide their morning meals. Right now, I think there will already be four of them coming today. I can pay you in advance, but the main thing is the long line for breakfast. Sometimes they need to leave pretty early and I was hoping I could reserve a table for them to come in and eat without standing in that line. If you're willing, could they come in as soon as you open and get served first? I know it is a lot to ask, but it would really help me out."

Catherine paused to consider this. "We should be able to help you, Mr. Smith. We really can't open before seven o'clock, but I could certainly set up a table near the back where your bullwhackers could come in and eat first thing. I guess they should come in the back door since anybody in line would get upset if they tried to cut in. Does that sound all right to you?"

Shorty laughed. "You're the only one in town who calls me Mister, Mrs. Callaway. I'd like to just stick with Shorty if that's all right with you. And thank you for helping me out. These men will fall all over themselves to use my livery once they have had a taste of your morning vittles. I'm only concerned that there could be even more than just the four, but we'll see about that. What do you think, Ma'am? Could we start today? I have money to pay you for the rest of the week right now if you want." He started to reach into his pocket.

This time Catherine laughed. "Why of course Mr., I mean Shorty. But let's work out the payment details later when I'm not so rushed. I will set aside a table in the back for four and, if you need more, you just tell me. Have them come to our back door."

Catherine started to move in the direction of the kitchen but Shorty wasn't taking the hint. Hands still in his pockets and feet shuffling, rocking back and forth on his feet, he looked even more embarrassed than before. Color was rising in his face, Catherine noticed uncritically. She knew he was quite shy and had noticed that this happened most of the times they'd spoken when she visited the livery horses in the past. She loved horses and had always thought she would get one of her own now that she was out west. There were miles and miles of high desert and mountain trails she could explore, but Patrick had told her they didn't have the money for a horse.

"Ma'am, you're a mighty fine lady, you are. I thank you. I do appreciate it." It looked like he was about to say more, but then he blushed even more and thrust out a gnarled hand covered with callouses from years of pounding hot iron bars into horseshoes.

Catherine was taken aback until she realized he just wanted to shake her hand to seal the deal. She gave him a warm smile and accepted his outstretched hand. "Shorty, I am sure this will work out well for both of us. Thank you for coming to me."

By this time, Shorty was nervously staring at his boots and mumbling something in response. Then he abruptly turned and left the saloon.

As she walked back to the kitchen, Catherine realized what a difficult conversation that must have been for him. He was much more at ease, self-assured and caring, with his horses. But this could be a good opportunity for the café. She liked many of the bullwhackers who had dropped in for drinks when Patrick had been at the bar; they were a rough looking bunch, but rarely rude and would be a good addition to their breakfast crowd.

Twenty minutes later, promptly at 7:00 AM, Catherine heard a gentle rapping on the saloon's back door usually only used for deliveries.

"Oh, Jay, unlock the back door please. I forgot to tell you, Shorty will be bringing the bullwhackers through the back door. Did you get a chance to set up two square tables near the back of the saloon? You can push them together if Shorty's group needs more than four settings. I'll go open the front door for the rest of the crowd."

"All taken care of, Miss Cat," Jay replied.

The crowd was just as big as it had been every day since she had started serving breakfast. If they were going to keep this up, Catherine thought, they may need that lumber out back for an addition after all. She wouldn't think about that until Patrick came back, but one thing was sure—she was paying for that lumber herself now and wasn't going to let Patrick build a gambling hall, no matter how profitable he thought it might be. She deserved her café. This crowd proved it could be a good venture and there wasn't any possibility Patrick could gamble away their hard-earned profits in a café. But these thoughts were pushed out of her mind for the remainder of the morning as the diners rushed in and cheerfully demanded to be fed.

Shorty came directly over with the money for six customers before he sat down with his group.

"We already have more than four, Miss Cat," Shorty said as the group walked in. "All five of them wanted to try out your homemade bread and biscuits and gravy. Thank you for making a table big enough for us." Shorty was beaming. He took a step closer and said quietly, "There could be a lot more of them wanting to use my livery once these five start bragging about the free breakfast. I'll have to build an addition onto my livery if this keeps up. I hope you'll still have room for them."

Catherine noted that he was far more comfortable with her now that there were more people around. She smiled and replied, "I'm sure we will figure something out."

The breakfast crowd was as boisterous as usual. The room was filled with the high energy talk of a large group of happy men and a lot of laughter. Mr. Anderson and Dick Chamberlain came in and asked Catherine if they could have a table near Shorty's group. She moved one of the last square tables over and placed it on the end of the two with the bullwhackers making a mental note to ask Henry if he would make a few more square tables for her. Round tables worked well for the drinking crowd because six could gather around a round table—more if they crowded together. But square tables were easier to combine for larger groups. The bullwhacker table was the source of most of the laughter she was hearing and it lifted her spirits.

The morning went rapidly and the bullwhackers stayed a little longer than she had anticipated. Apparently, they weren't hauling freight north today. She hoped they would come back for lunch. The laughter was gone from their corner and they seemed to be discussing something serious. She hadn't noticed this right away because of the general din of conversation throughout the room, but she became concerned there might be a problem. Before she had time to check on them, most of the bullwhackers had gone. Only Mr. Anderson, Dick Chamberlain, and one of the bullwhackers she recognized from earlier this year remained.

She hadn't seen Mr. Anderson since she'd presented him with the rumored possibility of a fire burning her business. The same day Fannie spoke of it she had gone to his office and the meeting had not been as difficult as she had imagined. He had softened a little toward her once he realized her café was thriving and he was going to get paid, and it helped that he really seemed to enjoy her food. She had not been convinced that he really believed her concern about the fire, but at least he had been somewhat polite.

"Was everything all right with your breakfast, gentlemen?" Catherine asked.

"As always," Mr. Anderson nodded. "Breakfast was excellent. You cook up corn muffins just the way my mother used too. I can hardly get enough of them. Mrs. Callaway, we have been discussing your situation. I believe you're acquainted with Odin Borgerson," he said, pointing to the fourth man in the group. "He has been regularly leading a group of wagons from Salt Lake City through Eagle Rock and northward for some time. He said he has been here often to have a drink with Patrick when passing through and remembers you."

Odin, a bear of a man, tall with broad shoulders, a barrel chest, and huge hands, solemnly nodded to Catherine. He had a huge, black beard that covered most of his face and hung down over his chest. Catherine had been frightened of him when he had first come to the saloon for drinks, but soon found him to be a surprisingly genial and considerate man.

In his deep, bass voice he nodded and quietly said, "It's gud ta be seein you again, Ma'am. Yoh vittles be maghty fahn."

"And it's good to see you again, Mr. Borgerson. I'm pleased you chose to come for breakfast, all of you." She waited anxiously to hear what Anderson had to say. He appeared more affable today, but their acquaintance had not been easy so far.

"Mrs. Callaway, reserving these tables for men doing business up and down the river does more than give them a good breakfast and an early start. It provides this community with a central meeting place. We have needed such a gathering point along the Snake. People need to know what's happening elsewhere in our territory. You are providing a much-needed service for this town. I'd be surprised if Mayor Armstrong doesn't commend you on this soon."

Catherine wondered what this was about. She was beginning to think about the lunch crowd to come.

"We have just been discussing the matter you presented to me several days ago. According to Odin, there are indeed rumors spreading throughout the Snake River Valley, but mostly about well-organized robberies that could disrupt the flow of merchandise and currency up and down the river. Such talk usually points to the Clancy Clan, but most of the bullwhackers believe the rumors to originate from communities south of Eagle Rock. There have also been rumors of arson here in Eagle Rock, but it just doesn't sound credible that the Clancys would try this. It doesn't make any sense. Pap Clancy is too smart to try something that isn't going to result in a good profit, and there's no profit in burning down a café," Anderson continued, "unless someone is paying him. It just doesn't seem right."

Catherine took a deep breath. How could she explain this without telling them she already knew it wasn't the Clancys, because Fannie had already heard all about it from Carl?

But Mr. Anderson continued before she could decide what to say. "I understand it may seem to some that this is a far-fetched concern from a single women, but don't misunderstand me. You have every right to be concerned. Dick, Shorty, and I have decided to discuss this with Luther Armstrong this morning. We don't understand why Sheriff Zane has not warned the town already. Whether or not there's truth to this, if a fire did break out, even if it was an accident, we have no way to stop it. The only water supply is what the railroad pumps to the depot water tower[33] to refill the steam engines. We need water for the residents. And we need water for fighting fires. We don't want to go the way of neighboring towns that have burned practically to the ground simply because no one took the time to develop a plan. Your concern has us thinking about how to ensure our town's safety and progress."

Catherine heard some slight encouragement in Anderson's unusually long speech, but nothing very immediate.

"In the meantime, I will provide a night watch on your saloon. I hope that makes you feel safe enough to stay and continue to feed this town your delicious meals."

Thank Heaven, she thought. "That's just wonderful. I know I would feel much safer if someone was watching the saloon." With that, the men stood, nodded respectfully to Catherine, and then followed Mr. Anderson out the door to express their concerns to Luther Armstrong.

That was far more than she had expected.

---

33   *See chapter notes.*

Chapter Twenty-seven

Saturday, 10:30 AM, July 19th, 1879

Later that morning, Catherine sat down on a bench in the small storage room behind the kitchen. She had brought the bench into the storeroom when the café first opened to give Crow Feather and Jay a place to get off their feet, but she wasn't sure they had ever even used it. Today she was tired and decided to set an example. If the owner could take a break she reasoned, they might feel more comfortable taking one as well. They had all been working twelve- to fourteen-hour days since they reopened after the Fourth and Catherine wasn't sure how any of them could up keep this pace.

But even though she was bone tired, she was also exhilarated. She sighed as much from satisfaction as exhaustion. Her café could be considered a roaring success well beyond what she had anticipated, but it had never occurred to her that it would also mean so much to the bullwhackers and locals needing a place to gather and talk while eating and drinking. At this rate, she would run out of supplies before the weekend again. She had tripled the amount of food and alcohol from her first order but needed to place yet another order yesterday. She would prefer to order food and alcohol just once a week but she kept underestimating how much she would need. This was a far cry from the months before the Fourth when Patrick's small monthly order was more than enough.

Catherine knew they needed more help in the kitchen but, for now, they had a good working routine. Fannie and Sandy handled the bar, Crow Feather prepared meals with Jay's assistance and Jay also washed dishes. Catherine greeted the customers, cleared the tables, and kept Jay informed on what was needed in the dining room. The breakfast and lunch crowd had settled into a somewhat calm and good-natured routine. In any spare time she had, she checked her inventory and, if she was lucky, took a minute to rest between breakfast and lunch. In the evenings, she occasionally spelled Fannie and Henry Willett had been dropping in to keep an eye on the crowd and knock a few heads together when necessary. Everything was going reasonably smoothly.

Catherine had made it clear to both Henry and Fannie that she did not want the sort of tension and fighting that her husband had reported was common at Potts' Saloon, and they seemed to be up to the task of keeping an acceptable degree of peace and order. That Fannie was tough, no matter how big and scary the men were. Not the least bit intimidated by the heavy drinkers, she had already escorted two unusually rude men out the door herself. The rest she just flirted with and they responded well to her charm. Catherine was beginning to wish she had a little more of that grit herself.

And Fannie's idea to contact Mr. Anderson had worked. After they talked he had checked with others, and had begun to believe that Zane might be behind this. "That sheriff of ours isn't worth the boots he walks in," he'd told Catherine after his meeting with Luther. Fannie admitted that Mr. Anderson wasn't accustomed to taking a woman into his confidence, so his candor was encouraging. "Since he hasn't made any effort to warn you, or anyone else in town, you might be right that he's behind it. Wouldn't surprise me. I can't believe Armstrong keeps him around. Our sheriff doesn't appear to have any concept of law and order, even the western variety."

Despite the progress, though, Catherine had broken down badly last night and cried herself to sleep. It had been more than two weeks since Patrick disappeared and just about everyone in town assumed he was dead. She had also gotten a telegram from her father, which honestly had only made things worse. In a kind way, but in no uncertain terms, he urged her to reconsider her decision to move out west with Patrick and to come home. As she sat there thinking about all of this, a lump was forming in her throat just as Crow Feather came into the room carrying a hot cup of tea.

"You drink," Crow Feather said in her plainspoken, kind way. Holding out the saucer with steam wafting out the top of the teacup, she appraised the weary Catherine. "You...sleepy. Rest."

"Thank you Crow Feather. I will. You should take a break, too."

Crow Feather gave her a small, closed-mouth smile, about the most she ever smiled, and bowed slightly with her hands clasped together in what Catherine had determined was a show of respect. "Rest soon," she said and went back into the kitchen.

Even on a hot summer morning, Crow Feather's hot tea and, really, Crow Feather's presence itself, comforted Catherine like a mother's touch. Or, how she imagined a mother's touch could be. Her stepmother had never tried to be comforting. The lump in her throat was gone after the first sip.

Reluctantly, she pulled the telegram out of her apron pocket. She had been so upset last night, she couldn't really recall all her father had written, so she unfolded it to read it again, noting the bottom of the page was tear stained.

CATHERINE DEAR SO SORRY ABOUT PATRICK/STOP/
WANT TO HELP/STOP/
DON'T WORRY ABOUT LOAN/STOP/
LONGER LETTER UNDER SEPARATE COVER/STOP/
MANY THINGS YOU DON'T KNOW ABOUT PATRICK/STOP/
WILL SEND MONEY/ PLEASE COME HOME/STOP/
ALL OUR LOVE/STOP/
FATHER

Another tear dropped on the telegram. She just wasn't ready to share the dilemma with her family. Ellington must have written to her father. That would have been the only way he could have found out. Even though she had eloped without telling any of her family, there didn't appear to be any judgment in the telegram, although the reference to things she didn't know about Patrick bothered her. She already knew that Patrick wasn't the man he had appeared to be when they met in Louisville. It also didn't surprise her one bit that it was her father who contacted her and not her stepmother or younger sisters.

She had never known her real mother. Elizabeth Marie Stubin had died during childbirth. Catherine, her first and only child, had been born in Lexington, Kentucky where her father and his brother had started a hard goods establishment. They were both Unionist southerners. The majority of their income was from the wholesale trade of everything from leather gloves to iron plows and wagon wheels. Most of their more profitable customers were in the upper Midwest, particularly central and northern Illinois around the booming town of Chicago. Henry had set up the business with various outlets across the region while his brother, Zachery, handled deliveries and logistics. Two years before the Civil War broke out, both men and Catherine moved to Springfield, Illinois, their most successful outlet, and participated in the Union war movement. They had an office right across from the Capitol and their business continued to expand rapidly due to the connections her father had made with William Herndon and Abraham Lincoln before Lincoln left for Washington.

Catherine had always been very close to her father. He had reared her with the help of a nanny, but without a mother for his only daughter, he had allowed her to become pretty much of a tomboy. Early on, they had traveled together during their many trips around Kentucky finding new outlets for his business. She had found the adventure of travel to be a very exciting part of her life. But this all changed abruptly when her father took as his second wife, the daughter of a Springfield aristocrat. Janette Elizabeth Brookfield's arrival in the family, along with her two teenage daughters from a previous marriage, severely altered Catherine's relationship with her father and her own self-confidence. Not only did Henry have less time for Catherine, but Janette was infatuated with the south and an avid Secessionist, making casual conversation within the family challenging. Catherine began to quietly withdraw into her own world to avoid any conflicts with her stepmother and tended to be less assertive about her own interests. Within months of the marriage, Henry announced to Catherine that she was going to have a new baby sibling. With that, Catherine's personality withdrew even further.

As soon as the war was over, Janette convinced Henry to move back to Kentucky, but they moved to Louisville instead of Lexington. Henry was not confident he would be well received in Lexington, and Louisville was a larger and better center for his business. His new wife agreed with the move since it would put her in contact with a much larger southern aristocratic community. She was adamant that her daughters be raised as true southern belles. Catherine resented the move and had no interest in becoming a southern belle, which caused her to become even more isolated in her own family.

Catherine had never felt any real affection from her stepmother, who tended to dote on her two considerably younger daughters and the new baby. Her step-sisters were at ease with the high society in Louisville while Catherine would have preferred continuing to live in Springfield where she felt more accepted. Horseback riding through the hills and woods that surrounded Springfield, western style, not sidesaddle, was much more to her liking than dress-up balls and garden parties. Catherine had felt like an outsider the moment they arrived in Louisville. That was one of the reasons, though not the main one, she had been so enamored with Patrick and had agreed to elope with him.

Catherine stood up, smoothed her apron, and walked back to the kitchen. *It's time to stop dwelling on the past and get back to work,* she thought to herself. She would warm up the last of her tea and see how Jay was doing.

He had finished the dishes and was stacking them on the counter so they would be ready for the noon meal.

"Jay, I'm concerned the two of you are working too hard. I am going to hire more help soon. You and your mother have been here since four o'clock this morning."

Jay smiled as he continued to stack dishes and sort silverware. "Actually, we would like to try something new, if you agree. I will help Ma prepare the dough for the bread and biscuits for tomorrow after lunch today. If we do that in the afternoon, we won't have to arrive in the morning until five-thirty."

"Well, that's still a long day, but at least you won't have to walk here in the dark."

Jay stepped over to Catherine and said quietly, "It's helping us, too, Miss Cat. Ma has never left this area of the Idaho territory and she wants to take a trip to visit some of her relatives on the Blackhawk Reservation down by Fort Henry. She's never been that far from home before. If we keep working, we can afford to take the train and have a little extra left over." He added quickly, "That is, if you will be able to give us some time off. We wouldn't need long. Maybe that wouldn't be possible as busy as it is. We wouldn't want to cause you any trouble, Miss Cat. We both really like working here. We're even getting along better with the people in Eagle Rock."

Catherine's eyes had become moist again, only these were good tears. She stepped forward and, still careful not to cause him any awkwardness by offering a hug, put her hands on his shoulders. "I cannot tell you enough how much both of you have helped me. I feel better today than I have for the last couple of weeks, and that is mostly because of what fine people you and your mother are. Jay, you could go far in the restaurant business, be a chef someday. I see how much you help your mother. You and your mother can go on a trip wherever you want and whenever you want. We will just close the café for a couple of days. And, who knows, I might even like to tag along. I'm going to need a break, too. What would you think of that?"

"Why sure, Miss Cat. We would love for you to come along. You could meet some of my relatives."

Crow Feather had been listening nearby and beamed with pride when Jay turned and explained what Catherine had just said.

"Thank you for the tea, Crow Feather. It's just what I needed," Catherine said. "And now my break time is over. I'll go out and see if Fannie needs any help."

As she turned to leave the kitchen, she realized that, at least for the moment, she really was just about as happy as she had ever been in Eagle Rock. And she hadn't even had one dreadful thought about Patrick in the last half hour. In fact, she had been so busy the last week, with the planning and all, that the terrible darkness she had been experiencing was starting to fade. Running the café was definitely lifting her spirits and Fannie was really running the saloon. She now had more friends in Eagle Rock than ever before.

But, befitting a possible widow, she assumed a more somber demeanor and joined Fannie, her new, good friend and mentor, behind the bar.

Chapter Twenty-eight

Saturday, 11:00 AM, July 19ᵗʰ, 1879

The saloon was much quieter than it had been earlier in the day. The breakfast crowd had left and only the die-hard drinkers were left. There were a few customers along the bar and a few more playing cards at some of the tables, but there wasn't the hubbub that had filled the room during breakfast. Fannie smiled at Catherine.

"Is there anything you need?" Catherine asked.

"Not really, but ask Jay to bring out another keg of beer from the back before lunch or we'll run out." Even Fannie called him Jay now. They had agreed that Slink was not a very proper name for such a hard-working young man.

"Oh dear," exclaimed Catherine. "I think that may be our last keg. I never imagined we would go through supplies so fast. I don't think my next load of supplies will arrive until Monday."

Fannie just smiled, raised both hands and shrugged as if to suggest, *Oh well*.

Catherine looked perplexed. "Well, what are we going to do if we run out of beer?"

Fannie continued smiling. "I think there is a saying. If they can't drink beer, let them drink whiskey! Or something like that."

After a brief startled look on Catherine's face, they both broke out laughing. Early on, Fannie had coached Catherine on the profitability of various types of beer and whiskey and she was already becoming far more business minded now that she knew the profit on whiskey was much better than beer. Most of the drinkers today were the ones who wanted the cheaper house whiskey which was their saloon's greatest profit center.

But their laughter stopped abruptly when Luther Armstrong walked in.

Catherine froze. He had only been in the saloon once before and that was to inform her that Patrick might have fallen off the new bridge. She straightened up, took a deep calming breath, and came out from behind the bar. Softly she asked, "Do you have news?"

Luther solemnly looked directly at her. "Yes. Is there someplace private where we can talk?"

Catherine sank into the nearest dining chair and murmured, "Oh no! You don't have good news do you?" Tears welled up instantly in her eyes.

"I really think it would be better if we found somewhere more private to talk. If you do not have a suitable place, I have cleared out the sheriff's office and we could talk there."

Fannie had come around the bar and was standing behind Catherine with a comforting hand on her shoulder. "For God's sake, Luther! The last thing she needs is to have Sheriff Zane and his flunkies hanging around her right now! You should know better than that."

Luther was unruffled by Fannie's comment. He spoke directly to Catherine. "Like I said, I have cleared out the sheriff's office. Zane and the deputies will not be there."

Catherine had gotten control of her sniffling and nodded. She got up and obediently followed Luther out the saloon doors. As they were walking down the street, she asked quietly, "You are going to tell me Patrick's dead aren't you?"

Luther looked at her, surprised she had gotten control of herself so quickly. He had been prepared for an anguished burst of wailing. Apparently, he had underestimated her. He would have to take this into consideration as he developed his story. This was his best chance to get her to leave town.

"Yes, but I'll wait to tell you what I've been able to surmise when we're not in such a public place."

Catherine nodded and kept pace with him, her head down, holding her skirt up off the muddy street and carefully placing her steps to avoid the piles of horse manure and puddles from the storm the previous night. "Thank you," she said quietly.

The sheriff's office was empty. It smelled of stale cigars and unwashed bodies. The door to the jail cells was closed, so anyone locked up wouldn't be able to hear their conversation. They both sat down and looked at each other.

Luther started out. "The sheriff found Patrick's body late last night quite a ways down the Snake River. It was clear he fell and drowned."

Catherine moaned and put her head in her hands. "Oh, he hated the water. He would have been so scared."

"It's precious little comfort, but he probably hit his head on one of those boulders under the bridge and died immediately or was at least unconscious when he died." Luther was winding up for the gruesome details.

Catherine was crying again.

Luther continued, "Before I go on, I want to tell you I've already spoken with Henry Willett. He and Jake had breakfast with me this morning and I said I was going to come into town to meet you. He wanted to be with you when you got this news, but I told him I wanted your permission. He's in the back hallway. Would you like me to have him come in?"

Catherine nodded between sobs and Luther let him in. Henry pulled up a chair next to Catherine and took one of her hands in his. "I am so sorry. This is awful, but you can get through this. We are all here for you." Catherine leaned over to rest her head on his shoulder. "Thank you, Henry."

After a moment, Catherine realized it might seem inappropriate for her to be comforted so much by Henry's presence. She stopped sniffling and straightened up, took a deep breath, looked squarely at Luther and said, "I need to know the rest. Where is he? I want to bury him in a proper grave."

Luther grimaced. "We haven't been able to bring the body back, yet."

"But why not?!"

Luther continued with the detailed version of the discovery of Patrick's body including a description of the storm and a fairly gory account of the men finding Patrick's body snagged on a branch in the middle of the river at dusk about thirty miles south of Eagle Rock. He explained how they identified his shirt, and how they had lost him again to the current during last night's storm. He explained that the deputies had gone downstream again this morning to see if they could find the body and might be back later this afternoon, but the body had probably been washed even farther down the Snake River.

Catherine had recovered her wits enough to ask, "But you are sure it was really Patrick? It could have been someone else. Maybe Potts, or just about anybody."

He returned to the shirt. "We were able to identify him by his shirt. He still had on what was left of his red, white, and blue Fourth of July shirt."

Catherine persisted. "But surely you could have seen his face. The sheriff knows what Patrick looks like. It must have been light enough for the sheriff to see Patrick's face."

Luther was pleased that her insistence made it easy for him to explain further, but outwardly he sighed. "I really didn't want to go into this much detail, but no. He had been in the water so long he was bloated and nearly unrecognizable."

Catherine's voice rose to a high pitch. "But his face! The sheriff saw his face, didn't he?"

Luther was silent for a moment to heighten the drama. "Mrs. Callaway, it pains me to say this, his face was gone. In fact portions of his body were missing. He had been in the water a long time and there are a lot of fish and birds of prey that feed off the river. They generally go for the face first. We only had the shirt to go by. I'm sorry."

Catherine jumped from her chair, tipping it over as she made a dash to the street outside where she promptly fell to her hands and knees and vomited. Henry and Luther came out but kept back until she was done. Henry reached down and helped her up.

Luther said, "I will want to talk with you more once you are feeling better, Mrs. Callaway. Tell Henry when you are up to meeting with me again, if you'd like. I am so sorry to be the messenger of such bad news. I'm sure you'll have a lot of arrangements for your return home to Kentucky, but I will be glad to help, and we'll see what we can do about a service for Patrick. We all want what is best for you."

Catherine was in no condition to respond to Luther's offer, so Henry put an arm around her shoulder and escorted her back to the saloon. As Luther watched them walking, he noticed a sign being put up in the front window. It read: "Closed at noon today." He smiled as he headed back to his ranch.

That certainly went well, he thought.

Where noted, permission to reproduce the following photos has been received from the Bonneville County Historical Society and Museum of Idaho. (MCHS/MOI)

W. H. JACKSON, Washington, D. C.

Photographer to the U. S. Geological Survey

Early stereoscopic 3D photo of Taylor's Bridge located in what would become Eagle Rock when the Utah & Northern Railroad built two steel truss bridges across the Snake River just south of this location. From 1863 to 1865, the only feasible crossing of this river was a ferry service nine miles north of this location. James

Views in Utah, Idaho, and Montana, 1871.

386

386—Taylor's Bridge, Snake River.

Madison Taylor built a bridge and collected tolls at this location in 1865, but it was washed out the following spring and rebuilt as seen here in 1866. (Courtesy BCHS/MOI)

Utah Northern Rail Road's Narrow Guage 4-6-0 Franklin

This wood burning steam engine was part of the Utah Northern Railway equipment under the ownership of the Mormons and was later sold to the new Utah & Northern Railroad under the Union Pacific's ownership. Narrow gauge engines like this were operated on many of the early railroad lines using small gauge track to lower initial investment and equipment costs. The Union Pacific widened the line by moving one rail over about 1-1/2 feet on July 25, 1887, to allow larger, standard gauge engines to run on the Utah & Northern RR all the way to the mines in Butte, Montana. (Courtesy BCHS/MOI)

Historical road marker along the right of way of the southeastern portion of the Utah & Northern Railroad.

Over many centuries, the Snake River formed what locals called the "Black Canyon;" a deep channel in the volcanic rock as the river descended the Teton Mountain range and traveled across the high desert of Idaho to the Pacific Ocean. These steep sides presented early pioneers a formidable challenge to get to the west side of the river and on to the west coast and Montana mines. In 1879, the Utah & Northern Railroad built these twin steel bridges designed for narrow gauge, wood-burning engines so the railroad could be extended to Butte, Montana. The small island made this possible and was called Eagle Rock for the eagles that nested on the few trees that had survived on this barren island. Taylor's Bridge is in this photo below the right side of the western (left) bridge. The owners of the bridge, which changed hands several times, continued to collect tolls from freight wagons and civilians for many more years. (Courtesy BCHS/MOI)

A photo of the eastern bridge of the Utah & Northern Railroad with Taylor's Bridge in the background. This photo was taken sometime between 1880 and 1886. To the right of Taylor's Bridge one can see the railroad maintenance buildings that were later relocated when the Utah & Northern picked Pocatello as a more central location for their maintenance shops. (Courtesy BCHS/MOI)

Early photo of typical shops probably located along the south side of the main street of Eagle Rock, initially called Railroad Avenue. Many of the shops were simply tents as early as 1879 and later replaced with quickly constructed wood frame structures once the railroad arrived. (Courtesy BCHS/MOI)

Typical wood frame, false front, commercial establishment along one of the streets of early Eagle Rock: The gentleman in the white hat appears to have been added to the photo later. The hand written note in the upper left corner states:

"This building reputed to be one of the oldest buildings in Eagle Rock days. It was taken by the banks of the Snake River by M. W. Keefer in the late 1880s where it had been used as a fur trader's store. False front was added later. Built with square nails." (Courtesy BCHS/MOI)

Early photo of the Anderson Brother's Bank and Dry Goods Store. Robert Anderson was the first mayor of Eagle Rock and founded the first commercial venture at Taylor's Crossing after the construction of the toll bridge. That structure was along the path to the toll bridge. This building may have been built later along the main street of Eagle Rock directly south of the railroad tracks. (Courtesy BCHS/MOI)

Chapter Twenty-nine

Saturday, 7:30 PM, July 19ᵗʰ, 1879

Catherine went directly to bed when she got back to the saloon. She was so distraught, she walked right past the "Closed at noon today" without noticing. So, when she woke up about six that evening, she was surprised at how quiet the building was. But she did hear some noise downstairs. Someone was down there, but certainly not the normal crowd. She washed her face in the nightstand next to the window facing south away from the main street and carefully stepped down the ladder into the storeroom behind the kitchen. Jay and Fannie were hauling barrels in through the front saloon doors.

As soon as Fannie saw Catherine, she came over, gently took hold of Catherine's arms, and looked directly into her swollen eyes. "How are you doing, Honey? This has been a bad day for you."

Catherine shook her head. "I guess I'm all right. Deep down, I think I knew." She looked around the saloon. "But where is everybody?"

Fannie led her to one of the tables and they both sat down. "We closed the café and saloon for the rest of the day. You looked just terrible when Henry brought you back, I knew you needed some time to rest. I decided we would close at least for today so you wouldn't be disturbed. You told me once how you can hear everything that goes on down here and we all agreed you just didn't need that right now. It actually gave us time to restock, and we were as quiet as church mice, or so I'm told."

Catherine was pleased. Fannie, as always had no pretense. She knew exactly who she was and didn't apologize for taking over. Irreverent even on a day like today, but it was *so* good to see her right now.

Fannie continued, "And don't worry about the food. Crow Feather put it all away for tomorrow if you want to open."

Catherine looked distractedly around the room and then spoke to Fannie in a subdued voice. "I don't know. I was still hoping Patrick would come walking through those doors. Now, I really don't know."

Fannie leaned forward and gave her a hug. "You really don't have to make any decisions right now. How about a cup of tea? Crow Feather made you some earlier and I can heat it up for you."

"I suppose that would be good," Catherine murmured. "Dear Crow Feather. She would think of that." She gave a small smile to Fannie. "Yes, thank you. I could use a cup of her tea."

As Fannie left for the kitchen, Catherine noticed Jay bringing in more barrels. "Jay, what is all this? I wasn't expecting our order so soon."

Jay set the barrel he was carrying down near the door next to a dozen others. "Your supplies came ahead of schedule. Mr. Edwards came over a little while ago. They were put on the four o'clock train. I think he's still upset that your last supplies had been misplaced. He personally came over to tell us that your supplies came early this time. We didn't want to leave them at the depot overnight."

"I'll have to make some decisions soon, especially with this huge order here already. I don't know if I can keep this up knowing Patrick is really gone. Not now that I'm truly alone."

"You are not alone at all," Fannie said as she walked back into the room with the tea and sat down next to Catherine. "Now, drink this and settle down. The whole town is concerned for you. You have made a big impression on everybody. We are all here for you. We should talk this out together in the morning."

Jay had not seen Catherine this upset since she first heard Patrick was missing. It upset him. "I will just put these barrels in the storeroom," he said, "and Ma and I can come back tomorrow morning. I wish you would try to get some more rest."

Fannie agreed. "Drink your tea and go back to bed. Jay and I will close up." She started to get up but stopped. "I almost forgot. You got a letter today. It's from Louisville. It looks like it's from your family. It certainly is a fancy envelope." She reached into the pocket of her skirt and pulled out the envelope with a large, embossed monogram in the left-hand corner. "Take the tea and the letter upstairs and get some rest."

Catherine was still distracted and tucked the letter into her apron pocket while making her way to the ladder. She realized she had been so upset when she went upstairs, she had never taken off her apron. After undressing, splashing a little water on her face, and putting on her nightgown, she climbed into bed and reached for the letter. She smiled at the monogram, the crest of her family. It was the letter her father had mentioned in his telegram. She noticed it was dated nearly three weeks ago. He wouldn't have known about Patrick's accident when he wrote this.

She smiled. She had always depended on his advice in the past, except of course, about eloping with Patrick. She had felt guilty about not telling him. Eagerly opening the letter, she began reading. She would have to make some difficult decisions by herself, but she wanted to see what he had to say.

Darling Catherine,

I have missed your sparkling smile and energy around our home. I wish you had told me you wanted to leave. I can't help believing I'm partially to blame and I am heartsick about it. I knew you weren't happy in Louisville, and that Janette and the girls were teasing you. I just hoped everything would eventually settle down. I see now I was wrong. I am so sorry for letting you down and not properly preparing you for womanhood.

"Oh no! He thinks he caused me to leave," Catherine exclaimed aloud. "Oh, this is awful! It was my fault. I let *him* down."

When your mother died, I should have tried harder to keep your nanny when we left for Springfield. Amelia always knew what was right for you, but she didn't want to leave the rest of her family and I couldn't bring all of them. I'm sure that was part of it. And I know our move to Louisville upset you. And then you met Patrick.

I believe all of these things caused you to leave abruptly, get married and start a café out in Eagle Rock. I hope it's everything you wanted when I arranged the loan for you. I finally found it on a map; it wasn't easy. Idaho Territory maps really show very little except mountains and unexplored land. I finally got a hold of a Union Pacific Railroad map and found your location. You are really in the middle of the Wild West, but I suppose that suits you. At least you no longer have to explain why you don't ride sidesaddle and I suppose you can ride just about anywhere you want. I am a little envious since I wanted to explore the West when I was your age, but I was too busy starting a business and taking care of your mother.

Dear Heart, this next part isn't easy for me. Please forgive my overly fatherly instincts but, when you eloped with a man I hardly knew, I felt I needed look into his background. What follows is a little disturbing, and you may not want to read this, but I'm concerned that he may not have been completely honest with you. I sincerely hope all is well, and that my concerns are entirely unfounded.

I hired a private investigator. His long report is distressing. It shows Patrick has a long history as a con man and serious gambler. He does not have the aristocratic background he claimed, and he was not born in 1854 near Central Park in New York. He was born in a rundown tenement building in Hoboken in 1848.

His Irish father was hotheaded and known to get into fights when provoked. His father, Brendan Callaway, was not in the banking business, as Patrick told us, but worked as a janitor at a boot and shoe factory. He spent most of his earnings on liquor and gambling. Eventually, his wife would send young Patrick to Brendan's workplace on Fridays to collect all but a little of his pay so the family could buy food and pay the rent. Patrick would only leave him a little drinking money from each envelope.

*After dropping off the money to his mother, Patrick would leave
again. He would claim he was going to spend Friday nights with
his friends, but really went back to the bars and gambling halls
his father frequented and watched his father gamble and drink.
His father was a terrible gambler and a quick drunk, but Patrick
had learned by age 14 to hold his liquor and win at cards, at least
partly because he was a very good at cheating.*

*At age 16, he left home and started traveling up and down the
east coast, perfecting his card cheating until his reputation began
preceding him. Owners ran him out of one gambling establishment after another. By the time he arrived in Louisville, he had
spent 12 years gambling in Pennsylvania, Virginia, North Carolina
and Kentucky.*

*I can see his attraction for a trusting, impressionable young
woman. He seemed quite charismatic in the little time I spent
with him. But he is much older than he claims to be, and he was
about to be run out of Louisville for cheating at cards just after he
arrived unannounced at our Thanksgiving celebration.*

Catherine recalled that Patrick's arrival at her father's annual Thanksgiving
party seemed like a mythical knight in shining armor riding in to rescue the
maiden. It was delightful to have such a charismatic and worldly man take
an interest in her. She had dreamed of being rescued from the boredom of
Louisville and carried away into the sunset by some handsome gentleman,
and the adventure of eloping to a new life in the West had been exhilarating.
But once they had arrived, his recklessness and self-centered personality had
quickly become apparent. So, this letter wasn't as shocking as her father might
have thought.

*I am afraid there are also several young women in Louisville
who are saying very bad things about him.*

*If you don't already know him to be the man I've described, but
have read this far, this has to be very distressing for you. If you do
know, your strong and virtuous personality must have brought*

about a change in his ways because I know you would not put up
with this behavior.

I wish only the best for you and hope everything is going very
well. But, if you want to come home, even just to visit, I will send
you tickets on the next train. I don't want you to think you are
trapped there. I am here for you and can help you start over if you
think that would be best.

No one else knows of this information and I will keep it secret
to avoid any possible embarrassment for you, but please think
of your own welfare and what you expect from the future. You
deserve the best and it is hard for me to believe Patrick is the right
man for you.

With all my love,
Father

By the end of the letter, Catherine was shaking. The idea that her father
thought he was responsible for her sudden departure from Louisville haunted
her. She could only correct this by telling him the whole reason she left. She
would have to leave Eagle Rock at once to tell him face to face, and she wished
he didn't have to know the truth. But she had no choice. She had to fix this.
Questions cascaded through her mind.

What would she tell Fannie, and Jay, and Crow Feather in the morning?
And how would she pay them now that her profits were all in the supplies?
And what was she going to do with all that food and liquor? What would
happen to Jay if she went back to Louisville? Could Fannie take over the
saloon and café? What could she tell Henry? In Louisville, Patrick's cavalier
demeanor and sense of adventure had been enthralling, but her time so far in
the West, particularly in Eagle Rock, had been far more fearful for her than
she'd expected. In quiet, unassuming Henry, she found the protector she had
needed in Patrick. In his attentive, tender way, Henry made her feel good
about herself, and safe, and he made her laugh.

The matter of her father's loan interrupted Catherine's appraisal of the
dependable Mr. Henry Willett. Would he really forgive the loan, especially

once he learned Patrick had built a saloon rather than a café? In her heart, she knew she had lied to her father. She'd had a pretty good idea that Patrick would want to build a saloon even when she had told her father the money was for a café. How could she face him?

Almost as bad, did she really want to go back and live with her stepmother and sisters? She wouldn't have any money of her own. How would she support herself? She would be giving up every bit of independence that she had earned here in Eagle Rock and would have to depend on her father's charity.

All that night, when she wasn't having bad dreams, she tossed and turned with new sets of problems. Hers was a living nightmare and she woke up the next morning far from rested.

Chapter Thirty

Sunday, 7:30 AM, July 20th, 1879

The next morning, Fannie arrived early as promised and found Jay and Crow Feather in the kitchen preparing a good breakfast for Catherine. When Catherine came down around seven o'clock, she explained she wanted to talk to everyone, so Jay went to find Henry. He was already heading for the café when Jay found him.

The group gathered around the new, large table Henry had found, including Crow Feather, who was so anxious about what Catherine was going to tell them that she overcame her reluctance to eat with white people. Each had a hot bowl of oatmeal with fresh berries picked by Crow Feather earlier that morning and a large cup of coffee. They were all very appreciative of Crow Feather's efforts to the point that she became a little flustered.

To take the unwanted attention off of Crow Feather, Catherine decided to break the news about her decision without any preamble. "I have to go back to Louisville. I suspect I won't be returning, so we have to decide what to do with the café and saloon."

After a momentary silence, everyone started talking at once, upset by her announcement.

"I know this seems abrupt, but you don't fully know all I have been going through." She turned to Fannie. "You were right. The letter was from my father and I have found out things about Patrick I would rather not share. For that reason, but not only because of that, I need to go back to Louisville. What we need to do is decide how best this can be done for all of us. I cannot possibly repay you for your efforts, but we need to come up with a solution that would help each one of you. I won't leave for at least week or two; I need to recoup the money I spent on supplies to pay each of you properly and not waste the food and liquor. I also need time to prepare and pack."

Through most of this announcement, Catherine had avoided eye contact with her friends, fearing their disappointment would weaken her resolve, so she didn't see them searching each other's concerned eyes for answers to their questions. The room had gone quiet again, except for Jay quietly summarizing the message for Crow Feather. No one was sure what Catherine would say next, but the direction of the conversation so far was very troubling for them.

"You have all been so good to me," she continued. "I want us to decide as a group what should be done with the saloon and the café. I have thought of two choices."

"Of course, I first thought of you two running the café," she said to Crow Feather and Jay. "You make the best food available north of Salt Lake City, and there isn't anywhere near here as well organized as our kitchen and storeroom thanks to the two of you. You would really be perfect, but I don't think the town would support you." Jay interpreted for Crow Feather and, recognizing the truth of the situation, the three of them nodded to each other.

"So, one idea would be if Fannie or Henry would like to take over the saloon and the café." She looked expectantly at both of them, but neither Henry nor Fannie seemed terribly interested by the idea, so she went on. "The other idea involves Luther Armstrong. He seems like a kind man and has expressed interest in this property. He might want to buy the property and maybe run the café. Being a Mormon, I am sure he wouldn't want the saloon."

Fanny frowned. "There is another option. There are rumors around town that Zane and that newcomer want to start a saloon, gambling hall, and brothel. He already has his eyes on this place, but nobody here should work five minutes for Zane Gunther. He is a horrible man. You can't trust him and I know he wouldn't treat any of us well, particularly Jay and Crow Feather."

Catherine didn't seem concerned. "A brothel? I don't think we have to worry about that. Mr. Armstrong wouldn't stand for it. He's a Mormon. That cannot possibly be part of the church beliefs."

Fannie looked at Henry. "You know him better than any of us, Henry. What do you think?"

Henry wiped his mouth with his napkin. He had been eating during most of this conversation. "I have only met with him a few times and I really don't

know any more than the rest of you. I have mentioned my concerns with
Mormons in the past, but I would be surprised if Mr. Armstrong allowed a
brothel this close to the future depot. Somewhere in town, yes. They're apparently very profitable. But having one at this location would not provide travelers with a good first impression of the town."

Henry pushed back his chair. "I have to meet with some of my workers at
Jake's house, so I need to leave now." Looking at Crow Feather, he said, "Thank
you for this delicious breakfast." Looking at Catherine, he asked, "Would you
like to talk more, later today?"

"Yes, I would, Henry," Catherine replied. "I do have more I would like to
discuss with you."

With that, Henry left the saloon.

"Doesn't look like Henry is very interested in taking over the saloon or
café," Fannie said to Catherine.

Catherine bit her lip. "No, it doesn't. Maybe when I talk with him I might
be able to encourage him to give it a try. But what about you, Fannie? You're
already managing the bar so well. I know you could run this place."

"Catherine, I appreciate the offer, I really do. But I don't have enough
money to purchase this property or even stock it sufficiently. And I don't want
a loan or a contract for deed. I have owed money to someone before and that
turned out badly. I don't have any intention of starting now. Do you really have
to go back to Louisville? Would you really be happy there?"

Catherine gave her a small smile, "I'm really not sure I will be happy there,
but I have made my mind up on that. Let's keep thinking about how to keep
this place going later and figure out what to do with all those supplies in the
back room. They won't earn us any money just sitting there. Anybody got any
ideas how we can cash in on that stockpile?"

Relieved to have something easier to deal with, they all started talking at
once about how the next week could go.

In the meantime, Luther was conducting a similar breakfast meeting at his
ranch. Two well-dressed gentlemen had joined him to discuss business.

"As I was saying, Mr. Lightworth," Luther said to the only other man present
who seemed completely at ease in his surroundings.

"Please, call me Jasper," the man across the table interrupted. "I prefer first
names with my partners. I think you'll agree it sets a more congenial tone."

Luther didn't consider congeniality a hallmark of his business dealings, but he was willing to give Lightworth the benefit of the doubt, for now. "Fine, Jasper it is, and you can call me Luther, but it is crucial that you remember I am never to be named at all outside this room. Is that clear?"

"Why of course."

Luther continued. "If we can reach an agreement, and I expect from the conversations we have already had that we can, your silent partner in this venture will be Ernst Fischer, Sr. from New York. That is the name by which my brother will handle all financial affairs on my behalf. I expect to be named bishop of the Mormon church in this area soon and, as such, some of my business dealings must be handled with maximum discretion."

Jasper jumped in. "And Ernst Fischer, Sr. will be receiving a very generous return on our prosperous business. We just need to get started." He didn't have enough experience with Luther to know how these conversations were expected to go, including Luther's pontificating.

Luther concealed his irritation with the man's impatience and glad-handing style as Jasper continued, "I understand you have access to several excellent properties, including the soon-to-be vacated Patrick's Saloon. I have a number of lovely ladies who are eager to start working."

Zane was the third member of the group and obviously uncomfortable in the string tie and jacket Luther had required. "This jus gonna be great, Luthuh! But, we gotta git goin'. Do ya think yor plan on runnin that fancy Mrs. Callaway outta town will take long?"

Luther smiled. "Jasper, your proposed, not-so-silent partner, can get a little jumpy." He looked at Zane. "Try to be patient. These things take time and there is still more to be decided. But yes, I have made arrangements to have control of the saloon very soon."

Jasper continued. "And there is a detail I've meant to bring to your attention. The girls and I have had all our meals at the café and there are some serious shortcomings with that building. It is too small and needs a second story so there can be a balcony over the main gambling area. That is essential to monitor the gaming tables and draw the clientele upstairs."

Zane laughed. "A balcony so ya can watch who cheatin the house."

Barely acknowledging Zane's attempt to join the conversation, Jasper asked Luther, "Do you know who owns the small lot just south of the saloon with that large stack of lumber? If we could have Patrick's and that lot, there might be room enough."

"Don't be concerned about the building, Jasper. My carpenter has already looked at the issues you just mentioned and advised me how to correct them. And acquiring the back lot won't be a problem. What we need to discuss is just exactly what share of the profits you are going to provide me for my investment."

"Yeah," Zane piped up. "And what ya gonna give me for keepin law and order in the place?"

The men discussed arrangements for another thirty minutes and everything seemed to be settled by the time Zane and Jasper left.

Luther signaled to Rachael to usher in another man who had been waiting quietly in the kitchen. Then, as he offered the new arrival a plate of steak, fried potatoes, and gravy, he asked, "How did your meeting go?"

"No, thank you," the man said. "I've already eaten. You were right. The letter from her father did just as you expected. She wants to leave as soon as possible, probably within a week. I don't know how you got her father to write that letter, but it did the trick."

Luther chuckled. "Would you believe, I didn't have anything to do with that letter? It crossed paths with my first telegram. To tell the truth, it has taken more to shake her up than I expected. I sent the first telegram to her father and thought his message back to her would send her packing. Apparently, it arrived after he had already sent that letter about Patrick. I'm glad I got to it before she did. I'd already sent him another more urgent telegram, specifically directing him not to mention me, so I had to open the letter and make sure he hadn't mentioned my involvement. Frankly, it was a combination of good timing and blind luck how this all worked out. It appears the letter got her sufficiently upset to finally decide to leave town, and the grisly account of Patrick's death might have been just the last straw. It is time for the final push to get her out of Idaho. I still have more plans for you on this. In the meantime, let's talk about your ideas for remodeling and expanding the saloon. You stand to gain a great deal from your efforts. I trust your judgment, and your discretion."

Luther gave his contractor a convincing smile. "There is a lot in this arrangement for you, Henry."

Chapter Thirty-one

Five days later, Friday, 2:00 PM, July 25th, 1879

The next five days flew by for Catherine with little time to think about much other than keeping up with the demands of the saloon and café. She had been taking breakfasts and lunches to Rebecca Mitchell each day and was about to deliver today's lunch. "Fannie, the lunch crowd has thinned out. Shall I take Mrs. Mitchell's lunch to her now?"

Fannie smiled. "Sure. If a late diner comes in demanding lunch, I'll just tell him he'll have to buy a whiskey and you will be back soon."

They both laughed. Catherine knew Fannie was doing a great job handling the drinkers. She was a natural. Alcohol sales were just as strong as the meal sales. Catherine suspected that was at least in part due to Fannie's seductive outfits and flirtatious behavior. She was so glad she didn't have to be behind the bar.

It was another dry, hot day in Eagle Rock. Tumbleweeds rolled down the street and a layer of dust covered everything. There was a pretty steady wind from the west that picked up just about anything loose. Stray hats, neckerchiefs, empty grain sacks, even small wooden barrels were bound to blow along with the tumbleweeds down Railroad Avenue, the main street past the depot and Patrick's Saloon. Catherine had to clear off odd articles that caught on her boardwalk every morning and evening. Once the sun came up, the heat was almost unbearable and even the dry breeze did little to help. The major rainstorm several days ago had temporarily cooled things off, but the scorching heat was back. Although she no longer had to walk through muddy streets, her walks into the constant hot wind to deliver Rebecca's afternoon meal were challenging. She tried to stay inside the café as much as she could until dusk but then she was normally too tired to really enjoy being outside.

On the way to the Rebecca's room, she reflected on her previous conversations with Mrs. Mitchell and her daughter. Mrs. Mitchell continued to be condescending and rude, but Catherine hoped she might become more sociable once she got out of that tiny room and started getting to know people here. Unlike Rebecca, her daughter Beth was very polite and reserved but quite curious about life in Eagle Rock.

In their brief conversations, Catherine had learned that Rebecca had grown up in in a very religious home in Macoupin County, Illinois. It was a rural area and must have been a very conservative community.

Although Rebecca had become a widow at twenty-three, she insisted on calling herself "Mrs. Mitchell" with everyone but Catherine. She had told Catherine just this morning that, since they seemed to be the only educated women in Eagle Rock, they should certainly call each other by their first names. Evidently she believed them to be equals surrounded by inferiors. She explained that she had attended the Baptist Missionary Training School in Chicago and was a fully self-supported missionary on what Catherine considered quite an ambitious quest to set up a Baptist church and school in an entrenched Mormon community. She behaved in a most arrogant, challenging manner but Catherine considered Rebecca brave and remarkably self-confident about her deeply religious ideas and goals, especially without a husband to protect her. Catherine certainly hadn't felt that comfortable in Eagle Rock, even before Patrick disappeared. She was a little envious.

When Catherine arrived at Rebecca's room, Rebecca was unusually gracious and asked her to join her. "I have made some tea and I hoped you would have a moment to talk with me. My students have left for the day and this won't take long, but I could use some advice."

Catherine was a little surprised. "Well, I have only been in town a short time myself, so I'm not sure I'm the best person for advice."

"Oh, please come in. Our tea is waiting and I am hungry. Of course Beth will join us, and I hope you don't mind if we start eating as I ask you some questions?"

Catherine knew she should get back to the café but agreed, wondering what the woman wanted. All three of them sat down at a little table by the window that faced the alley behind the building.

Catherine pulled back the sheer curtains and looked out the window. "At least your room has a view south to the mountains. The new depot is to be built just north of the building your room is backed up to."

Rebecca gave an exasperated sigh. "Well, if that is the case, I will have to find a new place to teach. The last thing I want is to be disturbed by the loud noises of construction every day."

Catherine managed to cover a small chuckle. She couldn't remember meeting another woman so completely unconcerned with anyone but herself. How did she become a missionary?

Catherine joined the women at the small table carefully set with china, silver, and a fine linen tablecloth. The teacups were set in matching saucers with a beautiful teapot. It couldn't have been easy getting all of this out here from Illinois.

"Your dishes are beautiful. They must make you feel more at home."

"Oh, this was a set I saw in the window of a Chicago pawn shop. It was the first time I'd ever even considered going into such a place but I walked past it day after day and just couldn't resist. Obviously, no one in the area appreciated this fine Haviland china, so I bought it for a song. It truly was an indulgence to bring it with me. Now, why did you laugh at my need for a quieter room?"

Catherine was a little flustered. Apparently, she hadn't covered that chuckle that well. "When my husband and I arrived in Eagle Rock, this street was a bedraggled assortment of boarded-up lean-tos and tents. Our building was one of the first permanent structures. I thought we had made a terrible mistake choosing to move to a town that was struggling to get off the ground. The railroad hadn't even arrived yet. When real construction finally started, we were relieved to finally hear the noise of more permanent buildings going up."

"Well then, I'm grateful for this chance to talk. I was right to ask you. And, may I say, this lunch is delicious. Thank you. As you know," she continued, "I plan to build a church and a school. Of course, I cannot do it all by myself. Who do you believe might back me locally, and what is the accepted way to conduct such business here?"

"Do you really think that is wise? So soon after arriving in town...or even at all?"

Rebecca had already finished most of the vegetable soup Crow Feather had made for the noon lunch. "My, I was ravenous. You are really an excellent cook."

Catherine waved her hand at the soup. "I've never made soup that good, even with the recipes I brought from home. That was made by my cook, Crow Feather."

"Crow Feather? Is she actually an Indian?"

Oh dear, thought Catherine. "Yes," she said firmly. "She and her son have been extraordinarily helpful in opening my café. I am very proud to have them in my business." She didn't add that she would be closing the café at the end of the week and they would be out of work and Rebecca would be at the mercy of the hotel kitchen again.

Rebecca stopped eating and leaned forward. "Would you please introduce me to her? I have wanted to talk to real Indians from the area. If they are working for you, they may be my in-road to setting up a school for Indian children."

"Oh, of course," was all Catherine could think of to say. She was surprised and a little embarrassed she hadn't thought of this.

"Could you introduce me to them today? It would be so helpful."

"Well, Crow Feather normally leaves around three o'clock, but they may still be there. I need to get back to make sure there are no problems at the café. Can you come now?"

Rebecca jumped up from the table. "Of course." She smiled at Catherine. "I'll just save this sandwich for supper. I'm so eager to meet them. So far, your meals have been about the only good thing I've found here, but I have an idea that is about to change. The Lord does work in mysterious ways. Let's go." She turned to Beth. "Go ahead and finish your lunch. I will be back shortly."

"They are both a little shy and can be put off easily so speak slowly and smile often. You will make a good impression on them if you compliment their cooking"

And the two of them headed back to the café.

As soon as they arrived, Fannie came out from behind the bar and asked Catherine to come into the kitchen with her. Catherine turned to Rebecca. "Let me speak with Crow Feather first. As I said, she can be shy around new people."

As soon as Catherine and Fannie were in the vestibule between the kitchen and saloon, Fannie grabbed Catherine's arm and stopped her from going any farther. "A very handsome, young gentleman came in for a late lunch and I felt I should get him something. Crow Feather had just enough left for a meal. He wants to talk with the owner and the chef. I told him the chef was busy, and the owner would be back soon. He said he could wait. What do we do? I don't know if Crow Feather will stand for this."

"Well, that makes two people who want to speak to the chef today. The lady with me just now is Rebecca Mitchell, the missionary. She, too, wants to speak to Crow Feather. I wasn't able to talk her out of meeting Crow Feather before she goes home for the day, so we might as well introduce both of them to her, although I think we should prepare Crow Feather."

As Catherine had expected, Crow Feather was not too happy about this, but eventually Jay talked her into staying long enough to at least meet the two visitors. Catherine went back into the saloon and over to the table in the back where the good-looking young man was seated drinking a beer.

"I am Catherine Callaway, owner of the saloon and café. I believe you wanted to meet me."

The young man stood. "Well, I'll be. What a great country this is. A lady saloon owner. Does that mean the chef is your husband?"

Catherine noted as he spoke that he had a strong accent of some sort. She looked at him quizzically. "No, our chef is a very talented Native American woman. My husband died recently."

The young man looked embarrassed. "No offense meant. Excuse me for not introducing myself." He bowed formally and continued. "Herman Joseph Berghoff of Dortmund, Westphalia, at your service. I'm called Joseph. I was so impressed with your combined saloon and café, I wanted to know who had been so resourceful as to put this fine establishment together. I am sorry about your husband. I shouldn't be intruding. You must have many more important things on your mind." He looked at her thoughtfully. "I just think it is marvelous that you have the courage to keep this enterprise going. I find American women are quite independent compared to the women from my country."

"Where is Western Follia? I am new here and I don't recognize that town."

Berghoff gave Catherine a broad smile. "Westfalia is a province in Prussia, a part of Western Europe. I have been exploring the wonderful states of America for the last decade and find the people grand and this vast country even grander. I wanted to meet the owner of this establishment as well as the chef who provided me with such a fine meal, particularly if she is a Native American."

"Well, as it happens, you are not the only one who wants to meet her." Catherine turned to Rebecca, who was looking curiously at Mr. Berghoff. "Mrs. Mitchell, you are welcome to join us in the kitchen now."

Once in the kitchen, Catherine introduced everyone. "Crow Feather, I'd like to introduce Mr. Joseph Berghoff, visiting from Europe, and Mrs. Rebecca Mitchell, who arrived recently from Illinois to start a church and school in Eagle Rock. Mr. Berghoff, Mrs. Mitchell, this is Crow Feather, our excellent cook, and her son Jeremiah, who does a little of everything else that we might need. And in the corner is our bartender, Fannie Smiles." Fannie gave Mr. Berghoff one of her beguiling smiles and ignored Rebecca Mitchell completely.

Both Herman and Rebecca started talking at once. Herman stopped and, with another of his gracious low bows and wave of his arm, said, "Forgive me. Ladies first, of course."

The two smiled at each other and Rebecca began again. "I wanted to tell you, Mrs. Crow Feather, that your meals this week have been positively delicious. Chicago has many fine restaurants, but your cooking is just as good and makes me feel at home. I also wanted to tell you I would like to start a school for children in this area and I am hoping you could help me explain to your people the benefits your children would be getting if they got a formal education so they could read and write and perform arithmetic."

By this time, Joseph was looking appreciatively at Rebecca. "What a wonderful idea! Another resourceful American woman." He turned to Crow Feather and Jay. "And I agree with Mrs. Mitchell. Crow Feather, your food is most satisfying."

Crow Feather was beginning to look alarmed and Catherine guessed she was not understanding much of this. Before she could intervene, though, Jay spoke quietly to his mother, translating what the two visitors had said. After a moment, Crow Feather slowly smiled and gave a little bow to both of them.

Jay explained, "Ma is happy you like her cooking."

Catherine felt she should add, "This is all new for Crow Feather. We will talk about your idea of a school later. They have usually gone home by now and they need to be ready early tomorrow morning, so they will need to go home soon. She can let me know if she would like more information from you, Mrs. Mitchell."

Joseph was deep in thought. "Jeremiah, could I come back tomorrow or some other time when I could talk to both of you? If you are willing, I would be interested to know what types of ingredients you and your mother are using in your recipes. I have never tasted food quite like this and I suspect that's because I have never eaten authentic Native American food. I worked for Buffalo Bill Cody's Wild West show for a year, but never had food this good. I would like to learn from you. Your food holds savory and sweet regional flavors and textures I can't quite identify."

By now, Rebecca was looking at Joseph. "Are you telling us you do some cooking yourself, Mr. Berghoff?"

"Oh, I'm not a chef by any means, but I do enjoy preparing a good, healthful, home-cooked meal when I have access to a kitchen. My recipes come from my mother, who prided herself on her hearty German traditions."

Rebecca smiled appreciatively. Not only handsome, but a gentleman with an appreciation for family, tradition, and food. Wonderful!

Herman turned to Catherine and continued, "And as much as I appreciate the food you serve here, Mrs. Callaway, I have yet to find anywhere in the West a really good beer. Germans are known for the quality beers they produce and I would be glad to make some suggestions that might expand your saloon business."

Catherine could see that Crow Feather was getting an anxious look in her eyes again. "I think we should call this a day. We will have time to become more acquainted, but we have bar customers who need our attention."

As the group filed out of the kitchen, there were several more comments about the good food and the hope of getting together soon.

Fannie was waiting by the door to the vestibule as the others left. When everyone was gone she spoke to Catherine. "Well, that was an interesting bunch. What do they really want? I want to be in that meeting with Mr. Berghoff."

Catherine was slow to respond. "I'm not really sure if they want anything else, but I am sure you are more interested in Mr. Berghoff than in his ideas about beer."

Fannie made a face of mock surprise. "Of course I want to hear his ideas about good beer…and other things."

Catherine smiled. "Well, this meeting does bring up some options I will have to think about, but it's nearing our prime drinking time. What do you need me to help with?"

And with that, Catherine and Fannie started preparing for the evening rush. In the back of her mind, Catherine was thinking about how she might be able to convince Henry to take over the saloon and café. He had been in every evening to help and she was convinced that he enjoyed it, or was it that he enjoyed being with her? She really wanted to know what his feelings were for her.

Perhaps this was the time to find out.

Chapter Thirty-two

Saturday, 10:00 AM, July 26th, 1879

Jay had been trying to get Catherine's attention most of the morning. He finally stopped her as they passed each other in the vestibule to the kitchen.

"Miss Cat, I had a chance to talk with Mr. Berghoff last night and he has some really good ideas. I think you should talk to him."

Catherine responded curtly, "Not now, Jay, please. We can discuss this later." As she went into the dining area, she felt bad about brushing past Jay like that, but she had a lot on her mind, and she was tired from a restless night of little sleep.

Last evening, Mr. Armstrong had come by with an offer to buy the café, but it was a pittance of what she and Patrick had spent to get the saloon built and started, and it wouldn't come close to repaying her father's loan. She was shocked at his miserly offer and had summoned the courage to tell him so, but that could have been a mistake. Right now, it was the only offer she had and she really didn't feel comfortable going back to Louisville penniless. After that meeting, she had gone upstairs to pack the things she wanted to take east, but her heart wasn't in it. She had ended up just sitting in the room by herself and crying quietly. So Catherine was quite pleased when Fannie called up to tell her that Henry had arrived. Collecting herself, she went down to meet him.

But that meeting didn't go very well either. Henry was not at all interested in taking over the saloon or café, even when she told him about Luther's low offer.

"Catherine, I would like to help, but I am in the middle of building a home for Jake, and several new arrivals in town have discussed having me build their homes as well. I enjoy the work and it could become a vocation I am really proud of. I just wouldn't have time to look after the saloon. If you are really leaving, maybe you should see if Luther will offer you a better deal."

Then, when she hinted to Henry that maybe he could take enough time off to escort her back to Louisville, hoping he might open up about continuing their relationship, he was supportive and tender but explained this also wasn't a good time for him to leave Eagle Rock. Perhaps, he said, he could consider it later in the fall when his work slowed down.

That was not what she had been hoping to hear.

After Henry left, she helped Fannie close and took the opportunity to tell her about the two conversations. Fannie agreed that Luther's offer seemed insufficient, but resolutely repeated her employment boundaries.

"Even if he does buy the café, I won't work for him. He will have that creep Zane manage the saloon. On top of that, neither of them would hire Crow Feather or Jay, so the food will likely be no better than the hotel's. So we would all be out of work soon anyway."

Fannie left abruptly after their discussion, and Catherine was even more lonely and unhappy as she finished closing up.

So, that morning, when Jay was so eager to tell her Mr. Berghoff's ideas, she couldn't muster any enthusiasm at all. As she walked into the dining room and heard Jake call her name, her first thought was, *What now?!*

"Mrs. Callaway, a letter came for you on the early train. Things are slow over there, so I thought I would bring it to you."

Catherine turned and wiped her hands on her apron. "Thank you, Mr. Edwards."

"Just Jake, Ma'am." He smiled as he handed Catherine the letter. "I also wanted to tell you I'm really sorry about Mr. Callaway. We always got along well. We sure are going to miss you around here."

Catherine laughed. "You mean you are sure going to miss Crow Feather's cooking."

"Well, yes, that too, Ma'am. But you sure have done a good thing with this saloon. You know, there were a lot of people in town who were sure you would just fly out of here as soon as your husband went missing. But you kept up the saloon, opened a café, and made a real go of it all. A lot of us are really proud of you and what you have accomplished. I can understand why you need to go back to your family and all, but don't forget us. I hope you'll come back and visit us some time."

He was looking directly and sincerely at Catherine as he spoke.

Tears formed in the corners of her eyes but she quickly brushed them away. "Thank you Jake. I will miss many of you and I will try to get back here, although it is a long way and an expensive trip."

"Just let me know when you're ready, Ma'am. You just send a telegraph to me at the depot and I will make sure you get a real good discount on your train fare and we'll have a place ready for your stay."

Catherine was touched and thanked him again before he left.

As she turned to go back to the kitchen, she looked more closely at the envelope. Much to her surprise she realized that the letter was from one of her sisters. She decided to go up to her room and read it in private. It was from Mary Jo.

July 2, 1879

Dear Catherine,

I hope this letter finds you well, although I can't say the same for Patrick (if that really is his name). I know Father has done some checking into his background and although he won't share that with anyone, he does not seem impressed. Actually, Annabelle and I both agree that we didn't think he was much of a catch. He seemed altogether too smooth for the likes of this southern girl! You should keep an eye on him or he might try to wander into the hills with some new conquest.

Guess what? I am preparing for the Louisville End of Summer Ball and Mama let me order a beautiful new gown all the way from Paris! Finally, it just arrived. Can you believe it? I'm so excited. It will be the event of the summer, and I'll be wearing a Parisian gown while you choke on dust out there in the Territory of Idaho. I hope that *doesn't sound mean. I really do hope you're getting along. I sometimes think you must miss our happy life here.*

Did Patrick ever build you a real house like he promised? I have new curtains and a new dressing table in my room. It's all so lovely. Do you miss our exciting life in Louisville? I can't imagine choosing to live out west; a world of dirt and sage brush, dust covering you every day, no real privacy, poor hygiene facilities. Do you even have a mirror? I guess you really don't need one out there. Poor food, no clean water; I just can't imagine living in those conditions. You did always prefer playing with the boys in the cotton rather than joining our tea parties and grand outings.

I digress... Back to the Ball!

I am being escorted by none other than Thomas Chambers! I am sure you remember him. He has already taken me to the Kentucky Derby at the Louisville Jockey Club track. He is so handsome, and funny. He owns a huge plantation outside of Lexington now. I'm so looking forward to entering the outdoor ball at the Crescent Hill Gate House grounds on his arm. Who knows what might happen next?

Catherine wadded up the delicate stationery into a tight ball and threw it as hard as she could across the room, exhaled sharply and screamed, *"Bitch!"* And then she promptly burst into tears, allowing herself a full-on pity party until she was spent. She didn't read the rest of the letter.

When she'd calmed down again, she picked up the glass that had shattered fallen off tit's stand by the window when she hit it with the balled up letter. When was the last time she had allowed herself to have a total fit like that? She had always tried to keep a tight rein on her feelings. She might swear about it later under her breath, but she had been reared with better manners than this. She sat, stunned at the anger she felt toward her sister. Not a catch...choking on dust...didn't need a mirror and all of that about Thomas Chambers. Oh yes, she remembered that man. She would never be able to forgive him for what he had done to her. Had Mary Jo always been so spiteful? What had Catherine ever done to her?

Sometimes, while she was growing up, Catherine had wished she didn't have sisters at all. Brothers would have been much better. At least she could have spent her days with a cane fishing pole and tin of worms at the edge of the Ohio River or riding bareback up and down the Louisville hills near her home. No dresses, no corsets, and no grand balls at the Crescent Hill Gate House! That would have been a life to return to.

And now Tom Chambers was taking her little sister to the Louisville Crescent Hill Gate House Ball for an elegant, outdoor evening of dining and dancing. Exactly what she and Tom had done at the 1877 ball. Tom had proposed to her that night at the ball and then the thing that completely changed her life had happened. He had claimed to love her so how could he have done what he did to her after he proposed?

Mary Jo could have him, but she might be in for even more trouble than Catherine was in right now.

Chapter Thirty-three

Sunday, 6:00 AM, July 27th, 1879

Catherine awoke with a start. She was sweating. The sheets were damp and tangled around her legs. It was hot and very still in the room, which only added to her discomfort. The night had been filled with bad dreams—Patrick crying for help in a rush of turbulent water, Jay and Crow Feather sitting alone in their hut with little work and no food, Fannie's disgust with Catherine's decision to close the saloon, the sour look on her father's face when she got home and told him the truth, and a string of very unpleasant memories of time spent with her sisters in Louisville.

Catherine always woke up thirsty and kept a pitcher of water and a glass on the nightstand under the window. Staggering over to the nightstand where she'd replaced her broken crystal glass with a mug from downstairs, she poured some water and took a long drink. As she set the mug down, she took a moment to look at the panorama outside her window.

The sun had just risen and it cast a golden light on the north faces of a few buildings erected along the next street. Beyond, there was the unbroken plain of high-desert sagebrush with the gentle movement of numerous tumbleweeds rolling along the ground, always heading east. In the distance, there was just the hint of mountains—pale, slight interruptions to the high plain like ghosts on the horizon. The early morning light cast long shadows, stretching out to the southwest wherever any tall, natural or man-made object broke the strong horizontal lines of the high desert plain.

There was little noise except the faint lows of cattle in the ranches to the west and the familiar morning calls of red-wing blackbirds. She noted a shade of vibrant blue she had never really noticed in the sky, which was threaded with wispy strings of thin, white clouds. She had marveled at the vastness of this valley when they first came, but the challenges of trying to please Patrick, the worries about the saloon and the strangeness of this land and its people had dampened all of those first impressions shortly after her arrival.

The harsh but subtle beauty of the land momentarily took Catherine's breath away. Did she want to leave this for the congestion, soot, and noise of Louisville? The city had grand mansions and beautiful parks but there was also the arrogant, stuffy atmosphere of people concerned only for themselves. Seeing her father again would be good, but she really had no interest in living alongside her stepmother and sisters. "I'm not ready to leave!" she said aloud.

Catherine began to smile, a genuine smile, for the first time in days and pulled a stool over to the small window. She would enjoy the rugged beauty a few more minutes before joining Jay and Crow Feather downstairs. Why hadn't she spent time at this window before? And why was the window so small? Probably because Patrick hadn't wanted this window at all.

"You will just be looking at the backs of buildings. We only need one window in the bedroom and it should face the depot across the street," he had insisted. But she had put her foot down and demanded that their bedroom needed another window to get fresh air upstairs. Patrick begrudgingly found the smallest window he could and installed it so close to the ladder that only a small table and stool would fit under the window. Catherine had to move carefully to avoid the ladder opening in the floor next to the window.

"If I were to stay, I would want a bigger window," she said to herself. She pursed her lips in thought. "*No!* I want a bigger *bedroom* with a *real* stair far enough from the saloon downstairs that I can go to sleep in peace before the saloon closes. And, if I can, big windows facing every direction!"

She spent the next fifteen minutes in front of the window sorting things out. When she finally got up, she realized she was feeling better that she had felt in all of the last difficult year. Rebecca Mitchell had made a significant impression on her. Rebecca was truly independent; a modern woman. She had control of her life. She didn't have to ask anyone for approval to determine how she spent her time. Of course, it was good to have someone to talk ideas over with, but you didn't have to be married to seek out advice. And Jake's kind words yesterday were very uplifting. He had gone out of his way to tell her what the community was thinking about her. And, the final straw, that rude letter from her arrogant little sister. It wasn't easy here, but why *would* she want to go back?

Her mind was made up. She would get presentable and have another talk with, well honestly, with her best friends.

Moments later Catherine was in the kitchen. Jay and Crow Feather could sense a new energy in her as soon as she walked through the door.

"Good morning. I have given this more thought and decided to stay. We are not closing and I hope both of you will continue to work for me."

As Catherine made her announcement, Jay's eyes brightened and he gave her a big smile. "Yes Miss Cat. We will! That's great news." He turned to his confused mother. "We are going to keep cooking here, Ma!"

Crow Feather stopped shaping biscuits, dusted off her hands on her apron and walked over to Catherine. "We happy keep cookin, Miz Cat."

"Jay, there is much to do. I have to go over to the train station and see about a refund for my ticket to Louisville. And you, Crow Feather, Fannie, and I need to prepare a new supply order for this afternoon. Jay, when you have time, could you go and see if Fannie can come in early?"

"Sure thing, Ma'am! Can I tell her why?"

"Yes, do. I will explain more this afternoon, but right now it's nearly time to open the door for breakfast. And Jay, I'm sorry I was so short with you before. I really do want to know what you learned about brewing beer from Mr. Berghoff. I certainly want to see if we can improve our beer sales. I'll be back soon."

Then Catherine headed across the street to the depot. She arrived just as the morning train was pulling in and had to wait while Jake attended to a considerable amount of freight and several confused passengers. When she finally got back to the saloon, Fannie had arrived and it was obvious Catherine's decision to stay had traveled fast. By seven-thirty there was a line almost as long as on opening day in front of the saloon. Catherine was glad she had decided to open for breakfast an hour later at eight on Sundays. Fannie suggested that everyone wanted to tell Catherine how glad they were she was staying. Rebecca Mitchell even came over. She marched to the front of the line and entered the café amidst much grumbling. She explained that she had just come in long enough to thank Catherine and say she had been very concerned about where she was going to get her meals next week.

"I see you are very busy. Could you please send Jay over with my breakfast when there is a break? I still want to talk to him about my school."

Once Rebecca had left, Catherine looked around the saloon and noticed a lot of new faces. She went behind the bar to talk with Fannie. "We seem to be more crowded than usual today."

Fannie smiled as she stacked clean glasses on the back bar in preparation for the ten o'clock crowd. "Everyone thought this would be their last day to get a good meal. Ellington was in earlier. He said a group of bullwhackers arrived late last evening. Now that the train is delivering freight all the way up to Eagle Rock, they only have to haul it by wagon from here to the mines in Butte. Apparently there is a little competition to see who can get to the early train freight first, but Ellington says there is so much freight being delivered here bound for Montana, there will be enough for all of them. But you know men. They can make anything into some type of competition."

Catherine nodded. "Yes, I saw all the extra freight and carts and men this morning when I went to see about my ticket. If many of them eat at the hotel this morning, we may have an even bigger crowd coming through here soon. We'll work on our order as soon as we get a break. I really need to find a supplier closer than Salt Lake City."

"I'm glad you're staying, Cat," Fannie said without stopping her work. "You'll make it. It's going to be okay."

Then Fannie turned to the immediate matter of the supplies order. "Now that we're going to be open, we need more of the cheap whiskey and we'd better get some more beer. As hot as it was this morning, I'm expecting a thirsty crowd this afternoon. This is the hottest time of year out here and the men drink even more than usual."

"Well that'll be good for business, if you can keep the rowdies under control."

"That's never been a problem before," she answered without a trace of irony. "I keep them in line, or they don't get to come back."

"Yes, you do," Catherine nodded appreciatively. "This afternoon, if Sandy can come over for an hour, I'd like to talk about our plans. We're going to need more help, and you both know more people in Eagle Rock than I do. Could you think about two more people who might come on part time? We need one to help with the bar during busy times and one to help both in the kitchen and in the dining area. Who knows? If they work out, they could become full time."

"Good. I already feel a need for a break once in a while, and it looks like we're just going to get busier. I might have a couple of ladies in mind who are looking for work and would do a good job with this crowd."

Catherine was delighted. "Do you think Sandy could come on short notice? This afternoon?"

"If you can manage the bar for about twenty minutes around two o'clock, I can probably have her here by three."

"Wonderful!" The double doors to the saloon opened and several men entered. "Well, here they come."

And with arrangements over additional help settled, Catherine gave a big smile to the group of five trappers who had just entered and took their order.

Chapter Thirty-four

Sunday, 11:00 AM, July 27th, 1879

"That damned woman!" Luther had slammed his fist on his desk when Zane brought the news to him that Catherine Callaway wasn't leaving. He was now unconsciously rubbing his right fist with a pained expression on his face. "What does it take to get rid of her? Are you sure of this, Zane?"

As he liked to do whenever he felt he had a bit of tasty news or an upper hand, Zane leaned casually against the door frame of Luther's home office. He was pleased to keep this war going and happy to experience Luther's wrath at someone and something other than him. "Ya know, Luthuh, if youdda just show up in town now and then, youdda have a better idea of the goin's on. Everybody right pleased she gonna keep that café open. Ya just shuddah lemme get riddah her long ago. She just too stubborn ta understand she don't belong here. Ya gimme the go-ahead an Ah gah-un-tee," Zane said guarantee as if it had three syllables, all unintelligible, "Ah can scare her off." The smirk on Zane's face told Luther he relished this idea, which, from what Luther could decipher, would mean Mrs. Callaway would have a violent encounter with a particularly crazy man. Zane leaned forward, strolled into the office, and sat in one of the chairs in front of Luther's desk, hoping he had enough bad news for Luther to continue this meeting a bit longer.

"Don't you get it in your head to do something reckless, Zane. We don't need any more attention around here. I just got a message from Jake that the Clancys are on the prowl again. He says the new U.S. Marshal has visited Raymond Clancy and his brother up on Willow Creek."

Zane didn't seem impressed. "Don't worry none about them, Luthuh. Ya know Ah kept their cattle rustlin in check befoh. You keep your eyes on me, Ah've got mah eyes on them. Ya got bigguh troubles."

Luther sighed. "Zane, this isn't just about cattle rustling. Marshal Dubois believes the Clancys plan to target our trainloads of settlers and provisions. It would be a smart move for them, more profitable and easier to dispose of than cattle or horses, and they can hit those trains anywhere up and down the line. We don't have enough deputies to watch the entire line. You and your men can handle any local rustling, but we may actually need the U.S. Marshal's help with the Clancys. I'll take care of that matter, but what is our immediate problem you mentioned?"

Zane looked a little disturbed over that. He leaned forward, put both his hands on the front of Luther's desk, and sighed. "Now Luthuh, Ah don't want ya ta take this wrong. Ah'm a patient man, but Jaspuh Lahtwuth be climbin up mah ass bout our saloon agreement. Ah saw'im this morning and he's about ta be makin other arrangements. And last night, another fancy Dan arrived with a bunch of very lovely ladies. They're plannin to start another brothel, an Jaspuh got a bug up his butt cause he say ya havnah done nothin to help him. He been talkin to the Anduhsons and say if we can't turn over Patrick's Saloon by this Monday, as ya told him ya would, he goin' ta purchase the old drugstoh and the next door lot for hisself. Ya promised that saloon ta him, and he say iffin ya don't make good, that drugstore will be the next best thing on Railroad Avenue for what he has in mind."

Don't make good? Luther thought with some displeasure.

Zane droned on. "The young couple in the drugstoh hasn't made it go and they behind in their rent to the Anduhson brothers. The brothers be ridin the kids to pay the rent money or clear out so the place can be sold. They want money ta build their new warehouse. Jaspuh's got money burnin a hole in his pants and he want his gals workin befoh he spend it all on their food and lodgin. Ah was kinda hopin we would be in business bah now mahsself. Ah got a hankerin for at least two of them ladies of his, and I shurnuff could use mah partnah-share of the profits. The sooner the better, if ya know what Ah mean."

Luther hadn't been listening for several minutes. "Damn it!" he said again and turned to look out the window over the high desert. The sun was directly overhead now and the landscape looked raw and hot. Other than midday, this view was perfect, but Luther was heading straight into a rant. "I thought she was going to be on the Saturday train. Are you sure she's not leaving?"

"Ah even checked with Jake. She had a mind ta ask for a refund! That lady's shurnuff got balls."

Luther turned and looked questioningly at Zane. "He didn't give her the damned refund, did he?"

Zane chuckled. "Ah knew ya would say that, but ya know Jake. He's an ole softy an Ah think he sweet on her ta boot. He diddin know he wasn't sposed to give her money back."

Luther just shook his head. "There are some things we don't need to bother Jake with. These things are just better if known only by you and me."

They both sat there for a few minutes as Luther considered his options. Finally he said, "I like your idea of scaring Mrs. Callaway out of Eagle Rock." A small smile formed on his lips. "I would like to scare the hell out of her too, so there could be some satisfaction in that, but let me think about it for a while. I don't want you doing something that might cause a problem for us later on. We will have to go along with Jasper's decision, but I want him to know I have really been trying to get control of that property."

"Well, ya can tell'im soon enough yourself. He said he would be lookin ya up this afternoon. And ya should know, there's another man in town lookin for a place to set up a saloon and gamblin hall. A man named Skoggs. Ah spect he will be callin on ya soon enough, too. Just what we be needin right befoh Ah go inta business. More saloons."

Neither man was happy with the outcome of this conversation. As Zane got up to leave, he turned and added, "The Clancys robbin the railroad could be some trouble. That ole man's a weasel. He might try bout anythin. How about Ah make a call on Beaver Dick?[34] He live up there, close ta the clan. Maybe he know somethin."

"Good thinking, Zane. That old hermit might be of use."

"Ah'll take a couple bottles of Flaming Eagle Whiskey and we can share stories bout the good ole days round the campfire with his squaw. Ah bet he tell me what we need ta know. Just leave it up ta ole Zane. Ya know Ah can always come through for ya."

---

34 *See chapter notes*

After Zane left, Luther pulled out his bottle of Old Forester bourbon and poured himself a small amount just to settle down. After his first mellow sip, he thought to himself that they wouldn't be having these problems if "good ole Zane" had actually followed his instructions from the beginning. Mrs. Callaway had become a real pain. He would have to think of something really nasty. But subtle. He didn't want it coming back on him with the bishop seat riding in the balance.

Probably Zane wasn't the best man for this job. He talked too much and he could get really cocky. Luther pictured him leaning in the doorway with a relaxed familiarity and conducting himself with that swagger of his. He would talk with Cloyd. Cloyd would know what to do, could do it without leaving any traces that could implicate Luther, and would enjoy doing it. He was a mean son-of-a-bitch.

In the meantime, Luther knew he had to take the warning about the Clancy Clan seriously. He really didn't want the new U.S. Marshal making a habit of visiting Eagle Rock. He knew enough about Fred Dubois to know that if he started poking around, he might think something wasn't quite right in Eagle Rock. Dubois thought too highly of himself to be bought or bribed. If he got wind of some of Luther's "off the books" business arrangements, he might be inclined to share them with the brass at the Union Pacific, who in turn might choose to share them with the Salt Lake Mormons.

Luther feared the Mormons even more than the Union Pacific.

Chapter Thirty-five

Monday, 2:00 AM, July 28th, 1879

Before going to bed Sunday night, Catherine reflected on all that she had accomplished in the last sixteen hours. So many decisions had been made and she felt good about all of them. The saloon and cafe were going to stay open and there would be guaranteed employment for Fannie, Crow Feather, and Jay. In addition, Fannie had located two women who could help out; Dixie Trix could start right away, and Sandy Turner would increase her hours, mainly working in the kitchen.

"I could learn so much about cooking from Crow Feather," Sandy had said when Catherine offered her a choice of the two positions.

Unlike the calm, steady Sandy, Dixie was a real character. She reminded Catherine of a young Fannie. She had the flirtatious manner of Fannie and was immediately successful with the drinking crowd.

It seemed like the whole town had turned out for Sunday breakfast and lunch, and nearly everyone, even some of the gruff trappers, went out of their way to thank Catherine for staying in Eagle Rock.

She had been disappointed about not getting to see her father, but she was sure she could make time to take a trip back to Louisville in the fall when she had enough money saved up to repay his loan. She might even be able to avoid explaining the saloon to him.

She went to bed still unsure of Henry's feelings about her, but there would be time now to sort that out. And her decision to stay meant she wouldn't have to live under the same roof with her stepmother and sisters. What a relief. It was really fortunate that Mary Jo's letter had come when it did.

Unlike the night before, which was filled with bad dreams, anxiety, and restlessness, Catherine went to bed Sunday night and fell immediately into a deep, satisfying sleep. She did have dreams, but they were pleasant and comforting ones. It was in the middle of that restful sleep and in the middle of a lovely and somewhat romantic dream about Henry, that she heard gunshots and someone yelling and pounding on the saloon doors.

"Fire! Fire! Catherine! Wake up! You need to get out now!"

She was so groggy from the deep sleep that she nearly tripped over the light robe she was wearing as she got out of bed. There were flashes of light coming through her small window. She stumbled over to the window and looked out.

"Oh my God," she gasped. "Zane has started a fire in my stack of lumber!"

Suddenly wide awake, she grabbed a shawl to wrap around her and made her way down the ladder. Her mind was working at top speed, but her body seemed to be in slow motion. Trying to rush downstairs holding her shawl in place, she almost missed a rung. It was just lucky that she didn't fall to the floor.

Damn it! she thought. *I have got to get real stairs. And an emergency exit.*

She could hear a growing commotion in her back lot where the lumber was stored. Men were shouting and she realized she really had heard gunshots as well as the sound of hooves galloping away from the saloon. The sound of gunfire was so common in Eagle Rock, she tended to sleep through it nowadays, but this time it was too close to ignore. She started to unbolt the back door and then thought better of it. Better not open the door into an inferno. Realizing now that it was Henry pounding on the door and calling to her, she turned and ran to the front doors. As she unbolted and opened them, she was thrilled to see him.

He grabbed her in his arms and gave her a bear hug. "My God, I thought you were never going to wake up. You could have been killed, trapped in your own bedroom!"

She was glad to be held tightly against him but her most pressing concern was the fire. "How can we put the fire out? I don't want to lose everything. Is there any water?"

Henry held her out from him, examining her fully to verify that she was really all right. She modestly pulled her shawl tighter around the top of her loose robe.

"Don't worry," he said. "Anderson's men and several others from town are putting out the fire. It should be out soon. It looks to be an accident. That drunk Smiley Jack seems to have dropped his lantern and set the whole thing off. I'm just glad you are out of the building and safe. We have to get you another way to get out of that death trap upstairs."

He put his arm around her waist and started guiding her around to the back of the saloon where there were at least twenty men in a line passing buckets from the railroad water tower to Anderson's men. Mr. Anderson himself was in the middle of the group but his watchman John was directing the work. It appeared that they had caught the fire quickly and it had never gotten a really good start. Some of the lumber was charred, but the fire was under control and most of the lumber was just wet and smoke damaged.

Henry grumbled. "Smiley Jack started this. The coward was hauled off by two deputies and will spend the night in the jail. Someone should have run him out of town long ago. He must have been so drunk he couldn't stand upright and he fell over and dropped the lantern right over there." He pointed to a shattered lantern near the worst of the scorched lumber.

"Oh dear! Was he hurt?" But Catherine was strangely relieved it hadn't been Zane trying to burn her out. Accidents happened. After all of the praise she had gotten yesterday, she was mortified at the thought that someone would intentionally try to burn her out. Few people in Eagle Rock were aware of the sinister arson rumor, and so far, Luther Armstrong had insisted that Zane was not a threat. It seemed he was correct.

As Catherine and Henry stood there, his arm still protectively around her waist, the commotion created by the fire was dying down. The fire itself was out and just one edge of the stack was still smoldering.

Just then, Jay came rushing up. "Are you all right, Miss Cat? I got up when I heard the noise and saw the fire. I came as quick as I could. Ma will be here soon. I'm glad we live so close to your saloon."

"Thank you, Jay. Yes, I'm all right." Catherine stepped away from Henry, concerned as always about appearances. "I have to thank everyone. Let's open the bar. Jay, will you please light the lamps in the saloon and check our stock of beer and whiskey? I want to give these brave men a round of drinks."

A few minutes later, a large crowd was in the saloon, drinking and sharing stories about the fire. The mood of the men had turned from desperation to levity as each tried to tell a bigger tale about his own bravery in the potential catastrophe. Fannie arrived and took over bar tending.

Catherine sat down at a table near the back of the room with Henry Mr. Anderson, now insisting she call him Robert, joined them along with his watchman John. John had been pretty quiet, about the only person in the saloon who wasn't in a merry mood.

"What's the matter with you, John?" Anderson asked. "Your efforts saved the day. You should be celebrating. In fact..." He turned to address the rest of the room and raised his voice so all could hear. "I propose a toast to the leader of the newly formed Eagle Rock Fire Brigade. It may have been started due to a rumor, but we now have a working fire patrol and a bang-up leader. Cheers everyone!"

John was slowly shaking his head. In a slow, gravelly voice he answered, "It wasn't a false rumor, boss." He continued in a grim voice. "That fire was set on purpose."

Everyone at the table stopped talking, the toast forgotten. There was a moment of silence. Then Anderson leaned closer to John. "It wasn't Smiley's lantern? Of course it was. He's cooling his heels right now in the jailhouse."

John was still shaking his head. "I'm sorry I didn't tell you earlier, but I was too busy fighting the fire. I saw just about all of it. It wasn't Smiley Jack."

You could tell Anderson was getting perturbed. "Well speak up. Smiley's in the jailhouse. Tell us what you saw."

John looked directly at his boss and then at Catherine. "You sure you want to hear this now with everyone around?

"Of course," responded Anderson. "Go ahead and tell us what you saw."

John looked around the table. "All right then. Just before two in the morning, I was making my warehouse rounds, checking all the locks, when I heard two horses passing behind our building heading east on Cliff Street. I was surprised that anyone was up and about at that hour, so I looked out the window. Two men on horseback were just starting to turn the corner and head north on Chamberlain toward Patrick's Saloon. And that's when I saw something odd. The lead man had something slung over his saddle and the more I looked, I was sure it was a body just hanging there, motionless. I ran through the building to get to a door facing Patrick's Saloon's rear lot where the lumber was stored. Before I could get the door unlocked, I heard a thump and then just a split second later, the sound of breaking glass. I assumed they had broken one of the saloon windows so I pushed open the door with my gun drawn only to find the body of a man lying in the street next to the lumber and a small fire. Now you got to remember it was pitch black out tonight, due to the cloud cover, so all I was seeing were shapes, but there was definitely a person sprawled in the street. I fired my rifle in the air to warn the two riders off and rushed to the body, which hadn't moved. Boss, it was Smiley Jack on the ground."

He paused to let this revelation sink in before continuing. "I turned and fired another round at the riders as they went around the corner of the saloon and headed down the main road out of town, but I'm pretty sure my shot went wild. It was just too dark for me to see much, but then the fire really took off. That's when I realized the glass breaking was the lantern, not a window." John looked around the table and saw that they were all dead silent and staring at him.

Anderson said, "Are you saying Smiley was out cold and dropped off unconscious? And strangers lit that fire and left him there?"

"Yessir. That's what I'm saying. I think one of the riders must have thrown the oil lantern onto the stacked lumber. I should've chased them down but I had to drag Smiley away from the fire. He was out cold and hadn't moved a muscle. Once I dragged him across the street and set him against our warehouse wall, I ran to the depot, sounded the alarm, and started hauling buckets of water to try to control the fire. Once we got a bucket brigade going, we were able to slow the spread of the fire down and finally put it out."

Anderson seemed completely unable to grasp John's meaning. "It still could have been Smiley."

"No sir, I'm sure it wasn't," John replied, "There was no lit lantern when I saw them behind our warehouse. Smiley was unconscious, draped over one of the stranger's saddles. He was already out cold and couldn't have lit the lantern."

"So it was the Clancys after all," Anderson said in a low voice filled with a mixture of consternation and confusion. "I just never believed they would stoop this low. To light a fire, leave a man to be burned alive, and gallop away. What would they have to gain from this?"

"I hate to disagree with you again, boss. I don't think it was the Clancy Clan."

Anderson had grown perturbed. "Well, if not them, who?"

"You know the Clancys ride pretty fine horses because they have to be able to outride anyone who ever tries to chase 'em down. These horses were sway backed, run-down crowbait.[35] They didn't so much gallop as plod along like farm mules. If I had tried, I might have been able to outrun them myself, at least enough to get a better shot at them. No, the Clancys wouldn't use horses like these to pull off a crime like this right in the middle of Eagle Rock. This was done by somebody else."

Henry broke in. "So you don't think Smiley had any real part in this?"

"He was being hauled to the site like a side of beef. I doubt he knows anything about the fire, but he might remember who he was with to get him so drunk. He certainly wasn't holding a lit lantern when he was draped over the saddle of those men. How did he get to the jailhouse and why is he there?"

Henry now looked concerned. "You know, two of Zane's deputies arrived and told me Smiley had started the fire and they would lock him up to keep him out of any more trouble. Or at least I thought they were two of Zane's deputies. Come to think of it, I've never seen them around here before, so I just thought they were new. Has Zane hired two new deputies?"

Anderson shook his head. "Zane goes through deputies so fast, who can keep track? You know, when I arrived at the fire, that's what someone told me, too." A frown formed on his face. "But how could these men have known Smiley started the fire? John, there were no deputies around when this started, were there? And if they actually were deputies, why didn't they come back to help put out the fire? All the deputies are part of the fire brigade. We never saw them again."

The group was quiet, considering all that they had just heard. Anderson got up from the table. "This just doesn't make any sense. And where is the sheriff? I think I need to go over to the jailhouse and have a talk with the deputies and Smiley." He chuckled. "Well, I guess I can talk with Smiley sobers up and can speak clearly enough for us to understand. Anyone want to go with me?"

John agreed to go and Henry said he would meet them there in a few minutes after he'd spoken with Catherine. As Anderson and John left, Catherine was simply staring at the table.

Henry stayed with her at the table. "Catherine, are you all right? I think everything is going to be fine now. They'll get it sorted out."

Catherine remained silent, but finally looked up at Henry and spoke with a catch in her voice, "It wasn't an accident, Henry. Someone wants to burn

---

35   **Crowbait** – *derogatory term for a poor-quality horse*

my saloon down. I could have been trapped and burned alive! I'm frightened! What am I going to do?"

Henry took one of her hands. "I think we have this under control. We'll get to the bottom of this. You are going to be all right."

Catherine's eyes were as big as saucers and she was clearly alarmed. "What if they come back? What can I do?"

Henry used his most comforting tone of voice to try to calm her down. "Would you be more comfortable if I stayed here on the first floor tonight? I could keep an eye on things."

"But what would people say?" Catherine said with some alarm.

"I think people would understand. Your building was attacked. But I will understand if you'd prefer I didn't stay here."

Catherine sniffed, took a breath and said, "Yes. I would feel much safer if you were here. Right now, I am truly frightened to be here alone by myself. You go ahead and talk with Robert and John. I will lock up and stay up to let you in when you come back." She looked around the saloon. "There really isn't a good place for you to sleep, but I will make up a cot for you. You need to rest, too."

"All right Catherine. I won't be gone long."

Catherine stayed still for a few minutes, staring at the table thinking about everything that had just happened.

This changed everything for her...again. What would her father think of all this? Especially, with a man sleeping downstairs in her saloon.

Chapter Thirty-six

Monday, 5:30 AM, July 28th, 1879

Zane was sitting across from Luther in his office, staring at his boots and looking terribly uncomfortable. He was thinking to himself that it might be time for him to move on from Eagle Rock. He was tired of these meetings with Luther, and Luther was turning out to be an intolerable ass.

Luther looked sternly at Zane. "It is taking entirely too long for you to answer the simple question I just asked you, so I will repeat it. Did you have anything to do with the fire that was started at Patrick's Saloon early this morning? I know we talked about scaring Mrs. Callaway out of town but I believe I made it very clear that you were to do nothing until I had thought about it further."

Zane sputtered, "Well, of course Ah had nothin ta do with it. When have Ah evvah let ya down befoh? Ya know me better than that." Zane mustered his most indignant look but Luther just stared at him. It didn't take long for Zane to start studying his boots again.

After a long silence, Luther continued, "I'd like to believe you, Zane, but there are a number of odd coincidences about this whole affair. Mr. Anderson told me a little earlier this week that several of his men traveling south of Eagle Rock heard you were telling people about the Clancys causing problems in Eagle Rock. Is that true?"

"Well of course it's true. The Clancys, they always causin problems. Ya know that yohsself," Zane said defiantly. "They the ones that probably got ole Smiley mixed up in this. They one sneaky buncha bastuhds."

"Well, maybe I wasn't specific enough. I was told you spread it around they were planning on burning Patrick's Saloon down. Is that right?"

Zane looked a little surprised at this. "Nah, nah. Ah'm sure Ah diddin say that. Of course, Ah tole folk how them Clancys was trouble makuhs and Ah wish they diddin homestead so close ta Eagle Rock. Ya know they are capable of anythin and Ah'm sure they started fires befoh. Who knows? Ah been thinkin they did start this themselves. But Ah don't remember tellin anyone the crazy tale ya just tol me." Zane suddenly became indignant again. "Who did tell ya that? Ah need ta talk and get this straightened out."

Luther was still looking directly at Zane and wasn't too pleased with his answers so far. "I'm not giving you any names, Zane, or letting you do something else stupid. I don't want to have to keep cleaning up your messes." Luther got up from his desk and stared out his window at the long shadows stretching to the southwest from the rising sun. He was trying to figure out how he was going to get the truth out of Zane. It was pretty clear that Zane was hiding something, but surely he hadn't started that fire. He could tell that Zane was pretty uncomfortable with the direction this little talk was going, and that meant he knew enough to have had some part in it. How much information did he have to give Zane to get the real story out of him, and still stay out of the spotlight himself from this mess?

Meanwhile, Zane, never comfortable with silence, started shuffling his boots. He finally stood up. "Now looky here, Mistuh Ahmstrong. Ya know as well as Ah them Clancys did set that fire. They's always lookin ta make trouble foh me. Ya just let me go up there and whack some heads. Ah'll get ta the bottom of this."

Luther turned and glared at Zane. "Absolutely not! You are not going up there at all. You'll wind up bringing the U.S. Marshal up here nosing around and asking a lot of questions. But you are going to tell me everything you know. There's enough suspicion right now to lead Fred Dubois, U.S. Marshal, straight to you. Do you understand?"

"Ah don't know what ya'll talkin about, Mistuh Ahmstrong, I truly don't," Zane pouted.

Luther sighed and sat back down at his desk. Maybe letting Zane know what he already knew would force him to admit his part in all of this. "Here's what I'm talking about. Mr. Anderson, a very respected member of this community, as well as many of his people, are sure you spread rumors about the Clancys while you were supposedly out looking for Patrick. You didn't mention it to me, but they have told me you were very specific that the Clancys were going to burn down Patrick's Saloon. Now we have a real fire at Patrick's Saloon started by two strangers nobody can identify. It was a sloppy job witnessed by reliable men in this town who can describe in some detail a crime that is unusual for the Clancy Clan, started by men riding nag horses the Clancys would never use. Add to that, your night watchman at the jail didn't bother to question the two men who brought Smiley in dead drunk. Some say it was his lantern that started the fire but, if your man had done his job, we would know who those two men were. Your deputy didn't so much as ask a single question about the strangers."

Zane had already heard more of what Luther thought than he wanted, but he had no other choice than to listen obediently.

"So, here is what I think. You are the only one who might really benefit from starting a fire at Patrick's Saloon."

"Now why wud Ah do such-a thing?" Zane exclaimed.

"Because you're liable to do just about any crazy thing without thinking of the consequences."

Zane started to get up and object, but Luther reached over and shoved him back in his chair. "Now, listen to me," he continued. "Yes, I want that woman out of Eagle Rock, but I want the saloon intact! I certainly don't want the building burned to the ground, you fool! And I don't want anything to happen to Mrs. Callaway that would throw suspicion on me. However, that is exactly what has happened. I think you hired those two dumb cowboys to start that fire. I have covered your ass time and time again, yet you continue to pull stunts like this and cause nothing but embarrassment and problems for me. The last thing I need is the sheriff of this town bungling up this investigation. I want you out of Eagle Rock in the next half hour. Make up some important task, take anyone who knows anything about this with you, and clear out of here! I don't want any of you around to be questioned. The whole town is in an uproar over this and I guarantee there will be an inquiry of some kind. I just hope I can keep a lid on this before Dubois hears of it. Come back under the cover of darkness one week from today and make sure no one sees you. I'll have a plan by then. Now get out of here! I don't want to see you again for the next week!"

Sheriff Zane had had enough and was quite ready to get out of Luther's sight. He left immediately without any further comments.

Luther sat for a long time thinking about how to handle this. Zane didn't complain about most of the tasks Luther gave him but he didn't follow directions very well, he was impulsive, and he talked too much. Cloyd could handle the real dirty work without implicating him, but everyone already knew that Cloyd was far too eager to kill to be a respectable sheriff. He could go ahead and let Cloyd take Zane out into the desert and get rid of him, but he didn't have anyone readily available as malleable as Zane to become the new sheriff and he certainly didn't want that nosy Bob Anderson involved in selecting the next sheriff. What he needed first was a scapegoat for the arson attempt.

He checked his vest pocket watch and realized that Anderson would be arriving soon, probably dragging along a frightened entourage. He would have Rachael prepare a big breakfast and congratulate everyone on the success of the fire brigade. Thank goodness he had had the foresight to follow up on Anderson's suggestion. He would also explain that Zane had left town to track down and apprehend the arsonists. Later he might have to pick a pair of scapegoats. Maybe he should instruct Zane to bring back the bodies of two deadbeats from somewhere south of Eagle Rock. He could claim that they'd confessed to starting the fire but then tried to escape. Zane should probably shoot them in the back as if they were running away. He could always send Cloyd out to give him the instructions. But he would need to talk to Bob Anderson first to get any other details he might need. He had several days to think this through and he would have to make it convincing.

Luther smiled to himself and reached for one of his cigars. He felt good about this decision and he could use Zane a little longer while he started looking for a replacement sheriff he could actually control.

Chapter Thirty-seven

Monday, 9:00 AM, July 28th, 1879

That morning, the café had an even longer line of diners. The talk of the town was the fire and who might have started it. Fortunately, Fannie had come back in early to help Jay and Sandy, so Catherine had enough time to talk with many of the guests. Almost everyone made an effort to tell Catherine how upset they were that anyone would dare to harm her saloon. Catherine had posted a large sign behind the bar thanking all the men who had helped put out the fire. It included a list of all of their names and an offer of a free breakfast for each. All anyone could talk about was how fortunate it was that Mr. Anderson had decided the town needed a fire brigade.

Mr. Anderson made it clear that it was Mrs. Callaway who had raised a concern about fire to him recently, and he repeatedly thanked the men for turning out quickly and performing admirably for their unplanned trial run. "I don't believe I have ever seen so many men wide awake at three in the morning as we had earlier today," Mr. Anderson exclaimed in his deep senatorial voice. "And it appears they all managed to drag themselves out of bed again in time to take advantage of Mrs. Callaway's offer of a free breakfast."

That brought about a round of laughter from the crowd.

The festive air and the hectic pace of the full dining room service helped take Catherine's mind off of the events of last night. And the turnout and support from the town made her realize again that this had, in its own way, become her new home. What still bothered her was who had attempted to burn her out. She wanted to talk with Mr. Anderson, but there just didn't seem to be an opportunity to single him out.

When Henry came in, she signaled him to meet her in the vestibule to the kitchen. "I want to know what you found out about Smiley last night," she asked him, once she was sure the general din of the crowd would mask her voice.

"I think it is best if you heard this directly from Bob Anderson. Stay here for a minute." He went out into the saloon and was back in a moment with Bob. Since it was crowded, they moved into the kitchen.

"Did you get to talk with Smiley?" Catherine asked.

Mr. Anderson grimaced before he responded. "We still don't know a lot, but Sheriff Zane has some explaining to do. After a lot of double talk last night with Allen Brown, the deputy on duty, it became clear he didn't know the men who brought Smiley in. You know Allen. He's not one of our brightest. Apparently, the men told him I had suggested Smiley be put in a cell to sleep off his drunk. They also told him that Smiley started the fire and the sheriff would be questioning him in the morning. Well, I certainly did not send him to the jail and John was right about Smiley. He was still out cold when we got there. He couldn't have lit that lamp or started the fire in the state he was in. He seemed barely alive. I got Doc up at four in the morning, which was a challenge in itself, and he looked him over. Doc said Smiley must have drunk more than just his usual cheap whiskey, but he would probably come out of it eventually."

Henry could see that Catherine was concerned about Smiley. "Bob and I agreed to leave Smiley in the jail where he couldn't get into any more trouble, and just as importantly, no one could get to him. Then, we went to check out Smiley's shack and there were two empty bottles of Flaming Eagle Whiskey tipped over on the floor. If he had drunk both bottles last night, he would be pretty out of it."

Catherine looked surprised. "Where would he get Flaming Eagle? Isn't that expensive? He's never asked for that at our saloon."

Bob shook his head. "That's just one of the questions we have for him. He normally drinks the cheapest whiskey he can find. I think someone had to have given that to him."

Henry nodded agreement. "If we can find that out, we may have a better idea who was behind this."

"Shouldn't we check on Smiley again?" asked Catherine.

"First, we need to talk again with Zane and he never shows up at the jail-house before nine," Mr. Anderson responded. "Henry and I are going over soon to see if Zane has any better explanation of what happened last night. He also has to explain where he was during all of this commotion. While he and his deputies are being paid to keep law and order in this town, it appears we have had two strangers causing all sorts of trouble. I suspect Zane will continue to claim to know little, if anything, and say even less that's truthful, but we have to start somewhere and we'll stick with it until we solve this thing. While we're there, I'll check with Smiley and see if he can explain what happened."

"Everyone here agrees your saloon and café is an important part of this town and we don't want you worried over anything. I will keep John on night watch duty to continue to keep an eye on things. You might want to consider having someone stay in your saloon as well. With everybody alerted to the possibility of a fire, I don't think anyone is dumb enough to try this again, but you never know about some of the dimwits we have around here."

After Bob and Henry left, Shorty Smith came into the saloon and wanted to explain that none of the bullwhackers had stayed over last night due to the early train's arrival yesterday.

"You just wuddin believe how competitive these fellas are. They all wanted to load up their wagons so they could head north at the crack of dawn. It'll just be me this morning, but I'll still be payin for the table and you can sit anyone you want at my table with me. I'm right proud to be a regular here, Ma'am."

Catherine smiled at the short, husky man. "Thank you Shorty, but we won't miss the bullwhackers today," she said, motioning to the crowded room. "It seems the whole town is here this morning. And you may sit wherever you'd like. You were here last night with the Fire Brigade and your breakfast is free."

This time Shorty smiled. "Thank you Mrs. Callaway. I appreciate it. And, if I may say, I've been missin your visits to the stable of late. You used to come like clockwork with an apple or carrot for my horses. Whitey, my lame horse, been missin you too. I don't git to spend as much time with her as I used ta with all the bullwhackers around. I hope you'll be droppin by soon."

"You know, I should. I miss Whitey and the others. I've just been so busy with the saloon and café, but I may just drop by this afternoon after lunch. It would be a good break for me. And Crow Feather is baking apple pie for lunch. I'll ask her to hold out a few apples for me. Now you go get your break-fast. You deserve it."

She smiled to herself as Shorty headed for his table, hailing a couple of his friends to join him. Even with all of the frightening experiences that were part of life in Eagle Rock, and the number of scary people who dropped into the saloon, there were still a lot of genuinely good people in this town. The truth be told, there were far more than she had encountered in Louisville. And even a good many of the scary ones, once you got over their poor manners, dirty clothes, and shaggy facial hair, were simple, honest people just trying to get by.

Catherine really did miss horseback riding. She would ask Shorty if she could do some riding, for pay of course. She turned back to the kitchen to tell Crow Feather she would need some apples before she got too busy and forgot.

Chapter Thirty-eight

Tuesday, 6:00 AM, July 29th, 1879

Catherine awoke with a start the next morning. Sunlight beamed through the small window facing south, but she had covered the front window with a blanket last night to muffle the street noise so the room was still fairly dark and it was difficult to know what time it was. Had she overslept? Was the café already open? She threw off her quilt, sat up, and listened for any sounds that would give her an idea of the time. When she got up and pulled the blanket from the window, early morning light flooded the room. It was later than normal for her to get up and Jay and Crow Feather were probably already downstairs, but there wasn't a sound from the kitchen. They were probably trying to be quiet so she could wake up on her own. Dear friends. What a restful night. And it was wonderful to be able to get up and feel good about the coming day with no looming problems.

As she dressed, Catherine remembered her conversation with Shorty yesterday morning. She had gotten busy and didn't have time to go visit the horses yesterday, but she would today. She would take the apples Crow Feather had left her after lunch to the livery stable. In fact, she would ask Shorty if she could ride one of the horses. She hadn't ridden anything but the hard bench seat of a wagon since leaving Ogden and had decided yesterday she would take some time for herself to ride a good horse again. She would ask him this afternoon and maybe even ride into the nearby foothills if he agreed. A well-deserved break would be thoroughly enjoyable.

A few moments later, Catherine marched into the kitchen and greeted Jay, Crow Feather, and Sandy with enough enthusiasm to cause them all to exchange smiles. She had been under considerable strain, and this was the most upbeat she had been for a long time. And Sandy was just as upbeat as Catherine. "Crow Feather let me make the dough for the biscuits yesterday afternoon," she exclaimed. "We tried them this morning and Crow Feather agrees they came out great."

"Well then, I certainly want to try some myself," Catherine replied. "You can spare a few can't you, Crow Feather?"

After showing due appreciation for the biscuits, Catherine asked Crow Feather if Sandy could help her set up the dining area for breakfast and then take charge of the dining crowd while Catherine focused on greeting guests and clearing tables. With Sandy's help, the morning routine had become much more congenial and better balanced for everyone. Catherine had really never had time to focus on the diners due to the hectic pace required just to keep up with the crowds. She wanted to become more familiar with the language and dialects of this diverse group of people, but their conversations had been lost to her in the general din that filled the cafe. It seemed to her that crowd of men each had their own language with terms and phrases that were unfamiliar— even strange, to her. Now that she was not so overwhelmed by the pace, she could finally pay attention to their separate conversations.

As she cleared tables, she heard one of the group of cowboys and ranchers say, "Well, I shor got it in the neck[36] when I bought me that hayburner. Nevva thought a horse could eat so much and come so short a'pullin.[37] Worse yet, that horse was Indian broke,[38] so I had to retrain it so I could mount it cowboy-like."

Another cowboy at the same table responded, "Well, at least your nag ain't owl-headed.[39] Mine keeps looking everwhere 'cept where we's a-goin'. The big auger[40] won' give me a cow horse so I'm stuck with a damn sorry, lop-eared, knock-kneed, barn-sore[41] critter not fit for a chuck-line rider.[42]"

---

36   *Get it in the neck* – *get cheated, mislead, bamboozle*
37   *Short a pulling* – *a horse unable to pull a good load*
38   *Indian broke* – *horse trained to be mounted from the right side. Cowboys mounted from the left side*
39   *Owl headed* – *a horse that won't stop looking around*
40   *Big Auger* – *ranch owner*
41   *Barn sore* – *a horse that loves its stall; speeds up the pace as he nears the barn*
42   *Chuck-line rider* - *unemployed cowboy who rode from ranch to ranch, exchanging a bit of news and gossip for a meal; grub-line rider*

At another table, a group of trappers shared tales of last night's events at another bar.

"And ya shudda seen him. Full as a tick.[43] Couldna even walk straight. He wobbled right up to one of those fancy ladies, thinking he was cuttin a swell,[44] and she jus dressed him down some dreadful awful. But he just wouldna shut his big bazoo,[45] so two big brutes finally picked'im up and threw him right out in the street," the trapper continued, laughing. "Now he was covered with horse muck. What a sight, caterwauling away in the middle of the street. Served him good and right. He's an odd stick, that one."

Catherine could make out the gist of that tale but, at another table, she was completely mystified by the conversation. One railman was in a dither about the new fireman assigned to his steam engine.

"That new man is just a damned diamond cracker[46] from the east coast and knows nothin about wood burnin engines. He's just a boomer[47] ashcat,[48] constantly complaining that his hands are sore because he can't use his banjo.[49] When the brass buttons[50] came up to tell him to get the blind baggage[51] off the train at the next stop, he looked like we were daft. Didn't even know what the man was talkin about. I tell you, I marched right into the buzzard's roost[52] at the next stop and told the brass hat[53] I wanted him off my train by the next trip down these rails. I'm not gonna put up with that kinda ignorance on my train."

But on the rare occasions when Jasper Lightworth treated his fancy ladies to breakfast out, Catherine avoided their table as much as possible. The ladies were loud and crude as they recounted in great detail their adventures in the upstairs rooms of their establishment just down the street. It made Catherine blush the few times she had gotten close enough to hear them.

---

43 **Full as a tick** – *very drunk*
44 **Cutting a swell** – *presenting a fine figure*
45 **Bazoo** - *mouth*
46 **Diamond cracker** – *locomotive fireman using black diamonds (coal)*
47 **Boomer** – *railmen who drifted from one railroad job to another*
48 **Ashcat** – *also a name for a locomotive fireman*
49 **Banjo** – *fireman's shovel; old style banjo-shaped railroad signal*
50 **Brass buttons** – *passenger conductor on railroad or streetcar line*
51 **Blind baggage** – *hobo riding the head end of the baggage car next to the tender, commonly called "riding the blinds"*
52 **Buzzard's roost** – *yard office*
53 **Brass hat** – *railroad official*

Yet, with all the poor grammar, slang, and jargon, the diners were, for the most part, good-natured, pleasant, and talked about simple things that were a part of their everyday lives. This was considerably unlike her experience in Louisville where she had been surrounded by stuffy, aristocratic gentlemen concerned more about the stock market, the price of gold, politics, and who might be bedding whom. The Louisville women were just as full of themselves, concerned about the latest fashions, hair styles, the price of silk, and, of course, who was bedding whom.

Just about the time Catherine was going to take Rebecca's breakfast to her, Rebecca walked through the door with Henry. She looked over the crowd, saw Catherine and marched over to speak with her. "Mr. Willett and I would like to make a proposal to you. Is there somewhere we could talk?"

Right to the point, as usual, and oblivious to the crowd and the armful of dishes Catherine was holding. Catherine couldn't imagine what both Rebecca and Henry would want to talk to her about. She looked around the saloon and noticed that the crowd was beginning to disperse and she had several tables empty near the back.

"Let me clear those tables in the back and we can talk there. But, we will only have a few minutes before the bar opens up. Are you sure you want to meet here?"

Rebecca frowned. "If I am going to live in Eagle Rock, I guess I will just have to get used to people drinking until they turn from godless sinners to God-fearing followers. Jesus was surrounded by sinners and weak-willed individuals, yet he ministered to all who would listen. I have been studying my Bible and am trying to keep his example at the forefront of my ministry. And that is why I decided to come here today with Henry. I think if we all work together, we can all meet our goals."

Catherine, who had just decided to stay and make her living from people enjoying beer and whiskey between, and sometimes during, meals, wasn't sure they actually shared a common goal. But she kept that thought to herself as Rebecca continued stalwartly on.

"I am so glad you have decided to stay and I have a plan to share with you that could make your café even more successful as well as eliminate the need for you to serve me meals in my stuffy little room."

Catherine looked at Henry but he was just smiling at her, so she responded, "Well, if you will just take a seat at the only clear table and let me clear and prepare the other two, I will join you."

Once Catherine had joined them, Rebecca shared her plan. "As I have said before, I think you should have a dining area for the café that is not in your saloon. You have a huge stockpile of lumber behind your saloon that I understand was to be used by your late husband to build a gambling hall addition to the saloon. I would like you to consider building a café addition instead, and I am prepared to help you if you will help me." A frown had now appeared on Catherine's face but Rebecca held up her hand to stop Catherine from interrupting.

"You have told me that you don't want a gambling hall and Lord knows, I don't want one either, but just about everyone in this town would benefit from a café expansion. You have also mentioned to me that while you may have the materials, you don't have the resources to pay for the labor, yet. Well, I think I can get that."

Catherine made a somewhat exasperated look at Henry who wasn't making any effort to stop this woman and then turned back to Rebecca. "I can agree with your thoughts about expanding the building to have a separate café, and your offer to help in some way is inviting, but I cannot pay you back at the moment. And how would you possibly benefit from this?"

Rebecca smiled. "Mr. Willett and I have discussed this and I am in a position to pay for the labor to build an addition on your property if you will allow me to use the addition as a day-school for children in the afternoon when the café is not in use and for Sunday morning church services."

"Oh my!" was all Catherine could say at first. She looked back and forth at Henry and Rebecca in amazement. "But how would that actually work?"

Rebecca continued, "I have the support for this mission from several generous sponsors from the east coast and may be able to get more support from my friends in Chicago. I will want to build a church eventually, but for now, there doesn't appear to be a suitable building in Eagle Rock. Once I have a place to teach and to preach the gospel, and with the continued support of my backers, I should be able to start raising money for a new building. But I have to start somewhere, especially to do anything worthwhile in the cold late-fall and winter months. This arrangement would allow me to begin in months rather than years. Henry and I have reached an agreement of how much this would cost and how long it would take once you give your approval. What do you think?"

Catherine was speechless.

Henry leaned forward to add to the conversation. "I know Patrick was planning on a second-story living space for you with real stairs and a second exit to avoid just the situation you faced several days ago. I have drawn up some plans that would include a small apartment on the second floor with a proper stair and a hallway to your present bedroom. Then the ladder would serve as your second way out. Mrs. Mitchell has agreed that she would pay for all labor needed to make this addition, but, since she would have no need for the second floor, she has stipulated that you should pay her back over time for the cost of the labor to build the second floor. This could be deposited into a fund to go toward the construction of her new church."

Catherine looked back and forth at both of them again. "I can't believe this. I have already imagined a café addition, and your offer sounds wonderful, but there may a problem you haven't considered yet. The lot behind the saloon is not even as big as this one, so the café would actually be smaller than the saloon is now."

Rebecca smiled. "Mr. Willett has already figured this out and he has solved it." She turned to Henry. "Tell her your plan."

"My plan is to make a large opening between the addition and the present saloon on the first floor. I am recommending two, barn-style rolling doors, one on each side of the dividing wall between the two spaces to help with sound control. In the morning, the doors would be open until the bar opened so you would have more dining space. Once the bar was open, you could close the doors for the lunch crowd, Mrs. Mitchell's classroom and for Sunday church services. With a short hall near the kitchen, you could serve lunch in both spaces since there will be some diners who are not bothered by eating lunch in the saloon. The one drawback would be that you could not open the bar until after the church services on Sunday morning."

"How long have you two been working on this?" Catherine asked. "It seems that you have thought of everything."

Rebecca responded, "I have been thinking about this ever since I got here and found the town's buildings in such disarray. I knew when coming here that it would be difficult to build right away, so I prepared my supporters for the need to rent a space once I arrived, but nothing suitable is available. Mr. Willet and I had discussed this in general terms but, with Patrick's whereabouts so uncertain, and your plans unsettled, I was reluctant to bring this up until you had made a decision to stay. Now I am eager to get started, so I ask you again, will this work for you?"

"Well, it is rather sudden. It will take me at least a little time to sort out. But, as you say, it does appear your ideas could be good for all of us if Henry has the time to build it." She looked questioningly at Henry, remembering how disappointed she'd felt when he declined to accompany her back to Louisville due to his schedule.

Henry also remembered that conversation and gave Catherine a knowing smile. "I happen to have enough time to take this on right now. Just yesterday I hired several more workers and a foreman. The projects I am presently working on are winding down but several more could start up very soon. For me, the timing couldn't be better. I expect this will change as winter approaches. New settlers are arriving every day and they will need some sort of shelter."

Catherine leaned back in her chair, hands folded in front of her, nodding as the idea started to take shape. "Really, it seems like a brilliant idea. I truly am running out of room for the diners, and I certainly need a better way to get out of my bedroom. I need a little time to think this over, but you both seem to have worked through any problems I could think of. Can we talk again tomorrow?" She turned to Rebecca. "I must admit, when you first came here alone and told me you would be starting a church, I thought you were unrealistically optimistic, but you have just proven you really are determined and a great problem solver. I want to support you in any way I can."

There was a growing crowd around the bar and Catherine was aware that Rebecca was looking increasingly anxious. "Thank you both so much for coming this morning. Rebecca, I will bring your breakfast over in just a minute but I do need to ask Henry something."

Once Rebecca was gone, Catherine asked Henry, "Can I do this? Will it work?"

Henry smiled and touched her hand. "This is a perfect solution to give you the space you need for diners. People aren't always going to wait in line outside, no matter how good Crow Feather's cooking is. But, more important to me, you will have a safe space to sleep and a lot more room. It should make you pleased that Patrick was thinking about a second floor apartment when he came up with the gambling hall addition. I already have plans drawn up. I can show you whenever you're ready to move forward on this project."

Catherine shook her head. "I suspect he was going to use the larger bedroom and stairs as a bargaining chip to get me to agree to his gambling room. I'm not sure that would have been enough for me to agree, but this is exciting. Can you really start right away?"

"As I said, it would be best for me if I could start quickly. Getting you a new stair as soon as possible is my highest priority. I was worried about you when that fire broke out."

Catherine blushed and put her hand on top of his. "I am so grateful for your concern and thoughtfulness, Henry."

"You should realize, though, that at least for a while, you will be living in a partially completed building. Security and a possible fire would be an even greater problem during construction. Zane is off looking for the arsonists and we still don't know who started the fire. Since I would be working here, I would prefer to sleep here as well if you don't think that is too forward. I want to protect the building materials and make sure nothing untoward happens."

Henry had been coming over early each evening to keep an eye on things, and they spent time after the saloon closed each evening to share the day's accomplishments and problems that had occurred in both of their lives. She was becoming more convinced that his feelings for her were about more than just friendship.

"Of course," she said. "I always feel safer when you're here."

Chapter Thirty-nine

Tuesday, 3:30 PM, July 29th, 1879

The remainder of the day, Catherine's mind returned to Rebecca's proposal whenever she wasn't fantasizing over going horseback riding. It had been an unusually busy day with diners coming in much later in the afternoon than normal, so she wasn't able to break away until three o'clock. She hurried up to her room to change into pants suitable for riding so she could get to the stable before Shorty Smith left for the day but found Jay patiently waiting at the base of the ladder when she came back down. She had put him off several times in the last few days and was embarrassed about not treating him properly.

"I'm so sorry, Jay. I know you want to talk about your discussion with Mr. Berghoff, but I need to meet with Shorty Smith at the stable right now. How about if we include Fannie and invite Mr. Berghoff over later this evening, about eight o'clock? I'll see if Sandy can spell Fannie long enough to meet with us. I think she should hear your thoughts, too."

Jay was slowly shaking his head. "Well, ah, I don't know if Mr. Berghoff could make it on such short notice. Ya know, he is out on the railroad gang up north and I don't know when he will be back in town tonight."

Catherine thought about this for a moment and said, "Well, I'm hoping to go riding today. I might as just well head north and invite him myself."

Jay looked startled. "You ride, Miss Cat? On a horse? Or do you mean in a buggy?"

Catherine laughed. "No, I'm not going to be riding in a buggy. I have always ridden on a horse. Can't you see I am even dressed for it?"

Jay's eyes widened. He looked a little embarrassed.

"You have a horse? You really ride in a regular saddle? I, well, I just didn't know ladies did that." Then it dawned on him. "Are you going to rent a horse from Mr. Smith?"

"That's right, Jay. And I know I may seem somewhat ladylike to you, but before I came to Eagle Rock, I did own a horse and rode frequently. And not so ladylike, I dare say."

"But you will have to leave town to get to the railroad gang. Are you sure you can find the way? Will it be safe for you?"

Catherine looked firmly at Jay. "Jay, all I have to do is follow the railroad tracks. I can't get lost."

Jay looked at his feet and mumbled, even more embarrassed now. "I don't know, Ma'am. I just never pictured you on a horse like that." He looked up at her. "I've always wanted to ride. It must be a great feeling."

Catherine was touched. What young Indian boy wouldn't want to ride? It just hadn't occurred to her that Jay wouldn't have access to a horse. "I'll ask Mr. Smith if he'll let me teach you to ride. Would you like that?"

Jay's face lit up. "Oh yes, Miss Cat! That would be great!"

"I'll see what I can do, but I must get to the stable now if I am to talk with Mr. Smith."

So Catherine hurried to the stable, definitely not ladylike, in hopes of catching Shorty before he left. As she rounded the corner of Capitol Avenue, she saw him closing the stable door, broke into a run, and then yelled, even more unladylike, "Mr. Smith! May I speak with you?"

Breathless from the short jog, she explained she had brought some apples for the horses. "Not whole apples, just pieces, from Crow Feather's pies

Shorty was all smiles. "Why shor ya can. Old Whitey would love a bite of apple."

Catherine showed him her burlap bag bulging with cut apples.

"Actually, I'm pretty sure I have enough for all your horses, but I don't want to trouble you if you have someplace you have to be."

"Oh my," he replied. "Why don't I just introduce ya ta all mah pets. I've not spent much time with them since I've had mah hands full with bullwhackers. Mah stable was full-up until Sunday when theys all rushed off ta Butte. Yor helpin me with breakfasts has been a boon foh me. It would be downright improper foh me not ta let ya see mah horses iffin that's what yor wantin."

Shorty took Catherine to Old Whitey first. Catherine's first impression was that the horse really did look old, but Whitey perked up the minute she smelled the apples. Her ears twitched, she nickered, and she stepped over to Catherine.

"That's a good girl. You do like apples don't you?" Catherine crooned.

Shorty's eyes went wide. He said in a soft voice, almost awed, "Why looky here. She ain't looked that perky in a coon's age. I shudduh been bringin her apples all along."

By this time, Old Whitey wasn't looking the least bit old and was attempting to get her muzzle directly into the bag of apples. Catherine laughed and said, "Now hold on there, Whitey. I need to save some for the rest of the horses."

Shorty was getting a little misty eyed. He continued to speak softly to Catherine as well as to himself. "I started mah stable with just Whitey an she wasn't even mah horse. She was mah wife's horse and a little old foh what we needed doin. Mah Mary always fed her apples an she always acted just like this. I don't know how I cuddah forgotten that."

"You have never talked about your wife before. When did she pass?"

Shorty sighed. "Mary passed away two years ago. I do miss er an I think Old Whitey must, too. I'd be mighty pleased if ya could hold back some apples for me when ya can. I need ta start payin more attention ta her. Look how happy she is."

"I'm very sorry about your wife, Mr. Smith."

Shorty looked a little uncomfortable and then changed the subject. "Thank you. We better move on if yor gonna have any apples left. I have more horses ta show ya."

Over the next twenty minutes, Catherine met all the horses in the stable along with a few mules, all the while chatting easily with Shorty about life in Eagle Rock. Obviously, Shorty didn't want to talk about his wife but he warmed up considerably to her and was beginning to talk without the shyness she had seen in him previously.

As they came up to the last stall, Shorty explained, "I've been savin this one for last. She is mah prize horse. A pure Appaloosa, and a fine one indeed. She's gentle, minds well, smart and, if ya let her," Shorty's eyes lit up and he continued in a whisper, "she'll run like the wind." With that gleam still in his eyes, he continued, "I don't hire her out for any of those wagon trains. Most of these horses are just work horses, but mah Marie is very special."

The sight of the horse took Catherine's breath away. She was looking at a beautiful animal with a reddish-brown front and several different shades of brown and tan spots on a cream background on her rump. The horse was alert, eyes bright, flicking her tail, observing Catherine. But what had caused Catherine to be so startled was Marie's amazing similarity to the very first horse her father had given her when they were still living in Lexington. Marie actually pranced over to look into Catherine's sack of apples.

"Did you name her after your wife?" Catherine asked.

Shorty gave her a warm smile. "Oh yah. I saw her last summer at Fort Henry and just couldn't pass up the opportunity ta bring her back ta Eagle Rock. The way she just reacted ta you proves I need ta pay more attention ta all these horses. I'm glad ya came today. It seems I've just been too busy ta treat these animals proper-like."

Catherine decided this might be the best time to suggest her idea.

"Shorty, I was hoping to do more than bring apples. You see, I rode horses all my life until I came to Eagle Rock. I have been busy myself, but with the opportunity to hire some help, I now have some time for myself. I would like to start riding again. I was hoping I could rent one of your horses for a short ride." Before Shorty could interrupt, she continued, "I also know a dependable young man who would like to learn to ride and I am sure, if you would let me teach him, he would be eager to come over regularly to spend some time with your horses, too. And of course, I would like to come over more often myself and bring treats for your horses."

Shorty was looking skeptical. "That really is a good idea but I'm not sure I have the equipment you need ta ride."

"What do you mean?"

Suddenly, Shorty was looking more like his old self, looking at the ground and shuffling his feet. He finally blurted out, "I don't have a proper saddle foh a lady like you."

Catherine started laughing. Looking around at all of the saddles hanging on the walls of the stable, she said, "Any of these will do. I don't ride side saddle. Any Western saddle will suit me just fine. Why do you think I came over here in riding slacks?"

Shorty looked relieved. "Well, then, of course ya can ride. I shuddah known ya was wearin them britches for a reason. In fact, I want ya ta ride Marie if ya think ya can manage her. Old Whitey is better left to short trips for someone not too sure of themselves, but she would be a good fit for your beginner friend. It would be great foh my horses ta git a little ridin time. If yor ready ta go right now, let's saddle up Marie. She's certainly been looking ya over an I know she would like a little fresh air."

It took another fifteen minutes to get Marie prepared, with Shorty giving instructions the entire time. But finally, all was ready and Catherine rode out of the stable toward Taylor's Bridge to cross the Snake River.

The moment she mounted Marie, it felt like a huge weight had been lifted from her shoulders and her heart was racing with the sheer joy of it.

Chapter Forty

Tuesday, 4:30 PM, July 29ᵗʰ, 1879

Once Catherine had crossed Taylor's Bridge, she put Marie into a slow canter heading due west. She knew she would come to the new railroad bed any moment and could follow it north to the railroad construction gang. Upon reaching the top of a small rise, she saw Mr. Armstrong's sprawling ranch spread out to the south. The view to the west and north was a startling contrast to the open vista and beauty of Armstrong's ranch. There, the alarmingly raw gash in the earth of the new railroad bed cut through the landscape like a raw wound. Although witnessing this accomplishment and the promise of expanding enterprises to come would inspire many, Catherine found it both jarring and ugly.

There was no sign of the railroad crew. Catherine suspected they were farther north. If she ignored the exposed bare dirt around the railroad tracks, the view beyond the new track was magnificent. Blue-gray mountains surrounded her on all sides. To the north and west, the mountains were a very distant, hazy collage of blues and purples. To her left, there were tall and majestic mountains that actually had remnants of snow on their upper peaks. Unlike in Eagle Rock, there was a steady breeze out of the west, free of dust. Even though it was hot, it was so much more invigorating than the dust-filled air blowing down Railroad Avenue in town. Catherine took a deep breath and let out a sigh. Except after occasional rainstorms, the wind in Eagle Rock was constantly blowing dust up from all the streets. She suspected it was actually soot from the railroad and dried horse manure ground down to a fine powder by animals and wagons. She still hadn't gotten used to it.

Catherine turned her face to the sun and took several more deep breaths. She leaned over onto Marie's neck and gave her a hug, nestling her face in the coarse hair and warm smell of the horse's mane. Speaking quietly to her so as not to startle her, she said, "Thank you for getting me out of town. We have to do this more often. It is great to be out in the open."

After looking around and getting her bearings to make sure she could recognize this spot on her return trip, she let Marie continue toward the tracks in the distance. As she got nearer, she was aghast at the debris and destruction left by the railroad workers. Deep scars in the landscape surrounded the railroad tracks left by heavy objects being dragged across the ground during the construction. Abandoned piles of dirt and rock paralleled the tracks for miles. Broken railroad ties, large iron spikes and various pieces of metal had been abandoned and left to rot or rust. The pollution and stench were terribly distressing. Broken wooden barrels, shattered glass, bits of canvas tangled in soot-covered sage brush, worn-out boots, rags, and an ever-present strong odor of smoke, oil, and even urine made an almost apocalyptic scene. Close up, it was a far cry from the more serene beauty she had witnessed from the ridge. Even Marie seemed a little anxious and shied away from the newly laid track. Catherine nudged her across the tracks and chose a route parallel but a little ways west of the track bed and debris.

It took them another half hour before they started hearing the distant sounds of construction. By the time they arrived at the southern edge of the construction gang, the noise of the train engines, shrill sounds of steam, billows of coal-black smoke, the hammering of spikes into ties, and the constant din of workers swearing and yelling at each other was even more distressing. This was not what Catherine had in mind when she had dreamed of a peaceful ride in the country.

She patted Marie on the neck to reassure her and said to the horse, as well to herself, "We will find Mr. Berghoff and get out of here as soon as possible. Be calm. This shouldn't take long."

But the railroad gang was stretched out over a few miles to the north and it took another half hour to find Mr. Berghoff working with a crew setting railroad ties near the north end of the construction. All the while, the workers' lascivious stares, jeers, and taunts in multiple languages, but with the same meaning, made it clear to Catherine she would not be safe alone around them. Of course, she realized, a well-dressed woman riding Western style on a fine

Appaloosa was not something these men saw frequently. Although she rode as far from the track as possible to still be able to identify Mr. Berghoff, she was causing quite a commotion all the way up the line. When she finally located him, she kept their conversation brief. Like all the men, he was bare chested and looked hot and sweaty, but he was pleased to accept her invitation to meet around eight o'clock in Eagle Rock. At last, Catherine could turn Marie west and ride farther west and away from the tracks at a canter again. It didn't take long for the disturbing construction sounds to be drowned out by the sound of the wind in her ears. She decided to let Marie choose her own pace.

After a moment of hesitation, Marie bolted forward into a full gallop. Catherine leaned forward into the wind, taking care to avoid Marie's mane whipping in front of her face, and let the horse go as fast as she wished. She lifted herself partially off the saddle and let her legs flex with the motion of the horse, keeping her body bent and steady as they raced across the sage-covered desert. This was the free, abandoned type of riding she had occasionally done in Illinois as a teenager with Spots, her own Appaloosa. Every once in a while, Todd, the stable hand her father insisted ride with her into the country, would let her race him, although her small Appaloosa was never this fast. It was also Todd who had taught Catherine how to groom and care for horses. The steady pounding of Marie's hooves, the horse's firm muscles flexing smoothly below her, and the wind in her face took her breath away. She felt more alive than she had since leaving Illinois.

When she noticed sweat forming on the horse's flanks, Catherine slowed Marie down to a walk. Catherine was hot, too. She knew her legs, arms, back, and butt would be sore tomorrow, but it had been worth it. It was wonderful to be able to ride again. Riding had brought back recollections of her childhood. Her life prior to her father's marriage to Janette was filled with pleasant memories.

As a child and young girl being raised by a single father with business interests in the region, Catherine went along on many trips. Initially, this meant riding in a carriage with her father. But, when she was older, he purchased Spots. Then they could ride together and make better time to communities less than a day's ride from Lexington, though she still rode in a buggy for the longer trips. These memories of her early life with her father had been fun, exciting, and comfortably secure. Her father's business provided a whole host of products he called dry goods to retail outlets in Kentucky, Illinois, and

Indiana. He bought and sold such farming supplies as settlers would need, including plows, nails, rope, barbed wire, shovels, oak barrels, tools, boots, clothing, and blankets, and just about anything else needed for a homestead or a wagon train.

His business had expanded rapidly, but the threat of a Civil War began to concern him. In 1858, he moved his primary business location north from Lexington to downtown Springfield, Illinois, with a storefront across from the new Capitol building. His store was located near the Lincoln Herndon law office where he had spent much time in the city prior to the move. While in Springfield, he had become a casual friend of Abraham Lincoln prior to Lincoln's election as the sixteenth president. This contact put him in a position to gain a Federal contract to supply the Union Army when the war broke out in 1861.

A sudden change in Marie's pace interrupted Catherine's reminiscing. Marie was limping! Catherine stopped the horse, jumped out of her saddle, and checked her legs and hooves.

"Oh Lord!" she exclaimed as she looked at Marie's left rear hoof. "You've thrown a shoe! You poor girl. How did that happen?" She wished she had stayed near the river where they could stop for a drink. Next time, she would be more prepared. She patted the horse's neck. "I'm sorry, girl. I wasn't thinking. We need to get you a drink and back to the stable."

Holding Marie's reins, she walked her back along the trail she had left in the sagebrush, but after several hundred feet, there still was no sign of the thrown shoe. Catherine muttered to herself, "I won't even be able to give it back to Mr. Smith. Now, we are just going to have to walk back to Eagle Rock. I can't continue to ride you like this."

She checked the angle of the sun. It was already early evening, later than she had expected to be riding, and now she had a long walk back to Eagle Rock. She could probably keep to the trail she had just made, but that would lead her back to the railroad construction site, considerably north of Taylor's Bridge. If she walked in a slightly southeast direction, she should come out much closer to Eagle Rock, avoid the stares of the railroad workers, and possibly get back before dark. The worst that could happen was that she would arrive at the banks of the Snake River before intercepting the railroad. Then she would just have to head north along the river to get to Taylor's Bridge.

She leaned up to give Marie a reassuring hug. "I'm sorry for not noticing your shoe earlier. It's my fault you're limping. And Shorty is probably going to be hopping mad. I will be lucky to get to ride you again."

Disappointed at how the day was ending and resigned to a long walk back, Catherine turned, struck a course on a slight angle to the south from their path, and started walking Marie back toward Eagle Rock.

Or so she thought.

Chapter Forty-one

Tuesday, 8:00 PM, July 29ᵗʰ, 1879

Rather than go home after making the bread dough for the next day, Jay told his mother he was going to stay in town to meet with Catherine, Fannie, and Mr. Berghoff. He was looking forward to sharing the information he and Mr. Berghoff had discussed about a new way to make beer that might boost their beer sales.

He spent the afternoon wandering around Eagle Rock and stopped by the stable several times to see if Catherine had returned. It was now seven. The sun was getting low in the sky and she had yet to return. Shorty hadn't seemed concerned, but Jay was growing anxious.

"The horse I gave her to ride, Miss Marie, is perfectly safe and knows her way around town," said Shorty. "She'll come back sooner or later."

Jay exclaimed, "But she rode out to the railroad construction crew."

With that, Shorty did show some concern. "You know, she probably just got interested in seeing all of them men working and just lost track of time. The railmen will be glad to escort her back into town when they're done working. Don't you worry, Slink. All she has to do is follow the railroad tracks back to Eagle Rock. How about I stay here and wait for her, and you go on back to the saloon and wait there?"

When Mr. Berghoff entered the saloon at eight and explained to Jay that he had met with Mrs. Callaway late in the afternoon and she had then headed west, both Jay and Fannie became concerned enough to inform Henry and Shorty. Henry was also alarmed and suggested Mr. Berghoff stay at the saloon while he went to see Shorty. It would be dark soon and it might be necessary to send out a search party.

Fannie was very upset. "She doesn't know the first thing about riding in the desert. She should have told me she was going out. I would have boxed her ears off before I would have let her go out there alone. Why would Shorty let her do that? I want to go with you so I can tell Shorty myself."

Henry and Berghoff looked a little surprised at Fannie's outburst. After a moment, Henry nodded to Fannie. "Of course you can come but I don't think this is the best time to blame Shorty. He may not even have known where she was headed."

Fannie wasn't convinced but agreed to not be too harsh with Shorty.

As Henry and Fannie were about to leave the saloon, she turned and looked back at Berghoff. with a flirtatious smile. "I'll be right back. You and I have plenty to talk about. I still want to hear all about this new beer-making process Jay is all wound up about. Dixie will fix you up with whiskey while you wait." She had been frustrated that Catherine had been delaying this meeting for several days now and she was convinced that this new beer-making idea was important. Actually, she had more than just the beer making on her mind. Carl had been noticeably absent lately and Fannie was missing their increasingly infrequent trysts in his cabin. She found Berghoff very interesting.

By eight forty-five, Henry, Robert Anderson, Mr. Berghoff, Shorty, Sandy, Fannie, and Jay were gathered around a table in the saloon organizing a search party. Several of Anderson's staff and many of the men who had been gathering to drink at the saloon all agreed to help.

"I don't expect any help from the deputies," Anderson began, "and the sheriff is still riding around the countryside looking for those two scoundrels who started the fire. It will just be us. I believe we should divide up into three groups. We will cross Taylor Bridge and head west, one group from Taylor Bridge, one group heading west from the railroad construction site, and the other heading west from farther south. Anything could have happened. She could be lost, hurt, or worse. And it's getting cold. This country isn't anything like riding in the green hills of Kentucky. There are pockets of exposed lava rock with dangerous crevices. Slipping into one of them could break a horse's leg. For all we know, her horse may have already stepped in one and she's out there pinned under her horse right now. And the Snake is treacherous in places and cannot be crossed except over Taylor's Bridge. We need to find her soon. At least we have some moonlight tonight. That'll help."

As everyone started teaming up, Mr. Anderson took Shorty aside. "Shorty, we'll need you to stay at the stable in case she does get past us. But first go over to Luther's ranch and see if you can get some of his leftover fireworks from the Fourth. Have him shoot them off as a signal if she returns, so the search parties will know to head back in."

Shorty was looking sick. Shaking his head he said, "I never should have let her ride. I just had no idea she was going to ride out of town." He turned to leave the saloon still shaking his head and mumbling to himself.

Across the river, Sheriff Zane rode into Luther's ranch leading two horses with bodies draped over the saddles. He went directly to the barn and left all three horses and the dead bodies there before banging on Luther's back door. When Luther opened the door, his first comment was, "I thought I told you to not come back for a week."

A haggard Zane stared back at Luther and said, "I caught'em. Ya gonna lemmee in?"

Chapter Forty-two

Tuesday, 8:00 PM, July 28th, 1879

After what had to be no more than a mile cross country back to the river and Eagle Rock, discomfort and the beginning of a nagging fear began to fill Catherine's thoughts. Her feet were developing blisters in her new boots. She had purchased them just before leaving Ogden and hadn't broken them in yet. Her riding pants were torn and covered with dust from walking through the sagebrush, and the muscles in her hips and legs, unaccustomed to riding, were burning. She had been startled twice by what she had thought might be rattlesnakes. She had heard bands of coyotes howling and chasing both far and near. The sun was considerably lower in the sky but still hot. She was quite upset that it had not occurred to her to bring water for her or Marie. All she could think of was what a foolish mistake it had been to ride out here alone. She really knew very little about the West. Her rides in the country in Kentucky and Illinois had been through farmland dotted with numerous homes and barns. This was hot, wild, untamed land. Although she tried not to think about it, she realized she might even run across Indians, *perish the thought!*

To take her mind off these frightening concerns and try to approach her present problems in a more constructive fashion, she considered what Henry would do in this situation. She really wished she had asked him to ride with her. He would know what to do. But worrying about what Henry might do was not calming her down. She was still overwhelmed by the proposal Rebecca and Henry had offered. However, having Henry in the café much more each day would be wonderful. She really should have talked with him before setting out by herself on her first horseback ride. He most likely would have talked her out of it and she wouldn't be in this predicament.

A blush began to form on Catherine's face as she thought about some of the dreams she'd had about him in the last few weeks. She had almost invited him upstairs on two occasions. Of course, that was totally inappropriate, but she couldn't explain the strong attraction she had for Henry. Ever since her terrible experience with Thomas Chambers in Louisville, her interest in men did not include a strong desire to sleep with them. Of course, she'd had to sleep with Patrick. He was her husband, but his brief efforts only brought pleasure for himself and didn't amount to a very good experience for her. The way Fannie talked, it seemed liked she found being in bed with a man quite delightful, no matter who it was. And from overhearing Mr. Lightworth's "lovely ladies" from the brothel over breakfast, they were simply amused by the bizarre adventures they had in bed with strangers. Who would want to do those things with a stranger? Yet, Catherine had found herself imagining entertaining some of those activities with Henry in her dream world! What kind of Christian women would have those thoughts?

But right now, just being held by Henry and letting him figure out how to get back to Eagle Rock would be wonderful. Assuming she actually made it back, she would immediately tell both Henry and Rebecca she wanted to start the addition as soon as possible. And she would accept Henry's offer to sleep in the saloon during the construction. Maybe she actually could get him to come upstairs. She would ask Fannie for help on that. Fannie would know what to do.

Her daydreaming was halted by the realization that the landscape they were walking through had changed. Large, black, weathered rocks jutted out from underneath the sage and scrub and Marie was limping more noticeably. She stopped the horse and squatted down to look closely at the ground, realizing these were the same rocks that were exposed around the river. They must be getting close. She stood up and looked ahead but saw no evidence that they were anywhere near Snake River. She also noticed that her shadow stretched out far ahead of her to the southeast. She turned to look back west and saw that the sun was getting close to the horizon now. It was getting late. How far had they run when she had let Marie gallop free?

She looked down at the rocks again and remembered something Jake had shared with her about the difficulties of building the tracks west of the river.

Ages ago, the west side of the river was a huge lava bed, and although dirt and sand had drifted in to cover much of the lava, there were still isolated areas where the lava was exposed. That would explain the black color of these rocks and why Jake had said the railroad would occasionally reroute the tracks around these treacherous, nearly impenetrable lava beds. Several workers had come back to Eagle Rock with sprained or broken ankles from tripping over the crevices. What would she do if she broke an ankle out here? How would she ever get back? And what about Marie? She didn't want the horse to step into one of those crevices either. She would have to find a way around this area and that would only slow her down even more. At this rate she would never get back before dark and she really didn't want to be out in the wilderness at night.

She checked Marie's hoof with the missing horseshoe and found that it was now bleeding. "Oh, what have I done? We can't have this." Looking up, she noticed a small leather bag attached to the back of the saddle she hadn't noticed before. She unhooked the strap and opened it to find a few odds and ends that could be useful. There was a small, sweat-stained rag, probably for wiping down the horse, but wrapped inside was a match tin. Much to her relief, it held several dry matches. This meant that, if she had to, she could light a fire to keep warm and scare off predators. Mr. Smith must have put this together as a sort of emergency kit. She would learn from him how to be more prepared for any future rides—if he would even allow them. Too bad there wasn't a canteen, but of course, anyone with any experience would know to bring fresh water. She also found some twine and a little tinder in a snuff box. There was a second snuff box full of tobacco. It was all dried out so he probably hadn't used this for quite some time but it could help to start a fire.

She tied the rag around Marie's bleeding hoof with the twine. As she was doing this, she heard the coyotes from the west again, but closer now. Whatever they were chasing, they sounded as though they were heading her way. She would have to pick up the pace. If she couldn't make it back to Eagle Rock, she would have to at least find the river before dark. She walked Marie away from the lava rock and turned north. Fortunately, she found a clearer path to the east not far from where she had stopped to put Marie's bandage on, so she headed east again in hopes of reaching the river.

As they were walking, she took more time to examine her surroundings. There was plenty of dry tumbleweed that could be used to start a fire, but she really needed bigger branches to keep it going. She had noticed that the riverbank around Eagle Rock was strewn with dead trees and branches that had been washed up during high water and gotten tangled in the rocks at the river's edge. If she could just get to the river soon.

Another hour later, the sun had disappeared behind the distant mountains and it was getting hard for her to see the lava when she finally heard the sound of rushing water. She guided Marie along a little more vigorously and minutes later came to a high bank above the Snake River. There was no sign of Eagle Rock and they hadn't encountered the railroad tracks, so she had gone too far south. Eagle Rock would be north of her now, but how far? The coyotes were much closer. She peered through the twilight up and down the river and noticed what seemed to be a low spot where the bank was eroded at a sharp bend not far north. Leading Marie that way she was pleased to find that a sandbar had formed on the riverbank and a large pile of wood had been caught in the rocks nearby. If she could start a fire on that sandbar with the river protecting her back, she should be able to keep any predators at bay for at least the night. She would worry about tomorrow later.

Once she found a way to get off the high bank onto the sandbar, Marie led them both to the water's edge. Catherine stepped out on a low rock in the river and scooped up water with her hands and they both drank greedily. Catherine finished by scooping up more water and splashing her face and the back of her neck. Once she knew Marie had had enough, she led the horse to a large pile of brush and tree limbs washed up on the sandbar and tied Marie to the largest she could find. With Marie secured, Catherine went back up on the bank and started gathering tumbleweeds for a fire. She also attempted to gather loose branches on the sandbar but was discouraged because although dry, most were too large to move. She didn't even have a knife. Another item for the kit she would make before she went out for another ride.

The sandbar was just above the current river level and surrounded by a rock ledge that protected it from the constant west wind. It had been a struggle to find a path down, but it made it easier to start a fire. She used only a small portion of the kindling in the snuff tin to get the fire started and was able to keep it going by putting more and more tumbleweed on. She also interspersed this with smaller branches she could break off the branch pile. Fortunately, she had a lot of experience in starting cooking fires from her time on the wagon train heading up to Eagle Rock. As her supply of wood started dwindling, she ran back up onto the riverbank and brought more tumbleweed and twigs down to her fire.

It was on one of Catherine's trips up onto the bank that Marie started acting up, snorting and pulling on the reins tied to the large tree branch in the sand.

"It's all right girl. You're all right." When Marie kept struggling to get free, Catherine looked around and saw several sets of yellow eyes watching her. The coyote band was stealthily closing in and had nearly surrounded her on the bank!

She leaped through an opening in the pack, jumped off the bank onto the sandbar and ran to Marie, leading her as close to the fire as the horse was willing to go. While stroking Marie's mane to try to calm her, she wondered what she was going to do now.

Chapter Forty-three

Tuesday, 9:00 PM, July 29th, 1879

Once the three groups had crossed the Snake River at Taylor's Bridge, Anderson gave a few last instructions. "I want the three search parties to stay in sight of each other's torches. That's going to limit the area we can cover, but if we spread out so everyone can see at least the torch from the man north and south of him, we can cover the most ground knowing we have looked as thoroughly as we can. If Catherine has been injured we may miss her, but we won't miss her horse and can assume the two are together. I don't know of any way we can do better on a night search. If we're unsuccessful, we will have to go out again in the morning."

He paused at the sound of distant barking to the north. "Sounds like a coyote band has found something near the railroad construction site. They likely won't approach our torches. We will head directly up to the construction site. All right men. My group— let's head north and hope we can pick up her trail in the sage. Henry, you, Jake, and Dick Chamberlain head south. Be careful of the lava rock. You may have to go a little west of the river to get around some of the large patches. John, you take your team and spread out right here in sight of each other's torches and head west. We will have nine men with torches spread out from north to south, all within sight of at least two others except for the two men on the ends. If anyone finds her, shoot off your rifle twice to alert the rest of us and wave your torch until you get an answering rifle shot and torch wave from the next man down the search line. Each of us on either side of you can signal the next man so we won't spend the entire remainder of the night wandering around in the dark after she has been found. Everybody ready?"

Jake leaned in his saddle toward Henry and spoke quietly. "I don't think we have much of a chance of finding her heading south. Why would she be coming back south of Taylor's Bridge?"

"She could be anywhere, Jake," Henry replied. "I doubt we will find her this close to the river, but we need to scan the whole area. I wondered about Anderson's plan at first but it actually makes sense. I suspect he has done this before. You're right, though. She probably realized it was getting late and followed her own trail back to the construction camp. If that's the case, Anderson's team will find her. As for us, we'll be the slowest team. I am concerned about the exposed lava beds. They are nearly impossible to see at night, so pay close attention to where you're leading your horse. I've not been around enough horses to trust their night vision. Dick, why don't you head west next, as soon as you feel you have traveled as far south as you can and still see the next torch rider north of us. Jake, you head west after Chamberlain and I will take the farthest southern route west. We can only hope she hasn't gotten so lost that she's even farther to the south."

They rode for a while and Dick Chamberlain left them to start searching west along a line parallel to John Anderson's southernmost rider. About the time Jake was going to start his search to the west, Henry stopped him. He motioned to Jake to remain quiet as he listened to the sounds in the night wind until he finally shook his head. "I must be hearing things. Don't mind me. It must be just the wind. You know, I'm really irritated that Catherine would ride off like this and not tell anyone. She's really just a city girl and doesn't truly understand how dangerous the high desert can be."

He peered ahead into the night. "I think I see a ridge up ahead of us. With this moon rising, we will be able to see farther from there, so let's split up once we get up top. If you were to head west on this side of the ridge, I would never be able to see you once I pass over it."

As they were nearing the top of the ridge, Henry stopped them again. This time there were definitely more sounds than just the wind.

"That's what I heard earlier! That's a band of hunting coyotes south of us over this ridge. That can't be the same pack we heard after we crossed the bridge. They have found something. I hope it's not Catherine!"

With that, both men spurred their horses to gain a better vantage point from the top of the ridge. Once there, they could see a small fire and hear the eerie clamor of the barking coyotes.

"They've cornered something!" Jake exclaimed as a figure brandishing a torch stepped into the light of the fire, holding onto the reins of a horse.

"Catherine!" Henry roared and, without any hesitation, spurred his horse off the ridge and down the slope toward fire. He fired his rifle in the air several times in hopes of scaring the coyotes away, but they didn't move.

"Careful, Henry," Jake yelled, following at a more cautious pace. "I see lava rock between you and the fire."

But Henry wasn't listening. He headed straight for the coyote pack and was now near enough to start firing at them. He was able to kill one and the rest of the band scattered.

Catherine screamed, "Help! Over here!"

Henry rode his horse to the ledge above the sandbar. "Catherine! Are you all right?"

"Oh my God! It's you Henry. Thank you! How did you find me?"

Henry turned to look back up the slope toward Jake. "What on earth is taking him so long?" he mumbled under his breath. Then he yelled at Jake. "Chase the last of those buggers away, Jake, and signal the rest of the teams. You will have to go back up on the ridge for them to see you."

After looking over the ledge at the drop to the sandbar below, Henry dismounted and carefully led his horse down to the level of the fire on the sandbar.

Catherine dropped Marie's reins and ran to him, wrapping her arms around his shoulders and sobbing. "I didn't know what to do! I was so scared!"

Henry patted her back gently. "I don't know how you got this far south, but you did the right thing. You used the river to protect your back and built a fire. Without a gun, you couldn't have done much more." He gently pushed her back enough so he could look directly into her sooty, tear-stained face. "You did really well for a city girl. Of course, you shouldn't be out here in the first place. What on earth were you thinking?"

Catherine was still sobbing. "I know. I know. I wasn't thinking. I'll never do this again." When she was able to stop crying, she looked up at Henry and added, "At least not alone."

Henry laughed. "You certainly are a stubborn young lady. You still want to come out here again?"

They heard more gunshots from the ridge and Henry let her know that Jake was signaling the rest of the search party. Catherine looked alarmed and drew back from Henry, realizing she still had him in a bear hug and both of their bodies were responding to the close contact.

"The rest of them? You meant there are more of them beside you and Jake?"

"The whole town is in an uproar over your disappearance, Catherine. Do you think that just two men could find you out here at night? Nine men volunteered to come out tonight and another party is being organized to come out tomorrow if we don't find you."

Henry turned her around to face west and pointed into the darkness. "The high desert is not very kind to single, unarmed, lost women, as surely as you have found out by now. You and I will have to sit down once you have recovered so we can reach an agreement on your future wandering behavior. But first, let's mount up and get you back to safety. You're shaking. That outfit you're wearing may be good for daytime riding, but you don't have on enough to protect you from a cold desert night." He took of his jacket and wrapped it around her shoulders.

"Thank you Henry."

As she went over to pat her horse's neck, Henry noticed the snug slacks and tiny waist that showed off her hips and the fitted blouse starting to come out of her waistband. Even torn and full of soot, the outfit on her was quite attractive. Rather provocative, actually. Up until now, he had only seen her in long skirts and aprons. After a lingering appraisal of her in her riding garb, he turned his attention to Marie and noticed the bloody rag tied to her rear hoof.

He pointed to the horse. "What happened? How did you get so far from town on an injured horse?"

"She threw a shoe somewhere west of the railroad construction site. I've been walking ever since. I can't ride her until we get her ankle properly wrapped."

"The construction site? But that has to be at least a couple of miles north of here. How did you end up down here? You could have just followed the tracks back."

Catherine came over to Henry, took ahold of his shoulders, looked directly at him and said calmly, "We can discuss this later, Henry. Right now we have to get all those men back to Eagle Rock and I need to make sure Marie is not seriously hurt. How do we get back?"

"All right. I can see that Jake is on his way back down here right now. You can ride with me. It won't be very comfortable but it will be better than walking all the way back to Eagle Rock. Jake can lead Marie."

He frowned as he looked at the odd route Jake was taking off the ridge. "I don't know why Jake is taking such a roundabout way to get down here."

"Henry, Jake is riding around the outcroppings of lava. You were the one who warned me about the lava rock. I don't understand how you got off that ridge and down to me without breaking your horse's leg and ending up falling yourself. That was dangerous." She gave him a knowing smile. "You and I will just have to sit down and reach an agreement about safe and responsible horseback riding." Then, looking more sober, she continued, "It's a miracle you came when you did. I don't think I could have kept those nasty coyotes away much longer."

Henry put his arm around Cat's waist and they turned, waiting for Jake to cautiously reach them at the now smoldering fire on the sandbar at the edge of the lava bed.

Chapter Forty-four

Tuesday, 10:30 PM, July 29th, 1879

While Henry and Catherine waited for Jake, Henry climbed onto the bank to survey the surrounding ground where the coyotes had been. Holding his torch high, he saw why Jake was taking such a wide route instead of coming directly down to them. Large, exposed lava rocks littered the path he had taken in his mad gallop down from the ridge. He called to Catherine to lead both horses back up onto the bank where they could meet Jake, who had finally picked up his pace. Shaking his head, he admitted, "I don't know how my horse got me down that slope. Either we were just damned lucky or that horse has much better night vision than I do. I had no idea I was galloping through a lava field, although I admit it was a rough ride down. I thought my horse was trying to buck me off, but I guess he was dodging the rocks. I was just focusing on those coyotes and you waving that tiny torch to try to chase them off."

When she was up on the bank with him, he put his arm around her waist again and hugged her close to him. "All I was thinking of was getting to you before the coyotes did."

Catherine smiled up at him. "Well you did, and I'm glad you did. I was terrified." She rested her head on his shoulder. "I'm really tired. This started out as such a wonderful day and ended so badly. I'm sorry Henry."

Jake joined them a few minutes later. "How in the hell did you get down here so quick, Henry? Glad to see you Mrs. Callaway. Let's get you back to civilization." He looked at Henry. "Why didn't you two just ride up to meet me?"

"Mrs. Callaway's horse is lame. She threw a shoe so they were walking back to Eagle Rock when the coyotes closed in."

"Oh my God! I'm sure you can't get home too soon, Mrs. Callaway. Henry, what do you want to do about the horse?"

"Jake, I'd like you to take the reins of her horse and lead her back to Eagle Rock. Mrs. Callaway is going to ride with me. We'll take it slow. With all the shots I fired at the coyotes, the search party is probably already heading back to town. I know Catherine would like to take Marie back to Shorty, but I feel she should go directly back to the saloon. Catherine, are you all right with that?"

"I have to see Mr. Smith. Please take me there, Henry."

"I'm sure there will be no talking you out of it. Jake, will you give her a leg up? She can ride behind me and we'll head back to the stable with you and Marie. I'll see that she gets home from there. Then I think we should all meet for breakfast and talk about how everyone else fared."

Once Catherine was settled, Jake led Marie slightly ahead and Catherine leaned forward against Henry's back. She moved her hands from his waist, wrapped them around his chest, and spoke softly. "Thank you for saving me. You have always been so kind to me. I'm sorry you had to come out here this late at night to find me, but I'm glad it was you rather than somebody else. I am so embarrassed to have caused so much trouble for everyone."

Henry put one of his hands over hers and squeezed. "Mind you, young lady. I'm going to have to keep an eye on you. What caused you to think you could ride out into the desert alone?"

So Catherine told him how one thing had led to another, the need to speak to Mr. Berghoff, the lewd workmen, the wonderful feeling of riding all out, the thrown shoe, and the terrifying night at the river—all while she was supposed to be meeting with Mr. Berghoff. "Oh!" Cat sat straight up with a start. "Mr. Berghoff! And Jay! And Fannie! They'll be so upset."

"You don't have to worry about Berghoff. He volunteered to be a part of the search party that went up north. And Fannie and Jay are worried sick about you."

"Oh my. I will apologize to them when we get back. And to Mr. Smith. Marie is really a wonderful horse. I hope he will let me ride her again, and I hope she'll trust me the next time."

"But how did you end up so far south? Surely you could have followed your own trail back."

"Well, it may seem silly of me, but that would have led me right back to all those men. I knew it was late and since we would have to walk, I figured I could make better time if I headed back a little south and end up at Taylor's Bridge without encountering the workers. I wanted to get back before dark."

She sighed. "Of course, I must have headed a little too far south. And when I heard the coyotes behind me in the distance, I decided to build a fire as soon as I got to the river and walk the rest of the way home tomorrow. I had no idea anyone would come looking for me."

Henry was silent for a while and then asked, "You still want to ride again, even after this experience? Do you really think that's a good idea?"

"Henry. I love to ride. I have been riding since I was a young girl. I truly feel like my old self when I ride, really, like no other time. And today was the most amazing of all, before I got lost, that is. It was the first time I'd ever ridden alone without a guide or teacher, or even the stable master from home, who I think was probably a little sweet on me, if I can say that without sounding arrogant. Tired as I am, I honestly can't wait to go again. But I will plan better next time."

"Yes, you will. And shouldn't we find you a riding companion, really? Maybe another stable master?" Henry chuckled. "I'm not sure I want anyone else to be sweet on you, Catherine, but I'm not surprised."

Catherine's blush got even deeper. After a moment she replied, "I like it when you call me Catherine, but you could call me Cat as well. Back east, my best friends always called me Cat, and I think you definitely qualify as a best friend. I might consider going riding with you, Henry." She gave him a hug and laid her head on his back again.

They had finally gotten around the lava field and were going downhill again. By this time, Jake was well ahead of them. They rode in a comfortable silence for a while, each thinking about what the other had said.

Henry broke the silence. "Yes. If you want to go riding again anywhere outside of Eagle Rock, I want to go with you. This is not the tame countryside of Illinois or Kentucky."

"Well, that is very thoughtful, but I don't want to keep you from your work."

"I have been working too hard and I need a break. I'm not a natural horseback rider like you and you could probably improve my skills." After a pause he added in a low, tender voice, "And I can't imagine anything better than spending more time with you."

Catherine's breath caught in her throat. She swallowed and after a moment answered, "And I would love to spend more time with you Henry. Forgive me for being so forward, but I've been a little lonely. Patrick was not a comfortable man to be around. I shouldn't be telling you this, I know, but I've been too busy to miss him much, except at night when I'm all alone above the saloon. And then only because I know he knew how to use a gun and he was very keen on protecting the money box under the bed. I always figured if I stayed near the money box, he would protect me, too."

They were both quiet.

"I guess I'm saying too much. I'm just very tired and need to get home."

It took a few moments for Henry to respond. "Catherine, I knew Patrick treated you poorly on the wagon trail. And I don't believe he had gotten any better once the two of you arrived at Eagle Rock. It's not my place to say anything, but I always thought you deserved better. I'd like to think I can offer you the loyalty and protection you hoped for from Patrick and I would be pleased to spend more time with you when you think that it is appropriate. I don't want to rush you, being a new widow and all, but things happen much more rapidly out here in the west. Partly just to survive. Two people of like minds are better than one when you are up against a hard country. I know you are tired so we should discuss this further when you are rested."

Catherine's mind was reeling from the implications of what this conversation might mean. She wanted to burst out, asking him to explain what he meant, but she decided to let him take the lead in his own time. Then the café addition came to mind.

"Henry, there's something else. I want to start the café addition as soon as possible. Your ideas are wonderful. Will you really build me a cafe? How soon can you start?"

Henry was taken by surprise by the sudden change of topic and burst out laughing.

Catherine was instantly contrite. "I'm sorry. I know you have many projects you're working on. That was rude of me. Whenever you can start will be just fine."

Henry was still laughing, but it was more of a chuckle. "No, you surprised me is all. I'm glad you're enthusiastic about it. I can start ordering materials tomorrow."

"But I already have all the materials stored behind the saloon."

"You have the lumber, but it takes quite a bit more to build a building. I think I have some of the supplies we'll need in a warehouse for another project.

If you'd like, after I place an order for replacement supplies, I can have my men come over tomorrow afternoon to start preparations for the foundation."

"Well, I won't insist, but I won't say 'no' either," she said with a smile. "I'm sure Rebecca believes it is important to start as soon as possible. And I certainly would be pleased as well. I won't ever object to having you nearby more often."

Henry reached back and pulled her waist tight up against his in the most reassuring hug he could accomplish while riding horseback.

"I guarantee I will be there every day, and I might want to drop in on you every evening to give you a status report and make sure you are pleased with the progress."

"That would be just wonderful, Henry." They were long past the lava rock field, but Catherine continued to hold him tightly.

Chapter Forty-five

Wednesday, 12:30 AM, July 30th

Catherine was relieved that no one had waited for them at Taylor's Bridge, but her relief was short lived when they arrived on Railroad Avenue and she saw the crowd in front of the saloon. They had stopped at Shorty Smith's stable, but he was not there and Henry had suggested he was probably at her saloon. "Oh dear!" she moaned. "It looks like the whole town has turned out. I'm never going to get to bed."

"We'll just tell everyone you'll bring everybody up to date in the morning, Catherine," replied Henry, in his calm, controlled manner. But they quickly found out it wasn't going to be that easy. Once they pushed through the crowd and entered the saloon, they found what appeared to be the rest of the town waiting for them inside.

Luther Armstrong and Sheriff Zane were the first to speak. "I'm so glad they found you, Mrs. Callaway," Luther began. "You have to be careful heading out into the desert like that. We had already organized another search party to look for you if the first team was not successful. Sheriff Zane has agreed to lead it but I am pleased that won't be necessary."

Fannie was behind the bar shaking her head in dismay. Catherine was going to tell everyone she was grateful for their concern and efforts but exhausted, and that she would see everyone in the morning, but Luther pressed on.

"We gathered here to welcome you home. Jake has filled us in on the ordeal you have endured and we won't keep you up any longer than necessary, but I have news I think will allow you to sleep much better tonight. I'll let the sheriff give you the news."

Zane sauntered forward, eager to take center stage with all of the townsfolk looking on. He was looking just about as cocky as he always did when he got to brag about himself. "Just as I was tellin all these folks, here, I found the treacherous bastards that tried to start the fire here at your saloon. Those cowards tried to frame poor ole Smiley, but they won't be botherin you any more, Mrs. Callaway. I caught'em braggin about what they done to your saloon down south and I tied'em up and was bringin'em back to justice when they tried to escape. They shuddna done that. I hollered at them to stop but they kept on runnin so they're dead now. No one escapes justice with Sheriff Zane around. I tied them to their horses and brung'em back ta ya, so you'd know ya safe now. If ya want, I can even show them to ya." He ended his short speech with a leer, seeming to dare Catherine to take a look at the dead men.

This was one shock to the system too many for Catherine. She was too upset to respond, so Henry stepped in for her. "I am sure Mrs. Callaway is very grateful for your efforts, Zane, I'm sure we all are. But she has been through quite an ordeal and she is exhausted. Let us respect her need to clean up and get some well-deserved sleep. She has offered to answer any questions you may have at breakfast tomorrow, and, of course, learn more of the men you apprehended."

By this time, Catherine was able to get her thoughts together. "Thank you all so much. I'm sorry to have caused so much trouble today, and I promise I've learned my lesson. I'm grateful for all of you. Breakfast is on the house tomorrow morning from seven until nine. I am sure I will be in much better shape by then. I really appreciate what everyone here has done for me tonight. You can be assured, I won't do that again."

Ellington started a slow clap and the rest of the crowd joined in. In the midst of the applause, Catherine's eyes started to tear. She went over to Fannie and asked her to come upstairs with her to help her clean up. With a smile and a wave to the people gathered in the saloon, she went into the kitchen and with Fannie right behind her, gingerly climbed the ladder up to her room, opening some of the larger scratches on her arms and hands.

Once upstairs, she quietly told Fannie, "You don't have to help me with these scratches. They're not very deep, but I saw what looked like you signaling me from the bar. Is there something you want to tell me?"

"I certainly will help you! You have blood all over yourself and it looks like some has already scabbed over. You are going to have a hell of a time getting out of those clothes and will probably open up all of those scabs again. What were you thinking riding off like that? What if you had run into Indians, or even the trigger-happy Sheriff Zane out there? You really put yourself in danger."

Catherine sat down heavily on her bed. "I know it was foolish, but I just don't have enough of my wits about me to explain right now. Let's just get these pants off." She tugged on one leg and grimaced. "Ouch, I guess you're right. I already have some large bruises."

Once Catherine had gotten cleaned up and into her nightgown, Fannie said, "I did come up here to talk to you. That smarmy Mr. Armstrong and his sidekick Zane were over here not long after the search party left. Of course, he wanted to see you to inform you of the grand thing they had accomplished, as if those dead bodies really prove anything. They said they would return as soon as you were found because they wanted to tell you face to face that this was all settled."

"Well, that's a relief," Catherine responded.

"Not so fast, Cat," Fannie continued, "I thought it sounded pretty fishy, so as soon as Anderson and John came in from the search, I told them what Luther and Zane had said. They didn't like the sound of it either, so they went over to Armstrong's ranch to find out more. Even Ellington went with them. They got back here just a few minutes before you arrived and wanted to talk to me privately. John is convinced that at least one of the dead men doesn't match the description of the men he saw start that fire. Mr. Anderson believes Zane just found some poor sods no one would miss, shot them, and brought them back so we would stop investigating this matter. That means someone out there may still want to burn your building down."

Catherine was speechless and clearly frightened.

"Now you get ahold of yourself. I know you have had a tough day, but this is a whole different matter. Don't worry, the whole town is behind you. We're going to get through this, but I'm staying here tonight so you can get some sleep. You might want to ask Henry to start spending nights here again. Anderson and John said they will be looking out for you as well. Even Ellington said he would help in any way he could. He seems like a pretty fine man to me and..." she paused, her serious side giving way to her suggestive style, as usual with a lusty look, "really good looking. You really ought to pay more attention to him. I just might myself." Both the women smiled and returned to the task of getting Cat comfortably settled into bed.

By this time the downstairs had finally quieted down, so the rest of the crowd must have left.

"Well darlin," Fannie said to Catherine, almost motherly now, "I do recall it only takes one long shot of good whiskey to put you down for the night. I brought one up earlier and you're going to drink it now. I'll stay up here with you until you fall asleep and then I'll go downstairs and keep a watch on the place. Sandy said she would come back about four and spell me. I'll see you in the morning. I'm so glad you're back, a little worse for wear, but safe."

Catherine finished her drink, closed her eyes, and fell asleep the moment her head touched the pillow.

Chapter Forty-six

Wednesday, 6:00 AM, July 30th, 1879

Ellington began an early morning with a cup of coffee in his office. Around seven o'clock, he planned to join the rest of the town for the free breakfast and search party recap at Patrick's. Until then, he wanted to have a brief conversation with Bob Anderson and John, who were just walking through the door. He hoped the three of them could make sense of Zane's performance in the saloon last night. The sheriff's claims regarding the arrest and subsequent death of the two supposed arsonists was most confusing, but he had received some information earlier in the evening that might help clear up some details. Being in the news business, even being in the rumor business, often created useful connections for Ellington.

In fact, rumors around town regarding Zane's absence and return just before the search party's return had stirred Ellington's curiosity last evening. He sent a telegraph message to Fort Hall on the subject before going over to the saloon to meet the returning search party, receiving word back almost immediately. He'd asked Anderson and John to meet him this morning before they all left Patrick's Saloon early that morning.

Bob opened without preamble. "Well, I was certainly intrigued by your comments last night, er, uh, I guess that was more like this morning, when the crowd finally left Patrick's. The sooner we can figure out what Zane is up too, the better I will feel."

"What I tell you this morning, gentlemen, I trust you will keep to yourselves," Ellington started out, always happiest when he could create a little drama. "To be frank, I did something a little unethical yesterday evening. Of course I strive to keep all transmitted telegraphic information confidential, and I hope you will not think less of me for breaking that trust today, but I felt a compromise in this case was justified and hope it will help us better understand if there is something unsavory, even illegal, going on between Luther Armstrong and his sidekick, Zane Gunther."

Ellington looked to both men for an indication he should continue. Bob gave Ellington a nod and said, "I have always questioned the relationship between Luther and Zane. Zane has never seemed the right person for the job but Luther has always stalwartly backed him, regardless of his bizarre behavior. We will keep this between ourselves, so go on."

Ellington continued, "Three days ago, a telegraph arrived for Luther. Obviously, in order for me to deliver telegrams, I have to know who to deliver them to, and right below the name of the recipient was the name of the sender. I couldn't help notice the telegram was sent from Fort Henry and was from Territorial U.S. Marshall, Fred Thomas Dubois."

That got raised eyebrows from both Bob and John.

Ellington went on, "Well, being a reporter, I just couldn't help looking over the message to see what this might be about. Dubois was requesting an audience with Luther to discuss the rumors regarding the Clancy gang and possible train robbery plans as well as the fire in our town. He also wanted to talk with the acting sheriff. He explained that he would be arriving on the afternoon train today and would probably stay the night. This means he will arrive around three o'clock."

Bob was clearly interested. "It would be good if we could meet him before he meets with Luther and Zane. I think he would get a better idea of the many odd things that are happening here if we could talk to him before Luther got a hold of him and attempted to grease the wheels of justice—not that Dubois would necessarily be susceptible to Luther's smooth speeches. But we can't be too careful."

"Those were my thoughts exactly, Bob, so last night I telegraphed him a short note and casually asked if he would be in the area anytime soon. I told him I had heard he was in Fort Henry and hinted that, as the local newspaper man, I was aware of some odd things he might want to know about law enforcement up here. I didn't know if he would get the telegraph in time to catch the early train but he would at least know there might be problems in Eagle Rock."

Both other men nodded. "Good thinking and it sounds like you didn't let on that you had read his telegram. Too bad we couldn't have gotten that message to him earlier."

"It arrived early enough," Ellington continued. "Apparently, Mr. Dubois is an early riser, and I got a return telegram about a half hour ago asking me to meet him at the noon train and arrange some place where we could privately discuss any issues I thought might be appropriate."

Bob and John both chuckled at that. Bob turned to John and said, "You just can't take the city out of a city boy." he turned back to Ellington. "You're pretty smooth, Ellington, and that is exactly what we need right now. Nice work. We need to firm up our understanding of what I believe is a slew of half-truths Zane tried to feed us last night. You noticed didn't you, that every time Zane explained what happened, it came out a little different? And Luther seemed to be correcting him to make it sound like a more consistent and believable story."

John was getting worked up and entered the conversation for the first time. "One of the men holding the lantern that night was overweight with a huge pot belly and neither of the men Zane claimed admitted to starting the fire was overweight. I think he just killed them to make it look like he solved the case."

Bob agreed. "And when I asked him where he found these two men, he claimed it was a saloon in Blackfoot called The Drunken Rooster. Well, I've been to that mudhole of a town a number of times and I am confident there is no saloon with that name or anything like that name. When I questioned him further, he became flustered and started making up names, got upset with me questioning him, and then finally admitted he didn't really recall the name of the saloon, but that wasn't as important as the fact that he found the men. When I asked him to explain when they said they had started the fire, after several different explanations that didn't make sense, he finally settled on that he had been told by someone in a neighboring town they had bragged about it during a poker game. Of course, he didn't know the name of the man who conveyed this information to him.

We would have had one a hell of a time trying to convict these two men on the basis of Zane's story and he knew it. I think that is why he killed them. How could two men trussed up with rope the way Zane described get loose and run away with no evidence of rope burns anywhere on their wrists or ankles? John went out to the barn and carefully examined the bodies while you and I were firing questions at Zane and he saw no evidence of them being tied up. I think when you add in the information about who we think may have started those rumors about the Clancys, Mr. Dubois is going to have some very pointed questions for Sheriff Zane. He should also be wondering why Luther is so willing to back him through all of this."

Ellington was busily taking notes as the other two men were getting more worked up. Once he had finished, he looked up and stated, "Sorry. I feel if we get this written down, we should be able to present it more convincingly. I don't want to give this to Dubois in writing. He has to understand that Luther and Zane could make things very uncomfortable for us in Eagle Rock if either of them knew we were the ones providing this information. But by writing this all down, I can make sure we can provide a complete account of these events to Mr. Dubois."

Bob nodded gravely. "You're right. Luther Armstrong has a lot of power behind him and Zane is just crazy enough to do anything if cornered. Got any ideas about how we should do this?"

"I have already telegraphed Dubois back and informed him that I will meet him at the train and escort him to this office. If anyone notices, they will simply think that as the gossipy local newspaper man I have grabbed him for an interview. I think the two of you should meet about half an hour before-hand in your warehouse and use your back door to the alley to get to my print room's back door so no one will see you. It is the most private room I could come up with. If I lock the front door when I bring Dubois from the train, we should be able to talk with him privately and undisturbed. I can tell you I am really looking forward to this since I have had orders in the past from Luther to print some ridiculously phony articles about Luther's community minded efforts on the behalf of the citizens of Eagle Rock. I want to make sure Mr. Dubois isn't overly influenced by the propaganda I have had to print."

The three men were silent for a while. Then Anderson stood up. "We are doing the right thing. And you did the right thing reading Luther's telegram. Right now, we need to act on behalf of the town of Eagle Rock...and for Mrs. Callaway. I am worried for that young lady. It seems like someone is trying to run her out of town. I don't like the idea of anybody being bullied like that and I have to admit I don't want Eagle Rock to lose the best food in the area, either. I for one would surely miss those good meals we've been getting."

Thoughts of the morning's free breakfast shortly lightened the men's mood as they stood to leave. Ellington nodded that he agreed. He added, "I think we should include Henry in these discussions. He seems to have taken a keen interest in her and I think he would be willing to help us watch out for her."

"Well, someone ought to look out for her, especially after that crazy ride out into the desert." Bob shook his head but continued, "I'll bet we can catch him in the saloon at breakfast, but let's not say anything to Mrs. Callaway. At least not yet. There's no point in getting her any more riled up. Let's head over, shall we? To think, it took the young widow from Louisville, Kentucky, to introduce us to the best food in the area, made by an old Indian woman we thought was only good for washing clothes. If we can keep a lid on Luther and Zane, Eagle Rock may have a much brighter future than we ever imagined."

All three left for Patrick's, thinking of Crow Feather's hot corn muffins and pleased to have a plan.

Chapter Forty-seven

Wednesday, 6:00 PM, July 30th, 1879

"I'm sorry, Henry," Catherine was saying with a look of frustration on her face, "I just can't picture it. I will just have to take your word for it."

"That's all right, Catherine." Henry replied. They were looking at some drawn-to-scale, freehand sketches he had made of the proposed café addition for her approval. "Lots of people have difficulty visualizing floor plans and I haven't had the opportunity to draw the elevations, yet. Fortunately, with these, my foreman will know what to do."

Catherine put her hand on his holding the plans and smiled one of her warm, endearing smiles that seemed to put a spell on him. "And that's all I need, Henry. I trust your judgment just as I trust Crow Feather's cooking. I'm sure you know what is right for me."

"Let's go outside and I will try to help you visualize this," he said. "I think you'll find it easier to visualize if we look at the space where it will be built." He clasped her hand and led her out the back door. It felt so right to be walking holding hands with her, he temporarily forgot what he was going to say next. As they stood there, in the back doorway off the kitchen storeroom, looking at the ground behind the saloon that had just yesterday been stacked with lumber, Catherine exclaimed, "What are those boys doing?"

"I haven't told you how helpful Jay has been."

Catherine looked confused again. "Jay?"

"Yes, Jay. He approached me yesterday and asked if he could help with the construction."

Catherine looked shocked. "But no! I don't want to lose Jay. We need him in the café!"

Henry laughed. "Don't worry. He made it clear he could only help after three in the afternoon, and he would be glad to work in the evenings. As you well know from your evening adventure," Henry said with a teasing nod, "it doesn't really get dark this time of year until at least nine. Of course, initially, I had no idea how I could use him, but he kept asking. When he saw my men moving the lumber and how long it was taking, he came to me and said he had two friends who could help and the three of them could do all the heavy lifting while my men started the footings. Well, I want this project to move as fast as possible and Mrs. Mitchell has been asking me repeatedly when it would be finished. So I saw no harm in letting the boys haul the lumber to the lot next door while my men started laying out the perimeter of the addition. Didn't you notice them working behind the saloon this afternoon?"

Catherine smiled. "I was so tired at the end of lunch, I simply went to bed. I just got up about half an hour ago and went down to help Fannie until you came. But the lumber is gone. What are they doing now?"

"These young men have turned out to be real workers. They cleared the site much faster than I had anticipated and wanted to continue working. Except for my foreman, Simon, my regular workers left at five to be with their families. Simon realized these three Indians were eager to work and convinced me to hire them on for any odd jobs we might need. Right now they are digging the holes for the footings that I had anticipated wouldn't be started until tomorrow afternoon. We are already ahead of schedule."

By this time, the three young men had noticed Catherine. Jay gave her a big smile and waved, but promptly went back to digging.

Henry, self-conscious of holding Catherine's hand in public, let go and laid his plans down on the ground. "This drawing is in the same orientation as the new addition is going to be. I am going to walk to the four corners of your café, here, here, here, and here," he said pointing to the four corners of the drawing in counter-clockwise order.

He walked to the southwest corner of the existing saloon. "I am now standing at the northwest front corner of your café, the first corner I pointed out to you on the drawing labeled First Floor."

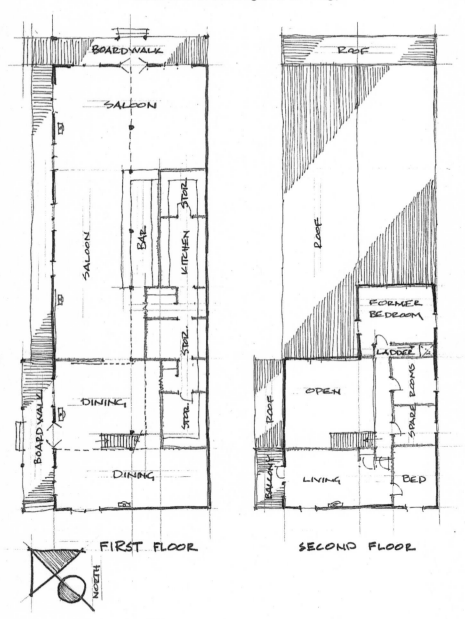

Henry Willet's floor plans of Patrick's Saloon and the café addition. The one-story portion of the building and the room identified as "Former Bedroom" in the right bottom corner of the second floor plan is the original building. The square, two-story addition is attached and immediately south of the saloon. This has a large dining area with Catherine's apartment upstairs, several extra rooms, and a grand stair to serve as the primary exit. The original ladder is still in the corner of the "Former Bedroom." Drawing by Ralls Melotte

He walked south and stood about thirty feet away near a hole one of the men was digging. "This will be the southwest corner of the front of your café."

Catherine's hands went to her face. "Oh my! It will be bigger than I had thought. Does it have to be that big?"

Henry was walking east to the next corner as he replied, "Things always look bigger at first. Not until you put in the chairs and tables will you really appreciate the actual size of the space. And remember, you thought it would be too small at first."

He had stopped walking at another hole that was being dug. "This will be the southeast corner of your café."

"It's so big!" was all Catherine could say.

"Not really. You need enough space on the first floor to seat the number of tables you requested. The café will be two stories tall but there will be an L-shaped second floor on the southeast and northeast side of the café. Look at the second drawing that's labeled Second Floor. On the southwest side, there will be a room that will be your living area with two windows, one facing southwest and one southeast. In the corner where I am standing now will be your bedroom with a window facing southeast."

Catherine said almost dreamily, "I told Patrick I wanted more windows. I just love this."

Henry had started walking back toward the southeast corner of the saloon. "About here, directly above me on the second floor, will be two small rooms that you can use as you see fit."

Catherine had a slight frown on her face over this.

"Do I really need more rooms? I only have a single room now and it suits me fine."

"I am building a balcony walkway from the top of the stairs that leads to the door to your new living area and to your present bedroom over the saloon so your old bedroom can be rented out if you wish. By tying the two additions together on the second floor, nobody will have to use the ladder except as an emergency exit, but you will have two ways out of the second floor."

"Oh, that's just wonderful, Henry, but can I really afford all of this?"

Henry was walking back to Catherine now. "With the arrangements that have been made with Mrs. Mitchell, the cost of the downstairs is covered. The second floor is an investment for your future. I suspect there will be a time when you really don't want to live directly above the saloon and café, and, with this arrangement, the second floor could be another source of income for you."

He had reached her and had a big smile on his face. He put his arm around her waist and turned her to look west at what would be the front of the new café. "We are also extending the covered boardwalk in front of the saloon down the southwest side of the saloon and across the front of the café so that if you continue to get even larger crowds waiting to enter, they won't have to stand in the dusty street. On top of this boardwalk will be an open balcony you can walk out onto from your living room to get a good look at the northern and western mountains and beautiful sunsets."

Catherine was silent for a few moments and then turned and lightly kissed Henry on the cheek. She was immediately embarrassed about how forward this must seem, but she was clearly moved by his plans. Henry's thoughtfulness for her stirred emotions she had not felt for some time.

Henry was knocked equally off balance by the kiss but did not make an effort to return it. There were at least three young men who were probably watching and he didn't want to embarrass Catherine any further right now. He took Catherine gently by both of her elbows and said to her quietly, "I hate to leave you at this moment since there are more things I want to tell you, but I have an appointment with several men and I cannot be late. May I come back and talk further once my meeting is over?"

It took a moment for Catherine to catch her breath. With a cough and in a low voice she responded, "Of course, Henry. You know you are always welcome here. I'll fix something for you to eat when you come back." She looked down for a moment to organize her next words, and then admitted, as she'd said before, "I always feel safer when I am with you. Thank you for all you have done for me. You are a wonderful man."

Henry smiled, gently squeezed her elbows, and said, "And you are a wonderful woman. I will be back as soon as I can." He turned and reluctantly left the saloon, thinking his departure couldn't have come at a worse time considering what he was about reveal to her. But this meeting was going to be important for her as well and might be the tipping point he needed to get her to agree to his next proposal, so he couldn't just dismiss it.

Chapter Forty-eight

Wednesday 7:00 PM, July 30th, 1879

When Henry entered Ellington's office, it was obvious that Bob, John, and Ellington had been discussing the marshal's visit and the possible outcomes.

Bob took a moment to bring Henry up to speed. "I told Ellington, I'll be real disappointed if Marshal Dubois does not follow up on this. I have been talking today with a number of people I trust in this community and they all agree. There has to be something going on between Luther and Zane for Luther to keep standing behind Zane's terrible performance. It is becoming clear that few in this community trust them. If the marshal can't see this, then we may have a real problem on our hands that we will have to handle ourselves. In the meantime, someone has to look out for Mrs. Callaway. Can you help with that, Henry?"

"I just left her and she seems a little skittish. I wonder if Fannie might have talked to her about a possible threat from Zane. That woman is pretty streetwise and I know she distrusts both of those men. You know I have started the construction of the café addition to the saloon for Cath...uh, for Mrs. Callaway. I would hate to have anything happen to that pile of lumber next to our project. I will be at the site daily and I would be willing to have one of my men, or myself, stay on the property at night if she wouldn't mind. One of us could camp out in the back of the saloon near the rear door and keep an eye on things if your men could watch the street around your warehouse, Bob."

"I think that's a fine idea. John can set up a rotating team to keep watch. We were damned lucky John was alert enough to spot the fire the last time before it really caught hold. Can you set that up with your night watchmen, John?"

"Of course. I'd like to catch the scallywag who's causing this trouble, but I still suspect that crazy Zane is behind it."

Just then, U.S. Marshal Fred Dubois entered the front door of the newspaper office. Ellington waved him into the back room with the rest of the group.

Dubois sat down on the empty chair Ellington had set out and gave a big sigh. After a moment to collect his thoughts, he opened the discussion. "Thank you all for setting aside some time for me. I've been talking to people all day and am ready to get off of my feet. It seems to me that not many of the residents of Eagle Rock think very highly of your sheriff. Some think he's just a loudmouth with big guns, and others think he causes more problems than he solves, although I will say, everyone seems to respect his skill with firearms, if not necessarily his wisdom in their use." He gave a pained look to the three men. "Does he really shoot off his guns throughout the day in town?"

Bob grunted. "Unfortunately, Sheriff Zane thinks of himself as a professional gunslinger and he is pretty accurate if he's not drunk. But I am surprised we haven't had more bullet wounds on Railroad Avenue since he does go through a lot of ammunition daily just for his own enjoyment."

Dubois shook his head. "That's not what a law and order man is supposed to be doing. And I have to tell you, I got a different story of what happened during his chase and arrest of those two men every time I asked him. I don't trust any of his answers and it seemed Luther was just trying to coach him to tell the same story twice. I think those two men must be hiding something."

"I agree," stated Henry, "And none of us believes that the two dead bodies he brought back are really the men who started that fire. That means there is someone out there who still wants Mrs. Callaway out of that saloon."

Dubois nodded. "Well, that's the main reason I wanted to meet with the three of you again. I too, believe there could be a repeat of some event to put her out of business and I wouldn't want anyone to get hurt before we can get to the bottom of this. I am going to visit the towns in which your sheriff claims to have witnesses who will support his story, although I'm not sure which of the stories he's talking about. I also need to spend some time determining what Mr. Gunther's activities were prior to being hired as your sheriff. So far, no one can tell me a thing about his past employment. I'm surprised that Mr. Armstrong didn't have a better idea of where Zane had come from before hiring him as sheriff."

Bob got up and started walking back and forth as he considered what Dubois was saying. "You know, Dick Chamberlain and I volunteered to share the sheriff's duties, but Luther wouldn't have it. He wanted one man to fill the job and neither one of us had the time. It should have been easy to get someone with acceptable credentials. When Zane was hired, we weren't really having any major problems in Eagle Rock. The problems seemed to arrive with the sheriff."

Henry finally spoke up. "I think you're doing the right thing to find out if there really are any witnesses to the events Zane has been telling us about and checking more thoroughly into his background. We have already decided that we will be putting a night watch together to make sure something else doesn't happen to Patrick's Saloon. We are concerned for Mrs. Callaway and for the locals she serves."

Dubois looked relieved. "I'm glad. I just don't have the resources to help you with that, but I certainly will be looking into Zane's activities. It does seem to me that your sheriff could well be causing more problems than he is worth."

"You might also want to look at Mr. Armstrong's reasons for putting up with Zane's shenanigans," Bob put in. "There has to be a reason why he doesn't fire the lunatic."

They talked a little longer and Dubois assured them he would keep in touch. Then he brought up another subject. "You should know that I'm also looking into the activities of the Clancy Clan. We have heard reports that they might be expanding into train robberies. There seems to me more of that going on around here lately. I don't believe Sheriff Zane's opinion that they had something to do with this fire, but I don't doubt they are up to no good and I wouldn't put it past them. Robbing trains is certainly more profitable than horse and cattle thieving. This was the only subject that really got Mr. Armstrong's attention, I suppose because he's the local representative of the railroad. If I were to send a telegram to this office, would anyone else see it? I want to know how candid I can be with any information I gather."

Ellington stood up and replied, "You are looking at the one and only employee of *The Register* and telegraph office. I assure you, only the four of us would be aware of any telegrams you send to my attention in this matter."

After more conversation about train robberies, Dubois headed off to the hotel. He said he wanted to get a good night's rest before catching the early train tomorrow, but he hoped he would have time for breakfast at Patrick's

Saloon. He said the one thing everyone he talked to in Eagle Rock agreed upon was that the food at the saloon shouldn't be missed.

After Dubois left, the remaining four men let out a sigh of relief. They agreed they were seeing progress and they split up soon after that. Henry, with a complaining stomach, headed back to Patrick's Saloon, just a little nervous about what he was planning to suggest to Catherine.

Chapter Forty-nine

Wednesday 6:00 PM, July 30th, 1879

Carl rolled over on top of Fannie and started to cover her with wet kisses.

"Get off me," she yelled and pushed him aside. Sitting up, she looked at Carl with a look of irritation. "I'm hot and sweaty, and no wonder, after all the gymnastics you just put me through. Haven't you had enough? I'm hungry."

She threw the covers back, got out of the bed stark naked, and walked to the cabin door, but then turned back to face him. "I'm going down to the creek to wash up. If you're still hungry for more, you've got to feed me first."

Standing in the doorway, naked and covered with beads of sweat, Carl couldn't help but openly stare at her. He slowly looked her over; from the top of her head to just above her thighs. And she was confident enough with herself to just stand there and let him.

She finally shook her head in disgust. "Stare all you want. I'm just too damned sweaty to put on clothes right now. Start thinking about supper."

Carl got out of bed, just as naked and sweaty, and continuing to leer at her. "Here's the deal," he drawled. "If I can git a hot meal ready foh ya by the time ya be gittn back, ya have to eat it befoh ya put on any clothes. I just love it when ya walk around bare assed."

Fannie snorted. "You can't make a *decent meal* in the time it takes me rinse off. But, if by some miracle you pull it off, it better be damned good. If so, I just might agree to your so-called deal."

She turned and headed down the short trail to a small pool in the creek where they routinely bathed together. Carl moved to the door so he could watch her ass as she walked down the path. Watching her hips move as she walked was pure joy for him. He had always liked staring at her body, coming or going, clothed or not. He shook his head once she turned out of sight. What a gal. But he did agree with her about the weather. It was just too hot for clothes. He wasn't going to put his on either. Maybe he could convince her to get back in bed after they ate.

Early this morning, he had made a stew out of the spare scraps he was able to find in his cabin before he had headed down to Eagle Rock to pick her up. He liked to call it "Whatever-ya-got stew," and she had laughed at the name the last few times he had made it, but she always ate it heartily. She had been in a somewhat grumpy mood when he picked her up, so, just before they had jumped into bed this afternoon, he had pushed the stew pot back into the fire to warm up.

At the fireplace he saw that the pot was just starting to bubble. He was going to stir it but had to step back quickly since the fire had gotten pretty warm and he was fully exposed. Standing as far as he could from the fireplace, he filled two bowls and was able to find two clean spoons. He arranged his small table with a large, well-used candle in the middle for a centerpiece. Just as he heard her coming up the trail, he remembered that Fannie had suddenly started insisting on having napkins with meals and he was able to find the two she had brought on a shelf below his washstand. Fannie had started complaining about his barbaric eating habits and had "borrowed" two cloth napkins from the saloon. He looked the table over with the two bowls of steaming stew and smiled since the addition of the napkins did make the table look better.

When Fannie entered the cabin, her stern face turned to mild shock. She walked over, picked up a spoon and took a tentative taste. Shaking her head, she looked up at Carl. "How on earth did you do this? And where are your clothes?"

Carl was still admiring her gorgeous body dripping wet from her dip in the creek. "I figured if ya were gonna eat supper stark naked, it would only be proper foh me ta be joinin ya."

She looked directly at him to see if he was really serious. The moisture on his body set off the strong muscles across his chest and tight abs, and then she looked a little farther down. "Well, I see I have your attention, so I'm going to be perfectly clear. Whatever else happens next, I am going to eat first. Your strange stew actually tastes pretty good."

She was about to sit down, then looked more closely at the bench she was about to sit on. She picked up her napkin, unfolded it, set it on the bench and very carefully sat on it.

"I guess I am going to have to borrow a few more napkins if we are going to eat at your place in August when it really gets hot. I don't want any slivers up my…well, you know."

Carl looked down at his bench, frowned and unfolded his napkin as well. He decided he would have to smooth out the bench tops better if he wanted them to eat naked again.

They were both ravenous, so there was little talk until the first bowls were finished. Carl got up and filled the bowls again, but Fannie could tell he had something more than just good sex on his mind.

He finally said, "When I went by yor saloon," he always referred to Patrick's Saloon as her saloon, "an I saw a lot of construction in the back. Is that a new buildin or is it an addition to the saloon?"

"It's not my saloon, Carl. And do you mean this morning when you were heading for Mr. Lightworth's brothel?" Fannie replied with a slight edge in her voice. "You forget that the ladies from the brothel frequent the café for lunch and boast about their conquests. You are apparently one of their favorites."

"Aw, c'mon, Fannie," Carl drawled, a little red-faced. "Ya know that means nothin. Us guys just have ta let off a little steam once in a while. It's hard bein' up in those mountains all alone day after day. It's just a little sportin, that's all. Ya know I think the world of ya."

From the expression on her face, Carl realized this clearly wasn't helping. "Don't go gettin all worked up about this. Havin a little fun with the ladies is just a guy thing."

"Well, your sportin with the ladies occurred just a few hours before you brought me up here. Is what we do just sportin?"

Carl suddenly realized where this might be going and got up from the table, leaving his untouched bowl of stew. Fannie recognized this in itself as significant since Carl never willingly left food.

He crossed around and stood behind her, rubbing her shoulders. "Yor right. Ah shouldna done that. Ah was actually pretty wound up knowin we'd be spending the night together and I just got carried away. I see I was wrong. But ya know, if that is an addition to the saloon, ya might want ta tell Mrs. Callaway about yor idea for a brothel. Ya have always said the only way ya would take that line of work up again was as the head madam, so ya could make sure the girls was safe. I gotta tell ya, Lightworth's brothel is rolling in cash. Nothing sells liquor faster than having some hot, willin ladies around."

Fannie smiled and put her hands on his over her shoulders. "Catherine would never go for a brothel. She is too much of a lady. But yes, it is an addition, and it will even have a second floor, a grand stair and a balcony overlooking the main room. I've overheard Henry talking about it. He's even building a small apartment for Catherine on the second floor, although I really think he's building a little love nest for the two of them.

"Man, that's it! A balcony foh the girls ta lean over and tease the crowd, a grand stair ta flirt at the men, and some small rooms upstairs ta take them back up foh entertainment. Henry has ta know that is a design that screams brothel."

Fannie was looking down at her stew with a confused look on her face. She said haltingly, "I hadn't thought of it quite like that. Henry just doesn't seem like the kind of man that would visit brothels, but you're right. With the addition, it could be an excellent brothel."

She paused. "But Catherine would never want a brothel. And what would she do about the café?" She dug into her stew again. "It's not going to be a brothel, Carl. That's enough talk."

Carl had moved back to his stew but continued, "You've tol me Catherine really doesn't want ta run a saloon. An you've told me the kitchen is already too small ta feed breakfast and lunch. What's gonna happen when even bigger crowds start a comin ta eat? Face it. Eagle Rock is growin by leaps and bounds now that the bridge is finished. In another year it could be twice as big."

Fannie could tell Carl had been thinking a lot about this. He was unusually animated about this subject. She listened quietly as he continued. "Ya gotta see it, Fannie. She is gonna need a bigger buildin with a real kitchen. I could help ya purchase the buildin and we could go in togetha on it. I've been lookin at my future prospects and, ya know, I don't really want ta keep gettin involved with mah family's plans. This could be a ticket foh both of us."

With that, Fannie stopped eating. Quietly she asked, "What do you mean by 'both of us' exactly? I don't have that kind of money and where would you get it? You know the U.S. Marshal is convinced that your family is going to start robbing the railroad. Don't you go getting involved in that! You'll end up getting locked up like your pappy. No brothels for you if you're in jail."

"That just what I'm meanin, Fannie. I got ta get away from mah brothers. Mah pappy knows Dubois is onto them, but mah brothers are all full of themselves an mah uncle is gettin them all fired up to start robbin trains. Pappy is holdin them back, but he won't be able ta do it much longer. I got to do somethin soon. I know mah pappy would back me on this. He doesn't want me robbin trains. His time in the poky really changed him."

Fannie noted that Carl still hadn't started his second bowl of stew. He must have been planning this discussion for some time. He never talked this much.

Carl took Fannie's hand and looked directly into her eyes. "I know this ain't comin out just right, but I'm doin mah best. I'm not a fancy talker like some of those men ya know, but ya see...," he looked down and then took a deep breath and blurted out, "I want us to be partners. You could manage the brothel and I certainly can manage the bar. It would be a dandy thing and I think ya would be mighty happy. I know I would. There's a fortune ta be made in this here town, and you and I are just the ones that could pull this off. We certainly could do a better job than that fancy pants Lightworth. What do ya think?"

Fannie was looking reserved and finally spoke. "When you say partners, tell me what you really mean."

Carl looked a little embarrassed and blustered, "What do ya mean, what do I mean? Ya know what I mean. What every man is wantin when he tells a woman he wants her as a partner."

Fannie kept looking at him. She shook her head slightly. "Carl?"

"Good God, Fannie! What do ya want me to say? I want ta marry ya, Fannie! And run a business with ya! For the rest of our lives!"

A small smile formed on Fannie's face. "And?" she asked.

Carl looked shocked, then perplexed, and then a small smile formed on his face. "And I will stop goin' ta brothels and spend all my energy on you."

Fannie's smile turned into a huge smile. "What a lovely thing for you to say, Carl. Of course, I will marry you. You just had to ask."

Chapter Fifty

Wednesday, 8:00 PM, July 30th, 1879

Catherine was helping Sandy tend the bar when Henry entered the saloon, but she motioned him to follow her into the kitchen. The room was uncharacteristically tidy with a welcoming, yeasty aroma of bread in the air. The table where Crow Feather prepared meals had a red and white checkered tablecloth illuminated by a kerosene lamp with place settings for two.

Catherine blushed as Henry stared at the setting.

"I don't have a dining area that is private so this is the best I could do. I have warmed up some of Crow Feather's lunch leftovers. It was nothing, really, but I thought you might be hungry and I haven't had a chance to eat yet, either. Is this all right?"

"All right? This is marvelous! Do you have any idea how long it has been since I've eaten a decent supper? Thank you, Catherine!" Seeing that she was a little nervous, Henry stopped himself before saying she'd managed to create a very romantic setting, even in the kitchen.

He adopted a charmingly formal, gentlemanly air and bowed slightly in her direction. "I would be pleased if you would join me, Mrs. Callaway." He smiled as he pulled out a stool for her. "I am at your service. Please have a seat Ma am."

Catherine smiled and replied, "You may call me Cat, sir, as my friends do."

"I would be delighted to call you Cat, Mrs. Callaway," and he gave her a wink.

That broke the ice and they both chuckled and sat down for a pleasant meal.

Once the meal was finished, Catherine took Henry's hands from across the table. "I'm hoping we can talk about the café addition. You have done a wonderful job and I like everything you have proposed, but it is just too much. I don't need an apartment. Maybe you could just make the café a one-story building and find a way to replace my ladder with a real stairway. Wouldn't that be easier?"

Henry firmly said "No! If I am going to build that addition, it has to be as I have shown you. I can pay for the second floor if you want, but let me explain first who I had an appointment with this evening. I think you will understand everything better if we start our conversation there. It shall all become clear soon."

He went on to tell her of the meeting with Marshal Dubois, Ellington, Anderson and John. When he finished, Catherine stood to clear the table. Her grim expression showed she understood the seriousness of her situation. She sat down again and nervously fiddled with the tablecloth. "So none of you, including the U.S. Marshall, think the two men Sheriff Zane brought back were really the men who started the fire. Fannie said as much, too." She looked up at Henry. "I could still be in danger!

"We all believe that Zane must be behind this. He is just crazy enough to think he might benefit from your building burning down. We think he expected to take over a saloon in this town and yours is certainly the biggest one."

"But why burn it down? Then he would only have a pile of rubble."

He might have been just trying to scare you out of the building with a small fire, but fires get out of hand. Cat, I, do think you are in danger. I would like to stay here at night as we discussed, starting tonight with your permission. I will sleep downstairs, of course. That way, Mr. Anderson's night watchman and I will be able to make sure no one tries something stupid again. I am aware that there might be talk in the town about me staying here, but I think everyone knows that someone is trying to scare you, if not actually harm you, so I think most of the people in this town would understand. I hope you are still comfortable with this plan."

Far from uncomfortable, Catherine was experiencing a dizzying combination of terror about Zane and exhilaration that Henry would be spending nights so close. Catherine was thrilled at the thought but, managed to keep the excitement out of her voice. "Henry, I've said it before. I always feel much safer when you are here. I trust you completely and know you wouldn't take advantage of the situation. But I don't think it is fair for you to have to sleep in the tavern. Isn't there something better we could arrange?"

Henry smiled and replied, "I intend to have the first floor completed quickly and could make an area in the café addition suitable for a bed fairly soon."

"Oh," is all Catherine could come up with. That was not what she had been thinking. "Well, I think it would be better for you to stay in the saloon until the addition is at least all closed in. I am very fond of you, Henry. I know you well enough not to be worried.

Henry smiled tenderly, "You really don't know much about me, Cat. You aren't the only one making a new beginning in the West. I don't think I ever told you I was married once."

Catherine was truly surprised by this. "No," she said hesitantly. "You never mentioned that before." Suddenly, Catherine wasn't sure if she was more alarmed by Henry's account of the day's meetings or amazed by his surprising news. For once, she just sat quietly and waited for him to continue.

"It only seems right that if I am going to be living on the first floor of your building, I should tell you a little more about my background." Catherine could see that he was having trouble deciding how to start, when in actuality, he had given this a lot of thought but didn't want to make a mistake.

"As a young boy, I was living in western Kansas with my parents and two older brothers when our homestead was attacked by Indians," Henry began. "I had wandered off into a deep creek bed in a gully fairly far from our sod home before the attack, hunting for frogs, and was too far away to know what was happening. My family was killed and I came back home that afternoon to find them lying dead all over our yard with their scalps missing. The raiding party had burned our house and the few outbuildings my dad had built. Fortunately, we were on a stagecoach run and I was found the next morning. That was my first experience with a major fire."

"Oh, Henry. That's just awful." Catherine picked up her stool and moved it around the table to sit next to Henry. "I'm so sorry."

"I was young and it was a long time ago. I have pretty much blocked it out of my mind. But a more recent fire has given me frequent nightmares. My grandparents in Paducah, Kentucky, took care of me after that, but it wasn't a happy household for me. We can talk about that later. I left them when I was sixteen and got a job in St. Louis. I met a bright young girl named Trish, who was just about as down and out as me, and we sort of took care of each other. I lied about my age; I was big for sixteen, and I claimed Trish was my wife so I could get us an apartment. I couldn't afford much but I found a single room on the fourth floor of a fairly run-down building not too far from where I was working odd jobs."

Cat had turned to face him as he continued. "The manager noticed I was good with numbers and suggested he might give me a raise if I could help him keep track of his inventory. Knowing our room was pretty meager, I told Trish we would be able to move soon. I could never figure out why she disliked the room so much since it wasn't really that bad. Then, of course, being young, curious and in the same apartment each night, she got pregnant. We had a little girl we named Jessica. With the arrival of the baby, I was finally able to get Trish to admit that she was afraid of fires.

"No problem," I told her. "I'm concerned about fires, too. I picked this apartment since there are two stairways to the ground, unlike most of the buildings in this area. No matter where a fire might break out, there is an exit we can use."

Catherine interrupted. "Did you ever really get married?"

"Well, not officially, we were too young. But, as far as we were concerned we were married. My explanation still didn't seem to console Trish. And when I finally got that raise, I was too busy with my new responsibilities to take looking for a new apartment seriously. But her concerns over safety only got worse. So, I decided to prove to her just how quickly she could get out of the building herself if she ever needed to. Right next to the door to our apartment was a door that led to a stair mounted on the side of the building. I opened the door to the stair and stepped out onto the landing, reaching back to bring her out with me. She turned white as a ghost and nearly collapsed in the hall. After several minutes of coaxing her, I realized she was also deathly afraid of heights. Even when I was able to get her on the landing, she was clinging to the rails with both hands and shaking like a leaf. It occurred to me then that she could never go down four flights of stairs holding a baby. That's when I started looking for a first-floor apartment more seriously."

Henry's voice caught in his throat and he had to pause a moment to get control of himself. Catherine was getting concerned. Henry took a deep breath and continued in a quiet voice, staring at the table in front of them. "I came home late one evening, eager to tell Trish all I had accomplished at work but stopped short when I saw the commotion in front of our building. When I saw the firemen in the crowd, I knew there must have been a fire. When I didn't see Trish in the crowd outside, I tried to run past the firemen to get to the fourth floor, but they grabbed me and held me back. Fire was coming out of the fourth-floor windows in the front of the building, but the back seemed to be fine. The fireman told me not to worry. They assured me that they had already vacated all of the residents, but I ran to the back of the building and was relieved to see the fire had not gotten that far.

I climbed the stair to the fourth-floor landing and tried to open the door, but there was no handle on the outside. I told the men again and again that I couldn't find my wife and baby and they might not have gotten out, but again they told me they had already accounted for everyone. I even tried to take one of the fireman's axes so I could break down the door on the fourth-floor exit, but the fireman complained to the police and accused me of theft and hauled me to the police station."

Henry was visibly shaking now and tears ran down his cheeks.

"Oh, Henry. This sounds just awful." Catherine drew close to him and curled her arm around his shoulders.

Sobbing, Henry continued, "The damned fire chief who claimed I stole an axe came by the jail that evening and told the police they weren't going to press charges. He told me he just didn't understand it. They found Trish huddled in a fetal position with her arms wrapped around her baby at the base of the door to the rear fire stair, but still inside the building. The door was actually partly open, he told me. All she had to do was step out on the landing. They just didn't know she was there. I found out later she had died of smoke inhalation. At least she hadn't burned to death."

"And the baby?" Catherine asked quietly.

"Dead, too," was all Henry could say.

Catherine leaned in and held him as he tried to get control of himself again. After several minutes he straightened up and looked directly into Catherine's eyes. "Now you know my overwhelming concern about fires and why I want to build you a safe apartment with two good exits. I think you know who much you mean to me, Catherine. I don't want to lose you. And I want to be on the ground floor of the building you are in until I know you are safe. This may not be the right time, but I want to be with you for the rest of my life. You don't have to say anything now. I know it's too early after Patrick's death, but I want you to think about it."

Chapter Fifty-one

Wednesday, 10:00 PM, July 30ᵗʰ, 1879

Patrick's Saloon was dark and quiet as Catherine sat in the kitchen, her mouth slightly open, staring at Henry and trying to take in what he had just said. There was a light knock on the kitchen door frame and Sandy spoke without entering the kitchen, "Catherine, the bar is closed and I'm about to go. Will you lock up behind me or do you want it left open?"

This shook Catherine out of her shock and she started to get up. She called back, "Wait. I'll be right there."

Henry leaned forward and lightly took her hand as she got up. Quietly, he said, "I shouldn't have blurted all that out. I'm sorry to startle you. I know you need time to think about all of this, but I mean what I said. I hope you will think about it."

Catherine regained some of her composure and replied, just as quietly, "It's all right, Henry. But it is a lot to think about. Give me some time. And let me see Sandy out. I'll be back in just a minute."

Smoothing out the wrinkles in her apron and taking a deep breath, she walked to the door, but turned and smiled at Henry. Then she walked into the saloon to meet Sandy.

"Thank you, Sandy, for filling in for Fannie today. I hope she is having a lovely evening."

Sandy looked skeptical. "I don't know about that, Cat. When I got here this morning, Fannie was in a grand mood, but that all changed over the noon hour. I don't know what happened, but she was pretty cranky by the time she left."

Catherine laughed and raised her eyelids. "Oh, you know how Fannie is. Her mood swings back and forth like the saloon doors. She'll be fine."

"Well, I certainly hope so, or Carl is in for a really rough evening." She pursed her lips. "I think I will come in early tomorrow just in case Fannie is a little late.

Both women laughed and Catherine closed the inside doors with a bar. She turned and recalled the last few sentences Henry had said. *I want to be with you for the rest of my life.* Those were his exact words. *What do I say to him that is proper?* she thought to herself. Of course the same thoughts had crossed her mind more than once, and she had wanted to know his real feelings. And, honestly, she'd been trying to seduce him ever since her disastrous ride on Marie. Now that she knew his real feelings for her, she would have to tell him about how she ended up eloping with Patrick. But what would he think of her if she was really honest with him? A dozen thoughts flew through her head, but she admitted to herself that she would have to tell him the truth. Resigned to the fact that this conversation might destroy any chance of a long relationship with Henry, she composed herself and walked hesitantly into the kitchen.

Henry had already risen and was holding the cot he used when sleeping over in the past. "I wanted to wait until Sandy left, but I will go now and get settled into the back of the saloon."

"Henry, we really need to talk some more. I have something serious I must tell you."

Henry shook his head. "Catherine, you don't have to tell me anything. I have burdened you with too much. Not the smoothest proposal, eh? Complete with a tragic sob story. It was too much."

Catherine took his free hand. "I really do need to talk. What you said was very sad and I am touched that you would share your life before Eagle Rock with me the way you have this evening. We have talked many times, but never anything so personal. I needed to know your background and of course I needed to know about your young wife and child. It means a lot to me that you were willing to share this with me. And, of course, I am touched that you would tell me you think of me in the way that you say. But it's been less than a month since Patrick went missing and, out of respect, even if we weren't the most loving couple, I must spend a little time mourning his loss."

Henry dropped his head in defeat, but Catherine continued, "But I do want to start thinking about the future, too. Things do move faster out here. I know you're not pressuring me, and I appreciate that about you, like everything else, Henry."

"Well, you know how I feel. Take your time to think about this and, if you make up your mind and agree it would be as good for you as I know it would be good for me, I would like the chance to ask for your hand in a much more... proper way."

"Henry. I know you're tired, and it's late. But please, please stay long enough to hear what's on my heart to share, just as you have. You were brave enough to share with me things you said you have not shared with anyone else. I have skeletons in my background just like you, only mine are much worse. It is not fair for me to hold back the terrible things I have done any longer. I don't want you to have any notions that I'm naïve and blameless. We can't talk about the future if I feel I've misled you in any way. Please stay."

Henry was more than willing but tried not to show too much emotion. "Like I said, you don't need to tell me anything. I hope you know that. But if you're determined, let's do go into the dining room where the chairs are at least a little more comfortable, shall we?"

"All right, Henry."

They took a minute to calm themselves, make a cup of tea for Catherine and pour a glass of bourbon for Henry, and sat down at a table in the corner to continue their conversation.

Then Catherine began. "Patrick had good reason to treat me the way he did. I had done a terrible thing and misled him. I've never been able to put it behind me. I know one thing for sure, whatever happens between us after tonight, I could not live with myself if I misled you. Once I begin, though, I want to tell all of it."

"You do what you feel you must, but for you, not for me."

She was silent for another moment, and then began. "I was very disappointed with Louisville. It was a much bigger and a considerably more formal town than Springfield. We didn't live on a farm in the country as Father and I had in Springfield. There really wasn't anywhere I could roam freely. My stepmother insisted we live in a grand mansion in an elite neighborhood. My father had been very successful during the war and we could afford a very nice home, but we were surrounded by neighbors who were, to me, cold and stuffy highbrows. Of course, my stepmother and my two younger sisters thought it was wonderful, but I hated it. Janette, as my stepmother wished me to call her, instead of 'Mother,' as her own daughters did, dolled us up in fancy dresses, styled our hair, and enrolled us in private classes to ensure we learned the required comportment of young ladies. Heaven forbid any slip in our etiquette embarrass her at social functions."

Catherine took a sip of her tea and continued. "Then we were paraded around to meet all of the high society ladies and gentlemen in our neighborhood. The tea parties were the worst. I never conducted myself to Janette's standards and soon came to find any way to avoid these ordeals. I started roaming around Louisville by myself, which made her even angrier. 'You'll never have the opportunity to meet a proper young man at this rate, young lady. You have hung around your father far too long and need training to be the least bit desirable to the opposite sex,' she admonished me.

"As far as I was concerned, the last thing I wanted was to meet some young man who was actually attracted to made-up tea party girls. Months passed like this, and then one evening, at a party my father held, I did meet an attractive young man. He was handsome, came from a wealthy family, and was just as uninterested as I with dreary society parties. My sisters threw themselves at him but, halfway through the evening, he took me aside, said he was bored to death, and asked if I wanted to slip out and take a walk with him. I'm not sure I would have agreed, but I thought it was hilarious that he would pick me over my sisters. To get back at them, we snuck out and took a walk in the early evening to downtown Louisville. In all of my wanderings, I had stayed away from the 'evil' downtown district my stepmother had warned us about. It was wonderfully exciting.

"His name was Thomas Edmund Chambers and although he was somewhat arrogant, he could also be fun and nothing like all the stiff, young men our stepmother chose. He had money and plenty of time to treat me to all kinds of delightful experiences. Over the next few months, he took me to plays, we wandered in parks, shopped in Louisville's nicest stores, and took rides in his own, shiny-black, gilded carriage pulled by four beautiful matching black horses. All the time, he was generally quite proper. Of course, I never told Janette who I was with. She would have approved of the company but insisted I have a chaperon to keep appearances up. I just didn't want to be under her thumb and I trusted Thomas and made sure we kept our rendezvous secret."

Henry watched Catherine with fascination as her features and body language changed, the deeper she went back into her past. For herself, Catherine was now oblivious to Henry's presence at the table. She felt every detail of her account as if it had all happened yesterday. It felt good to finally let these feelings out. Her face was tense and her eyes were dark as she went further inside.

"Thomas sent me private notes of locations where we could meet and I would take off from home, claiming I was just meeting girlfriends. And then one day, he invited me to the Louisville End of Summer Ball. It was the most talked about social event held every year in Louisville. That year it was to be held on the grounds of the recently completed Crescent Hill Reservoir. When I told Elizabeth and my sisters I had been invited to the ball, Janette was stunned and both my sisters were unbelievably jealous, which made me even more pleased with myself. I had learned how to be petty and rude from my sisters and I was happy to return the favor."

Henry wanted to assure her none of this seemed the least bit out of character for a young girl growing up in a difficult situation, but he remained quiet and didn't interrupt.

"The evening of the ball was magical. My dress was an exquisite, pale pink embroidered silk, and I was allowed to wear my own mother's beautiful pearl necklace and long ivory silk gloves. Thomas picked me up in the late afternoon for a leisurely carriage ride to Crescent Hill, and a stroll through the grounds before supper. I truly felt like Cinderella—complete with two jealous stepsisters. It started out blissfully, and the ball was more beautiful and wonderful than any party I could have imagined. I was swept away by the music, the glamorous landscaped grounds, and the equally glamorous people. Thomas was the perfect gentleman, and for once, I felt like I fit in. This was the first time I liked being in Louisville. As other couples were doing between dances, he suggested we sit down in a pavilion nearby to catch our breath. The grounds were sparkling in the light of what must have been a thousand twinkling candles as he guided me to a beautiful pavilion spot next to a large tulip tree near a beautiful fountain. I thought he was going to try to kiss me. Instead, he got very serious, got down on one knee and proposed to me."

Henry wasn't surprised. What young man wouldn't?

"I was flabbergasted. I couldn't speak. It was like he had been reading my mind all that evening and knew what I wanted. I couldn't imagine a more wonderful life than living with a man like him and spending my time in the Louisville I had come to know through his eyes. It was all a young woman's dream come true. I wanted to think about it, though, and I thought he understood. But he was so elated he decided on the spot we should leave the ball and go home to tell his parents. They were going to leave on the early morning train to go to their racehorse estate outside of Lexington and he wanted us to see them before they left. Although I would have preferred to stay a little longer, I rode with him in his luxurious carriage, wondering what his house would be like."

"We found the house to be completely dark. Thomas looked disappointed and explained that they may have taken the late evening train instead and asked if he could show me around anyway. I was a little nervous, but no more so than any young woman walking into a rich estate, accompanied by a young, eligible man. I knew he had snuck off a few times at the ball and I could smell alcohol on his breath although I hadn't had a drop. And, honestly, the night had already been so intoxicating, I ignored any warning bells that were telling me to leave. As he lit the lamps, rich tapestries and oil paintings came to life, imported carpets in old, dark-wood-framed room after room filled with opulent furnishings. I had no idea his family, or any family, could be this wealthy. We even went upstairs, but he admitted it wouldn't be proper to show me his room. As we walked, he explained he would be getting an advance on his inheritance once he got married and would build us a home just as grand as this one. I asked how long it would take to build such a home, but his plan, he said, would be for us to live in a separate house on the estate grounds while our new home was being built. 'Let me show you,' he said."

Henry was beginning to see where this was going.

"So we walked out into the spacious, landscaped back yard. What he had described as the small cottage where we could live was bigger than the farmhouse my father and I had lived in in Springfield. He explained that the housekeeper lived here but she would have traveled ahead of his parents to Lexington to make sure the estate was ready for them. He took me all through the home until we reached what he said would be our bedroom. 'Of course, you can have it redecorated to meet your standards,' he said. 'Shall we try it out?'"

Catherine paused, took a deep breath, and finally looked at Henry. "That's when he changed. He grabbed me, held me tight, and gave me a long, deep kiss. I struggled and he just laughed. 'Come on,' he said. 'A little pre-marriage roll in the sheets will be a practice run. My family has a long history of horse racing and, as we Chambers say, you don't win a race with a horse the first time out of the gate. I need to know how good you are going to be in bed.'"

Catherine faltered but continued. "I struggled and got away from him and headed for the door, but he had apparently locked the house after we entered. He managed to catch me in the dining room and knocked me to the floor." She paused, swallowed, and continued. "He raped me there on the floor of the dining room."

Henry sat quiet and motionless until Catherine again raised her head to look at him. "I'm so sorry, Catherine," he said. He extended his hand to her, letting her show him if she needed a comforting touch. But she went on and he slowly pulled his arm back.

"When he rolled off of me, he said I was certainly a fighter but he liked that. I got up, bruised and bleeding, ran to the first room I could find and locked that door, only to find that the windows were barred and I could not escape. I spent the rest of the night curled up in a ball on the floor.

"The next morning, I peered out the door. The house was quiet and Thomas was gone. I walked back to my house, burned my gown, and went to bed for the day. I made up a story about the evening to satisfy my sisters and waited for Thomas to contact me and apologize…He never did."

Henry could feel Catherine's pain, and shame, but let her continue without trying to make this all go away.

"I walked to his home on Monday and the housekeeper answered the door. She knew nothing about me or my family. When I asked about Thomas, she explained that the family was at their Lexington estate. When I explained that Thomas had escorted me to the ball on Friday, she said Thomas had taken the early train to Lexington Saturday morning. Then she looked at me more carefully. I think she knew by my miserable expression what had probably happened. But no self-respecting housekeeper is disloyal. She didn't say a word against Thomas and offered me no encouragement. I knew right then, this wasn't the first time he had been so despicable."

Henry wanted to put Catherine out of her misery and put an end to this sad saga, but he decided he'd better let her finish. She'd said as much before she started.

"In the following weeks, I started each morning with an upset stomach. Soon I was throwing up every day. Of course I was pregnant, but so naïve I didn't realize it right away. Really, when you think of it, who would have taught me? Not my father, not my stepmother. There weren't books for me. I thought I had caught something and it took a while before I realized what my problem was. I didn't tell anyone what had happened, but I knew I would be showing sometime soon and had to think of something I could tell Father.

"I met the charming storyteller, Mr. Patrick Callaway, the third month of my pregnancy at a Thanksgiving party my father sponsored. I was distraught, but somehow, Patrick managed to sweep me off my feet. For the next two weeks he called on me daily and talked about all the wonderful things happening in the West. He was planning to leave soon and start a new life full of adventure. When he talked, he had a way of making me forget all about my troubles and that wretched city of highbrows and hypocrites. I began to look forward to his visits."

Ah, Henry thought. The arrival of Patrick Callaway. A young vulnerable woman, a dashing charmer. *No wonder*, Henry thought again.

"Then one evening when he called on me, he seemed anxious. He said he had a business opportunity that had come up in Salt Lake City, Utah. He said he wanted me to come with him. This was another hurried proposition, but I saw a way to avoid telling my father he was going to be grandfather to a baby born to his unwed daughter. 'When can we leave?' I asked. It turned out Patrick was pretty sure of himself—he had already bought tickets for the two of us on the Union Pacific Trans-Continental Railway leaving that same night."

Catherine took a deep breath and leaned back in her chair. "I never told him I was already pregnant. I handled it badly, I know. But I was so devastated by what had happened and what might happen to my baby, I didn't think it through. Patrick had bought us tickets for a sleeper. So I told him I would not stay in the same room with him unless we were married. I thought this would give me a little time and distance from Louisville to figure it all out. He let me sleep in the sleeper that night and apparently went to the dining car and found a minister to marry us on the train the next day. We were married just outside of Denver and I still hadn't the courage to tell him."

They were both silent for a while.

"And then, I had a miscarriage on that train before we arrived at Salt Lake City. I had to tell Patrick at that point. He was first stunned, then angry, and then furious with me. I won't get into the details, but he was ready to divorce me on the spot. He found me a room in a hotel and disappeared for about a week. When he returned, he had decided to make the best of it. Being in

Mormon country, he reckoned, his business prospects were better if he was married, so he wouldn't divorce me. He would treat me as if we were married in public, but I wasn't to expect any more than that. And we had been living that way ever since. He actually blackmailed me, using my pregnancy on several occasions to force me to do things I didn't want to. One of them was to borrow money from my father to build his saloon in Eagle Rock. I could tell my father anything I wanted to get the money but, if I didn't, he would go to my father, tell him he had married his already pregnant daughter, and try to extort the money himself. I just couldn't put my father through that."

"My dear Catherine. You have been the victim twice, really, both times from men who took the worst kind of advantage of you. I hope in time you can come to forgive yourself."

Tears were starting slide down Catherine's cheeks, "But what do you think of me, Henry?"

He got up, gently pulled her to her feet, and put his arms around her. "I see before me a strong, beautiful women I would be proud to call my wife and protect as my own."

Catherine was sobbing on Henry's shoulder now as he gently patted her back. In between sobs, she said, "I think I could fall in love you, Henry, but I'm finished with sudden decisions. Let's take some time together to work this out."

Chapter Fifty-two

Thursday, 9:30 AM, July 31th, 1879

Henry pushed his chair back from the table and gave Luther the smile of a man who has lost a friendly bet. "You've finally done it Luther. I just can't finish your excellent breakfast this time. There's enough here for lunch and supper both."

Luther laughed, appreciating what he took as a compliment. "Well, I'll ask Rachael to bring out some coffee and we can move to my study where the chairs are more comfortable."

Henry had already eaten a light breakfast after his long night at Patrick's Saloon before he came over the river for the meeting he had requested with Luther. He had anticipated Luther's grand breakfast service, but underestimated today's spread of bacon, bran muffins, and fresh squeezed orange juice, a rarity in the west, just for starters. That alone would have been more than enough for Henry. Then Rachael brought out the main course of thick-cut sirloin steak, fried potatoes, and freshly baked bread with orange marmalade. Henry had only been able to eat half of what was on his plate and was uncomfortably full. He thanked Luther for the gracious hospitality and followed him into the study.

Once they were both seated, Luther leaned back in his chair behind his elegant mahogany desk, and folded his hands. "So Henry, I understand that you've had a productive conversation with Mrs. Callaway. Am I to assume this was about your future relationship with her?"

"Yes," Henry replied. "Now don't misunderstand me. Nothing is final at the moment, but I am confident she will accept my offer of marriage soon. As she pointed out to me, Patrick went missing less than a month ago and, even out here, a proper lady must show some respect for her deceased husband."

Both men stopped talking as Rachael came in with cups and a pitcher of coffee. She poured them each a cup, smiled and left the room, leaving the door slightly cracked open. She liked Henry and was interested in knowing if he would be dropping in on Luther more.

After taking a sip, Luther leaned forward and spoke in a low, ominous tone. "I've been trying to get control of that single piece of property for some time now. As far as the folks in this town are concerned, Mrs. Callaway could have jumped in bed with the first cowboy she found at her bar once we had evidence that her husband was dead and nobody would have thought a thing about it. Relationships form fast out here and I need that property!"

"Well now, Luther, Mrs. Callaway is from the sophisticated metropolis of Louisville and that is just not the way she was brought up. If I push her, she's just going to back off. But don't worry. She made it clear to me that she liked the idea and just needed a little time for appearances. She is not as young and impressionable as you might think. She won't be pushed around."

Luther looked a little irritated. "I just fed you a magnificent breakfast, which I will point out, you didn't even finish, thinking you were ready to enter into a contract with me. What are we to talk about?"

It was Henry's turn to lean forward. "So far, our conversations have all been in generalities. Now that I know I can perform my half of the bargain, I need to be reassured of just exactly what you think my efforts are worth."

Luther laughed. "Just like Bob Anderson. You're all business, Henry, but I respect that. There is no point in not settling this here and now, but it has come to my attention that we need to address some issues that have been raised about our agreement. I was living in Utah at the time the Idaho Territory was established by the Federal government. I checked to verify that the Idaho Territory constitution was based on Common Law principals of marital property rights. Having confirmed that, I didn't pay much attention to the Idaho Territory legislature after that. Apparently, in 1867 while I was still in Utah in the middle of one of my land acquisition project in Corinne, the Idaho Territory legislature quietly passed an Act doing away with Common Law Property Rights and adopting the Idaho Community Property System. This means we will need to adjust our plan to insure that you will have the right to sell me the saloon and cafe once Mrs. Callaway becomes Mrs. Willett.

Henry was clearly aggravated by this. "We had an agreement sealed with a handshake! Are you suddenly backing out om me?"

"Not at all, Henry. We just have to make some modifications that will not change our agreement much and will be to your benefit."

"Well, I'm not at all pleased that you would bring this up this late in our plans. You had better spell this out for me. I don't understand how I can sell that property if Mrs. Callaway still owns it."

Luther leaned back in his chair and thought for a moment. "It is really quite simple. As long as you acquire majority ownership of the property *prior* to the marriage, you will have the final say in what happens to the property."

"But, how on earth do I do that?"

"It is my understanding that you are covering the cost of materials and labor for the second story of the café, at least temporarily, and Mrs. Mitchell is providing funding for your construction of the first story in exchange for the limited use of the first floor for teaching and worship services. All Mrs. Callaway is contributing is the lumber that Patrick purchased before his accident. You don't want to be obligated to Mrs. Mitchell, so why don't you suggest that she pay you once the project is complete? By then, you will be married and can explain that the building has been purchased but she will not owe you any money and she can use it to fund her own building. This puts you in a position to be the majority owner of the café."

Henry didn't seem completely pleased with this suggestion. "Well, I didn't know how I was going to break the news to Mrs. Mitchell that she wouldn't be able to use the café anyway, so that would solve one problem, but I don't have the funds to pay for all of the construction and what about the saloon? It looks like I could be sacrificing a lot with this new plan."

"I have a plan for the funds, but let's talk about the saloon first. It is my understanding that Mrs. Callaway took a loan from her father so Patrick could build the saloon. Why don't you privately explain to her father that you want your new marriage to start off on a secure financial foundation and you will pay off the loan in advance of the marriage? This leaves you as the majority owner of both the saloon and café. I can help you make this happen by advancing you the funds you need and then we will just adjust the price of the property to account for those funds. I will agree that the funds you receive are sufficient for you to build the dream home you are planning for your new wife."

"Consequently, once Mrs. Callaway becomes Mrs. Willett," Luther said, "I will negotiate with you to acquire Patrick's Saloon. Since I know you don't really want to run a saloon, I believe I can make an offer for that property that you would find worthwhile. You will make a tidy sum for your, uh, sacrifice."

Henry nodded agreement but raised a finger. "Luther, we need to get down to brass tacks and talk numbers."

Luther swung his chair around to look out the window behind his desk as he contemplated how to respond. He turned back with a smile on his face. "You are a shrewd negotiator, Henry, but yes, we can address this now. Actually, I will want to put it in writing so we don't have to have this discussion again. How does that sound?"

"That's just what I had in mind."

Luther steepled his fingers before him as he considered the best way to go about this. "Let me see if I remember clearly your talking points when we first met. You want to build a small cattle ranch with a few outbuildings on very reasonably priced property west of the Snake with frontage on the Snake. You will not only need the property, but you need enough for the supplies and materials to build a respectable home for you and the new Mrs. Willett."

"I will be purchasing a horse for Catherine as a wedding present," Henry interjected, "so I'll need at least fifty acres on the ranch with access to the river for my cattle and space for her to ride. The desert is fine as long as it is not covered with exposed lava beds."

Luther looked mildly surprised. "Well, I was thinking of a smaller parcel north of my ranch on the river, but the land to the west of that should meet your purposes and there really is no value to that land other than grazing. I can do that. I am proposing that the land be separate from the cash payment for the saloon since I have control of the Union Pacific property that was granted to UP by the federal government along the rail right of way. You can consider it my wedding present to the two of you. And I understand that you need to be reimbursed for the added value of the addition you are presently constructing. I was able to look again at the plans you have developed and agree that the second floor and grand stairway will work well for my uses. The partner I have picked to manage this new business was quite specific about the need for a second floor, balcony, and stair. I trust Mrs. Callaway had no problems with that?"

"It was not to her liking initially, but I talked her into it."

Luther pulled a slip of paper from his desk and wrote something on it. He turned it so Henry could read it and pushed it over to him. "How does that look?"

Henry looked at the paper but was silent.

After a long pause, Luther shook his head. "You know I think that is a very fair price, Henry. And I really can't offer much more."

Henry smiled at Luther and said, "Actually, you can, Luther."

Luther was clearly becoming irritated.

Henry leaned forward again. "You see, Luther, I know that the Union Pacific wants to build a maintenance facility in Eagle Rock to maintain all the engines and railroad cars. You will need a roundhouse, a maintenance building, lodging for the engineers, and of course, there is also the new depot. I suspect they are going to give you the authority to decide who builds these facilities. I simply want a guarantee that I will be your builder of choice. You know I am the most qualified contractor around and you have seen me stay within budgets without shirking on quality. I want to be able to tell Catherine that I have enough work so she need not worry about losing the income from the saloon. I will be able to provide for her needs and she can comfortably stay at the ranch, and be a proper housewife, and ride her horse whenever she wants on our property. I don't want her behind a bar any more or being exposed to those roughnecks who frequent a saloon. That's no place for a lady and certainly not for my wife."

Luther's irritation faded into a small smirk. He thought for a minute and then responded. "That's very forward thinking, Henry. But you have to understand that I have had to put a lot of my own money into getting this town off the ground. I need to find ways to recoup some of that."

He paused for a minute then continued, "I will have to let you in on something that can only be between us. If you agree, I think this could work. I have been negotiating with the management of the UP for several months about the costs of what they want built. I have put together numbers that are higher than they expected, but I explained that just getting materials and good labor out west is expensive. Of course, what I am asking for is a pittance of what they would have to spend in the east, so these numbers are inflated but shouldn't raise any red flags. I have just gotten a reluctant approval of my budget, but I really don't want to spend all of it on railroad infrastructure. I am looking for a contractor who can not only stay within this budget but is interested in sharing a percentage of the funds remaining after construction with me. Of course, we cannot be seen as building poor quality construction, but, as you just said, you have proven yourself to be very resourceful in the projects you have completed to date. Is that something you might be interested in?"

"What percentage are you thinking of?"

"I think twenty-five percent would be very generous."

After another cup of coffee and a half hour of negotiations, both parties finally agreed on the details of the arrangement and Luther said he would have a written draft ready for signatures the following day.

When Henry left, Luther pulled out his decanter of Old Forester and poured himself two fingers of the caramel-colored liquor. He held it up to the light and smiled. A salute to his success. He had been mortified to discover he hadn't known of the legislative change to the ownership of marital property and had been in a nervous turmoil for the last several days, but, as usual, where there was a will , there was always a way. He took a sip, smiled, and congratulated himself on the successful negotiation with Henry. He had expected that Henry would not want to have any paperwork for this transaction, but the new twist on the funding to assure him majority ownership had moved him to agree to a contract. And, of course, he was ready to split the profits with Henry, if needed, to make sure he finally owned that property. Even the final number that they had agreed upon was less than Luther had been willing to go to.

Just another successful day in the life of the rapidly-rising property tycoon in Eagle Rock.

In the meantime, Henry was happily whistling to himself as he crossed the railroad bridge back to Eagle Rock. He had managed to convince Luther he was worth another five percent, making his share of any money he could save on the construction thirty percent, and now all of his plans were in place. He was confident that he and Catherine would be sleeping in the new apartment as soon as it was finished and marriage would come quite soon after that. Once he explained how much he wanted her to be safe in their new, one-story, modern ranch house across the river, and what a relief it would be for her to no longer have to deal with the saloon lowlifes, she would be pleased with the new arrangements. Having home-cooked meals every day when he arrived home would be a wonderful change for him. He was tired of living at the hotel. He had already made arrangements to buy that horse she had ridden from Shorty Smith. When he asked about a saddle, he was surprised to find out that Shorty had been a leather worker and would make a custom saddle for Catherine. He even said he would include saddlebags so she could keep emergency supplies with her on her rides. Henry had made sure Shorty understood this was to be a surprise and he couldn't tell anyone.

Henry had left St. Louis with dreams of making his fortune in the west, and it was all coming true. With multiple contracts for the railroad buildings in Eagle Rock, he could put enough money aside to expand his operation to other parts of the territory. Who knew how far he could go with this enterprise and a new wife to keep the home fires burning. His imaginative story about Trish had really finalized his future for him.

Chapter Fifty-three

August 4, 1879

Dearest Father,

I must apologize for not writing you much earlier. I have been overwhelmed this last month in getting my life back to normal since Patrick's death. Although this will sound terrible, Patrick's demise has made the uncertainty of life out here a little more manageable for me. He was not the man I thought he was. I appreciate the efforts you made to find out more about Patrick as well as your attempt to break the news to me gently in your letter, but I had already determined that most of what Patrick told me were lies. I found him to be a reckless risk taker who endangered both our lives. He was very difficult to live with. This probably sounds very hard-hearted, but being single has helped me get myself back together again.

I have always been embarrassed about leaving Louisville so abruptly and not telling you more about why I left. Above all, I want you to know my departure was not caused by anything you did. It was because of events you had no way of knowing. I would prefer to tell you more in person. What I can tell you now is this. When you were so gracious to lend us the money we needed to build a café in Eagle Rock, I had hoped that once we were established, I could come back to Louisville to talk to you privately or you might even want to come out to see what we had accomplished.

Needless to say, our café endeavor did not go as I expected. It turns out, Patrick never intended to build a café at all but planned to build a saloon with your money instead. Then, I found out after his death that he had already ordered materials to add a gambling hall based on the assumption that the profits we made on the 4th of July would be enough to pay for the materials and labor.

Once I saw what he was really going to do with the loan I had requested from you, I was even more embarrassed and unable to bring myself to tell you. I will admit now that I should have talked with you about my plans before ever leaving Louisville.

Not all of this is as bad as it may seem since my life has changed for the better since the 4th of July. I now know that I should be able to pay the loan you gave us back within the next several months, and I have been able to manage my own life much better now that I no longer am encumbered by Patrick's unpredictable lifestyle.

I have found a wonderful woman with good experience in operating a saloon to help me. Fannie, my new dear friend, is managing the saloon and, with the help of an excellent local cook and her son, I have started serving breakfasts and lunches in the saloon. Although I was shaken deeply by the news that Patrick had drowned, since then, I have been forced to make my own decisions and they have generally proven to be good ones.

The saloon is doing well under Fannie's guidance and the meals have been well received. We are even starting to make a profit. I think I may have inherited some of your entrepreneurial genes after all!

I want you to know that I am very happy here and don't really want to live in Louisville, but it would be nice to be able to see you more often. The townsfolk here have been very supportive and, although certainly not the well-educated people you are surrounded by in Louisville, these people are very down to earth and to be around.

Managing my own business and making my own decisions has brought me a whole new and wonderful outlook, too. I think I can be very happy here in Eagle Rock. Unlike my stepmother and sisters, I did not find that kind of acceptance or caring attitude in Louisville. I hope you understand, Father.

Through some amazing developments, a very dear man, Henry Willett, is building an addition to the saloon for me for a café. Once completed, we will be able to provide meals in both the saloon and café addition. Right now, we are very crowded and the addition will certainly help my bottom line. I have known this man for some time as a true friend. He traveled to Eagle Rock with Patrick and I and was a tremendous help to me even before Patrick's death. I am thinking seriously of making him a part of my life as more than just a friend, but I would really like you to meet him before I make any final decisions.

We will be having an Open House for the café in early September and I am hoping you will be able to come and be a part of the celebration. I would love to see you and we could really talk. I would be delighted if you could come.

You may be pleased to know that I am using the sweet nickname you gave me as a child while you and I were traveling around your early circuit selling hard goods around Lexington, and I'm going to name my café the same.

I plan to call it Cat's Café.

With much love,
   Your devoted and loving daughter,

        Cat

P.S. Please look into Thomas Edmund Chambers' background. I know my sisters are enamored with him, but I know firsthand he is an evil man.

Author's Note

Although this book is fiction, the story is built upon actual events and real people in the late 1800s during the formation of the new town of Eagle Rock, which is now called Idaho Falls, Idaho. Many of the fictional characters I've portrayed would have had strong dialects and little formal education. I have attempted to pick up the flavor of their conversations by using phonetic spellings of the words they might have used. In addition, we have incorporated traditional Western slang of the day. The generally accepted definitions for the slang used come from multiple sources.

- General Characteristics of Printed Cowboy Dialect
  - ▷ Dickheaberlinwrites.com
- Cowboy Slang, Lingo, and Jargon
  - ▷ Ira Koretsky
- A Writer's Guide to the Old West
  - ▷ compiled by G.M Atwater, January 2001
- The Long Riders Guild Academic Foundation
  - ▷ Long Rider Douglas Preston
- The Glossary of Railroad Lingo
  - ▷ Railroad Avenue, Freeman Hubbard, 1945

Chapter Notes

Chapter One ~ Taylor's Crossing and Eagle Rock

The Snake River, running first west and then south out of the Teton Mountain range, carved deep channels through numerous ridges of the ancient lava beds of the Idaho high desert before reaching an area near Pocatello where it veered west across the southern portion of Idaho to Boise. This often turbulent river was dangerous to cross and took the lives of many pioneers attempting to head to the Pacific Northwest from the plains on the Montana Trail. The lava bed forced the river into a narrow channel at the present site of Idaho Falls. In 1865, Matt Taylor built a rough-hewn lumber bridge at this location. The bridge was washed out the following year by a spring torrent that came out of the Tetons, but, with the assistance of Bob Anderson, he built a second stronger and higher bridge at the same location in 1866 and collected tolls from travelers wanting to cross the river. This location became known as Taylor's Crossing, later Eagle Rock, and presently Idaho Falls.

Matt Taylor and Robert Anderson had opened a trading post at Taylor's Crossing in 1865, hoping to take advantage of the traffic that would be generated at this location. Having acquired a large portion of land east of the bridge, they were briefly partners in the endeavor but Taylor eventually headed back East and Anderson stayed to take part in the development of the small community of Eagle Rock that formed in the late 1870s.

When the Union Pacific Railroad (UP) purchased the bankrupt Mormon-built Utah Northern Railroad (UNR) and changed it to the Utah and Northern RR (U&N), hoping to connect the Transcontinental Railroad with Montana, their surveyors selected Taylor's Crossing as the most economical location for the railroad to place a bridge over the Snake River to get to the Montana mines. Just south of Taylor's Crossing, the river divided at a small resistant island of lava which made it the best location to build a pair of bridges. This island was used as the midpoint of the railroad crossing. It was home to eagles and thus was called Eagle Rock. The UP decided to use a location just east of the river at this location for a division point for their new railroad line. This quickly became the town of Eagle Rock as the railroad completed the line north into Montana.

I chose the site for my fictional Patrick's Saloon from an 1884 map of the small town. The location is the southeast corner of the intersection of Railroad and Chamberlain avenues, although those streets no longer exist at that location. In 1884, the entire town west to east was contained between the Snake River, Capitol Avenue, and Chamberlain Avenue (now Park Avenue.) North to south, the town included Cliff Street and Railroad Avenue with the depot and yard north of Railroad Avenue now the site of the Idaho Falls Public Library. Present-day Chamberlain Avenue bends to the west about a hundred feet from Cliff Avenue and turns into present-day Park Avenue. The railroad tracks are still there. The double railroad bridge can be seen spanning the river and the island in the center is now the site of the Japanese Friendship garden. Taylor's Bridge would have been just a little north of the railroad bridges. A replica of the bridge is there now and used as a walking bridge to the island and Japanese garden.

Chapter Three ~ Railroads and fortunes

The Utah Northern Railroad (UNR) was sold to the Union Pacific (UP) in a bankruptcy sale on April 3, 1878 but, as early as November of 1877, the UP had already started construction of a new line from Franklin, Idaho, the northern terminal of the UNR heading further northward. The new Utah & Northern Railroad (U&N) construction crew arrived at Eagle Rock in April of 1879 and started the construction of the twin bridges over the Snake River. The steel bridges had been prefabricated in the east and shipped out to Eagle Rock by rail.

I chose July 4, 1879 as the date for a celebration held in Eagle Rock at the completion of the new pair of railroad bridges across the Snake River. In actuality, the first steam engine crossing occurred on Tuesday, July 1, 1879. I have no information on whether there actually was such a celebration, but certainly they must have celebrated Independence Day and the completion of the bridge which was a major accomplishment for the railroad and the beginning of a rapid expansion for the town.

The Mormons had started construction of the Utah Northern Railroad in 1871, anticipating Mormon settlers setting up homesteads throughout northern Utah and Idaho, but they only completed a portion of the line to Franklin, just inside the southern Idaho border. The Union Pacific proposed bridge construction to cross the Snake River approximately midway between Salt Lake City and the mines in Butte, Montana, and built a railroad town to act as the division point for the new Utah & Northern Railroad. With the Union Pacific Railroad building the infrastructure necessary to maintain their railroad stock at this location and rumors of gold in the hills north and east of this new town, it was inevitable that the town would grow rapidly and be a destination point for all sorts of fortune hunters.

Chapter Four ~ A way of life destroyed

Looking back at the rapid western development of the United States, it is clear that the indigenous peoples were never treated well and were often treated very badly by the new American settlers and the U.S. government. Two government actions in the early 1880s that turned over Native American lands to private ownership were extremely detrimental.

In 1862, the Idaho Territory was organized and Congress passed the Homestead Act. This allowed American citizens to settle on up to 160 acres of unclaimed public land and receive title to the land after making improvements and residing there for five years. In 1864, the Second Pacific Railroad Act was passed by Congress. It doubled the size of land grants to railroad companies and improved subsidies for every mile of track laid. All of these actions turned over Native American lands to private ownership.

So, In the space of a few years, a series of events as unfortunate as they were intentional destroyed much of the life and culture of the Native Americans in the central-western United States.

In 1862, Cheyenne Chief Black Kettle met with U.S. Army officers outside of Denver and agreed to lead his people back to their Sand Creek reservation in order to restore peace in the area. Yet, that same year, a volunteer force led by "The Fighting Parson," Henry M. Chivington, massacred nearly 200 men, women, and children in the Native American encampment.

In 1868, General Philip H. Sheridan took command of the U.S. Army forces in the West and proposed to bring peace to the area by exterminating the herds of buffalo. "Kill the buffalo and you kill the Indians," Sheridan decreed.

George Armstrong Custer announced the discovery of gold in the Black Hills of Dakota in 1874. This set off a stampede of fortune hunters in the most sacred part of the Lakota Territories which, according to the 1868 Fort Laramie Treaty, were to be protected against White settlers. However, federal authorities protected the miners instead. By 1875, federal authorities had ordered the Lakota chiefs to report back to their reservations. Sitting Bull, Crazy Horse, and others refused.

In the area around Eagle Rock, the prominent First Nations were the Lakota, Shoshone, Lemhi, and Bannock tribes. Many had already moved to the Fort Hall Indian reservation near present-day Pocatello. Some remained in the areas where they had grown up but were not treated well by the settlers. The heavy influx of gold-seeking miners in the hills east of Eagle Rock contaminated the streams. Trappers, looking strictly for furs, exterminated much of the wildlife that was the source of food for the indigenous people. The loud, unnatural sounds of the railroad and the constant airborne soot frightened away the rest. Native Americans were forced into reservations and encouraged to change their lifestyle from living off the land to looking for work. Rampant racism against Native Americans and foreigners resulted in them finding nothing but the most menial jobs, if any.

A note about timetables

The times I have indicated below each chapter title are a general guide of the times of the events presented in this book. It wasn't until the passing of the Standard Time Act of 1918 that the current time zones were established. Consequently, prior to 1918, each community established the time for their location based on "local solar time," setting noon as the time when the sun passed the local meridian. At one point, this resulted in more than 300 separate time zones in the nation. This became a problem once railroads were introduced since it was difficult to set arrival and departure times for sites along each rail line. Railroads had difficulties setting meaningful schedules since the times in adjacent towns could be as much as a half an hour different. Most towns were connected by a single rail line used for travel in both directions, so the timing of trains running in opposing directions had to be correct. Early on, two trains actually collided, both going by the time found in the town they had just left. Initially, each railroad line established its own definition of what the time was in the stations they served, but this posed a problem for larger towns served by multiple railroads. The introduction of the Standard Time Act of 1918 was the beginning of standardized time now used throughout the world.

As a guide to how people used their daylight hours in 1879, I used a useful online table indicating when the sun rose and set throughout the nation on any given date. It became apparent that this table had to be adjusted to take out the current, built-in use of Daylight Savings Time. Another table allowed me to establish the phases of the moon for nighttime events.

Chapter Five ~ The Mormons

Accuracy, objectivity, and fairness without interpretation in these notes is of supreme importance to me. If something doesn't look right, please let me know. It's a challenging subject, to be sure.

References of note cited in various sources I read for Brigham Young and the Mormon Church, particularly the notes for chapters 5 and 6, are primarily from excerpts of works by Thomas G. Alexander, Franklin M. Gibbons and John G. Turner found in Wikipedia. The specific books by these authors can be found in the bibliography at the end of this novel.

References of note cited in various sources I read for Joseph Smith and the Mormon Church, particularly the notes for chapters 5 and 6, are primarily from excerpts of works by Richard L. Bushman, D. Michael Quinn, Robert V. Remini and Dan Vogel found in Wikipedia. The specific books by these authors can be found in the bibliography at the end of this novel.

A brief usage guide to the names Brigham Young and Joseph Smith -- Histories referring to Brigham Young senior generally use Brigham Young, whereas his son Brigham Young is written as Brigham Young, Jr. I have followed that practice in the book's chapters, but I have specified each with a suffix in parentheses for these notes. On the other hand, the elder Joseph Smith is generally referred to as Joseph Smith, Sr., and his son who would become the first leader of the Mormons, as simply Joseph Smith. I used their names in the chapters accordingly and, again, added parenthetical suffixes to keep them straight in these notes. I hope this will help clarify the different generations.

Brigham Young (Sr.), often referred to as the "Mormon Moses," led his followers on an exodus across the western plains of America to what would be called The Promised Land. He had stepped in to lead the Mormons when Joseph Smith (Jr.) and his brother were murdered in 1844. Brigham Young, Sr. was a polygamist and autocrat. He instituted a church ban against conferring the priesthood on men of African descent and participated in the Utah War against the Federal government. When he died in 1877 his sons and others upon whom he had ordained as priests, continued the leadership of the Mormon faith from Salt Lake City, Utah. To understand Brigham Young's (Sr.) leadership and accomplishments, one must understand the origins of this new faith.

Joseph Smith (Jr.), the first leader of the Mormon Church, was born to Joseph Smith, Sr. and Lucy Mack Smith on December 23, 1805. Throughout his early years, his mother was preoccupied with the subject of religion and was desperate to find what she felt was the "true religion" or "true church." Joseph and Joseph Jr. did not accept any of the conventional religious creeds or churches of the period either, but were at odds with Lucy nonetheless on this subject.

Religious harmony was not the family's only struggle. Although Joseph Smith, Sr. and Lucy had started out their marriage comfortably as landowners of a farm in Tunbridge, Vermont, their financial situation had deteriorated six years later in 1802 when Joseph Smith, Sr.'s mercantile venture exporting ginseng root to China failed. They were forced to sell their farm and become tenant farmers, ultimately moving seven times in the following fourteen years due to various failed farming attempts and other ventures. Joseph, Sr. would try employment as a cooper, farmer, teacher, and merchant, but ran into financial difficulties with each vocation.

A paper prepared by C. Jess Grosebeck states, "From then on [1802], it was though [sic] he [Joseph Smith, Sr.] was a dreamer who detached himself from reality, becoming preoccupied and fascinated with money digging, probably in an attempt to recover a loss he could never fully accept. Through money digging [including actual hunting for buried treasure], he expected to become rich and to find the security he had always wanted for his family." Joseph (Sr.)

and his sons started seeking buried treasure and became interested in magic, common practices in the northeast at that time.

As the parents struggled to find a faith that suited them, they shared their religious visions with Joseph Smith (Jr.) It is not surprising that when their son had what he believed to be his first revelation in 1820 at the age of fourteen, they supported him and encouraged him to follow it.

Joseph (Jr.) claimed to have dug up inscribed golden plates from a hill not far from the farm they were working and explained to his parents that he had been told by an angel named Moroni to translate the message written in "reformed Egyptian" on the plates using "seer stones" called the Urim and Thummim, which had been buried with the plates.

In 1830, Joseph Smith, Jr. created the Book of Mormon which revealed the 1,000-year history of the Israelites who were, it was written, led from Jerusalem to a promised land in the Western Hemisphere. The resulting 588-page book resembled the Bible in describing the life and times of these people, including a visit from Christ after his resurrection. It went on to explain that around 400 years after the birth of Christ, the last of the Nephites were eliminated by their enemies, the Lamanites, presumably the ancestors of the American Indians.

Joseph Smith (Jr.) organized several dozen believers, including his father, into a new church following the guidance from the golden plates. This body of believers was later organized as The Church of Jesus Christ of Latter-day Saints or LDS Church. Male converts were ordained and sent out throughout the world in an extensive missionary program that resulted in tens of thousands of converts by the end of Joseph Smith's (Jr.) life. For their religious training and protection, these new converts were to gather in settlements called Cities of Zion. All converts were expected to tithe 10 percent of their income to support the aggressive mission program and land acquisition.

The Mormons were not welcome in the communities they moved to because of their beliefs, practice of polygamy, and the dramatic effect of their politics in each community. They were instructed from the pulpit to vote in accordance with the direction of their religious leaders and they represented a large voting block that threatened the remainder of the inhabitants of the community. Joseph Smith (Jr.) and his brother Hyrum were eventually arrested for treason in Carthage, Illinois. During their incarceration awaiting trial, they were shot to death by a mob of angry non-Mormons on June 27, 1844. Since it had been expected that Hyrum would be Joseph Smith's (Jr.) successor, the Mormons were left with a sudden lack of leadership.

Brigham Young (Sr.) was able to convince followers of Joseph Smith (Jr.) that he should take over the leadership of the Quorum of the Twelve Apostles. Brigham Young (Sr.) organized the journey of the Mormon pioneers to the Salt Lake Valley, a part of Mexico at the time. His hope was to avoid any more conflicts by starting a "City of Zion" far from the established territories of the United States where they could peacefully expand their religious brotherhood in near isolation.

Brigham Young (Sr.) was successful in establishing numerous new settlements throughout what is now known as the state of Utah. During his tenure as leader of the Mormon Church, he established many controversial religious policies including the Adam-God doctrine which explains that Adam returned to earth to become the biological father of Jesus. He also expanded the doctrine of polygamy, having possibly as many as fifty-five wives himself, and he successfully organized numerous caravans of converts from all over the world to move to the Salt Lake City region.

Besides acting as the religious leader of the Mormons, he was an impressive political and financial leader. Although implicated in the 1857 Mountain Meadows Massacre and other confrontations with the U.S. government, he still managed to negotiate an understanding with President Abraham Lincoln during the Civil War wherein the Mormons sided with the Union and protected the telegraph service that ran through Salt Lake City in exchange for the government not enforcing the Morrill Anti-Bigamy Act of 1862. During Brigham Young's (Sr.) tenure over the Mormons, he directed the founding of 350 towns in the southwest and became the single most successful individual in colonizing the vast arid west between the Rockies and the Sierra Nevada.

Chapter Six ~ The Mormons, continued

Accuracy, objectivity, and fairness without interpretation in these notes is of supreme importance to me. If something doesn't look right, please let me know. It's a challenging subject, to be sure.

I have not found historical evidence that Eagle Rock celebrated the 4th of July or that John W. Young, son of Brigham Young (Sr.) spoke at this event. But, if the mayor of the town was hoping to become part of the Mormon brotherhood of bishops, it seems likely that he would have made efforts to include someone from the Mormon leadership to encourage further Mormon settlement in the area of Eagle Rock.

Upon Brigham Young's (Sr.) death in 1877, his two oldest surviving sons were John W. Young and Brigham Young, Jr. John W. Young had participated in the early construction of the southern portion of what had become the Union Pacific-owned Utah & Northern, but would have been unable to participate in the fictional 4th of July celebration due to his actual involvement with another railroad project southwest of Salt Lake city at the time. Since Brigham Young, Jr. had become increasingly in conflict with the leadership of the Mormon Church due his residency in New York City and his business practices there, he had more to gain by agreeing to speak for the Mormon leadership so I chose him to speak at Eagle Rock. By 1881, he would lose his position as one of the Quorum of the Twelve Apostles. Eventually, he would fall sufficiently out of favor with the church that he was not reinstated as a member of the Apostle of Twelve leadership.

As noted, the speech I have presented in this chapter is actually a collection of excerpts from a speech given by Brigham Young (Sr.) to the Utah State Legislature in 1852. Although Joseph Smith (Jr.) treated black men of African descent equally, Young (Sr.) is generally considered to have instituted a church ban against conferring the priesthood on African Americans, and, as stated in his speech, it would appear of anyone of foreign or minority descent.

These excerpts are in the order they appeared in the original speech and were not taken out of context and can be found throughout the speech.

It also appears his opinion was the same for all minority races present in the West at this time. Note that this ban was lifted after his death, but Mormon records reveal that there were few African-Americans who achieved priesthood until nearly a century later.

I have included this speech because it reflects the general attitude embraced by many Americans in the late 1800s toward non-White people and minority ethnic races. African-American, Native American, Irish, Italian, German, Jewish, Polish, Asian, Hispanic, and Pacific Islander persons were treated with disdain and as a lower class of citizen in general.

Chapter Seven ~Not much law, not much order until Winn

Sheriff Zane Gunther is a fictional character based on two historical individuals who did serve as sheriff in the vicinity of Eagle Rock around the time I've portrayed. According to the book *Images of America, Idaho Falls* by William Hathaway (see bibliography), on May 24, 1863, Sheriff Henry Plummer was elected sheriff for a large area that included Eagle Rock and the Snake River plains. During the brief period in which he was sheriff, more than 100 people were murdered in eastern Idaho and western Montana in less than a year. Prior to his selection, Plummer had been the secret ringleader of San Francisco's infamous gang of stagecoach robbers known as The Innocents. He was advised he would be commissioned as the new Idaho Territory U.S. Marshal, but locals, disgusted with the violence, hanged him and several of his gang members shortly before the official commission letter arrived.

Ed F. Winn became the first Eagle Rock resident sheriff in 1880 and later became a deputy U.S. Marshal. According to Hathaway's *Idaho Falls*, Winn wore pearl-handled .44-caliber six-shooters mounted on swivel holsters and was involved with several deadly gunfights. It is said he was recognized for his ability to regulate cattle thieves in the area, a prominent member of Eagle Rock most of his life, and became a partner with Dick Chamberlain in several business ventures.

The back cover of Hathaway's *Idaho Falls* states, "Taylor's Crossing began as a wooden toll bridge over a narrow spot on the Snake River for travelers along the Old Montana Trail. By 1883, it was known as Eagle Rock, a dusty outpost for railroad workers, bullwhackers, and miners…'We cannot claim an orderly town,' the newspaper reported. The reckless firing of firearms at all hours of the day and night is a nuisance that should be stopped."

Chapter Eight ~ Cigars, chicanery, and collusion

Martinez-Ybor started his small cigar manufacturing company in Havana, Cuba in 1856. His *El Principe de Gales* brand soon became quite popular and his factory was producing 20,000 cigars a day. When the 1868 Ten Years' War broke out in an effort to win independence from Spanish colonial rule,

Martinez-Ybor supported the Cuban rebels. When faced with potential arrest from Spanish authorities, he fled with his family to Key West, Florida. Martinez opened a new factory in Key West. He employed many of the Cubans who had left their war-torn homeland and continued producing *Principe de Gales* cigars but renamed them "Prince of Wales" since he had a corner on the American market. He was the first to manufacture and market a "Havana clear" or "Cuban clear" cigar. This was a cigar made with Cuban tobacco produced by Cuban workers but manufactured in the United States, thus avoiding the high tariff the U.S. imposed on cigars imported from Cuba.

The true story of railroad politics, manipulation and deception, and even the role of polygamy in the Mormon Church at this time and in this region, is so complex, so labyrinthine, that the best treatment here would be a collection of maps, a list of characters with photos and links to online biographies, a detailed timeline, and possibly a word bank. And it would be worth every inch to include a thorough treatment of how intertwined became the Mormon Church leaders and east coast investors and barons.

It's worth noting that even scholarly printed histories disagree on the events and motivations of this period of history. This version is the very best I have found, albeit abbreviated here. Here we go.

In the 1860's there was a huge push to complete, and then extend with spurs, the Transcontinental Railroad, with incentives and bonuses to be the first to reach the midpoint. Owners hired Chinese workers to help build the Central Pacific line east from the Pacific Ocean through the Sierra Nevada Mountains and on through Nevada. Many other groups, including freed African Americans, Confederate soldiers, and immigrants from Europe were hired to build the Union Pacific west through the Great Plains, Native American lands, and the Rocky Mountains. At that time, the anticipated midpoint was Salt Lake City where the Mormons were well established. This is where the Mormon interest comes in.

If Salt Lake City were the Transcontinental Railroad midpoint, the Mormons would be perfectly positioned to move freight east and west between the two competing railroads (Central Pacific and Union Pacific) as well as run a spur north to the fertile Cache Valley where farm families could prosper.

So, when Jay Gould and his cronies with interest in the west-bound Union Pacific approached the Mormons for help, a deal was struck. Mormon laborers would help finish the project in exchange for help building their spur north to the Cache Valley. Perfect? Not so fast.

Dwindling funds, deceptive practices, and dubious measures eventually wound up cheating the Mormons out of the northbound railroad extension and their payment for labor they had provided to the Union Pacific; AND the Union Pacific chose to alter the midpoint of the Transcontinental Railroad away from Salt Lake City to a little town named Ogden. The Mormons had been swindled.

Adding insult to injury, Jay Gould's Union Pacific had built the town of Corinne as a railroad town that prided itself in being Utah's largest "Gentile" community. As such, and with the added benefit of being closer to the overland wagon trail to the Montana mines, Corrine became a major freight center, a goal Brigham Young (Sr.) had had for Salt Lake City. In 1872, half to three-quarters of a million pounds of freight rolled out of Corrine each week in wagon trains driven by bullwhackers to the Montana markets —and the Mormons had to build their own spur to connect to the Transcontinental.

In the end, the Mormons finally gave up waiting for fair play. About a decade later, they built their own line, the Utah Northern Railroad, using volunteer Mormon labor to the Cache Valley and financial assistance from east coast investors. Unfortunately, this short line was *too* short to make a profit and the investors eventually forced it to close in bankruptcy court.

Little did the Mormons know that the Union Pacific had their hand in this as well and profited from the bankruptcy sale. Not even my fictitious character Luther Armstrong whose story actually links the wide, shady, cast of characters involved over several years of railroad development and chicanery, made money until copper emerged as a profit center in Butte, Montana and Luther was finally able to convince the Union Pacific to extend the line north.

All of this was, at the time, totally unregulated enterprise. Theodore Roosevelt was the first President to seriously address the sorts of monopoly issues that arose in America's Industrial Age. More information on the Union Pacific's fascinating acquisition of the Utah Northern is widely available online.

Chapter Ten ~ Copper control, corporate greed, alternating current, and a massacre

With the exception of Luther's roles in these chapters, the events leading to the Union Pacific's acquisition of the Utah Northern Railroad and transforming it into the Utah and Northern Railroad accurately summarize the historical events of 1877 and 1878. The expectation that electricity would be the next new profit opportunity made controlling the transportation of copper exceedingly important to the Union Pacific. In order to enhance the general public's awareness of the potential for the Utah Northern to go bankrupt while simultaneously buying up all available stock at a fraction of its worth, a reputable person in the Salt Lake City area would be needed to spread the rumors convincingly.

The federal government encouraged the rapid expansion of railroad lines all over America. In the West, indigenous populations were moved to reservations to make way for the railroad and the government gave incentives to railroad companies by offering them land for not only the right of way but an additional strip of land on either side of the rails for future development. To take advantage of this, railroad companies advertised the "land of milk and honey" available in the West and built railroad towns along their routes. It was part of a railroad strategy to populate and control the territory along its line. Successful or not, a railroad town was a tool of ambitious corporations to manipulate people and resources, to control space, and to consolidate their own position in order to maximize profits for the company. In the 1860s and 1870s, "every terminus of track laying became a city; wicked, wonderful and short-lived," wrote a former railroad agent in *Harper's Magazine* of one such place at the end of track in western Kansas. The writer found that "the Pacific railways have been responsible for more and worse towns than any other single cause… These shabby towns were the personal creations of railroad builders and their companies, everyone's favorite symbols of greed and corruption in the Gilded Age."[54]

---

54   Gilded Age – *a term used to describe the tumultuous years between the Civil War and the turn of the century. In fact, it was wealthy tycoons, not politicians, who inconspicuously held the most political power during the Gilded Age.*

Thomas Edison and George Westinghouse – Although Thomas Edison is normally recognized as the man who developed the light bulb and electricity for public use, it was actually Nikola Tesla that introduced alternating current (AC) electricity that is used today. Edison, with Morgan's financial backing, was developing direct current (DC) electricity and proposed that large generation plants be built so electricity could be distributed throughout New York and eventually the nation. Edison was recognized as a genius inventor of his times and obtained 1,093 patents during his life. Tesla was an assistant to Edison and strongly urged him to consider AC electricity over DC but Edison was unmoved, so Tesla approached George Westinghouse for assistance in competing with the Edison/Morgan approach for the best form of electrical distribution. The competition led to an intense and divisive marketing between the two teams, nearly causing Westinghouse to go bankrupt. In the end, Westinghouse convinced the 1893 Chicago Fair to use AC electricity to provide the first fully lighted World Fair. This was a huge success and, in turn, convinced builders of the largest electrical generation plant being built at the time at Niagara Falls to use AC electricity. With that, AC became the new standard for electricity in the nation.

The Mountain Massacre – "The Massacre, in 1857, was one of the most explosive episodes in the history of the American West—not only were 120 men, women and children killed, but the denouement of the so-called Utah War set Utah on the path to statehood and the Mormons on a long and fitful accommodation to secular authority, but the Mountain Meadows Massacre remained the focus of suspicion and resentment for decades." (SmithsonianMag.com, February 29, 2012 by Gilbert King.)

The Mormons had moved from the United States in 1847 to an area governed by Mexico (which, unknown to them would shortly become the Utah Territory) to avoid the hostility of members of other religions. Six months later, Mexico ceded the land to the United States and hostilities became a concern again for the Mormons.

But, in 1857, when a Mormon apostle named Parley Pratt was murdered by the legal husband of one of Pratt's plural wives, Joseph Young (Jr.) declared martial law and made it illegal to travel through the Utah Territory without a permit. When the Baker-Fancher party, a large group of American settlers passing through the Utah Territory, set up camp in Mountain Meadows, they were surrounded by Paiute Indians as well as Mormons dressed as Indians. The battle lasted five days until John D. Lee of the Mormons approached the camp under a white flag. The Mormons arranged a truce whereby the members of the Baker-Fancher party were promised safe passage if they would put their weapons down. When they did, the entire party, including the remaining men, women, and older children, were executed with the exception of seventeen young children. Although the Mormons disavowed any participation in the massacre for 150 years, leaders of the church issued the following statement on the sesquicentennial anniversary of the massacre:

> "We express profound regret of the massacre carried out in this valley 150 years ago today, and for the undue and untold suffering experienced by the victims then and by their relatives to the present time. A separate expression of regret is owed the Paiute people who have unjustly borne for too long the principal blame for what occurred during the massacre. Although the extent of their involvement is disputed, it is believed they would not have participated without the direction and stimulus provided by local church leaders and members…"

Chapter Fourteen, All the news that fits …

William E. Wheeler was the first newspaper man in the eastern Idaho Territory. He founded *The Blackfoot Register* in 1880 in Blackfoot, the anticipated territorial capitol. When it became clear that Eagle Rock would be more likely to grow rapidly due to the presence of the Union Pacific headquarters, he moved to Eagle Rock in 1884 and changed the name of the paper to the *Register*. Unlike my fictitious newspaper man, William Wheeler was quite outspoken and printed numerous attacks in his weekly paper. According to research for Hathaway's *Idaho Falls*, in 1894, he described "a fizzled attempt to establish a stage line to St. Anthony: Antone Edingher … brought a dilapidated old worn-out coach and a few skinny horses and made no attempt to run a stage line. He knows about as much about stage lines as a hog does about music."

Later, according to *Idaho Falls*, "…the *Register* reviewed the Independence Day arrival of a traveling circus. 'Idaho Falls was visited on Friday last by the most gigantic fake gang of surething gamblers, thieves and pick pockets [sic] that ever spread a tent in this city ... the only redeeming virtue being their good horses.'"

Mr. Wheeler was apparently more inclined to tell things as they were than my much younger character, Ellington Harper, Jr. The reason for Ellington's reticence will become clearer in the Eagle Rock Trilogy books two and three.

Chapter Twenty ~ Hello telegraph, goodbye Pony Express

In the early 1800s, Leopoldo Nobili invented the Astatic Galvanometer, an instrument that could measure variations in electrical transmissions. It was a predecessor of the telegraph. Later inventions using twenty-six electrical lines were invented to transmit distant signals but proved too clumsy for practical use.

In 1843 the American government financed the construction of the first telegraphic communications system developed by Samuel Morse. This system used only one wire, and the use of his code allowed practical communication between more distant points for the first time. The railroads made arrangements to install telegraph lines along all their routes. Since national time zones weren't agreed upon until 1918, railroad companies utilized the telegraph to coordinate rail traffic. This was essential since almost all railroad lines were single tracks accommodating traffic in both directions. The telegraph soon also became a tool for businesses to conduct trade over long distances. During the Civil War, Lincoln used telegraph to keep up with the various battles and communicate directly with his generals.

The telegraph put the Pony Express out of business. In the mid-19th century, mail overland by stage coach took twenty-five days to reach California or months by ship. The Pony Express had an average delivery time of just ten days. In March of 1861, Abraham Lincoln's inaugural address was delivered from Nebraska to California in seven days and seventeen hours by Pony Express. Despite this impressive achievement, the Pony Express only lasted a year and a half before going bankrupt. When Western Union completed the transcontinental telegraph line in Salt Lake City in October of 1861, the Pony Express ceased service two days later. In the nineteen months of its existence, Pony Express riders had delivered nearly 35,000 pieces of mail.

Chapter Twenty-one ~ Whatever it takes for a paycheck

Saloons and Brothels – A western saloon, often raucous and unruly, was an important gathering place for locals and visitors alike. In the early day's of a town's development, numerous saloons in the same time likely featured false fronts, bat-wing doors, stand-up bars, gambling, entertainment, drinking, and gun fights. In 1883, the town of Livingston, Montana, boasted of 3,000 residents and 33 saloons.

Competition between saloons across the West became quite fierce and the saloons soon began to specialize to accommodate specific types of customers. Many started out as just tents with dirt floors offering cheap, home-made liquor, generally whiskey, while others were elegant dance halls with live entertainment, lavish back bars, and large mirrors brought at great expense all the way from the east coast. Besides whiskey, they served unrefrigerated beer, which was only slightly cooler than room temperature and had to be drunk very quickly before went flat. In the late 1800s, Adolphus Busch was among the first beer barons to prepare lager beer, which required some form of refrigeration.

In most Western towns, with single men outnumbering the single women by a hundred to one, the most popular—and profitable—form of entertainment was women. In many of the more respectable "dance hall" saloons, the "girls" were there simply to sing, dance, flirt, and encourage the customers to purchase more liquor. But combining a saloon with a brothel was the most profitable and popular business.

In 1876, shortly after Deadwood was established in South Dakota, the well-known wagon train headed up by Charlie Utter brought Wild Bill Hickok, Calamity Jane, and several "working women," including Madam Dirty Em and Madam Mustachio to this frontier town. "Respectable" women who came west with their husbands or fathers, who, in turn, were later killed as the result of a mining accident, lost in the wilderness, or shot down by a gunslinger, found there were few prospects to sustain themselves and many turned to prostitution for survival or headed back east if they could afford it. Others were lured to the West with promises of respectable employment only to arrive and find themselves stranded without any options other than prostitution. These women faced violence and a form of slavery that pushed many of them to turn to drugs and alcohol as a means of escape. Opium, laudanum, and morphine were provided by the local doctors. An article about the Deadwood "painted ladies" explained that a doctor under the employ of the brothel owners always carried a stomach pump whenever summoned in the middle of the night.

Brothels performed a very significant benefit for the rough and rowdy men of the west but brought great hardship to the women.

For more, Legends of America online presents this subject in much greater detail.

Chinese Immigrants – The competition to complete the Transcontinental Railroad caused the two competing railroad companies, the Central Pacific and Union Pacific, to look for more workers. Railroad construction was dangerous, hard, physical labor conducted on the plains and mountains in the midst of angry Native American tribes, but many desperate men needed work. When the Civil War ended, there were plenty of former Confederate soldiers without a livelihood and a large proportion of Irish immigrants who were finding work hard to find on the east coast due to racism and prejudice. In addition, newly freed slaves were willing to do just about anything to earn a living. The Union Pacific grabbed these men but put them on separate crews to distance them from each other since there was considerable hostility among these groups. The former Union soldiers also looking for work were drawn to railroad construction. On the west coast, the Central Pacific hired Asian immigrants to work with their White crews, but quickly found they too had to be separated.

When the Transcontinental Railroad was completed at Promontory Point in 1869, these men were out of work again and homeless. Since they had experience in railroad construction and there was a considerable amount of railroad building in the West, many stayed in the area. The Mormons used volunteer Mormon farmers to build the Utah Northern railroad but, by 1878, the Union Pacific was willing to pay the workers and rounded up as many unemployed men they could find to complete the Utah & Northern extension to Butte, Montana.

In the construction camps, the various ethnic groups tended to stay together as a group, for the sense of safety in numbers as well as the opportunity to share similar foods, a common language, and familiar stories around the campfires at night. Many of the Chinese, who were willing to perform the more menial tasks such as laundry, butchering, and cooking, left railroad employment to set up their own small shops, first near the construction camps and later in the local communities along the railroad line.

Chapter Twenty-two ~ Rebecca Mitchell

References of note cited in various sources I read for Rebecca Mitchell, particularly the notes for chapters 22, are primarily from excerpts of works by James H. Hawley, Mary James Fritren and Molly Draben. The specific books by these authors can be found in the bibliography at the end of this novel.

Missionary Rebecca Mitchell, born in 1834, was a real person mentioned in several sources — but often with little information about her early life. However, Todd Wood, a Master of Divinity residing in Idaho Falls and currently conducting a pastoral ministry at the Providence Downtown Church, provided an informative blog about her that fills in a number of details.

According to Wood, Rebecca Mitchell was the devoutly religious daughter of a farming family residing in Macoupin County, Illinois, about sixty miles south of what would become the new Illinois Capitol in Springfield. She married a farmer when she was nineteen and they had three children together. When Rebecca was just twenty-three, her father and husband both died. Common Law in Illinois, as in many states at that time, required her to purchase all the property they had owned as a couple with the exception of her Bible and hymn book. She found it very upsetting that, had she died, her husband would have automatically gotten possession of all of their property with no regard to the rights of any of their children. This was aggravating enough for her to dedicate her life to improving the legal status of women. By the turn of the century, she would become well known for her influence on women's suffrage in Idaho.

Mitchell's two older children were boys. Once they married, she went to Chicago to attend a short training program at the Baptist Missionary Training School of Chicago. She served several years as a missionary and church worker in central Illinois but felt held back by the restrictions placed on women in conventional church organizations. Consequently, in June of 1882, she and her daughter Beth headed west for Rebecca to serve as a self-supporting missionary for the Baptist Church. She had enough money for them to get to Eagle

Rock, deep in the heart of Mormon territory. With few suitable accommodations available for herself and her daughter, they ended up in an abandoned saloon, which she transformed into a Sunday school and schoolroom. Three years later, she constructed the first church in Eagle Rock and named it the Providence Mission. For the purpose of this novel, I have advanced Rebecca's arrival in Eagle Rock to July, of 1879.

Chapter Twenty-six ~ Free enterprise, western style

Livery stables in the east were locations where one could rent a buggy and horse, or board a horse for a designated period of time. In larger cities, because liveries many times catered to wealthy individuals, but not so wealthy that they had their own stables, these facilities could be very prestigious and offer many forms of service. In the West, they were more likely to be small operations and would provide a variety of services for working horses, mules, and oxen. A livery in the West was normally a one-man operation whose owner might be skilled in making and putting on horseshoes and reworking worn saddles, halters, reins, bits, harnesses, and other forms of horse tack.

James Madison "Matt" Taylor is credited to be the founding father of Eagle Rock, which was first called Taylor's Crossing. In 1865, Matt and several partners built the first bridge across the Snake River with the intention of charging a toll to travelers using the California Trail and its northern leg, the Montana Trail, leading to Oregon. Matt lived alone near the bridge but asked his wife's brother, Robert Anderson to assist him in running the toll business. In the fall of the same year, Robert and Matt's wife and children arrived to become the sole occupants of the remote village. The bridge was washed out the following spring but Matt and Robert rebuilt it higher and stronger.

Within two months of his arrival, Robert was appointed as the first postmaster and later as the first chairman of the village board and mayor of the village. An article from *Idaho Falls Magazine* states: "During [Anderson's] tenure, the board passed important ordinances defining misdemeanors punishable by fines: riding a horse or mule recklessly through the village, shooting firearms from horseback, lying drunk on a public street, fighting and even threatening to start a fight."

Robert opened the Anderson Trading House and later the Anderson Brothers Store and Bank. The building served as an early form of department store, offering groceries, boots, shoes, hats, and dry goods, as well as a bank and post office. By this time, his brother, Jack Anderson, had moved to Eagle Rock and bought out Matt Taylor's shares of the toll bridge. Matt and his family left the area to go back to Missouri and the Anderson brothers purchased additional land around the bridge in hopes of building up the town. When Union Pacific chose the area near Taylor's Crossing for the new railroad bridge for the Utah and Northern Railroad, Anderson's Oneida Road, Bridge, and Ferry Company granted the Utah & Northern Railroad a right-of-way 100 feet wide on each side of the proposed tracks in what would become the downtown of Eagle Rock as well as 102 acres of downtown property for the railroad buildings. The Anderson Brothers Trading Post and Bank stayed in business until 1900 when it was sold to a company based in Saint Louis.

Dick Chamberlain was another of Eagle Rock's early entrepreneurs. When Sheriff Henry Plummer was hanged (see Chapter Seven Notes), Dick Chamberlain became a self-appointed law enforcer with Ed F. Winn. Dick was known locally as Captain Dick, Uncle Dick, D. F., Dan, or Dave. He owned a saloon that was described in a history written for the Daughters of the American Revolution by Eldora Keefer, as "a rough house…many fights and shooting scrapes took place in his building." According to *Images of America – Idaho Falls* "By 1882, he owned a two-story building with a saloon and billiard hall on the ground floor and an organ upstairs for dances, while next door there was a 10-pin bowling alley."

Steam engines require enormous amounts of water that must be carried behind the engines in an engine tender. This tender also carries the fuel, which at this time would have been wood. It would be important for a division point on a railroad to have ready access to water to supply these engines. With the Snake River very close to the depot, early on, the U&N built a small steam pump to move water from the Snake up into the water tower. From there, it was fed by gravity into the steam engine tenders. As a benefit for the new residents of the small community and as part of their aggressive marketing program to encourage settlement, the U&N piped water to many of the buildings along the streets near the tower. Although the volunteer fire brigade wasn't actually formed until 1885 after a fire burned down nearly all of the frame shacks on

Eagle Rock Street, for the sake of the story, I have given Mr. Anderson credit for having the foresight to form a fire brigade earlier.

Chapter Twenty-seven ~ Early Illinois

The early settlers of Springfield, Illinois were mostly southerners drawn to the fertile open fields of central Illinois. Large areas of relatively flat land with enormous fields of prairie grass and few trees to cut down were considered an ideal area for farming. As early as 1818, trappers and fur traders found the Sangamon River to be well populated with deer and wild game. The town was initially called Calhoun after Senator John C. Calhoun of South Carolina but, in 1832, Senator Calhoun had fallen out of favor and the town was renamed Springfield for Spring Creek which ran through the area. The Illinois Territory's first Capitol was in Kaskaskia, along the Mississippi River in the southern portion of the territory. During a catastrophic flood in April of 1881, the Mississippi destroyed most of Kaskaskia and the course of the river was altered to pass on the east rather than the west. Since then, Illinois travelers have had to drive into Missouri to get to Kaskasia, Illinois. When Illinois was granted statehood, the capitol was moved north to Vandalia in what was still fairly southern Illinois. Springfield became the third capitol in 1839 largely due to the efforts of Abraham Lincoln and his eight associates named the 'Long Nine' due to them all being over six feet tall.

Although the majority of the early population had left the South to settle in Illinois, a large contingent of northeastern settlers moved to Springfield once it had become an established city. This caused a real problem at the time of Lincoln's election to the presidency. The city was very divided on the concept of slavery. As an example, the First Presbyterian Church in downtown Springfield was divided about the Civil War even though Lincoln was a resident of the city and a member of the congregation. Many of the church members were southern sympathizers, which eventually led to the church splitting and a second Presbyterian Church being established for the northern sympathizers, later becoming the Westminster Presbyterian Church.

Thus, in such a divided city, it would be quite possible for our fictional character, Henry Stubin to become enthralled with the southern belle wannabe, Elizabeth Marie Sabin.

Chapter Thirty-one ~ Two pathfinders

I could not find any information suggesting that Rebecca Mitchell had a particular interest in teaching Native American children, but there is no doubt there were few if any opportunities for Native American children in the West to obtain a formal education. Rebecca did have a strong desire to educate children and she did establish a school in Eagle Rock very shortly after arriving, yet this brand new frontier town would have had very few children. I have taken a little license in suggesting that she would have a desire to educate anyone she could and, having grown up in rural, southern Illinois, she might not have been as fearful of Native Americans as Catherine.

Another historical character, Herman Joseph Berghoff, was born on November 13, 1853 in Dortmund, Westphalia, Prussia, current-day Germany. In Prussia at the time, only the eldest son could inherit his father's estate. This was a policy throughout Europe since there was little unowned land available and the wealthy aristocrats did not want to water down their wealth by spreading it over multiple sons. Daughters were not entitled to inherit their father's estates. Herman was the third of seven children and, with few prospects, he decided at age seventeen to sail to America with the hopes of better opportunities. According to the *Berghoff Family Cookbook*, as a boy, he had been "captivated by tales of the American 'Wild West' and had fancied that he might share those adventures and strike it rich in the process."

As a young man coming to America, Berghoff worked several jobs before getting to the West, including as a deck hand and pastry chef on a small freighter, a field hand on a sugar plantation, and numerous other odd jobs. When he finally was able to get to western America, he took a job with Buffalo Bill Cody's Wild West Show and spent time working on western railroads. By 1874, he had moved back east to Fort Wayne, Indiana to settle down.

Although Herman would have already left the west by the time Eagle Rock was formed, I wanted to introduce him into our story since, coming from Prussia, he would have been accustomed to the better quality German beers and lagers from his homeland. By this time in eastern America, the lager beers from Germany were becoming quite popular. Our Herman will be influential in interesting Jeremiah in the art of German beer production, which required some form of refrigeration, and in turn, slowed down the production of this type of beer in the West.

Chapter Thirty-two ~ Lavish locations

Construction of the Crescent Hill Reservoir in Louisville, Kentucky started in 1874 and was completed in 1879. The reservoir was built to replace a smaller reservoir built in 1860 and could store a two-week supply of water for the Louisville area residents. This facility and adjacent land became an instant tourist attraction with numerous amenities to handle the many visitors who came by train, horse, and buggy to visit the grounds which were surrounded by large, privately held estates. In 1884, a visitors' building named the Gatehouse was constructed with the modern addition of water closets and bathrooms and a large common area. I found no evidence that balls were held here, but the grounds were well landscaped and the site was a popular destination for well-to-do Louisville residents, so I made it the site of a glamorous but fictional outdoor 'End of Summer Ball' held adjacent to an open-air shelter.

The reservoir is still part of Louisville Water's Crescent Hill operations and the Gatehouse was fully restored in 2015. At least prior to Covid 19, it was open to tourists from 11 AM to 7 PM the second Wednesday of the month from June through September.

Meriwether Lewis Clark, the grandson of William Clark of the Lewis and Clark Expedition, traveled to Europe in 1872. While there, he attended the famed Epsom Derby horse race in England. He also spent time with members of the French Jockey Club who had developed the Grand Prix de Paris Longchamps horse race. Clark was sufficiently impressed that he convinced his uncles John and Henry Churchill to gift him land to build a ten furlong (1¼-mile) long, oval, horse racetrack in Louisville. He formed the Louisville Jockey Club to sponsor the track and the first Kentucky Derby was held in 1875. This event drew approximately 10,000 spectators and started a tradition in Louisville that continues to this day. In 1883, the name "Churchill Downs" was first used to landmark the racetrack that is the home of the Kentucky Derby. Apparently, the track was modified to a one-mile oval—its present form.

Chapter Thirty-four ~ Local residents, western whiskey

The real Eagle Rock did have a saloon, which was named the Skogg and Wallenstein Saloon, although it is not clear when this saloon actually opened for business. Hathaway's *Idaho Falls* has a photo of the front of the saloon next to J. Oley's Barber Shop. The photo also shows a billboard advertising Eagle Rock Lager Beer.

In 1858, mountain man Richard "Beaver Dick" Leigh came to the area in 1858, in the vicinity of where Eagle Rock would eventually form in 1879. Beaver Dick was an Englishman who had become a fur trapper and was probably the area's first permanent settler. He married a sixteen-year-old Shoshone named Jenny, who was a maiden of Chief Washakie's people. He chose to live in the wild, long before other White settlers arrived. He and Jenny embraced the life-style of the Native Americans and reared three children. Because he was fluent in both the Bannock and Shoshone languages and reasonably knowledgeable in Native American sign language and smoke signals, he was asked to assist with the U.S. government's first geological surveys of the area and served as a guide to many notable Americans, including Theodore Roosevelt. The Grand Teton National Park's Leigh Lake is named after him and the park's Jenny Lake is named for his wife.

As described in the Chapter Two Notes, whiskey available in the West in the late 1800s was of generally poor quality, was made locally by individuals with little knowledge of whiskey brewing, and contained many dubious ingredients. The main goal was to produce a cheap alcoholic beverage that had a real punch, many times to the detriment of the drinker. Whiskey was normally transported in ceramic jugs of varying capacity, sometimes known as "little brown jugs." Until the late 1860s, glass bottles were too expensive to produce. When hinged metal molds were invented to make bottles more economically, a few of the more prominent whiskey producers started bottling their whiskey in these bottles. In 1870, George Garvin Brown started selling his Old Forester bourbon exclusively in sealed glass bottles. It was generally understood that a bottle of Old Forester was a special treat for anyone who could afford it.

Chapter Thirty-eight ~ The fare to Franklin

The Baptist Church denied Rebecca Mitchell the opportunity to become a funded missionary in Illinois because she was a woman so she took her daughter and headed west with no clear idea of where she would end up.

She took the Transcontinental Railroad as far as Salt Lake City and checked in with the local Baptist leader who advised her that teaching skills would be useful in Bellevue, Idaho. Although she was informed that she and her daughter could take the Utah & Northern railroad as far as Franklin, Idaho, and catch a stage coach from there to Bellevue, she discovered at Franklin that the stagecoach would cost the two of them fifty dollars, but she only had a little more than twenty-five dollars left.

After explaining her predicament to the stagecoach sales lady, she was told there was a brand new town on the rail line that was all saloons and brothels and could use a church. The cost of traveling for both of them by rail on the U&N railroad would only be a total of twenty-five dollars. Thus, Rebecca Mitchell and her daughter Beth arrived in Eagle Rock.

They were nearly destitute and could not immediately find housing. She found what is described in some accounts of her life a "weathered board shanty," and in other sources "an abandoned saloon," to set up housekeeping facing the alley behind one of the buildings on Railroad Avenue. The first weekend after her arrival, she was able to open up her "shanty" to offer Sunday school classes and shortly later, a day school. She had success in getting at least some of the homesteads in the area to attend her temporary church by visiting every family dwelling in the area. She made it clear that she wanted to establish a true church building and worked hard to get local funding. She also contacted Baptist organizations in the East and had success in obtaining many generous donors from the New England states. The Anderson brothers eventually donated the land for the new church.

Chapter Thirty-nine ~ Side to astride

The idea that a woman should ride sidesaddle dates back to 1382 when Princess Anne of Bohemia rode sidesaddle across Europe on her way to marry King Richard II. It was understood that men rode horses and women were merely passengers who sat behind the men or rode in a carriage or buggy. Due to their long, heavy skirts, it was impractical for women to ride astride a horse so they had to ride with both legs over the same side of a horse. Riding this way didn't give women much control of their horse and, by the sixteenth century, Catherine de Medici had developed a more practical design by placing her right leg over the pommel[55] of the saddle. This gave her much better control of her horse and created less likelihood of falling off. It also was said to show off her shapely ankle and calf to their best advantage.

Riding attire for women was altered dramatically in 1875 when the first "safety skirt" was invented. Women could have serious accidents if their full skirts got caught on the saddle and caused them to be dragged by their horse if they fell. The safety skirts were buttoned along the seams to break away under the pressure of a fall. The women wore breeches for modesty.

Finally, by 1930, riding astride had become a somewhat acceptable way of riding for women, yet it was mostly daring women who enjoyed riding astride a horse to give them complete control long before it was considered completely fashionable.

Chapter Forty-three ~ Hell's Half Acre

There is a large, exposed lava field located west of Idaho Falls. Hell's Half Acre lava flow erupted about 4,100 years ago and covers 222 square miles. The Snake River used to flow across the northern portion of the Snake River Plain, but now flows along the southern margin of the plain. The river was pushed there by successive lava flows. At a point southwest of Idaho Falls, the exposed lava field rises about twelve feet above the surrounding ground near a bend in the Snake River. The immediate area around this exposed flow is filled with outcroppings of lava that can be hazardous to travel through, particularly on horseback. Although the area I have Catherine riding through is not in the Hell's Half Acre site, it would be close enough to come across numerous outcroppings partially hidden by the soil. This lava rock is similar to the exposed lava found in the Hawaiian Islands and is extremely sharp, glassy, and fragmented with open cracks, lava tubes, and caves.

---

55 **Pommel** – *the rounded knob on the front of a horse's saddle that a rider can grip with one hand*

Chapter Forty-six ~ Fred Dubois

Jesse Dubois was highly recommended by Abraham Lincoln to become the auditor of public accounts for Illinois in 1856. His family, including his son, Fred Thomas Dubois, left Crawford County in southeastern Illinois to move to the state Capitol in Springfield, Illinois. Jesse purchased a home just down the street from the Lincolns and his son inherited the interest of the family tradition of public service and politics due to the friendships he formed in Springfield.

Through family contacts, Fred won an appointment as secretary of the Board of Railway and Warehouse Commissioners in 1875. He served one year and left shortly after his father's death. Not pleased with the opportunities in the Midwest, he decided to try his luck in the West and moved to Idaho. After a brief stint as a cowboy on cattle drives, Dubois found employment at Fort Hall doing a variety of tasks. Using his contacts in Illinois, including Secretary of War Robert T. Lincoln, he received an appointment as the United States Marshal for the Idaho Territory. Dubois would go on to become Idaho's representative in Congress and eventually serve two terms in the Idaho Senate. He is best known for his opposition to the gold standard and his efforts that disenfranchised Mormon voters by demanding a stop to the use of polygamy by the Mormons as a requirement to gain Idaho statehood in 1890.

Just like Rebecca Mitchell, Fred Dubois did not actually come to Idaho until after the period of time portrayed in this book, but I wanted to introduce both these historic characters in Book One since they will be significant figures in the remainder of this trilogy. Fred Dubois as U.S. Marshall did spend considerable time in the Idaho Territory and was responsible for the establishment of law and order in his early years in Idaho.

Chapter Fifty-two ~ Property law and voting rights

The *Michigan Law Review*, Volume 61, Issue 3, provides an in-depth evaluation of the initial constitutional laws in territorial courts of the United States. Our character Luther Armstrong explains to Henry Willett a reasonably accurate summary of women's rights regarding ownership of property in Idaho in the early 1860s. The U.S. Constitution at that time had provisions for establishing laws and the appointment of judges in territories. These laws, written into the U.S. Constitution in 1788, were based largely on the common laws established in England at the time. Under English Common Law, women could not vote and could not own property, and a married woman did not necessarily inherit the property of her husband upon his death, so territories were still established in the United States using the Common Law rights offered women found in the late 1700's in England. Thus, single women were allowed to own property but that right was transferred to the husband upon marriage. He became her guardian and legal representative and was responsible for all her legal and financial interests. Essentially, a married woman had no legal identity and was required by law to let her husband make all important decisions for the family.

Although territories could develop their own statutes to clarify issues of law, the federal government had to approve them. States had the right to issue clarifications to Common Law and most states did provide a more liberal opinion of women's right of ownership as early as the mid 1800s, although none allowed women to vote. Because broad ownership of land was important to the Mormon Church and it also established a greater headcount for the territory, Brigham Young (Sr.) passed territorial laws in 1870 in Utah allowing women to own land and vote without obtaining the consent of the U.S. government. This was abolished by an act of Congress in 1887. Women's rights in the Utah Territory reverted to the archaic interpretation of Common Law and women's rights found in the U.S. Constitution provisions for territorial law until Utah became a state in 1896. The Utah State Legislature immediately reinstated the right for women to vote.

In 1863 when the Idaho Territory was established, like Utah, it started out with a constitution that spelled out Common Law provisions for property ownership. What the *Michigan Law Review* does not explain is that, for reasons never well documented, the Idaho Territorial Legislature abandoned the Common Law system of marital property rights in favor of a community property system in 1867. To quote the "Origins of Idaho's Community Property System" found in Digital Commons @UidahoLaw published in 2009, "there is a noticeable lack of information concerning the motives, intent, and reasons for its enactment in the Idaho Territory..." By passing the Community Property Act, the territorial legislature altered the property relationships that existed between husband and wife and departed dramatically from the dominant common law system of marital property law prevalent in most other states."

As part of the fictional aspect of this book, it is plausible that Luther was not aware of this Act in his focus of bringing himself into power with the Mormons and the Union Pacific during the late 1860s and 1870s. As suggested by Luther in Chapter 52, if Henry really did obtain ownership of a majority of the property Catherine might own as the result of Patrick's death *prior* to their marriage, the vagueness of the proper interpretation of laws at that time might turn over the property to Henry. Luther was confident he had sufficient contacts within the local judicial system to ensure that Henry could get ownership of the property.

To find out how this all resolves itself, I encourage the reader to read Book Two of the *Eagle Rock Trilogy*.

Brief Bibliography

Berghoff Family Cookbook, Carlyn and Jan Berghoff and Nancy Ross Ryan, Andrews McMeel Publishing. 2007

Bonneville County Heritage Association, Chapter 12 – "Transportation"

Images of America, Idaho Falls, William Hathaway, Arcadia Publishing. 2006

New Perspectives on the West, PBS.org

Rocks, Rails & Trails, Paul Karl Link & E Chilton Phoenix, Idaho Museum of Natural History. 1994

The Smiths and their Dreams and Visions, C. Jess Groesbeck, 1988

Lava Trail System (Hell's Half Acre), U.S. Department of Interior, Bureau Land Management website

Brigham Young and the Expansion of the Mormon Faith, Thomas G. Alexander, 2019

Brigham Young, Modern Moses, Prophet of God, Franklin M. Gibbons, 1981

Brigham Young, Pioneer Prophet, John G. Turner, 2014

Joseph Smith – Rough Stone Rolling, Richard Lyman Bushman, 2005

Early Mormonism and the Magic World View, D. Michael Quinn, 1998

Joseph Smith: A Penguin Life, Robert V. Remini, 2002

Joseph Smith: The Making of a Prophet, Dan Vogel, 2004

History of Idaho: the Gem of the Mountains, Vol. 2, James H. Hawley, 1920

Eagle Rock City of Destiny, Bonneville Historical Society, Mary Jane Fritzen, 1991

Glimpses from My Life – Rebecca Mitchell, Biographical Sketch of Rebecca Mitchell, Prepared by undergraduate Mary Draben

The Iron Trail to the Golden Spike, (Utah's Role in the Pacific Railroad, Chapter 7), John J. Stewart, 1969

The History of Utah's Railroads, 1869-1883, (Chapter 6 – The Northern Railroads), Clarence A. Reeder, Jr. 2000

The Aftermath of Mountain Meadows, Gilbert King, Smithsonianmag.com, 2012

A Preview of Book Two of the Eagle Rock Trilogy

July 7, 1879, 5:30 am

"You quit that bickerin and get outside," Samuel yelled at his two boys as he swatted the nearest one on the back of his head. The boys charged out the opening that served as a door in the squat, sod cabin, looking back in fear that their pa might follow them.

"And you keep your voice down," Pearl ordered, "or you're going to wake the baby. I was up half the night with that little screamer and I don't need you makin such a ruckus."

"I'm hungry. Where's breakfast," he answered, growing more irritated by the minute. The morning was already hot, the house was full of biting bugs, and tempers were running high.

"Quiet, you fool," was all the answer he got from his wife.

Samuel muttered under his breath, "I might as well go check on the herd."

"Samuel," Pearl called after him. "Don't forget it's washin day. You said you'd fetch me water. I need two full buckets or you'll have to go back for more."

Samuel shook his head and was about to tell her what he thought of being the water monkey but a loud squeal stopped him short. The baby had awakened. No point in hanging around now. He grabbed two buckets, headed out the door, and walked into a wall of hot air. The sun was so bright he had to shield his eyes, and he could already see heat waves rising off the land. He took a shallow breath of the dusty air and headed toward the river as his wife's voice rose up to an even higher pitch.

Glad for a reason to put some distance between himself and the squabble, Samuel picked up his stride. He could still hear Pearl yelling at him. "Two buckets Samuel. Two *full* buckets, and remember to keep them wet so they won't leak again, damn you!"

She was generally not very happy, and was particularly unhappy with their new homestead near the railroad. The Union Pacific had sold him the land for less than he had expected for a ranch, although you could hardly call this arid plot of sagebrush and six cattle a real ranch. He'd saved enough to buy more, but Pearl had not let him spend all of their savings so they were stuck on this miserable piece of ground without any real prospect of profit from their few cattle or enough resources to start the farm Pearl wanted. And if he tried to convince Pearl they needed more cattle, she would insist they turn right around and go back to Utah. He would just have to find a way to come up with more money.

Pearl was always against his good ideas and plans to become independent. She just had no imagination. And clearly, less faith in him every year. At least this land had access to the Snake River and he didn't have to haul water for the cattle. But he had never planned on having to haul water for his wife. What kind of man would agree to do that? Still, it was usually a good way to get out of the shack and avoid any other chores she dreamed up. He would check on the cattle and then walk a little upstream to the bend where it was easy to dip out a bucket of fresh water. He knew if he collected the water near the cattle, Pearl was going to complain that it was full of cow manure and he would have to make another trip and suffer more of her scorn. Then, after he delivered the water, he would head to The Pony for his morning poker game with the boys and wash down some of this irritation with a little Old Glory whiskey. That would keep him away from Pearl and the baby for most of the day.

Sweat was already running into his eyes as he left the garden they had managed to eke out of this desert, and he'd forgotten his bandana. With more than ample sun, it should have been up and thriving, but it was withering in this damn drought. It wouldn't survive much longer if they didn't get some rain. No one had told him it was going to be this God-awful hot and dusty in Idaho. They had traveled days to get north of Utah and he had expected it to be a little cooler up here. Didn't it ever rain? The ground was so dry in Pearl's small patch of corn it was full of jagged cracks and the corn was drooping badly.

Fortunately, he had the cattle and that was what he really wanted. He certainly didn't want to be a gardener let alone a farmer. He spit onto the dry cracked earth just thinking about farming. Pearl had insisted on the corn. Did she think they would want to eat corn every meal? Silly woman. Thanks to his wisdom and keen mind, they would have steaks and eat like kings! He chuckled as he thought about that. *She should be thanking me for planning ahead. You just can't bring a woman to think like a man.*

He wiped the sweat off his forehead again with the back of his hand and surveyed the property for his cattle. *They must be down on the sand bar at the river. Probably getting their fill of water for the day. And there is actually some grass down there. That's where they'll be.*

But it took another half hour to find his cattle. They had wandered far off his property and were gathered together around a small scrub tree at the water's edge down river a half a mile.

"Someday I gotta put up some fence. I wonder why they wandered down here. Boy it's hot today," he grumbled aloud.

He began yelling and banging his water pails together to herd the cattle back to his property. That took another half hour. As he approached the sandbar where his cattle normally went to drink, he saw something at the edge of the river washed up close to the shore. *Probably just a pile of rags hung up on that old fallen tree in the water.*

For some reason the cattle were shying away from their drinking spot and kept turning back down river on him. No amount of shouting seemed to get them to go to the water. Frustrated and hoarse from yelling, he decided he would have to pull those rags out of the tree so the skittish cattle would go and drink.

As he got closer, he realized it was more than just a pile of rags. Looking more carefully, he was so startled he dropped the buckets and stared. It was a body, face down in the water. There was a torn, colorful shirt bunched up on the back of the body and covering the head. It must have gotten hung up on a limb of the fallen tree.

He stood stock still, thinking about the situation for a moment. He really didn't want to get his boots wet, but the body could have something worthwhile to salvage. He might find a silver belt buckle, some cash, or even a gun for his trouble. After considering his alternatives, he gave up and waded into the river and attempted to pull the body free, but something under the shirt was holding the body firmly. After another short struggle, the body suddenly came free and Samuel gave out a loud yelp. He could clearly see a huge knife sticking out of a man's back. And it was as fine a Bowie knife as he had ever laid eyes on.

More mindful of his good fortune than concerned about the corpse, he was feeling quite a bit more energy than he'd had all morning. *Why, that knife has got to be worth a small fortune!* He pried and twisted the knife in the bloated body. It had gone in deep. Once it was free, he could see that it was truly an expensive knife, with the initials PGC carved into the handle. He sat down at the river's edge to think.

His friend John had told him that some sheriff from up river in Eagle Rock came callin at The Pony with a story about a man that had fallen off a bridge and got himself drowned. He was wearing a red, white and blue shirt. *This has got to be that man. And there's a big reward for anyone that can find him. But Lawdy, this man didn't just fall off a bridge and drown. He was stabbed to death!*

Surely, someone in Eagle Rock would want to know about this. And a man with the initials of PGC must have killed this guy with this knife. This is my lucky day! I just found the missing body and solved a murder, all before breakfast. That's got to be worth a lot of money! Pearl will never believe just how clever I am!

But then he frowned. *But what if the sheriff don't do what's right? Tries to keep the reward for hisself?*

After a moment he broke into a sly grin. *If the sheriff don't see fit to give me more than the reward, I'll just tell him I'll go to Eagle Rock myself and tell the town folk I know who killed this man and collect the reward myself.*

Samuel knew he could outsmart the sheriff. He was just as sure the sheriff would see the light and give him what he wanted by threatening to go directly to the people of Eagle Rock. He got up, dragged the body out of the river, and turned to go back and tell Pearl about their good fortune. *Boy, will she be proud of me.*

By the time he left, the cattle had already headed down river again, and the buckets were forgotten, tipped over, and drying in the sun.

About the Author

After graduating from the University of Illinois, Urbana-Champaign with a Bachelors of Architecture, Melotte began a professional career that would span fifty years. He and business partner Richard Morse founded an architectural office and stained glass studio, and built the business into a successful collaboration of architects, scientists, artists, craftsmen, and social entrepreneurs serving the region with new construction, historic preservation, environmental hazard remediation, major stained glass art collections, and legislative development that became foundational to present-day regulations. Melotte retired in 2019 and moved to his beloved home state of Wisconsin to pursue his life-long love of writing.

Cat's Café is Melotte's first published novel.